THE CASE FOR KILLING

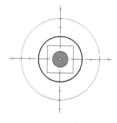

Peter Fritze

THE CASE FOR KILLING

Peter Fritze

ISBN 978-0-9937025-3-2

ISBN 978-0-9937025-2-5 (eBook)

CHAPTER 1

I want Peter Bradley dead.

There — I have written it, after complaining in this journal for so long.

I know him all too well. He may have his charms, but really he is a snake. He slithers around in search of his next prey, and when he finds it, he seizes it for his sole benefit. Then he lies curled up, digesting his victim, fat in the stomach and satisfied in the ego.

PB angers me so much that I have a fantasy of how I would kill him. First, I would tie him to a chair pushed up against a wall in some remote building where no one can hear his screams. Then I would take out a handgun and serenely show it to him, describing what will happen to him when I pull the trigger. The handgun should be new because, in its life, I want it to have a single shot and purpose — to cover the wall behind PB with his brains and blood. Before pulling the trigger, I would stuff the tip of the barrel in his mouth and hold it there until he starts to gag and squirm. At the same time, in his ear I would whisper some last-minute reflections on the treachery and uselessness of his life. I want his final moments to be ones of humiliation and doom — without a shred of hope of changing things. Then I would pull the trigger, very slowly and deliberately, his concluding seconds stretching to eons of unending torment. A huge bang — does he hear it? A huge body recoil — does he feel it? And then the snake would slump into his last curl, the back half of his head blown off.

Do I feel guilty about my thoughts? I probably will later, but not as I write these words. A little disturbing, I know. But this is the dark place I am in right now.

Undoubtedly, PB has some virtues, but for the moment I just can't think of any. Simply put, he is a fraud, a man without bearings, moral or otherwise. His outward success is a lie. Inside, he is mess of self-centredness, insecurities and depravity.

My thoughts are becoming more powerful. Maybe it was easier to suppress them in the past. I can't tell. More and more, I see him as a person who deserves the pain that he hands out so easily to others. This is what I hear in my head: "It is time — bring on the tortured end."

Stop this already! It really *is time to let this stuff go. After all, my fantasy is just that: a fantasy.*

Right?

CHAPTER 2

Peter Bradley felt he was a good man. Occasionally he wondered if anyone could doubt it. Say Abrams, for example. Maybe him. From the desk in his corner office high above downtown Toronto's congested streets, Bradley stared out at Lake Ontario. He absorbed nothing of the lake's playful glint in the September sun. Instead, he imagined sitting at lunch in a few minutes with Abrams, telling him of his decision. It was the right decision, but not an easy one. Abrams might be upset — he often was. The question was whether he would be left harbouring doubts about Bradley as well.

Turning back to his messy desk, Bradley thought half-heartedly about organizing a few papers for his assistant, Margaret, to file. Instead he irritably wiped the palm of his right hand down his bloated, horse-like face, for a moment grotesquely stretching the heavy lids of his grey eyes, his bulbous nose and his thin lips. After a deep sigh, he followed with a derisive push of his fingers through a thick crop of wavy, grey-etched brown hair. He *was* a good man. What were his efforts on the board of the hospital charity if not the work of one? Board meetings, great advice, even a donor — incontrovertible, he thought. And there was his work for the competition law section of the bar association. Without him, the submissions on all the legislative changes of the past few years would have been an embarrassment. *A complete embarrassment*, he repeated, shaking his head. And all this without mentioning the Rosedale home he had bought his wife and the endless support he had given her blood-sucking brother. "Huh, not a good man. Give me a break," he muttered.

At the same moment, in an awkward, lurching motion, Abrams stuck his head into Bradley's office. Quickly manufacturing a large, ingratiating smile, Bradley looked hard to see if Abrams had heard his utterance. It seemed not.

"Ready to go?" Abrams asked. "I made reservations at Chartrand."

"Always the best for you," Bradley said, getting up from his desk and slapping the outside of his jacket to check for his wallet.

"They're not rated number one anymore. Giorgio's is now. Did you know that?"

For goodness' sake, Abrams, it was a joke, Bradley thought. *Lighten up*. He joined Abrams at the door.

"I didn't. Let's go."

"Yes, last month's *Food and Drink*."

"Interesting. Why aren't we going to Giorgio's then?"

Abrams shrugged. "I was there yesterday."

Large numbers were trying to get out of the Bay Wellington Tower at the same time. Eventually, Abrams and Bradley were able to press themselves into an elevator for the twenty-nine-floor ride down to street level. Released like sardines out of a can, they walked west along Wellington Street, working their way into the hurried lunchtime crowd. Striding next to one another, each in a nondescript blue suit, they formed an odd pair: Bradley, tall and heavy-set with a large chest and spindly legs, next to the diminutive and spry Abrams. Bradley straightened his back to accentuate his height advantage.

As they continued trivial chat, Bradley revisited old ground. Leonard Abrams had become a great litigator at an astonishingly young age. But in times of unprecedented challenge for Collins, Shaw LLP, he was too inexperienced to have been made managing partner. Even so, Ted Collins, grandnephew of one founder and Chair of the Management Committee, had anointed Abrams, and what Ted wanted, Ted got. Bradley and Collins may have started at the firm together twenty-four years earlier and always enjoyed each other's company, but Bradley was losing his respect for Collins. Goddamn Collins. Instead of embedding cronies, he should be worrying about fixing things.

They cut across Wellington to the TD Bank Tower and took a broad set of steps down to the underground network. Once through several sets of glass doors, they saw the usual Friday lunch lineup at Chartrand spilling out the front door. Collins, Shaw lawyers brought steady business and the maître d' had moved mountains to accommodate Abrams' last-minute reservation request. When he saw Abrams and Bradley arrive at the back of the lineup, he energetically waved them through the crowd into his care.

"Right this way, Mr. Abrams," he said. "I have an excellent table for you."

They sat at a table for two in dim light off to one side of the restaurant. Conversation was strained, and their eyes frequently diverted to scrutinize other guests. By the time they ordered, Bradley had had enough of small talk.

"So, how are we doing this year?"

Abrams gave a half-hearted smile. "We're still making far more money than we deserve."

Bradley looked quizzically at Abrams. He sure was a hard guy to understand sometimes. Either Abrams was serious, which was preposterous, or his sense of humour was worse than Bradley remembered. Not only that, he could use a new tailor and a stylist to tame the sprouts of hair below his bald spot.

"Seriously," Bradley said.

"Seriously, we're doing fine," Abrams said with a light toss of his shoulders. "What can I say? We're doing better than the street, that's what I'm hearing."

"No details for me? You got all the numbers — but my gut is telling me that we're not keeping up. My area excluded, of course."

A sardonic smile drifted on and off Abrams' face. "Naturally, your area is fine," he said. He gently rotated his glass of water, watching the ice cubes swirl. "It's been a good year, despite the shrinking number of quality clients out there." Abrams looked up at Bradley with a tilt of his head. "I don't usually share specifics with individual partners — it's better to present the same stuff to everyone at the same time. But you're one of our most senior lawyers. I have no problem slipping you some details. What do you want to know?"

Bullshit, Bradley said to himself. In court, Abrams was known as a wolf — a killer. Words only left his lips after the most careful calculation.

"Well, how are the individual departments doing?"

"So far this year, corporate is doing fine. All the sub-groups in corporate are doing fine, too — but you probably know that from the deal flow you're seeing. Outside of corporate, things are a bit slower. Tax could be doing better. I don't understand why, given the deal flow. And litigation, they miss me, what can I say?"

Bradley sighed impatiently. "You know, between you and me — and I've been saying this for years — we need to gut that tax department and bring in some really good people. Every year — I swear, every year — it's the same story. Tax should be doing better. I mean, how many chances do they get?"

Abrams put up a hand in submission. "I know, Peter. You're not the only one who says this. Trust me, I know. It's just these things take time, what can I say? It's not like great tax lawyers are banging our doors down."

"They should be," Bradley said as salads arrived. "They really should be."

"And then there are the personnel issues. Who do you get rid of? And it's getting rid of people, right? It's very unpleasant."

More bullshit. Abrams and Collins — both killers. Anyone they didn't need or want was tossed out on the street so fast, they didn't have time to shred their business cards. Bradley was getting irritated; it was time for Abrams to get to the topic of Walter Anand.

"And litigation is slow, too? Maybe you need to be there — part-time, I mean."

"You know what? Litigation will be fine without me. A couple of big cases came in this week. And I don't have time to be there. I can hardly keep up with our internal sexual harassment cases — and I'm almost not kidding. But you know, I miss it. Maybe I wasn't cut out for this managing partner stuff. I shouldn't show you my weakness, but there it is."

Bullshit, bullshit, bullshit. Undoubtedly, Abrams had his purpose in sharing a vulnerability, but Bradley couldn't guess what it was. It didn't matter. It was time to get to the point. *Carpe diem.*

"So let me guess, Leonard," Bradley said, flashing an engaging smile at Abrams, then crunching into his salad. "Is it Walter Anand you want to talk about?"

Abrams interrupted salting his mixed greens and looked at Bradley. "Actually, no," he said. "But now that you mention him..." he added, resuming snaps of the salt shaker.

Bradley was taken aback; his trusty instincts had let him down. And he had trapped himself into talking about Anand when he hadn't had much interest in the first place.

"I think he has to go," Bradley said.

"Really?" Abrams said, astonished. "Why?"

"You know, I've been at this game awhile —"

Abrams pointed a fork at Bradley. "Nineteen eighty-eight, first year with the firm, out of law school, right?"

"Yes," Bradley said, mildly gratified by Abrams' command of his personal details. "So, obviously, I've seen my share of files come and go. Now, don't get me wrong. Anand is a capable lawyer, but he is not great. He carries files to conclusion quite well, and most of the time I admit the clients are happy. But he doesn't have those moments of inspiration — you know, those times when he develops a completely out-of-the-box argument that separates him from others. And frankly, that's been my goal with the competition group. People should be coming to us because no one else on the street can help them."

"So, right now, in your practice area, we're showing what on the website? Ten lawyers?"

"Nine. But of course it's padded. I think four of those are litigators who dabble. No offence, Leonard, but they dabble."

"No offence taken."

"Another two are young associates who I can rely on here and there. One seems quite serious. Really, the core of the group is me, Walter and Carolyn Murphy."

"And you're saying that not only would you not make Walter partner, you would let him go?"

"He won't stay if he doesn't make partner this year. He'll go somewhere else where he can be. Good riddance, probably. He can be quite whiny and pissy, actually."

"I'm surprised. I hear many good things about him. If we have the business case to make him partner — I mean, to lose him now, after everything we've invested in him?"

Again, Bradley looked quizzically at Abrams. "*I* have invested a lot in him. But I assure you, I can make any bright, motivated associate every bit the competent competition lawyer that Walter is. I need more brilliance and inspiration."

"I take it you don't think that these moments of inspiration — your term — can be taught? Can't you talk Anand through some examples?"

One waiter whisked away the half-eaten salads and another arrived with pasta for Abrams and seared tuna for Bradley, who leaned in and lowered his voice.

"I'm sure I don't have to tell you, Leonard, this stuff isn't just taught. Look, he's worked on lots of files with me where he's seen what I'm talking about. It's really the stuff of instinct or genetics or I don't know what. But, you know, you either have it or you don't. That's my view."

Abrams tilted his head from side to side and compressed his lips. "I tend to agree with you on that, although — although, someone who works really hard and is open-minded and a good learner, well, that type of person shouldn't be underestimated. I can think of a few litigators who, you know, with just a bit of direction, really got better. A couple of them became great, actually."

Bradley did not hesitate. "I don't see that in Walter."

For several moments they ate in silence. Then Abrams cleared his throat and looked across the table. "In terms of the inspired ones in competition law, who in the city, or the country, has that? Present company excluded, naturally."

Bradley took Abrams' last statement as fact, not flattery. But his question struck Bradley as odd. What interest could there be in lauding competitors?

"Tony Amato at Bergheim's, I suppose; he's sharp, kind of a lone wolf. Greg Schulz at Adams, Morison has thrown the occasional good argument my way and built an adequate group there. And maybe Christie Blanchard out west. That's who comes to mind. Of course, lots of other lawyers pretend to be anti-trust lawyers these days — mostly just technicians, as far as I'm concerned."

Slowly but assertively, Abrams nodded. He put down the fork and spoon with which he'd battled his pasta and wiped his mouth clean with a cloth napkin.

"Which brings us to the reason we're here," he said, lowering his voice. "I have news that may come as a bit of shock." Abrams paused, looking Bradley straight in the eyes. "Tony Amato wants your job. And we think he should get it."

CHAPTER 3

Instantly, Bradley felt his blood start to boil. So that was why Abrams had shown vulnerability about being managing partner — he'd been trying to ingratiate himself with Bradley before releasing bad news. Now he wore an impish grin that Bradley thought looked disrespectful.

"What the hell are you talking about?"

"Well, maybe not right away. I'm having a bit of fun with you — couldn't help myself. But in all seriousness, Tony Amato approached us earlier this week to see if we're interested in having him join the firm as the second partner of the anti-trust group. And once you retire, Chair."

Bradley knew his incendiary anger well. Sometimes it was friend and other times it was foe, and occasionally he could not predict which. He stared hard at his food and decided getting more information would calm him.

"What's the problem at his firm?" he asked tersely.

"Problem, why does there have to be a problem? We're a great firm, what can I say? A lot of people would like to be part of it. Really, his approach is a compliment to our firm and to you in particular. But it's also fair to say that he thinks he can do better with us. He doesn't feel that he's getting the support at Bergheim's that he deserves."

"Is his book better than mine?"

"It's a really good book — if we are to believe what he tells us.

About ten percent better than yours, actually. Not all of it would come over to us, of course; some would stay at Bergheim's. He has two great clients, so he has a lot of concentration risk. He thinks he can bring them over — all their anti-trust work and maybe more..."

"Is that what this is really about — those two clients?"

"Peter, no. It's part of it, but a secondary part, though I have to say, they would be two outstanding clients, and like I said, they're hard to come by these days. No, the MC thinks that it's important for your group to grow and that Tony would be a great addition, both to your group and to the firm. Of course, there's a lot to look into still, and all the financial details to sort out. Tony has his own diligence to do, too, but it seems like he's made up his mind. And needless to stay, your thoughts are extremely important."

Bradley ground his teeth, wondering why he didn't have a veto over Amato's proposal. "Look," Abrams continued, "I understand if you might be feeling a bit defensive, but —"

Bradley interrupted. "Leonard, I don't *need* a Tony Amato. I built this thing from nothing, absolutely nothing. I know how to grow this area and I know exactly where it's going."

"Peter, you've done a great job —"

"I mean, why the hell didn't Amato talk to me about this?"

"He said he was pretty sure he had your respect. He wanted to explain to Ted and me his issues with Bergheim's so we're comfortable he's not going to jump on us. And I know him a little — he was a year ahead of me in law school."

Bradley shook his head dismissively. "Do you have any idea how hard it was to get support to practice in this area twenty years ago? All I kept hearing was that no one could build a practice in this area and that there never would be enough work. Well, obviously that was wrong but it was lonely proving it. I wonder how many times the Management Committee had getting rid of me on their agenda. So now they want me to hand over our great client base and reputation? Does that make sense to you? An odd way to express appreciation."

"He's bringing his own clients."

"Even if some come over, he's getting privileged access to what we have here."

Abrams sighed and peered at Bradley. "Peter, candidly, you're looking at this the wrong way. I'm sorry that you didn't get the support you feel you deserved, but I can't fix the past. You know what our number one problem is right now?"

"The tax department?"

"No. The law business is going international. At least our type — corporate, securities and all the related litigation — is. We've tried to ignore this for twenty years and we're right on the cusp of getting left behind."

"That's Ted's fault. He said we'd be fine as long as we had the best transaction and litigation lawyers and the right alliances. Now suddenly everyone wants to join an international firm. Ted and the MC have to come up with a plan. It's not really my problem."

"Ted's looking at all the options. And it's everyone's problem. This much we know: if we have the best lawyers, then we have the best options and bargaining position. We can't afford to be territorial right now —"

Bradley was going to interrupt again but Abrams waved him off.

"No, it's true. You're being territorial, and frankly I expected it. But I'm telling you that kind of attitude is dangerous. Anti-trust has become really important — we get that at the MC now. We can see how tough the Competition Bureau has become. That's great for business and really differentiates us. And adding one of the best anti-trust lawyers in the country can only help."

"There's only one 'best', and you're looking at him."

"Peter, of course no one can touch you. But Amato's got a great reputation and he was a smart guy in law school. Look, Tony understands that this will be a big change for you."

"And what's this stuff about being Chair?"

"For the time being, of course, you stay Chair. There's no issue around that."

"For the time being?"

"Don't pick at my words, Peter. As I said, until you retire, you're Chair. Then, barring some disaster, its Tony's turn. He's as ambitious as you are and he's ten years younger than you — naturally he wants to be Chair one day. Why would we hire a guy who wouldn't want that? Look, we've done things like this in the corporate department several times. Lots of great lawyers and big egos and it all works out. We need to make sure that we're growing your group into the best on the street. Adding Amato can only help. Frankly, you need Walter Anand, too, just to get the work done, especially if Tony comes over."

"So, could I say a few things?"

"Yes, of course, tell me what you think."

"First of all, it trivializes my reaction to call it territorial. It makes it sound like a pissing match between dogs. I am proud of what I've built here and believe me, it *is* the best competition group on the street. And one wrong move, especially something as big as this, could ruin it all."

"Point taken," Abrams said quietly.

"Second, I happen to think Tony Amato is something of an asshole."

"But an inspired asshole?"

Bradley raised his hand. "My turn, ok? My turn."

Abrams said nothing.

"Amato has been so aggressive on some files, especially some litigious ones, that I thought it bordered on unethical. I am very serious when I say that. I sincerely don't know if I want him as my partner or representing my group. And I think the Management Committee will have to ask itself that as well. And lastly, I work hard, very hard, and so do Walter and Carolyn. We can grow this practice area just fine on our own. Everything is under control. The firm is going to continue to make lots of money from us. Everyone — including every international law firm — is and will be envious. We don't need Tony."

The maître d' sidled up to the table. "Gentlemen, sorry to interrupt, but is the food not to your liking? Some more drinks, perhaps?"

Wrestling with agitation, Bradley ignored the maître d' but Abrams gave him a gracious smile. "The food is lovely. I happen to be talking my partner's ear off, that's all."

After a few half-hearted stabs at his cold pasta, Abrams resumed talking, his tone all business. "So, to be clear, now you're saying Walter stays? As a partner?"

"Better than Amato — that's my first reaction."

"But you'll think about it?"

"If I must," Bradley said, not meeting Amato's eyes.

"Ok, then here is what I suggest we do. We told Amato that we'd get back to him early next week after having lunch with you and giving you the weekend to think about it. I'll tell the MC that you and I had a good discussion about the idea; that you're neither for it nor against; and that we agreed we would talk first thing Monday. Let's aim for 10:00 a.m., ok? In the meantime, call me if you have any questions about what Amato said."

Bradley's eyes darted between Abrams and his plate. Once again, Abrams put down his cutlery, wiped his mouth and leaned in across the table toward Bradley.

"But, Peter, there are three things you need to know. First, you must keep this confidential. No one in your family, no one in your group, no one at all, can know. Amato will be dead at his firm if this gets out. Agreed?"

"Obviously."

"Ok. Second, the MC will really need to be convinced if you don't think that this is the best way to go. Having the very best people we can find at the firm — that's the only way to beat off the competition and stay relevant. And the MC has already decided we should differentiate ourselves in anti-trust. You should be the one leading this. I am telling you as a colleague and a friend, if all I hear Monday is stonewalling, without leadership —"

"I get it," Bradley said tersely.

"Let me finish here. The way the MC looks at it, having Amato and you together would be a coup. Like having Gretzky and Crosby on the first line together. Or De Niro and Streep in the same movie. You know, it could be really magical — these two brilliantly inspired lawyers working side by side, feeding off each other. So please, look carefully at the opportunity. Then lead us one way or another with a plan."

"And third?"

Abrams shifted in his seat and his face went blank. For the first time, Bradley thought, he looked uncomfortable. In an even quieter voice, Abrams said, "This part comes from Collins. He's back next week, so maybe he'll have more to say. He thinks he knows you very well — you started in the same year, right?"

"Yes."

"He certainly predicted your reactions accurately. Anyway, he wanted me to remind you that not only have you been a good friend to the firm, but that the firm has also been a good friend to you. So, personally, he would appreciate if you would keep an open mind in thinking about this."

Bradley looked hard at Abrams, his anger escalating again. "I don't understand what the hell that means."

Abrams looked back unflinchingly. "I think you do. The Christmas party and those girls — that hasn't been forgotten, regardless of how many years ago that was. What no one knows about — and I only got an overview — was how much Collins helped you out. There was quite a group that wanted you out. Anyway, that's what I know and it's mostly between Collins and you. So as a favour to Collins —"

"I have your point. I'll talk to Collins."

"I'm expecting him to be there Monday."

"Fine."

As lunch came to a lurching stop and they walked back to the Bay Wellington Tower, it was all Bradley could do to stay civil. When they parted ways, Bradley returned to his office and, with a large smile, closed the door in Margaret's face, ignoring her plea for attention to some pressing client inquiries.

He fell heavily into his large leather chair and wiped his face hard with his right hand. It was an absolute outrage to bring up those old issues, he thought; that stuff was supposed to be dead and gone. His jaw was tight as a drum and his molars were locked in an unrelenting grind. He leaned forward to grab a pencil, and holding it horizontally, one end in each hand, he slowly bent it until it snapped in half. Idly, he tossed the pieces into the garbage, then took two more pencils from a cup on his desk and repeated the vaguely gratifying exercise.

Bradley wondered what more he could do to release his inner havoc. He told himself that he had all weekend to work out a solution, but that did little to help just then. Instead he chose to do what he often did when he was severely agitated: he called the escort agency. They were happy to arrange for two girls to visit around five thirty. Slowly, the anticipation of his end-of-day visitors distracted Bradley, and after a few minutes he buzzed Margaret to find out what the clients were fussing about.

CHAPTER 4

It was close to 10:00 Friday night and, except for some dim street-lights and the blue vertical neon sign ahead that shone "Maximus", Queen Street West was dark. Amy hurried toward the club entrance at the east corner of Fennings Street, shivering slightly in the brisk fall air. When she reached the smoke-coloured glass front door, she snapped it open, then, before ducking in, paused to look back west along Queen. All kinds of men, from gentle to fearsome, had followed her since her early teens, and since parking on Dovercourt she had suspected another. A figure emerged from under a streetlight ten yards away: well-dressed, at least six feet, with a strong, angled face and a self-assured gait. Discreetly, she watched him stride by. Her worries had been misplaced and for a moment she felt an odd pang of disappointment. With a flick of her free hand she banished the emotion and entered Maximus with the same thrust of excitement she had felt on her first visit.

After the glass door, there was a darkly lit foyer with a pair of floor-to-ceiling blue velvet curtains at the end. Amy took off her sunglasses, intended only for evening camouflage, and let her eyes adjust. She made out the form of a tall, striking man in his late twenties wearing all black. A greeter to some and a guard to others, he smiled as he recognized Amy and said, "Welcome back, Ms. Klein. I trust you enjoyed your visit with us last week."

Amy was impressed that he remembered her name. She

thought the pseudonym had a good ring to it, sounding much more elegant than her real name. The ambiguity was clever, too, possibly telling of a European Christian or Jewish background — not that any of that mattered at Maximus.

"May we take your coat?"

"Yes, please," Amy said, noting the dryness in her mouth.

The greeter handed the coat to a girl at the check-in and returned a token to Amy. With an over-the-top flourish and an engaging, non-judgmental smile, he parted the curtains to let her into the body of Maximus.

A few steps in Amy came to a momentary stop. She stood at the threshold of a large rectangular room with a dark grey slate floor. The room's front half was dissected by a black marble bar in the centre with rows of wine glasses hung above and silver stools tucked under the outer perimeter. The back half was a lounge area with several puffy black leather couches facing glass-and-chrome coffee tables. Gentle techno caressed from speakers in the low ceiling and a dim glow of lighting permitted glimpses of other members without drawing attention.

If Amy was certain of one thing, it was her physical allure. It was a natural advantage she had accepted unquestioningly about the time she had learned that day follows night. She decided with the help of a neighbouring mirror that, at thirty-six, it showed few signs of letting up. A cascade of long hair transformed quickly from light hazel at the scalp to dazzling variations of blond. A provocative twinkle emitted from large ice-blue eyes set in perfect symmetry below etched brown eyebrows and above an aquiline nose. Full lips beckoned with an open poutiness.

Amy shifted her shoulders so the red silk blouse accompanying her short black skirt and giant stilettos opened invitingly at her breasts. With a black leather clutch held tightly at one side, she started toward the bar, the hips of her tall, hourglass figure churning manipulatively as one long leg stepped decisively in front of the other. When she reached the bar, the lengthy slender fingers of her free hand, its nails lacquered smooth red, confidently grabbed the nearest available stool. Slipping on top, she tossed her hair to one side then flung a casual glance around the room. For a second, mute excitement made her eyes flutter larger.

Every person in the bar and lounge areas took Amy in, the men with long, hungry looks, the women more subtly and warily. She ordered a vodka and orange juice and ignored the bartender's three attempts to engage her in conversation. The captivating question was whom she would pick that evening. She didn't plan on hurrying that decision — the anticipation and filling of her pores with attention were half the eroticism. She assumed that some evenings there would be no one. But the first evening there had been a youngish, disarming couple, and she saw no reason why a similarly new and satisfying experience couldn't happen again.

Beyond her attractiveness and ability to manipulate, Amy had little self-awareness. Things came to her too easily for introspection to offer value. With precision, however, she knew how she would make her choice. It was all about the eyes and the touch. With a single glance, the eyes should show ardour and daring. If it was all craving, she was not interested; that was available at a moment's notice, any place, any time. An offer to take care of her for the rest of her life was also uninteresting; she already had that and, at least financially, it was working out quite well. She wanted lust with mystery and a hint of safety. And the touch confirmed that. Neither harsh grasping nor ambivalent stroking sufficed; the touch needed to be calm, strong and purposeful.

The first to move was a man sitting at the bar with a woman, seemingly his partner, both dressed to kill. Casually, he separated from his companion and slid over several stools with his drink to sit next to Amy. There was no chance that she would accept an invitation from him or them — it was too early to make a choice — but she was interested to see what he would bring. It wasn't much. Diffident, anguished grey-blue eyes flicked back and forth between Amy and the bartender. For a few magnanimous moments, Amy spoke with her new friend. But at the first suggestion of more, she chopped him down. "There's no way that's going to happen." Speechlessly, he skulked back to his old seat.

And so it went, as it had the first evening, for an hour or so. Several couples and a few single men and women approached Amy. She chatted with each for a short time then turned them away. One woman did spark Amy's interest — briefly. Avoiding glib lines, her repartee was more engaging. And, like Amy, she seemed to use eyes to judge. She stole several long, intense looks at Amy. The first was mildly captivating, the second invasive. Unsettled, Amy excused herself and went to the washroom.

Using the mirror in the small, cream-coloured room, Amy preened and assessed. Then, with a sharp nod, she decided she was ready for the second room. Re-emerging, she peered toward the far end of the lounge area. The entrance to the second room, discreetly marked by a lamp on a side table, was down a few steps in the right back corner.

Languidly, Amy moved toward the lamp's red-orange glow, enjoying the sense of eyes following her. At the top step, the first whiff of carnality in the air, Amy could not resist a brief, flirtatious glance toward the lounge area. She did a hard, involuntary double-take. Seated in one corner of a couch, holding a drink and introducing himself to the woman beside him, was the man who had passed Amy at the entrance to Maximus.

CHAPTER 5

Amy squinted to make sure she was not mistaken. Hadn't the man continued down Queen? The angular jaw, the well-fitting suit — she was sure it was him. For a moment his eyes caught hers then quickly reverted to his new companion. A bit too quickly, Amy thought. She collected herself and moved down the steps as fast as her stilettos allowed.

At the bottom, another smoke-coloured glass door revealed a second foyer, much like the first but with a final door, not curtains, at the end. Again, a striking man dressed only in black was there to greet Amy. However pleasant, he was an enforcer, ensuring rules were honoured: members or guests only; single men with a couple; no one inebriated; everyone well-dressed; everyone with a current disclaimer form.

"Hello, Ms. Klein. Lovely to have you," he said.

"Yes — thank you," Amy said.

The hesitation in Amy's voice caught his attention. "Is everything all right?"

Uneasily, Amy shifted weight from one stiletto to the other and back again, but the enforcer's concern convinced her to confide. "It's just that — I almost think I'm being followed."

"Followed?"

Amy saw the confusion in his face. "I mean, I *know* that inside here, everyone follows people. What I meant is, followed inside the club from the street."

After pausing, he asked, "Who is it?"

Amy described him and where he sat. Moving around Amy, the enforcer opened the glass door a sliver, then gave a slight nod. "He's a new member. I'll make sure everything's ok," he said. "But if there's any trouble, my name's Carl."

"Yes, I remember."

"I'm one of the owners. As I said, I'll make sure you're taken care of."

Reassured, Amy entered the heart of Maximus carefree. The lighting was subdued, and house music tamped down the din of chatter. In the centre of the room, another long bar hosted a group larger than in the first room, roughly split between men and women. Along the sides and at the back of the room, long pairs of blue velvet curtains hung floor-to-ceiling, with middle partings offering the only access behind.

Amy's heart beat rapidly and she moved to the side to avoid attention. For some time she watched people slip behind or emerge from the curtained areas: massage on the left, one-on-one at the back and group on the right. Around the bar, frowns and glares ensured that ubiquitous little black dresses and blue-grey jackets were not shed prematurely. But in the boutique rooms behind the curtained areas, where the senses were vivified and sometimes overloaded, clothing was an optional prop.

It was time for Amy to put herself on display. She walked suggestively to the back end of the bar, took one of two free stools and ordered another drink. Glancing around, she spied several people of interest. With a smile and a flick of her head to the empty stool next to her, she picked the person farthest from her. Returning her smile and nodding, he took his drink and walked over. He had played a bit too eagerly but she liked the confidence of his casual stride.

"May I?" he asked, pointing to the free stool.

She glanced into his eyes. To her surprise, their colour was unremarkable and radiance dim. She told herself she deserved better, and dropping the visual connection, she turned away from him.

"I'm sorry —" she began.

The words stuck. Just passing through the doors into the second room was the man Amy had pointed out to Carl. She watched him matter-of-factly take in the room's activity, then drift off to one side. Pursing her pouty lips, she hoped Carl had made appropriate inquiries.

"I didn't hear what you said," the man next to her said.

Amy looked at him again. She had no reason to settle for a washed-up, been-around-the-block man and unashamedly did not hesitate. "I'm sorry. I've changed my mind. You're very charming, but I had something else in mind."

He looked at her with surprise. Members and most guests knew they were in a place of minimum banter and quick decisions, but even by these standards, rarely had he been sent to slaughter so quickly. Amy was scanning the bar. Rather than fight the odds, he anticipated better luck elsewhere and disappeared as quickly as he had arrived.

Amy felt a pang that the evening would disappoint. She looked amazing — it should not be difficult to get the proper attention. Her eyes settled on a man she had not noticed before, in conversation with the same woman who had tried to glance her soul in the first room. The woman was cute but not in Amy's league. A mocking grin formed on Amy's lips that soon evolved into a full smile of enticement.

It took a few seconds, but he was soon snared. The woman next to him kept talking, unaware of his distraction. He looked straight at Amy, tilting his head slightly. Amy nodded and again looked at the free stool next to her. He wound down his conversation and made his way to her. As he drew close, Amy observed the other woman deduce his destination. A scowl crossed her face, and grabbing her drink, she marched away from the bar. *No one will care if you leave*, Amy mused, *not a single soul*.

"Hello," he said with an attractive smile, offering his hand. They shook. "Are you here alone?"

"For now," Amy said. His handshake was dead on: dry and steady. "I hope I didn't take you away from interesting conversation."

"Ah, no. A lot of talk — and indecision."

Amy looked closely at his eyes. They were a strong brown with a hint of green at the edge, quite intense and focused solely on her. She felt she could trust.

"You won't have that problem with me," Amy purred. She scanned the room again for the man she thought might be following her. He was nowhere to be seen. "Are you with someone?"

"My significant other and I are members. She's off doing her own thing."

"I see. What do you like to do — here?" Amy asked.

He soaked in the side of her face and took a large breath. "I prefer to get know one woman in an evening — usually starting with massage."

"I see, massage," Amy said quietly, forcing the man to lean closer. She turned toward him again, meeting his eyes as her right hand eased across the bar to grasp his left. "You think you have a good touch, do you?"

Smiling, he said, "As a matter of fact, I do. In fact, I guarantee it."

Amy slipped off her stool, and leaving their drinks behind, she led the man by the hand from the crowded bar to the velvet curtain in front of the massage area. She parted one side and pulled him through.

Behind, there was a row of ten small rooms. Those in use had closed doors with red plastic cards hung from the handle showing two female hands clutching a man's ass. Amy chose a free room at the end. She hung a plastic card and closed the door; ambient music swelled through the room and suffused lighting replaced the glare of phosphorescents. Dark-stained oak flooring married well with lighter, wood-panelled walls, and a king-sized bed was set against the wall across from the door. Small night tables with lamps were on either side, one with an assortment of oils, lubricants and condoms, and the other with a silver cooler, glasses and drinks. The room looked and smelled spotless.

"You're a lucky man," Amy said. "Today I happen to be in the mood for a massage." Standing facing the bed with her back to the man, she gracefully undid the front buttons of her red silk blouse. When she was done, she flicked the blouse off her shoulders, letting it crumple to the floor. Her long blond hair scattered across her back, concealing most of a lacy black bra strap.

The man placed his hands on the outside of her shoulders and ran them down the sides of her arms, letting them come to rest on top of her hips. "Do you want my wife to join?" he asked.

Amy raised her head slightly and with eyelids half-shut absorbed his touch. She found his hands and drew them around her, pulling his front to her back, hearing his breath next to one ear. "As you said, she's off doing her own thing."

Amy pushed the man back and crawled onto the bed, lying prone at an angle. She undid her bra strap, letting each end drop to the bed. Then she spread her arms above her shoulders and rested her right cheek on joined hands, facing away from him, eyes closed. Her hair spread to give glimpses of her narrow back, and her black skirt was hiked up several inches, exposing a long stretch of slim legs down to her stilettos.

"Well?" Amy said.

He let a few more seconds pass. "Which oil do you prefer?"

"Any is fine. You choose."

He hung his jacket on the door and returned to the side of the bed, rolling up his sleeves. After examining several bottles of oil, he selected one and guided a generous arc of oil into his right palm. Leaning over the bed, he pushed Amy's hair away from him. Then he spread the oil across her shoulders and began to caress the muscles at the base of her neck.

"Hmm, obviously you've done this before," Amy said, relaxing, her nerve endings stirring.

He put his hands together at the top of her spine and began a gentle circular rubbing. Slowly, he eased his hands apart to the sides of her body. At each vertebra, he repeated the process. A third the way down her back, he encountered the bulge of her breasts and he paused, maintaining the circular motions. Amy raised her head and shoulders from the bed, exposing more of her breasts. He slipped a hand under each until she slumped back into the bed, forcing his hands back out. He resumed his massage all the way to her lower back, stopping at the crest of her hips.

"And what about my legs?" she asked coolly.

"Oh, I'm getting there," he said with a sly laugh.

Dripping oil on each calf, he applied long, penetrating strokes that caused her legs to part. His hands rose to the lower part of her thighs, first rubbing the outside, then the back and finally the inside. He worked with the earnestness and deliberation of a professional, and for the moment she was taken in. When his hands met her skirt, they snuck under, keeping to the softness of her skin. They drew up her skirt exposing the edge of thin white panties, until, pinned between her stomach and the bed, the skirt became taut, and he couldn't move his hands higher.

From under her head, Amy withdrew her right hand and laid her arm straight along her side. She ran her hand slowly up and down his thigh. Then she slipped it between his legs, searching for signs of arousal. An erection tented his pants and she stroked it with the back of her fingers.

"Your skirt and panties are in the way," he said, his voice raspier.

Amy accommodated, raising her hips using her knees and elbows. He pushed her skirt to her waist then curled a finger under each side of her panties and pulled them to her knees. He drew his fingers back up her thighs to her buttocks. Stopping for a few more drops of oil, he began small, leisurely circles near her hip bones. Amy arched her ass as he moved his hands inwards, easing her legs apart as far as her panties allowed. He dipped between her legs, beginning a slow, repeated slide up and down the wet ridges of her lips. She moaned with a growing desire to be parted and filled.

"More?" he asked. He took her right hand and moved it along the outline of his erection.

"Um-hm."

Amy prepared to give in fully, to be unremittingly satisfied. Instead, shock rolled through her body as someone grabbed the handle of the room's door and threw the door open. Full lighting came on and the ambient music stopped. She imagined herself prone and exposed. Without looking at the intruder, she scrambled to the other side of the bed, lunging for one of two housecoats at the bottom of the side table.

"Oh jeez, oh jeez. Really sorry," the intruder said. "Wrong room — really drunk. So sorry." As quickly as he'd arrived, the intruder stumbled back out, mumbling more apologies and closing the door heavily.

The lighting dimmed again and the music restarted, but they only aggravated Amy. "What the fuck!" she shrieked, scrambling to cover herself with the housecoat. Standing next to the opposite side of the bed, one palm open with oil, the man looked at the door with mild surprise. "Seriously, who the hell was that?" Amy demanded, arms flailing.

"I don't have the slightest idea," the man said.

Amy felt a surge of suspicion. "Was he — was he, I don't know, about six feet, well-dressed, really angular jaw?"

Half-heartedly, the man shrugged. "I didn't get a good look at him. Wearing boxers. Kind of short, actually. I don't really know."

Amy's suspiciousness fell away, only to be replaced by indignation. "That kind of thing should not happen. That's crap."

The man looked at her a bit helplessly. "You know, shit happens. Can't we —?"

"There should be a lock on the door, that's what I think."

"They don't want people behind locked doors for obvious reasons. Can't we, you know, rekindle the moment?"

Amy ignored the man. "And you know what else I think? There should be a panic button here. That's what you should get at a place like this."

"It's right over there," the man said, pointing to a red button next to the bed's headboard.

"Well then," Amy said, and leaned over to give it a smack.

"Oh, for Christ's sake. Here we go." The man moved away from the bed and began looking for a towel to wipe his hand.

"Do you mind looking the other way?" Amy asked. "I want to put this on properly."

"Not at all," the man said with a sardonic smile and turned away.

Amy got up from the bed and drowned herself in the coat's soft fabric. Within seconds footsteps approached the room, followed by a sharp knock.

"Everything all right in there? We are going to come in," a deep voice said.

"Please do," Amy said. Two muscle-bound men in the usual black entered warily. Amy got off the bed and faced them, arms crossed, an involuntary scowl savaging her facial symmetry. "This guy just walked in on us, while we were, you know, in the middle of something," she explained rapidly, her arms flailing again. "Just walked in."

A moment later, Carl peered in from the doorway.

"He was kind of drunk," Amy's erstwhile companion said, putting on his shirt and jacket. "No big deal, really."

"It *was* a big deal," Amy corrected.

Carl was brought up to speed. He adopted a demeanour of deep understanding. "I am so sorry, Ms. Klein. We don't permit inebriation here. If either of you could point out who it was, I would be most pleased to speak to him."

"We didn't see him that well," the man said. "Anyway, I am really out of here. Goodbye all."

"Is there anything I can do to make this up to you?" Carl asked.

"Don't worry about it," the man said and left.

Amy sighed irritably at his lack of understanding. As soon as he left, she walked up to Carl and said in a low voice, "I was wondering if it could have been that guy who was following me."

Carl narrowed his eyes slightly. "The guy you pointed out to me?"

"Yes," Amy said, watching Carl closely.

"I don't think so, Ms. Klein," he said quietly. "I took the liberty of having someone keep an eye on him, and he did very little other than to talk to a few people. I don't think he was following you, actually."

Amy absorbed the information. "Ok," she said, nodding. "Ok. Thanks, Carl. That makes me feel a little better, actually."

"We will see you again soon, Ms. Klein?" Carl asked.

Amy thought for a moment. With a stab of sadness she saw the evening as a statement of how pathetic her marriage had become. "Yes, probably," she said after a few seconds and started to scan the room for her clothes. "Or I might look for something even more interesting."

CHAPTER 6

His ringtone was "Smoke on the Water". "Yes," he said, trying to hide his disquiet.

"Just reporting in. So, she went to a club called Maximus. Just left. Following her in my car now but appears to be on her way home."

"What kind of place is that?"

"Maximus? It's a swingers' club. For couples mostly, but singles can get in, especially women. You have to be a member."

He caught his breath as anger poured into his veins. "And what the fuck does she do there?"

"As I explained, it's a swingers' club."

"I *know* that. But what does she *do* there?"

"She picked up a guy and went to the massage section."

"And?"

"And? I don't know. It's behind closed doors. I can't get in there. They weren't there long. So maybe not too much. Or maybe — who knows."

He stayed silent, grinding his molars mercilessly.

"I got a few pictures of her on the phone, at the bar, talking to a few guys. Want me to email them to you?"

He tried to imagine the pictures. "No. I don't really want to see them."

"Ok." There was an awkward pause. "Is that all for me?" No answer came. "Well, I'll send my report in a day or two — and my invoice."

Peter Bradley hung up. For several minutes he sat almost motionlessly. In one day, he'd been pricked by two troubling revelations, and for each a gamut of tormenting responses vied for his attention.

CHAPTER 7

It was another of those irrelevant sidebar thoughts that constantly wormed their way through his cranium. Words or phrases ending in "off": usually bad. Not always — "liftoff", "playoff" and "stroganoff" were fine. But "cut off", "brushoff" and "showoff": trouble in the air. And "rip-off" — ominous.

Which was how he thought of his purchase of weed the night before. An outright rip-off by the dealer he had known for years, no less. "Sorry," the dealer had said. "Friday evening. Supply is low." The dealer had probably sensed his urgency, caught out by friends visiting unexpectedly, and intuitively raised his prices. And worst of all, what remained of the weed now seemed lost.

Reggie Faxner's rental unit was in a condo tower on Brunel Court off Spadina Avenue among a thicket of similar planning calamities. Suite 2012 was less than four hundred square feet and could have used a coat of paint and some curtains, but the Hong Kong-based owners had no interest in such niceties. To the right of the front door there was a tiny kitchen and to the left a washroom and closet. The remaining square space was dining room, living room and bedroom in one. At the end, sliding doors opened to a balcony elegantly placed above the roar of the Gardiner Expressway. Most of the living room was consumed by a digital audio workstation in the right corner — laptop, two monitors, speakers and mikes on a semi-circle of tables centred by a swivel chair. In the left corner there was a flat-top TV, angled toward a sofa bed shoved up against the kitchen's break-fast nook. Clothes, towels and random items were strewn across the carpeted floor; unwashed dishes and half-consumed bags of chips and cookies cluttered the kitchen. And somewhere in all of this were a bag of weed, a pipe and matches, still concealed despite a fifteen-minute search.

Reggie stood in the centre of the condo, arms crossed against his tall, thin, slumping frame and disdain on his face, surveying for his missing possessions. He accepted that life had its pre-dicaments, but the steady stream of them got him down. He closed his eyes. What had he done last night? He'd started a new track. What then? His friends had shown up at the door. Off to the dealer. Then they'd smoked some of the weed, complaining about its quality, and listened to his tracks and some other music. Later — he couldn't recall exactly when — his neighbour had complained about the noise and said she would call the police. And they'd decided to hide the weed in a place where they were sure the police would never find it. *Where?* Reggie slammed his forehead with his right hand. *Where, where, where?* It was coming back, it was at the edge of consciousness, it was so close — *yes!* At the bottom of the garbage in the kitchen, that was where. Oh god, he hadn't really, had he?

Reggie sprinted over discarded clothing into the kitchen. He opened the right cabinet door under the sink. Stretched across a metal frame screwed to the door and topped by a plastic lid was a grocery bag, sagging with waste. Reggie lifted the lid then turned away and slammed it shut again as a repulsive smell poured into the kitchen. For a few moments he stood disconsolately in front of the sink, considering how he might rummage through the re-fuse.

Spying another plastic bag on the kitchen counter, Reggie muttered, "Not so stupid after all." He put his right hand into the bag and knotted the upper edges along the top of his forearm. Holding his nose with his left hand, he lifted the garbage lid again and eased his covered hand to the bottom of the bag. Almost instantly he felt the shape of his pipe, then the outline of his bag of weed. He withdrew both and delicately put them on the kitchen counter. Triumphantly, he stood in front of his finds.

In seconds, his sense of triumph dissolved. Here he was, standing in front of a bag of weed and a pipe covered with rancid garbage in a rented, minuscule condo that was top-to-bottom chaos. Once again, the tape began to run in his head. Twenty-six and still living off his sister, or more accurately her husband; an artist-in-waiting, prospects never panning out and only a few good ideas left in him. For Christ's sakes, he had to get his shit together.

The tape continued. When the judge had fined him for possession and Peter Bradley had paid for it, Bradley said to him, "Don't worry, it's just a game. Think of it as a payoff to society. But don't let it happen again." And in the oddest coincidence, later the same day, Amy had said to him in a confiding voice, "Peter can afford it. Don't worry about it. It's one of the payoffs for me being with him."

Get in the game and master it, he snarled at himself. *Get in it now*. It was about payoffs — politicians, lobbyists, corporations, the entire Russian oligarchy — everyone was greasing the others' hands and he was missing out. And why? Because he had nothing to give. Amy had her looks; Bradley had his profession and money. Reggie had nothing.

His cell phone stopped the tape running. It was Amy.

"Sis?"

"What are you doing?"

For a second he didn't know what to say. "I'm taking the garbage out."

"Fascinating. I just phoned to see how you are. I haven't

heard from you all week."

"I'm ok, I guess. I, ah, I started a new track last night," he said half-heartedly. "Just gonna listen to it, actually."

"Good — very good. What happened to the tracks you sent to the elevator music company?"

"I haven't heard anything. And I won't. On their website they say they get hundreds of thousands of submissions a year — so you don't even get an acknowledgement that they got your music. If they like your stuff, then they contact you. Otherwise nada. It's a total long shot, sis."

"Hundreds of thousands?"

"You know what I mean. A lot. I've kind of lost hope."

Amy knew her brother better than any other person. She could sense the start of personal demolition work. "And what are you doing today?"

Dominic, I'm meeting Dominic for coffee. Can't tell Amy that.

"I'm meeting someone for coffee at two. Someone who knows a DJ who might listen to my stuff."

"Ok," Amy said, trying to sound hopeful.

"And, you know, the usual club stuff in the evening. Maybe I can get someone to play one of my tracks. I need someone with connections. Amy, you sure you don't know anyone in the music business? A DJ, a producer? Or somebody who knows somebody else? Anybody?"

"Reggie, you know if I did..."

"Couldn't you — couldn't you come with me to the club?"

Amy's voice became icier. "Reggie, I don't go to clubs anymore."

"But, you know, the DJ might play a track if it comes from you..."

"No, absolutely not," Amy said tersely. "We've been through this. I'm thirty-six. I'm too old for clubs and I'm not going to flaunt myself for your music. This is your thing. You make your own success, just like I had to."

Yeah, right, Reggie said to himself but shied away from a confrontation.

"Anyway," she went on in a more soothing tone, "I also called to see if you'd like to visit me tomorrow afternoon. Come by midafternoon — any time after one. I'm bored; I hardly get out. And I want to talk to you about a couple of things."

"I don't want to be there if Peter's there."

"He won't be. He'll be at work — like every Sunday."

"I scored some dope last night. Want me to bring it along?

"If you like."

"Ok, I guess I will. See you tomorrow."

Reggie tossed the cell phone on the sofa bed and wondered what to do next. He still had an hour and a half before meeting Dominic. He remembered telling Amy he might listen to his new track, of which he remembered little. But he checked himself; his mood wouldn't be served if the track disappointed him. He couldn't imagine that it was more than another house beat and bass line. The hard part was an original melody or effect, which rarely came to him. Reggie decided to focus on the week's earlier realization: that his destiny lay in returning to writing. And also getting some money, quick.

Reggie grabbed items of clothing on the floor, looking for something clean to wear. It was a good thing Amy called, he told himself. He was sure he could get her to lend him rent tomorrow, despite swearing never again last time. After a few minutes he found a pair of jeans and a T-shirt that would do.

With little to fill his time, Reggie left his condo and began a slow walk north on Spadina and west on Queen to the coffee shop at Tecumseth Street where he was meeting Dominic. After ordering a cappuccino, he chose a discreet table. He appreciated the time to calm himself. Reggie had always felt wary around Dominic. It wasn't his textbook suburban look: the cropped dark hair and beard, the workout build stuffed into a black T-shirt and jeans, the sunglasses that never came off. No, it was because Dominic was unsavoury and didn't know the line between right and wrong. Many times Reggie had intimated as much to his sister, but she always ignored the point, and Reggie had instead learned to keep his distance. Except now. Dominic's unsavouriness was exactly what he was after.

CHAPTER 8

Predictably, Dominic was fifteen minutes late. After passing through the front door of the coffee shop, he paused, garnering attention from patrons while casually scanning for Reggie. Eventually he saw Reggie's hesitant wave and eased through the small room into a chair across from Reggie. Slumped and saying nothing, Dominic looked slowly from side to side to see whose attention he had caught.

Reggie tried to wait for Dominic to start talking, but he couldn't hold out.

"Hey, Dominic, what's going on? It's been a while."

Without a glance at Reggie, Dominic said, "Nothing's going on little brother, nothing." Reggie was immediately irritated by Dominic's tag for him, a condescending relic from more than fifteen years ago, when Dominic had first gotten to know Amy.

"What are you up to these days?" Reggie asked.

"Same old. Taking care of this and that. You know."

"I don't, actually."

"Don't what?"

"Know what you do, exactly," Reggie said with an awkward laugh.

For the first time since coming into the coffee shop, Dominic seemed to look at Reggie but Dominic's sunglasses made it hard to be sure. Reggie decided to change the topic.

"I saw you at Fantasy last time, about a year ago — remember?"

"Ah — no, not really." Dominic looked away again. "Look, Reggie, I don't know what this is about, meeting here. I'm doing this as a favour for old times, but, you know, I got to be somewhere by three. So, what's up?"

Reacquainting himself with how patronizing Dominic could be, Reggie was put off and hardly wanted to talk about his idea. But he had gone to this much trouble and come this far.

"Well, I guess I'll get right into it. There's something I was hoping you could help me with."

"Me?" Dominic said caustically. "I don't give help, little brother, I sell it. Understand?"

Reggie attempted to ignore Dominic's swagger. He leaned forward slightly, and trying hard to keep his eyes on Dominic, he asked, "Do you know anybody who — who, you know, kills people for a living?"

Dominic's mouth fell open and he jerked to attention. Reggie was delighted he finally had his attention.

"What the fuck did you say? And please, for fuck's sake, lower your voice."

Reggie looked around to see if anyone had heard him and nervously concluded not.

"I said, do you know anyone who kills people for a living — like a contract killer? You know what I mean."

Dominic took off his sunglasses. Reggie couldn't remember the last time he had seen Dominic's eyes: small, beady and nervous, like a rat's. They blazed brown-black at him.

"Why would I know what you mean? Why would I even *tell* you I know what you mean?" Dominic slumped back into his seat but kept his angry stare. "What kind of bullshit question is this? Do you seriously expect me to answer this?"

Reggie felt his mouth grow dry. "I just thought you would

know —"

"I repeat, *why* would I know what you mean? Not a complicated question, Reggie, but I'm sure I know the answer. You think because I'm Italian, right? That's what you're saying — I'm Italian, therefore I should know people who do the kind of thing you're talking about. That's bullshit."

"Not because you're Italian, Dominic. That's got nothing to do with it. It's your background and all. I just thought —"

"My background? What the fuck do you know about my background? Is this all some sick joke? Seriously, little brother, just fuck off."

Dominic stood up to leave.

"Don't go, man," Reggie said, turning open his palms, appealing for understanding. "Let me explain. Just hear me out. Come on, give me a few minutes, that's all."

Dominic glared at Reggie, curled his lips to one side and reluctantly sat down again. "You got two minutes, and keep your voice down. I'm doing this for Amy — for no other reason, got that? And I can't help you. But tell me fast and straight up what the hell you're talking about."

"Dominic, I've always wanted to be a writer. My idea —"

"A writer?" Dominic interrupted. "You? What kind of writer?"

"My idea is to write a book about a contract killer," Reggie said, talking rapidly. "I want to understand how he thinks, you know, when he's hired and when he plans and when he actually does the deed. And I want to understand what's going on in his head when he's *not* working, you know what I mean? How does he live with himself? How does he do what he does without feeling *guilty*? Guilty till it kills him.

"That's what I want to write about, and I need to do some research, right? I've read a few books, autobiographies about contract killers," Reggie lied, not having picked up a book since high school, "but an interview with a real one, anonymously, that would be different. That would be original, that would put me on the map, know what I'm saying?"

Dominic stared at Reggie, registering complete disbelief. "You're serious? Am I right?"

"Yes, absolutely, of course I'm serious. I just thought —"

"You keep fucking saying that. What? What did you think?"

"Amy told me a few times, years ago, that you know a lot of people." Reggie searched anxiously for words to appeal to Dominic's vanity. "You know, important people, from all walks of life, real connections."

"Of course I do. I'm *very* connected. But I can't help with your crazy idea. Even if I knew somebody, why would they do this?"

"I think they'd like to read their story. I'm not gonna name them. I don't even want to know their name. But they might like their side of the story told. People would read this stuff. You know what I mean?"

Dominic snorted. "I'll tell you the only reason they would do this: money. Understand? Money. Makes the world go round and all that stuff. Do you have any? You don't look like it."

"No — I guess — no, no money."

Dominic snorted again. "I don't even know what to say." He looked around the coffee shop, throwing his hands up in the air as if expecting consolation from other patrons. Then, after a shake of his head, he asked in a quieter tone, "So, how is Amy anyway?"

Reggie was thrown off. "She's good, I guess," he said tentatively. "You know she's been married for a bunch of years now."

"Of course I know that," Dominic answered. "Our paths have crossed."

"They have?"

"Sure, little brother."

"I'm seeing her tomorrow afternoon. Do you want me to pass a message on or something?"

Dominic paused then said, "Tell her that her little brother is fucked up." He got up to go. "But I'm guessing she already knows that."

Reggie half stood up, again opening his palms for understanding. "Please think about it, Dominic. It's a good idea, you know? Call me."

But Dominic was already walking out the coffee shop. He slowed only for a smile and imperceptible nod to a table of attractive women near the front door.

Five minutes later, Reggie began the walk back to his condo, hands in his pockets and shoulders slumped. Halfway home, crossing Victoria Memorial Square, he spotted something unusual: a folded one hundred dollar bill, caught among some dandelion leaves. Reggie regarded luck with suspicion; it usually meant that disproportionate hardship was around the corner. He came close to leaving the bill where it was. But he recognized that it solved a problem; he needed money that night to get into the club and to buy some booze or drugs. Warily, looking in all directions, he pocketed the bill.

At home, he called several friends to meet him outside Fantasy around ten. All were noncommittal and Reggie started to feel an unwelcome solitude. The day, like so many recently, was evaporating into nothing. Meeting Dominic had been a huge mistake. Of course he'd known that his idea was outlandish, but it was exactly the kind of idea that would attract an audience, and he'd been convinced that Dominic would buy in. Instead, Dominic had ridiculed him.

Reggie took a cloth and cleaned the garbage off his bag of weed and pipe on the kitchen countertop. He stuffed the pipe with bits of leaf and stalk, lit it and sucked in the smoke from the embers. He wondered what it was like to be Dominic. Most of his characteristics Reggie could take or leave, but he grudgingly acknowledged that he admired Dominic's self-confidence and bravado. A puff later, he decided that he had it all wrong. However much Dominic had mocked his idea, he had clarified that money could make it work. That was how Dominic analyzed everything and presumably how he prospered. Money — the stuff of payoffs — and not personal characteristics was what was important, Reggie told himself with a knowing nod.

He lay on the couch and listened to music for several hours. Then a new idea struck him. He booted up his laptop and listened to some of his own house tracks at high volume on his headphones. He knew the weed made them sound better, but he'd only smoked one pipeful and thought he could still be objective. His music was pretty good after all, probably as good as anything he would hear that evening at the club. He chose the three tracks he thought were best and put them on a USB stick. Around a quarter to ten, after finding his only remaining clean party clothes, he left for the Entertainment District.

None of his friends showed at Fantasy but Reggie was undeterred. He joined the lineup under Richmond Street's dim lights, and in exchange for promising to buy some drinks in the club, he convinced a few girls to say he was with them. Within an hour they were all in Fantasy. Reggie lived up to his promise, supplying each girl as well as himself with a drink, leaving him with fifty found dollars. He abandoned the girls, modestly surprised one seemed disappointed. But his goal that evening was different, and the girl dropped from his thoughts.

As the club filled, Reggie stayed on the sidelines, watching the DJ closely and listening to his selection of tracks. He observed the DJ coolly take the occasional request; a few nineteen-year-old girls in short skirts even earned a smile and a bit of conversation. When he guessed that the DJ had arranged an extended selection of tracks on his controller, Reggie sucked back the rest of his drink and approached the front of the staging area.

"I have a favour to ask," he said to the DJ.

"What?" the DJ yelled back, one hand holding a headphone speaker to an ear and the other waving at the volume of sound around them.

"I said, I have a favour to ask," Reggie repeated, much louder. Holding the USB stick in the air, he asked, "Could you play the first track?"

"What is it?"

"It's mine. It's good. Listen to it."

"I only play tracks from people I know, man," the DJ said and flipped his headphones over both ears.

Reggie was undeterred. Placing his fifty dollar bill under a clip on the side of the USB stick, he reached across the DJ's table and dropped the stick under a small LCD lamp that lit the controller. At first the DJ recoiled from Reggie's unexpected invasion of his space. Then he saw the bill, and after looking back and forth between Reggie and it several times, he said, "I'll only listen, man. No guarantees I'll play, ok?" The fifty slipped from sight.

"Yes, fine. Great. Go for it," Reggie said, feeling a surge of excitement.

Returning to the sidelines, he watched the DJ intently. Bodies surged, lights throbbed, the DJ swayed — but Reggie's USB stick was nowhere to be seen. *Patience*, he lectured himself, *patience*. But after an hour Reggie began to taste the bitterness of his naiveté. He felt helpless to do anything about it; the will to confront the DJ escaped him.

And then there it was: an opening effect he had reworked countless times, a bass drum pummelling at one hundred twenty beats per minute and the gradual emergence of a heavily distorted bass line. It was his track and it was being played for hundreds of people. How he'd missed seeing the DJ insert his USB stick and listen to his tracks, he didn't know. But it was irrelevant. Elation swelled from his core and rolled through his arms and legs in waves.

Reggie had to move. He threw himself into the sea of dancers. Leaning his face back to look at the ceiling, then closing his eyes, he spun around more than twenty times with outstretched hands. It was pure glee and Reggie wished it would never end.

After a minute, it did. His track faded into another and dancers yelped in approval. Reggie came to a rigid stop in the middle of the dance floor, blinking in confusion. His track hadn't reached the first chorus. Deep hostility rose in him. Rudely, he pushed dancers aside and aimed straight for the staging area.

"What the hell?" Reggie yelled. "You stopped playing my track."

The DJ looked surprised then shrugged and ignored him.

"Hey, I'm talking to you. Play the whole damn track!" Reggie pushed as close to the DJ's equipment as he could. For a moment he thought about making an end run around the staging area and confronting the guy face-to-face.

The DJ raised a hand toward the side of the dance floor to catch someone's attention. Then he tore off his headphones. "Look man, no guarantees, remember? You're lucky I played what I did. It was shit, ok? People were leaving the dance floor. I get paid to make them dance, not leave, get it?"

"Shit? It was *not* shit. It was just as fucking good as the shit you're playing right now. Asshole."

"Leave me alone," the DJ said. "Your stuff is crap," he added derisively, putting his headphones on again and focusing on his laptop.

Reggie had not been in a fight lately, but he was ready for one now. The staging area was not large. Quickly, he circled around the right side and began lunging up three steps to the DJ's platform. Before Reggie cleared the steps, a large hand grabbed his left arm's bicep and pulled him back. His neck snapped with the violent change of direction.

"Not so fast," the bouncer said.

Reggie only caught a glimpse of him but it was enough to see that he was a cliché: broad-chested, muscular and tall, with skin much darker than Reggie's and a look of utter intolerance. The insult Reggie had been dealt, the offence he had suffered, required some action. *This guy will do just fine*, Reggie thought as the bouncer pulled him toward the back exit. He clenched his right hand and landed a sucker punch across the side of the bouncer's face. The punch was more successful than Reggie had anticipated and the bouncer doubled over in pain.

A few minutes later, when Reggie regained consciousness, any feelings of success had long vanished. He was prone in the alley behind the club, grit from the rough pavement puncturing the skin on his right cheekbone. His head throbbed and his left eye was swollen shut. His only thought was that a real payoff required more money — a lot more money — and he was prepared to do whatever it took to get as much as possible, soon.

CHAPTER 9

One of my earliest memories, involving my mother, is from a hot summer day at an island cottage we were visiting. I think it was near Parry Sound, but I don't remember now. What I do remember in a hazy, dreamy way, is blue-green water peaked by lapping waves and emergent pinky-beige granite with east-tilting pines. It all was unlike anything I'd seen before. To one side of the island, someone — I assume it was the cottage owner — had built a rock garden. Intersected by three paths and built over a large mound of granite strewn with rocks, it seemed endless to my eyes. Lupins had finished blooming while white and yellow daisies and wild roses were starting.

My mother had warned me that there were snakes in the rock garden. Stay away, she'd said. However, the garden summoned and I began to explore once I lost my mother's attention. More or less in its centre — at least this is my memory — was a particularly large boulder that rose out of the foliage, rounded with a smooth, clean surface. I followed a path to the boulder and, of course, wanted to climb it. It was as tall as I was then and I could only see the top by clambering onto a smaller neighbouring rock. This took a lot of effort, and when I finally was able to see the top of the boulder, I was surprised to see something that looked like a thick black rope. Then I saw a small rattle at one end that twitched and a diamond-shaped head. It dawned on me that this was a snake, the first I'd ever seen with my own eyes. I didn't know how to react; my mother's warning rang in my ear but this creature seemed docile and calm, a natural part of the surroundings.

I suppose the snake was sneaking some sun, maybe slumbering, and I took it by surprise when I poked it with a stick. It was a gentle prod but instantly the snake lashed out at me with enormous speed and animosity, open-mouthed and fangs exposed, and then it was gone in the brush. It only clipped my neck but the pain and swelling came fast. I tore out of the rock garden, screaming for my mother's help. I remember little after that except for a lot of fuss and the new experience of wariness.

That's why I liken PB to a snake. One moment he lulls you into thinking he's on your side, that he is there for you, and the next he attacks and disappears without warning. You can't trust him. And when he betrays you, it's not in an incidental, unimportant way; he maliciously goes for the jugular.

Last entry, I said my fantasy was to blow his head off with a gun. I don't have a gun, so I would need to buy one, which would mean leaving a purchase invoice at a gun shop or meeting with a gang member. A knife would be better. It's easier to purchase and discard. A pristine, razor-sharp knife — that would certainly do the trick. Tied down, he would watch me put the knife to his neck and then feel me go for his jugular.

It seems to me that the divide between thought and action is growing narrower. That's ok. It actually looks passable.

Could I do this? I think I could. Do I want to? Depends when I ask myself.

CHAPTER 10

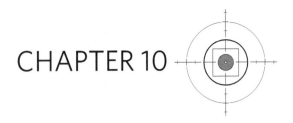

When the load was heavy, Bradley often spent Sunday in the office and forced an early afternoon meeting on Walter Anand and Carolyn Murphy. After Friday's lunch with Abrams, he had been unproductive for the rest of the day, and pressure on a merger file had grown intense. Sunday morning, wearing an old, coarse blue shirt and tan pants, he had arrived at his office at ten thirty, even earlier than normal, and thrown himself headlong into the file.

His was a coveted corner office, dominated by a sprawling desk and a large leather chair. The desk and chair faced the office door from the right, angled into the corner where the southern floor-to-ceiling glass of the Bay Wellington Tower met its counterpart from the west. To the left of the door was an oval meeting table with four matching chairs and along the wall a bookcase of rarely touched legal texts.

Through the morning and early afternoon, Bradley raised his head from his desk only to check for sounds of Anand or Murphy's arrival. Their meeting was for one, but when each arrived a little early, Bradley heaved himself out of his chair and found Anand in the office next to his and Murphy one office further east. He told each they should start early.

A few minutes later Anand and Murphy arrived together at Bradley's office. Bradley had changed seats to the oval meeting table. His bulky upper body was huddled over a pad of yellow legal-sized paper, a pencil in his right hand and a large stack of documents to his left. Anand and Murphy each took a seat, placed smartphones on the table and set up their laptops, then waited motionlessly for direction.

The weather was dour. Mist enveloped the twenty-ninth floor, obscuring any view of Lake Ontario and even the Hockey Hall of Fame below. Rain spat against the western glass but Bradley didn't notice. Instead he racked his brain for the right words to respond to concerns of the Competition Bureau on the merger file. As Anand and Murphy stared at him, he became faintly aware of an unusual tension at the table. He wondered why it always was up to him to find the right words.

"What if — what if *this* just went into the submission to the Competition Bureau?" Bradley mumbled. In a paragraph he had written on the yellow pad, he scratched out some words, inserted a few new ones and relocated others. "Yes, that'll work. What do you think?" He handed the pad to Anand. "It's simple but right to the point." Bradley drummed his fingers on the table, waiting for some feedback.

"Seems fine to me," Anand said, his smooth voice tinged with an English accent. "Simple is good, as you always say."

"Carlisle called me late Friday," Bradley continued. "He said Oshwegan desperately wants to close the merger with Carter Packaging at the end of October. So we need to get the Bureau's approval, fast. The Bureau was clear in our calls — their issue is monopoly in the Lower Mainland market around Vancouver. That's why they sent the Supplementary Information Request. So let's make sure Oshwegan gives the Bureau all the information they want but also explains why they're not analyzing that market properly."

"I like it," Murphy agreed after taking the pad from Anand. "And it ties in with Oshwegan's internal studies and the additional sales statistics they just sent."

"I think it's very clear Oshwegan won't monopolize the Lower Mainland after buying Carter," Bradley continued. "There are other suppliers customers can go to — there's no way Oshwegan can impose sustained price increases." He sighed. "I warned the client, though. There's no overlap in markets anywhere except Vancouver, where they're number one and two. The optics there are wrong. Walter, did Dave, ah, Dave Griz —"

"Gryzbowski?" Murphy said.

"Yes, whatever, did he get that letter from the Vancouver customer? Describing who they'd switch to if Oshwegan raised prices?"

"Yes," Anand said. "But it's very vague. I'm sure the customer is worried about getting dragged into something. Carolyn, you were going to speak to Dave to see if he could get it strengthened."

"I called Friday but he didn't call back."

"That has to go in the package to the Bureau," Bradley said, rubbing his face with his right hand, "and the package has got to get out pronto."

"Did you call him a second time?" Anand asked Murphy.

"No, I didn't. Remember, we had that other client's panic to deal with?"

"We should have," Anand said.

"But I did follow up at the end of the day by email. Let me see if he responded."

"I didn't see anything," Anand said testily.

As usual, Anand looked sharper on a Sunday than most male lawyers did during the week. His shirt, jacket and slacks fit and matched flawlessly, and his face and jet-black hair were perfectly groomed. His composure was what Bradley liked best about him. His parents, immigrants from India via England in the mid-eighties, had had the same calm when Bradley met them two years earlier. Bradley speculated it was the Hinduism, though he knew he didn't have the knowledge to judge. Today, though, Anand's composure was awry and his voice had an uncharacteristic edge.

"Come on, come on," Murphy muttered, rapidly scrolling through emails on her smartphone.

She was smart, efficient and professional to the point of being an utter bore, Bradley thought. Unlike Anand, she eschewed style for plainness. Her mousey brown hair was perpetually cropped. Coal-coloured eyes, centred by a marginally pudgy nose and tense, thin lips, compelled people to keep their distance. And too many pounds on a short frame, together with a preference for flats and tight clothing, made her curvaceous body seem stout. Bradley shook his head imperceptibly. What did he care how his juniors looked? What really mattered was that he had a team of knowledgeable and dedicated lawyers supporting him, and both Anand and Murphy offered that.

"Got it," Murphy announced. "Ok, let's see."

All of which, Bradley barked internally, should be more than enough for the Management Committee. As it had all day Saturday, his mind jumped unannounced into a wary deliberation of his meeting the next morning with Collins and Abrams. Sitting up tall in his chair and trying to discern the lake through the mist, Bradley felt his heart race. Fifty beats later, he reached the same conclusion as every other time: Tony Amato offered him nothing. He needed to make Collins and Abrams understand that the group he'd already built would be the dominant anti-trust team on the street for years. File flow had increased dramatically in the last five years, and revenues had increased fifty per cent. What more did they want? If he had to, he would happily hire one or two new junior lawyers every few years and give them all the mentorship they required. But at least the team would be organized as he wished, with the people he wanted. It had always been his team — and it had to stay that way.

"Peter?" Anand said, interrupting Bradley's ruminations.

"Yes?"

"I said, Dave did respond to Carolyn. He said he would try his best to get a stronger letter from the customer."

"Try his best? Well, obviously, that's not good enough. We *have* to get something — and by tomorrow. I don't want to be the group holding up closing. I know they need court approval for the merger, but the hearing's in two weeks." Bradley was immediately peeved. It was just this kind of inattention he despised. He got up from the oval table and started to pace.

Anand and Murphy looked at each other, knowing this was not a good sign. "Peter," Murphy began after clearing her throat, "it was just late Friday that Dave responded. I'll talk to him when he gets in tomorrow. If we get the submission to him in the afternoon, I'm sure he can send it to the Bureau Wednesday. He said he wants a day to review it."

"Tuesday. He has to send it Tuesday," Bradley said, trying hard to hide his displeasure. "If we don't get the Bureau onside with our views quickly, I'm worried they're going to want Oshwegan to exclude the Lower Mainland market from the merger — and that's a non-starter I'm told. We could even lose Oshwegan as a client." Bradley came to a sudden stop. "In fact, I know it's Sunday, but maybe Dave's at work and we can talk to him now about that customer letter. Carolyn, do you have his number?"

"It's on the contact list. I'll just get the hard copy in my office."

Murphy, in jeans that were too tight, squirmed out of her seat and darted down the hall to her office. Tersely, Bradley said to Anand, "We need to be on top of these things."

"I thought she was —" Anand began but stopped as Murphy hurried back into Bradley's office.

"Here it is," Murphy said, "but I just remembered that Dave

said in his email he's not available today. Wedding in his home-town in California."

Anand stepped in. "I'll redraft the customer letter and send it to Dave this afternoon and leave him a voicemail. I have a good precedent, I think. And I'll revise their submission to the Bureau using your new words, Peter, and send him that, too. If the customer signs off tomorrow, Dave can courier everything to the Bureau Tuesday."

"And I'll make sure the new stats are formatted properly for the submission," Murphy said. "But otherwise, the appendices are in good shape. You can review them today."

Reluctantly, Bradley nodded his approval.

"There is one other thing, though," Murphy said in a strained voice. Bradley and Anand looked at her with poorly hidden im-patience. She took a breath, as if summoning strength for re-solve. "My boyfriend and I — we've been together for one year and my parents are hosting a dinner. I can check the formatting tomorrow morning first thing or even much later today, but I'd appreciate if I could head home for the dinner shortly. It's nearly two already."

Anand eyed Bradley dubiously as Bradley sized up the situa-tion. *She certainly is frumpy*, Bradley thought. Boyfriend for one year — that was a surprise. He knew his reputation for being difficult on issues like this. He thought of reciting his mantra: "The client comes first because the client pays the bills. Every-thing else is secondary." However, just then Bradley felt a needle of empathy for Murphy's circumstances. It surprised him, and he wondered vaguely if it sprang from the yawning cleft between Amy and him, but he couldn't see how. Amy was a problem — something else he needed to solve.

"Sure," Bradley said after a few moments. "Head home now." Murphy could not hide her astonishment and Anand did little better. "But Walter, we have to get the submission and customer letter out this afternoon. And formatting done by nine tomorrow morning, Carolyn, all right?"

"Yes, thanks so much. I will get that done for sure," Murphy said. As she gathered her things, intent on leaving before Bradley could change his mind, she added, "Good luck with everything. Call me if you have any questions."

"I'm not sure what luck has to do with it," Bradley began, but Murphy was halfway down the hall.

By four, Anand had sent the redrafted customer letter, and Bradley and he had finished reviewing Oshwegan's submission. As Anand emailed Murphy with a few requests for supporting information, Bradley tidied up the meeting table.

He then went to his desk, and standing in front of the leather chair, he began to sort through mail. Anand continued to sit at the meeting table, shuffling papers. Bradley turned to the most recent *Ontario Reports* and Anand got up.

"Peter, there is one thing I'd like to chat with you about." Bradley looked up. A tense and restless Anand stood at the other side of his desk. "When you have a moment. It doesn't have to be today, of course."

Bradley had the oddest thought — that Anand somehow knew about Amato's approach to the firm. "That's fine. What is it?"

"Well, last week, at the weekly firm luncheon, we sat together at a table. I don't know if you recall —"

Bradley didn't but he wanted to be gracious. "Ah, yes, I think so."

"Of course there were others. You spoke mostly to Phil Kressler."

"Last Tuesday, you mean? Sure, I remember."

"Exactly. Well, there was just one thing you said that I wanted to ask you about." Bradley grew apprehensive. "Phil was commenting that the new partners would be announced soon, in early October, of course. And you said — well, you said something to the effect of 'I wonder if anyone will make partner in corporate this year.'"

Bradley instantly saw where the conversation was going. He swiped a hand over his face. Whatever his sentiments toward Walter Anand had been Friday, they'd changed. He needed to be careful. "Ah, I see what might be concerning you."

"It's just that — well, I'm sure you'll appreciate that I've had my eyes set on partnership since joining the firm. Of course, last year I was passed over but I've worked very hard to make up for my perceived — for my perceived shortcomings, and frankly I'd be disappointed if the firm didn't see fit this year —"

Bradley waved him off. "I understand completely. My comment to Phil was off-the-cuff. No reflection at all of my thoughts about you. Of course, I can't speak for the firm. There always has to be a business case."

"Yes, I understand that completely. But I am wondering if —"

"If you have my support?"

"Yes, exactly."

Bradley assessed the situation in a nanosecond. Amato's inquiry was throwing a wrench into everything. Bradley needed Anand in his pocket if he was going to tell Collins and Abrams that adding Amato was a waste of time. But Amato's interest in Collins, Shaw might blow over and Anand would be expendable again. The trick was to leave Anand feeling confident but also preserve an escape hatch. As always, Bradley thought he had just the right words.

"You've done good work, Walter. So I am certainly inclined to give you my support," Bradley said calmly.

A few creases of worry on Anand's face dissipated, but not

all. "Thank you, Peter. Thank you for your support." He paused. His body became still and his eyes focused resolutely on Bradley. "Just so I understand, when you say *inclined* to give your support —"

Bradley sat in his leather chair. He swivelled to watch the rain pound against the west windows and leaned back as far as he could. He didn't appreciate being pressed by Anand, not just then. "One of the things we talked about during your last annual review was thinking laterally, out-of-the-box," Bradley said, as measured as possible, not diverting his gaze from the windows. He pressed his fingertips together above his lap. "I've seen some of that but I'd certainly like to see more."

Anand stared at Bradley. "Maybe I don't understand what thinking laterally means."

Bradley turned to look at Anand with obvious surprise. "I'm sure you do. Think of the Pillar file in spring. How did I get the regulators to stop talking about price-fixing charges? By applying the very same argument they'd bought five years earlier with Notea. Remember? We threw the Notea debacle at them. It wasn't obvious Notea could help us with Pillar — different sectors, right? But there it was, ripe for the picking. And the folks at the Bureau are very smart. Once they saw the parallels, it was easy to resolve things. That's an example."

Anand hesitated. "I thought — I mean, I took the Pillar file, and the use of Notea, as a fairly collaborative effort. Not just involving me. Litigation helped a bit, too."

That was absurd, Bradley thought. Anand was pushing his patience. "That's not how I remember it. Your technical work on Pillar, though — first class." Bradley paused, seeing Anand still rigid in his spot. "I'm going to give a bit more thought to things over the next few days. Don't be too concerned. You know I think highly of you."

Bradley opened a file on his desk as a broad hint that the meeting was over. Anand held his position. "Maybe what I'll do, Peter, if you don't mind, is collect together the files where I think I've shown lateral thinking and send you an email on them tomorrow morning. As a reminder."

"I have several meetings tomorrow morning," Bradley said quickly. The Amato problem darted into his mind again. It was an affront, he thought. And now Anand was pestering him. He should be spending time on files, not these sorts of things.

"Just look at it when you can," Anand countered.

"All right, I'll do that," Bradley said. He hadn't conceded anything; any file Anand cited would demonstrate *his* skills, not Anand's. Any important anti-trust file at Collins, Shaw would.

"Thank you." Seeming somewhat appeased, Anand turned and began to leave Bradley's office. But Bradley had one more question.

"Tony Amato. You've had a few files with him, I think. What's your experience with him been?" When Anand turned to face Bradley again, Bradley could see he was puzzled. "I have one issue with him that I'm trying to sort through. I'm interested in your thoughts — confidentially, of course."

Anand took a moment to think. "Great judgment, very fast and very clever is what I think," he said. "Certainly an excellent lateral thinker," he added with a rueful laugh.

Bradley looked hard at Anand. "No particular problems then?"

"No, apart from conceding that he represents his clients very well."

Wishing Anand had never entered his life, Bradley said, "Thanks," and proceeded to ignore him.

CHAPTER 11

As Peter Bradley liked to put it, four years earlier, he had bought the house on Gregory Avenue in ritzy Rosedale "for Amy". It had taken a shocking amount of money and a risk-happy banker to be among the gentry. Faux-Tudor with prickly neighbours, the house was far too large for the two of them as far as Amy was concerned, but she'd never had the heart to tell her husband. What she did like was the renovated, generous master bedroom. Together with its ensuite washroom and walk-in closet, it was nearly as large as the house in which she grew up. The bedroom had a soothing view of the landscaped backyard garden, and a plentiful seating area where Amy had her work desk. Unlike the other rooms in the house, it made her feel at ease, and when she was alone she spent most of her time there.

Amy awoke Sunday morning around eleven, an hour after Bradley had left for work. Her first thought was that she had time for a long bath followed by a tanning session in the backyard; Reggie wouldn't be by until he was finished sleeping into the early afternoon. Crawling out of bed, leaving the bedroom curtains drawn, she went into the ensuite washroom for self-pampering. An hour or so later, she located one of her two-piece bathing suits in the walk-in closet and put it on in front of a six-foot mirror, critically eyeing her body for fault lines.

More or less satisfied with herself, she grabbed a towel and headed along the upper centre hallway, then right and down the stairs. At the bottom, near the front door, she reversed course. She went down the first floor hallway, past the living room to her right and the formal dining room to her left, and into the expansive kitchen at the back. The drapery and dim lighting of most rooms barred the outside elements, but the kitchen had three sides of generous windows that welcomed in the backyard. At its threshold, Amy came to a sudden stop. For the first time she realized it was raining.

"What the hell?" she said, adopting the look of a forlorn child. "What am I going to do now?"

After a few minutes' agitation she reluctantly decided to make a cup of coffee. Mug in hand, she called Reggie to remind him that she was expecting him in a few hours. Predictably, he didn't pick up, and she left a voicemail.

Amy returned to the master bedroom and changed into a blouse, jeans and sweater. At her desk she preferred a tablet over a laptop and curled into a comfortable neighbouring chaise. She began to revise a note called "Projects", as she had done each day since creating it two weeks before. And like the previous days, she concluded that all five projects were intriguing. But the first two, art gallery owner and antiques shop proprietor, easily seemed the best. Each took advantage of her Master's degree in Fine Arts, even if she had completed it more than a decade earlier. And she could see herself in either scenario, charming clients with her looks, engaging personality and knowledge, and persuading them to consume unnecessarily.

She would need to lease a space in the best part of town, maybe on Davenport Road, and certainly not far from home. It would have to be sufficient for some proper inventory, but otherwise intimate. A staff of one or two pretty young things would be sufficient, though they couldn't look better than her. And she would make her own hours, whether greeting visitors from behind sleek furniture at the leased space or meeting clients with sample catalogues at their homes. Her plan of purpose and independence was coming together nicely. She only saw two problems: choosing the project and getting the start-up capital.

Amy decided that it was down to the art gallery and antiques shop, and that this was the day to choose. For more than an hour she pondered which, sometimes curled in the chaise, other times wandering the master bedroom or visiting the kitchen for a snack and coffee refill. On the brink of deciding for the milieu of an art gallery, the doorbell rang. It echoed through the house like a bell in a church.

When she arrived downstairs and opened the door, Reggie, carrying a knapsack, strode past, avoiding her eyes. "I don't want to talk about my face," he said sheepishly.

Amy did not miss the blue-yellow swelling around her brother's eye. Catching up to him, she grabbed one of his arms and forced him to turn so she could see him head on. "Reggie, what happened to you? You look awful. Let me see."

"Thanks. Like I said, I don't want to talk about it."

"You're going to talk about it — I want to know. We need to get some ice for that eye." Amy hurried to the kitchen and Reggie trailed. "Have you seen a doctor?" she asked.

"A bouncer took exception to me punching him last night. Those guys are too sensitive."

"*What*? You're skin and bones and you're fighting bouncers?" Amy put some ice cubes in a kitchen towel and handed the bundle to Reggie.

He let the skin and bones reference pass. "And no, I haven't seen a doctor. I didn't really think about it."

"Put that on your eye and tell me what happened. And you have to go see a doctor. Tomorrow morning. Promise?" Comforted by his sister, Reggie dutifully iced his eye. "Sit and explain," she said. They each sat on a stool next to the kitchen island. Amy drew her knees to her chest and hugged her lower legs, eyeing her brother intently.

"Sure, I promise," Reggie said, looking away. "I went to Fantasy last night, like every Saturday. I took a USB stick with my three best tracks. I thought maybe I could get the DJ to play one."

"Ok," Amy said in a dubious lilt.

Reggie heard the doubt. "And he actually did."

"Really? Seriously, that's awesome."

"Yeah — but he stopped after a minute. So I, you know, confronted him — asked him why."

"Let me guess — that didn't go well."

"Well, if you're gonna play a track for one minute, you might as well play it to the end, you know what I mean? He said people were leaving the dance floor — which was bullshit — and that the track was crap — which was *more* bullshit."

"Oh, Reggie," Amy said with a condescending shake of her head. "I don't even know if I want to ask. How did the bouncer come into it?"

"What do you mean 'Oh, Reggie'? The DJ couldn't handle things on his own, I guess, and called him over. The bouncer just pissed me off more. I wanted a piece of him. Who wouldn't?"

"Everyone else in the world? Seriously, you always do this," she said. Dropping her knees and leaning toward Reggie, Amy put a hand on each shoulder and drew him closer. "You get in over your head. All the time."

"I do not."

"Yes, you do. You'll never get in that club again."

"I don't care. I don't want to go back."

"The number of scrapes and problems I've gotten you out of since Mom and Dad died. Seriously."

Reggie didn't know what to say. "Whatever," was all he could muster.

Amy leaned further and hugged him. "But I still love you," she added before releasing him.

"Anyway, I brought the weed over," he said, hoping to divert her. "Do you want to light up?"

"Maybe just a bit," she said. "I don't want the house to smell. Peter will get pissed off."

"Really — I'm shocked," Reggie said, deadpan. Reaching inside his knapsack, he pulled out the weed bag and pipe, put them on the kitchen island, and partially filled the pipe. "How is Attila anyway?" Lighting the pipe, he passed it to Amy. After drawing some smoke, she crinkled her nose and passed the pipe back.

"Why does that pipe stink?" she asked.

Reggie ignored the question. "Still cutting me off?"

"Absolutely," she said with a snarky laugh. "I stopped telling him months ago that I give you money."

"I don't know what his big deal is. It's just a loan anyway."

"Really? I wonder how big that loan is now."

"Probably pretty big, but I'll pay you back — or I guess I should say, pay Peter back."

"And I won't buy any more shoes this year."

Reggie smirked. "Tell me, sis. Is your husband a jerk *all* the time?"

Amy paused for a deep sigh. "Seriously, Reggie, sometimes I just think I've made the biggest mistake a woman could make. Some days I don't even understand what I was thinking when I married him."

"It confused a lot of people, sis," Reggie said. "Of course, you know what they were saying."

"Well, that's crap, it wasn't what everyone thought. So he was a lawyer. So he had money. At least I think he does, not that he ever shows me. It wasn't about that."

"It wasn't? Not even a bit?"

"Of course it was a *bit*. I mean, we didn't have much, right?"

"No, we didn't," Reggie agreed. "You know, I didn't notice so much. You were taking care of everything. But it's true — it never felt like we had anything."

"Two hundred and fifty thousand from the car accident, that's what we had."

"Seems like a lot, actually."

"Not for ten years, Reggie."

"I know, I know."

"That and whatever we earned from jobs, which wasn't much."

"You worked a lot more than me," Reggie said a bit awkwardly.

"You needed to get through high school," Amy said with a shrug.

"And I kept cratering. I'm an idiot."

"No, you're not, Reggie. I don't want to hear that."

"I'll make it one day, sis. Soon."

"All the money was gone when I met him. Ten years after the accident — no wonder."

"And the shitholes we lived in."

"And the shitholes we lived in," Amy said, nodding. "I mean, you can only take so much of that, right? But truthfully, I loved Peter. At least I think I did. I almost can't tell for sure anymore." She looked to the backyard garden. "I had options, you know."

"I know you did. Not Dominic, though. He wasn't an option."

"Of course not Dominic. You remember him, huh?"

"Hard to forget him. An asshole, really."

Amy giggled. "A lot more exciting, though. And I think he's probably just as successful as Peter in his own criminal way. Anyway, six years ago, I thought Peter was the one."

"Whatever that means," Reggie said, feeling a bit giddy from the weed.

"And now I can't believe how he's treating me. It's insulting."

"You know what I think these days, sis? It's all about payoffs. I'm killing myself to be a successful artist — and it's about payoffs. You know what I mean? Getting people to do things for you."

Amy looked mystified. "What are you talking about?"

"If you have something people want, they'll do stuff for you to get it. I paid that fucking DJ to play my song last night. That's right, Amy, I paid him. And it worked. I just didn't pay him enough. Because I never have enough. So he played one minute of my track. I bought a minute's worth of his time. That's what happened."

"Take it easy on the weed, Reggie," Amy said a little sternly. "Anyway, I'm feeling very confused about Peter right now, and very trapped. For one, he's never around. And when he is, he's very controlling and judgmental and very — very *odd*."

"Odd? What do you mean?"

"Sexually, I mean."

Reggie squirmed on his seat. "Ok, I don't really want to know about that. Don't you have a girlfriend to talk to about that or something?"

Amy's opportunities for meaningful female relationships had been rare; women always seemed to take an instant dislike to her.

"We moved around a lot before I met Peter, remember?"

"And there always were boyfriends."

Amy studied her brother. "What was it like with LeeAnn?" she finally asked, recalling the thin, mousey girl who had interfered in her relationship with Reggie. Amy had never understood why Reggie fell for her; purely sexual, she assumed, his first serious girlfriend at age twenty and, as far as Amy knew, his last.

Reggie was glad that he was stoned. "What was what like?"

"The sex."

Reggie ran his hands through his hair. "I don't know. It was a long time ago."

"You do know — you're just embarrassed. I can't believe it."

"Come on, sis, what do you expect?"

"I mean, was it regular and fun?"

"I guess. It really was a long time ago," Reggie said. He looked down at his knapsack, searching for any point of focus other than Amy's face. Sensing the topic wasn't exhausted, he asked reluctantly, "And it's not with Peter?"

"Not really, no." Amy wondered how much to share with her brother. "He is — really inconsistent. Very interested for short periods, then not at all, often for a long time. And he really likes to be dominant. Which — which I accommodated for a while, but at some point you want some connection."

She looked at her brother for understanding. He stared blankly at his pipe. "Sometimes he's just too extreme," she continued. "Quite honestly, I don't care if he has sex with me at all." Reggie's legs bounced on the stool. He reached to relight his pipe, offering her another smoke. "No, I'm ok. And don't smoke so much here. I'm serious. I don't want Peter to smell the weed when he comes home. Not that he cares if I smell someone else's bullshit perfume on his clothes."

"You do?" Reggie asked, surprised.

Amy put up her hands as if to protest. "He's not having an affair. He wouldn't know what to do with it. I'm pretty sure I know what's going on. A slut hanging onto his shoulders during his deals, trying to tease him. Anyway, some slut somewhere, that's what I think. I can't believe he lets that happen."

"She won't get anywhere, Amy. You're way too attractive and smart," Reggie said, doubting the point as he made it.

"He lets it happen — that's what's aggravating. Peter always knows exactly what he's doing. Jerk."

A scowl crossed Amy's face and it made Reggie anxious. "Amy, there's something I need to tell you."

She eyed her brother carefully. "You need rent money, right? Remember what I told you last time?"

"That's not what I was gonna talk to you about, actually."

"What then?" The rain pelted the kitchen windows. "Gosh, it's pouring," Amy said, looking outdoors, appearing to relax.

"I had coffee with Dominic."

She snapped her head back to look at him. "Why?"

"I know you said he was off limits and everything. But I have this idea to write a book. And it's about something — I just naturally thought of Dominic. So I called him and had a quick coffee."

Reggie expected Amy to protest vociferously, but to his surprise she didn't. After a few moments reflecting, she said, "I really don't care, Reggie. Dominic is from a long time ago. So you're interested in the world of illegitimate gain, are you?"

"Yes, although he denied he was anything but a normal guy."

Amy laughed. "That's part of his routine. He steals but gets very upset when you call him on it. I think he's convinced by his own denial. Is that your project — writing about a life of mundane crime? I'm not sure anyone will find that very interesting. And didn't you give up on writing? What about making music and DJing? What did we spend on all that electronic crap you bought?"

"Amy, I need to do something with my life."

"You keep telling me that."

"No, it's true," Reggie said with a flash of anger. "I really need to and I'm gonna. I just need time and I need to build some cash. The music — I'll keep doing that. Although it's just so competitive —"

"There are thousands of writers out there making nothing."

"I know, I know. But this is a really good idea. I think even Dominic thought so."

"He said that? What does he know about writing?"

"Just listen to my idea. I want to write a book about a contract killer. But not just about what he's done. I want to know what goes on in a head like that. How they do what they do and keep on functioning. So I thought I need to interview a real hit man. He'll stay anonymous and everything, but I want to learn about his background, his clients, how he *lives* with himself. Do you know what I mean?"

"They're psychopaths — they have no feelings."

"That's what everyone thinks, but we don't know. That's maybe the most interesting part of the project. Are they just built differently than you and me, or has something else changed them?"

"And Dominic is going to help you with this?" Amy said incredulously.

"No, he didn't say that," Reggie said with a sigh. "He basically laughed at me first. He was a real asshole. But he left the door open a bit. What he said was if I paid enough money, it could happen. I don't even know if Dominic knows a hit man."

"I bet he knows three. And Dominic will take his share of the action. Seriously, watch out. And I guess you're looking for money from me again? Is that it, Reggie?"

"Sis, actually, what I need money for first is rent. I'm sorry."

Amy buried her face in her hands. "Reggie, I thought you said it *wasn't* about rent. I can't keep doing this. Seriously. I'm on an allowance. That's how Peter does it. He gives me a fucking allowance every month."

"I know, I know, you told me about that."

"Reggie, listen to me, get a job. You're twenty-eight. Be a courier again if you have to. Use my old car, I don't care. It works.

I keep renewing the license plates and insurance, so use it. Just get a job."

"I will. I promise I will. I'll do my résumé today. Really." Reggie looked at Amy pleadingly. "It's only fifteen hundred. Just this month. I'll pay you back."

"Oh, yes, the loan. Great," Amy said, shaking her head. She grew quiet for a few seconds. Reggie felt an uncomfortable stare. "I will do it if you help me with something."

"Sure, absolutely. Name it."

Amy paused, wondering again how much to disclose to her brother. "I have a project I want to do, too. I — I need to get independence from Peter. It's as simple as that. My own career, my own money. Anything with money, he gives it to me like a father giving money to his daughter to go buy an ice cream cone. It's — it's humiliating."

"The project, sis?"

"An art gallery owner."

Reggie deliberated for a moment then nodded approvingly. "I could see that."

"Yes, so can I. I'd start working at another gallery. Peter could probably help me find a job, with his connections. I'd work there for a year or so and learn the business. Then I'd open my own gallery. I think I could do it. I've got the right education. I've got the right personal qualities."

"Well, that's a relief — I think."

"What is?"

"I thought you wanted help with a divorce."

"How would you help me with that?"

"Stand by your side and all that stuff."

Amy bit her lower lip. "I have thought about it. A lot. It would be so awful. I am so close to where I want to be. If I divorce him, who knows where I'll end up. It would take *years* to get a settlement from him. He has all the money and power, and I don't have either. How do I fight that? What happens to me in the meantime? Peter would just make life miserable for me."

"But you'd just find another man, wouldn't you? Like always."

"That would drive him even crazier."

Reggie nodded. "So you should totally do the gallery, sis. That would be right for you."

Amy looked at Reggie hopefully. "It would be, wouldn't it? It would make me a lot happier, too. And then I could just sideline Peter." She sighed. "There is one big problem, though. I don't have the money to start it with. Not enough, anyway."

"I thought you said Peter would help you with the gallery."

"Help me get a *job* at one, yes. But I don't know if he'll give me the money, and frankly, I don't want to ask him. It would be so painful, and if he does give it to me, he'll want to take control." Amy's voice became shrill, and her arms began to flail. "I *know* him. In no time at all it will be his gallery and he'll be telling me what to do. And then I'll be right back where I started. To hell with all that." She paused and then in a lower voice, she said, "No, I need to get the money another way. Which is where your favour comes in."

CHAPTER 12

Reggie squirmed on his seat some more. "Favour?"

"Relax," Amy said, averting her eyes. "It's not that serious."

"Well, what is it?"

Amy looked at her brother again. "Peter might be a great lawyer but he's a terrible financial manager. He should be investing his money, but he keeps most of it in one chequing account and one savings account. Other than what he put into this place and the cottage."

"How do you know all this?"

"His financial adviser comes over here twice a year. I'm not included, of course. Except for the part where Peter has him explain to me how Peter is taking care of me — the deal, as he so romantically calls it. But I, you know — happen to be around —"

"The deal?" Reggie interrupted.

Amy waved Reggie off. "What I'm saying is that I happen to be around and happen to hear quite a lot of what they say. And it's the same every time. Why do you keep your money in those accounts? You should invest it in stocks and bonds for your retirement."

"I don't get it, sis."

"What don't you get? Peter's money is in two accounts. There's probably a lot of money there. He doesn't watch these accounts ... do you see?" *Man, he's slow sometimes*, Amy thought. "In other words, Reggie, he won't notice if there's a transfer of a hundred thousand to my account, say ten thousand a month for a while. I — I just need his password."

Reggie got up from the island stool and walked to a kitchen window to watch the rain. "You're sure he won't notice that much money leaving his account?"

"Reggie, I live with this man. He doesn't keep track of money. It doesn't interest him. He cares about being a lawyer at the top of his game and his political connections. And occasionally, when it suits him, he wants me by his side — you know, as his trophy wife, though I hate that phrase so much. That's the deal by the way, Reggie, if you want to know. I'm his trophy wife, he looks good with me in public, and once in a while I give him access to this body, if I can stand it. And dead or alive, he takes care of me financially."

"So that's your payoff," Reggie blurted.

"Payoff?"

"For being his beautiful young wife, he makes you part of the rich and famous."

"Call it what you want, Reggie. If transfers are done intelligently — seven thousand here, nine thousand there, he won't notice, I'm sure."

"So you want me to help you steal his password? Is that what you're saying?"

"I need help getting it. I don't know enough about tech stuff."

Amy got up from her stool and joined Reggie at the window. She stood close to him, staring at him intently. A little intimidation now wouldn't hurt, she thought. "There must be a way to get his password without him knowing."

"Just stand beside him when he logs in."

"I thought of that. He wants to be left alone when he's in the study."

"He's gonna wonder where you got the money for your business."

"I'll tell him it's from my savings. He doesn't know what I have or don't have. And I *do* have savings — just not enough. And frankly, I think he should pay for this one way or another. You know, for me putting up with him and doing everything I do for him."

"Sis, it sounds — it sounds illegal, you know."

"That's crap, Reggie." Amy surprised herself with the vigour of her tone and softened it. "Reggie, Peter has me on a leash. I'm like his little dog that he trots proudly around the park. I deserve better. *We* deserve better. And — and I'll give you ten thousand to help you for a while. That will be rent and whatever idea you're working on. We can do this — we *should* do this. It's not my fault that he doesn't treat me right. Once the transfers are done, so am I. Then I have my own business and I'm independent."

Hesitantly, Reggie said, "Does Peter know much about computers?"

"Reggie, *I* help him with questions about his computer. He didn't even know what a USB stick is until I showed him a few weeks ago. That's how bad it is."

"Then it would probably be easy. I can think of a couple of ways."

Amy smelled success. "Reggie, when can we do this?"

"In the next few days, I guess."

"Wonderful," she said, planting a kiss on the sore side of his face. He winced and she gave him a replacement kiss on the other cheek. "Why don't you have the ice I gave you on your eye?"

"It's melted."

Amy went to the fridge to replenish the ice cubes in the wet towel. She noticed her brother becoming quiet. "What are you thinking about?" she asked, anxious to maintain their connection and his commitment to her favour.

"I guess part of me always understood how things worked between Peter and you. I mean, he's so much older than you, and I always knew he was taking care of you," Reggie said. "But another part of me thinks he really loves you. This all seems so —"

"Crass? Welcome to the real world, Reggie. There was some romance between us — once — but there also was calculation. And by the way, I think he does love me."

"So the running joke might be right."

"The joke?"

"That Peter is worth more to you dead than alive."

"Maybe you're right. I'll have to check his life insurance policies — again," she said with a mocking laugh. "That's terrible. I can't believe I said that."

But she knew why. It reflected a more recent calculation. It was dark to think of her husband's death, but not as dark as thinking about divorce. Much less humiliating, and much easier to get on with her life.

A half hour later, Reggie stood at the Rosedale subway stop. When the train arrived he chose an inconspicuous corner in the back car; he was tired of people looking at the rainbow swelling around his left eye. Once seated, he looked at his reflection in the window. He was indeed hideous, even though the ice had reduced the puffiness enough for him to see through a small slit. Probing the swelling with a finger, he rapidly sucked in air from the pain, generating a sharp hiss. The noise caught the attention of a few mid-car riders who shot him a glance, then quickly looked away. Amy was right, as she so often was. He should go see a doctor.

And he should do his résumé and get a job. And he should shave and get a haircut. And he should believe in himself and make a life. Should, should, should. Reggie wondered, *Where do people get the strength?* Money, luck, knowing the game, being in the game, being connected – all items that cascaded in his brain like a wad of bills thrown in the air, floating to the ground. All things in Peter Bradley's life and not his, he told himself in disgust.

The subway rolled into the construction nightmare of Union Station, Reggie's stop. For the last ten minutes he'd let Amy's idea drift in and out of his mind. In his gut, he felt a tremor of distrust. Could it be as easy as she thought to access Peter Bradley's money? But he told himself, *Amy is smart, and she does live with him and she knows how to do things.* And she was right — they *did* deserve better. With ten thousand dollars, there was so much he could do and so many people he could impress. And maybe, with a little persuasion, it could be more. A lot more. Then it would be *his* moment. Exiting the train, excited and scared, he let the thought stick.

On Front Street walking toward Spadina, Reggie heard the ringtone for a text. It was from Amy. *"Talked with D. Will help with your idea. Calling you shortly. PLEASE be careful. PLEASE. Call me when you can. A."* Yes, this could definitely be his moment. Time to be seizing the day, or whatever the phrase was, he told himself.

CHAPTER 13

Carolyn Murphy knew that her mother and father were the most loving parents imaginable. Unlike her own affections, which tended to be conditional, her parents had given her what she wanted when she asked for it. Despite it putting them years behind in their retirement plans, they had helped fund her university and law school. Thankfully, it had ended six years earlier, but their pride in their daughter, a lawyer no less, meant they were at peace with their future.

Nonetheless, taking her place at the dining table in her parents' small home in Etobicoke, Murphy felt a grating irritation. Often she felt suffocated by her parents' love, and dinner that evening was one of those times. It was as if they were intent on breaking down the careful distance that Murphy, an only child, liked to maintain. Of course, on a Sunday afternoon their company was much better than Peter Bradley's. But in a week or so she intended to break off her relationship with Kyle, something she had only just decided and not shared with anyone. Then the dinner would seem embarrassing. Life would be simpler if she was at home reading a useless, smutty novel and her parents weren't *fussing* so much.

Murphy's mother was still busy in the kitchen. Her father, who loved the food at family gatherings, had long seated himself in the dining room. Kyle sat with Carolyn on the other side of the table.

"It's so nice to have a Sunday dinner like old times when you were young, Carolyn," her father said. "You're going to like what your mother's cooked for us."

Murphy could have guessed the dish two weeks earlier when her mother had called with the invitation.

"Lasagna, Dad?"

Her father looked at her with feigned surprise. "How did you know?"

She smiled. "What she makes every time — with garlic bread. And I can smell it, too. Get ready — when she comes out, she's going to tell everyone it's my favourite dish."

"At least you have a mother who cooks for you," Kyle said with a derisory laugh.

The old story, Murphy said to herself. She didn't bite but her father did.

"What do you mean?"

"Kyle's parents separated twenty years ago and his mother disappeared off the face of the earth," Murphy said to her father.

"Oh yes, I'd forgotten, Kyle. Getting old."

"You're all of fifty-six, Dad."

"Still..."

Murphy's mother burst into the dining room, her hands in oven mitts that held a large square ceramic pot. "Carolyn, I've made your favourite, lasagna," she announced proudly. Ignoring the laughter, she carefully set the hot pot on the dining table, and applying her heavy-set frame cut the lasagna into four large pieces. "Bring in the salad and garlic bread, would you?" she said to Murphy's father.

"You see, Carolyn, I'm like a slave around here," he said light-heartedly. Quickly, he returned with the food.

As they began to eat, Murphy's mother looked at her daughter. "You look tired, dear. I suppose you were at work again today?"

"Of course, I'm part of the Peter Bradley and Walter Anand show. That's what we do — work. We're kingdom builders, you know."

Murphy's father stopped attacking his food and held his fork in mid-air. "You see, that's what I mean," he began. "I know we've talked about this before, but I feel like talking to someone at your firm about this. You just can't work people to the bone like that. It's counterproductive. They'll leave, burn out, or both. Not healthy, I'd say."

Murphy stared impatiently across the table at her father. *Oh, to be curled up with a paperback*, she thought.

"I know, I know, you don't think I know what I'm talking about," her father said, feeling his daughter's glare. "I'll just keep eating," he added and dove back into his meal.

"Maybe he does know what he's talking about, dear," her mother said.

"He doesn't, Mom," Murphy said. "And don't you dare talk to anyone at my firm, Dad. Can we please not talk about this? You can't change things there. Hard work is the culture, it's the measuring stick. It's not a unionized public sector environment."

"Touché," said her father, a life-long civil servant. "What do you think, Kyle?"

Murphy wondered why her father thought Kyle would have an opinion.

"You know, I mean, Carolyn works a lot harder than me. I hardly see her sometimes."

This kind of self-centred crap was why Kyle had to go, Murphy thought. After knowing her for a full year, he still was blind to her desire for success.

"What I don't get," Murphy's father said, "I mean, really don't get, is why anything that has to be done on a Sunday can't wait till a Monday? Can someone explain that to me?" he said, alternately looking at his wife, his daughter and Kyle.

Kyle made a motion to speak but Murphy didn't give him a chance.

"And I quote the eminent Peter Bradley," she said mockingly. "'The client comes first because the client pays the bills. Everything else is secondary.'"

"I don't get that guy," her father said, staring at a large chunk of lasagna at the end of his fork. "He's a bit —"

"Insane?" Murphy blurted with a laugh. "Yes, Dad, he's a megalomaniac. He's hell-bent on being the centre of the competition law universe, and you know what, in this city he's done it. Incredibly motivated. I think it's admirable, really. It just would be better if he wasn't such a dick."

Kyle laughed.

"Do we have to use that language here?" Murphy's mother interjected. "I agree with your father. Sundays should be off limits. And Saturdays, too."

"Look, whatever I say, I'm happy where I am. I have things I want to accomplish — things that are important to me. It's just a lot of work. And a lot of perseverance."

"I just worry that you're trying to prove something," her father said. "That you're worthy. That kind of stuff can kill you. You *are* worthy. I've told you that a hundred times."

Murphy thought Kyle was getting far too much information. "Trust me, one day, well — it'll be worth it. Who knows, maybe *I'll* be the centre of the universe."

As her father shook his head and scanned the table for more food, her mother said lightly, "That would be wonderful, dear."

Silence fell over the table. Kyle offered Murphy a heartfelt smile of support, and in return she summoned up her best half-smile. Her parents did not fathom her desire for a career — and how could they? She was in a crazy profession working for a crazy man. More likely, she thought, they would understand why Kyle was not the man for her — not for commitment, not for children. But even that was far from certain.

* * *

As Carolyn Murphy was sitting down for dinner, Walter Anand was arriving home from the office. Instantly, Anita knew to leave him alone; his mood was foul and he hardly acknowledged her. She held off passing the baby to him, though she desperately wanted a break from the child's incessant demands. Within a few minutes, Anand had barricaded himself in their small home office to hide his anger.

Lateral thinking; out-of-the-box thinking — Anand had never heard such inanity. If Bradley were responsible for identifying Notea as a precedent for Pillar, then he was responsible for Bradley's cholesterol levels. Plainly, Bradley took what wasn't his. Anand shook his head; he saw no way to fight such a predicament.

When he stepped out of the office to go to the washroom, his wife was waiting in the hallway, gently swaying the baby in her arms to hold off another colicky cry.

"What's wrong, Walter?" she asked anxiously.

"I don't want to talk about it," he said.

His wife watched him walk down the hallway. "But you have to! Why won't you tell me?"

At first Anand continued walking, waving his hand behind his back for his wife to end her persistent inquiries. Then he stopped and turned around.

"I'm telling you, Peter Bradley will be the end of me."

"Why? What happened now?"

"I asked him, Anita. I asked him, as you and I discussed, if he was going to support me for partnership this year. And do you know what he said?"

His wife waited, bracing herself.

"He's inclined to support me. *Inclined*, for goodness' sake. After all the work and all the false promises, after eight years at that bloody firm, he only has an *inclination*. Why? Do you want to know why?"

Again, his wife simply waited. The baby caught the strain in Anand's voice and began the anxious gasps that usually preceded crying.

"Because I'm not a lateral thinker, because I'm not an out-of-the-box thinker. I don't think he has the slightest idea what he's talking about. Do you want to know why I think that?"

"Yes," his wife said meekly, swaying the baby more forcefully as the cries began.

"Because the example he gave is completely wrong. Utterly and completely wrong. He has the gall to take credit for lateral thinking that *I* did on a file and then use that very file as an example to me of the type of thinking *I* should do. I tell you, he's insane. He is taking good work that is mine and attributing it to himself. And as you know, he's done it before. I've fallen into his trap one more time."

"But didn't you tell him it was your work this time?"

"Of course, Anita. The man does not listen to me. He has his world, and in that world he is the only brilliant thinker. I think he's going to pull the rug out from under my feet just like last year. Two years waiting for partnership. Do you know how awful that will look?"

Anand finally went into the washroom, closing the door heavily behind him. He stared into the mirror and tried to imagine telling his parents that he had been passed over for partnership a second year. He could hear his father's warnings from last year. *I wonder if you can trust this man*, his father had said about Bradley. Anand had remonstrated that he could. He shook his head at the thought that his father might have been right.

Anand's parents would not understand; neither would Anita. And the obvious truth was neither did he. He would put together the best email he could, outlining the work he had done. After that, he did not know what he would do. Perhaps he needed to start over at another firm. Anand couldn't conceive of such a defeat. He could ask for an audience with the Management Committee. But Bradley would never forgive him. He looked at the strain etched on his usually placid face. "Hell," he said out loud to himself. "You've really and truly been made a fool — again."

CHAPTER 14

Almost three hours after Anand left Bradley's office, Bradley was still at his desk. It was nearly seven, and rainless clouds hung heavy in the day's fading light. As usual on Sunday evening, Collins, Shaw was quiet. It was a time Bradley commonly used to get work done, undisturbed. Usually he prepared for the week ahead since Mondays could be chaotic. That evening he was finishing off some notes to himself for his meeting with Collins and Abrams at ten in the morning.

His smartphone's silly ringtone startled him. As he searched for the phone in his leather briefcase, he guessed it was Amy inquiring about dinner. As much as her wandering Friday evening had chewed a hole in his gut all Saturday, he hoped it was her. A desire for retribution remained just below the surface, but what rose above, barely, was a hope for reconciliation and a return to stability. However difficult, that evening he would push down his anger and reach out to his wife.

It was not Amy. It was John Carver, a friend since university and for the last two years chief strategic adviser to Ontario's premier. It wasn't unheard of for Carver to call on a Sunday evening, but it was rare, a portent of crisis.

"Hello, John," Bradley answered with vague excitement.

"Peter, caught you. Good. Very sorry about bothering you on a Sunday evening."

"I'm just finishing off at the office before going home. Good timing."

"Thought you'd be at the office." The premier must appreciate the time savings from Carver's trademark clipped phrases, Bradley mused.

"Big favour to ask. Something's come up I need to run by you — as soon as possible, as in yesterday if I could do it."

"Talk away."

"Face-to-face would be much better. Awkward situation. Would Amy forgive me if I came by your house in half an hour or so? Won't take long to discuss — an hour maybe."

"I'm sure she won't mind," Bradley said.

"See you around seven thirty."

Bradley called home with the news, asking Amy if some dinner could be delivered. She was quiet and closed off but said she would see what she could do. Later that evening, he thought, he would be peacemaker.

Less than fifteen minutes later Bradley walked through the front door of his house. He called out Amy's name but Carver rang the doorbell before Bradley found her. He answered the door, and Carver, tall, erect and surprisingly well-dressed, strode in with a confident and youthful air. Amy emerged from the second floor to begin a slow walk down the stairs.

"Right behind you there, Peter," Carver said. Seeing Amy, his dark brown eyes enlarged, and with a snap of his neck he flung his similarly coloured hair back from his forehead. As a broad smile sent creases across his high cheekbones, he raised his voice and said, "There she is. As beautiful as ever!" Compared to the proper environment in recent years of a law firm, open flirtation seemed to Bradley like a vestige of the past. Eye-catching in a wispy summer dress, Amy arrived at the bottom of the stairs and lit up with her best smile.

"Peter said you were coming over," she said, moving close to

Carver and giving him a light kiss on the cheek. "At least you're not one of his boring friends," she added with a laugh. A few seconds later she threw a quick glance at her husband and ran two long fingers along a shoulder. "How was your fascinating work?" she asked. Without waiting for an answer, she added, "And why are you still wearing this silly old shirt?"

Bradley grimaced. "I think we're going to meet in the study," was his best response. "Can you let us know when dinner arrives?" Amy nodded and began a slow, deliberate walk toward the kitchen. Bradley started climbing the stairs. Peripherally, he saw Carver cast a lingering glance at Amy's swaying hips before following him.

Bradley opened the study door and turned on a light. When the house was renovated he'd given special thought to the study. It was a salutation to maleness. Grabbing the eye first were a goliath desk and sumptuous chair, as ostentatious as the ones in his downtown office. A small fortune in panelled wood lined the left wall floor-to-ceiling, and matching bookcases were mounted behind the desk. Off to the other side, a maroon leather couch and chair sat engagingly around a dark wooden coffee table. Bradley took the chair while Carver sat at the near end of the couch.

"The bloody bounciest couch I've ever sat in," Carver said with a laugh. "Where do you get this stuff?" For several seconds, he bobbed like a child at a playground.

"Drink first, maybe?" Bradley asked.

"Sure. Any Scotch on hand?"

"Of course."

"The older the better."

Bradley got up and poured two Scotch on the rocks from the small bar behind his desk. While waiting, Carver picked up a miniature bust that sat on the coffee table.

"Who is this again?"

"Caesar."

"Thought as much. Where's he from?"

"Italy."

"Very funny."

"Passed down to me from my grandfather. Never met the man, of course."

"Who, Caesar?"

"Equally funny. My grandfather. I know much more about Caesar than him, actually."

When Bradley returned to the seating area with the drinks, Carver had set down the bust and grown still.

"Little mess on our hands," he began after a sip. "Premier knows I'm here, of course. Remembered I like to run things by you occasionally. He trusts you implicitly and all that stuff."

"As he should."

"When he thinks to ask, I remind him you've been a party hack longer than me."

"Second-year university. Long time ago now. I transferred the bug to you."

"Always say it would have been better never to have met you," Carver said, snorting as much as laughing. "Anyway, Carol Mc-Leavey got a DUI charge earlier today. Not too far from here. Hasn't hit the press yet, amazingly. Escaped all the social media because she was in a residential area, nearly home. She wants to resign. Premier — well, the premier doesn't know what to do. *Really* can't afford to lose her." Carver paused for another sip.

"Resign?"

Carver held up a hand to hold off more questions. "All the facts first. Carol's eldest daughter, Beverley —"

"— was convicted of a DUI last year. I remember."

"At the ripe old age of *sixteen*, no less. She was in the car as well — obviously had a few herself — again. Got quite upset, told the police to let her mother go and what they could do with themselves. Pissed them off. Just doing their job, really."

"Where the hell were they coming from?"

"Carol's father's eightieth birthday. Those Scots and their drink. In fairness, Carol blew just slightly over. She's hanging her head very low. Premier's fussing. Some statement needs to be issued, no later than tomorrow morning."

Bradley began to see the pressure to resign. "So the minister with the health portfolio — I'm trying to imagine now what her enemies will say — drinks and drives. An activity that is not only illegal but also potentially harmful to her daughter, who she has in the car with her at the time. Dangerous to others on the road, too, without mentioning McLeavey herself. And the daughter is drunk in public twice, underage. One time she's driving and the other time she's abusive toward the police. In other words, both the Minister of Health and her daughter are acting unhealthily and with poor judgment. Not a great picture."

"Family out of control with booze. That's what Carol thinks it looks like. Consequently, she can't be in a position to run a health portfolio, perhaps no other portfolio, but certainly not a *health* portfolio."

"I see. And the premier —"

"Just wants the problem to go away. Speculation here, but there's something in the premier's past that makes him impatient with people with a drinking problem or an apparent one. Don't fully understand that part. Thinks the daughter may have a problem and is now wondering about Carol. There's lots of stigma regarding drinking, of course, and lots of pressure from families who've suffered calamities from drunk drivers. He sees lost votes."

"And she's been making such great progress negotiating with the nurses' union."

"Guiding the hospital association behind the scenes. Mc-Leavey's been a stalwart in the cabinet. And with elections only six months away —"

"— the premier badly needs a win on that issue. He needs McLeavey to continue, in other words."

"Exactly. But she doesn't want to. And the premier isn't quite sure he wants her to, either."

"Is the fight with the nurses' union getting to her? Maybe this DUI is an excuse to get off the portfolio."

"Asked her that point blank. No. Shame, Peter, that's what she feels. A DUI in this day and age — almost unforgiveable, you know. Very uncomfortable about her daughter — feels like she's letting her down somehow. And afraid of the public roasting ahead. No fear of the union, though." Carver paused while Bradley digested the situation. "There's a bit of good news in this, though," Carver continued. "The premier has already talked to a possible replacement who would help in a pinch."

"Who?"

"Malkiel."

"Oh, god forbid," Bradley said derisively.

"Not as bad as that as far as I'm concerned, but certainly not optimal. Not optimal at all. The real problem is that, with a change of ministers, the negotiations with the nurses will derail and end up at arbitration. And if we get a bad deal there, you can imagine what the right will say about our failure to deal with the deficit."

Bradley got up and reached for Carver's glass. "Top up?"

"Just a splash."

There was silence while Bradley refreshed the drinks. As he sat down, handing Carver his drink, he said, "In public, Mc-Leavey comes across as a tough nut. I don't know her. What's she like, really? And what's her daughter like?"

Carver shrugged. "Carol *is* tough. Much tougher than most in the government, I'd say. But fair-minded and not at all venal. Can be empathetic, too. Very much so. I think that's why people like her. Sticks to her guns but a decent person."

"That fits with what I see."

Carver took a sip of his drink. "As for her daughter — what can I say? Teenage girls — there's no greater plague in the world. You don't know them like I do, though you might have. Maybe Amy and you will have children, I don't know." Bradley said nothing and Carver continued. "Anyhow, my two are trouble inside and out. Never content. As for Beverley — you know, I've only met her twice. She's an angry young woman. More than usual, I'd say. Don't know why — her mother's not like that at all. Doesn't surprise me a bit that she'll take a sip or two."

"And at the party today, any idea if Carol knew Beverley was drinking too much?"

"The way Carol described the scenario, Beverley was sneaking drinks on the side."

The doorbell rang. A second later, Amy called up that dinner had arrived.

Bradley licked his lips. "John, here's my view," he began. "We *need* McLeavey to stay. We have to convince her of that, and the premier too, though I don't think it will take much convincing on his part. As you say, a statement needs to go out in the morning, before the press gets hold of things. Carol can refer to a family celebration and say that she didn't realize she had too much to drink, that she was slightly over the limit and that she is deeply regretful. And regarding her daughter, we need to generate sympathy for Carol. A very decent person who happens to be Minister of Health, and a great mother who is having problems with one of her teenage children. Who can't relate to that? So in the statement, we add one sentence which simply says that mother and other family members — everyone will know we're referring to her daughter but we don't need to name Beverley — are seeking proper family counselling that will include discussing alcohol use. They'll have to do it, of course. If the premier gets too much flak after the statement is released — which I doubt — he can say that the minister did talk about resignation but that he refused to discuss it because personal matters are involved that do not affect McLeavey's ability to handle her portfolio.

"John, my gut tells me that this is a family matter for which sympathy is appropriate, not excommunication. That's the theme."

Amy summoned Carver and Bradley to dinner a second time. They got up slowly from their seats with their glasses, Carver running Bradley's proposal through his head.

"Yes," he said slowly as they left the study and started down the stairs. "Premier could go for that. Carol, I'm less sure. She's very upset by this. Possible, though. She and her family deserve sympathy, not blame. She's taking the right steps by taking time out of her busy schedule for counselling."

"I have another thought to add," Bradley interjected as they got to the bottom of the stairs. "If we get the right organization to provide the counselling, and the right people, then we could leak a few details of it — and it would show how serious Carol is about dealing with this problem. The inference the public will draw is that she deals earnestly with government problems, too. I'll have a word with my sister tonight. She might know which organization to use. In fact, why don't I try to reach her now?"

"Pass on my apologies for bothering her as well on a Sunday evening."

"Start dinner with Amy — I'll try to reach Dottie now."

Bradley bounded back up the stairs. He was exhilarated by successfully handling the role of trusted adviser to John Carver. When he was on his game, his insights were fast and sharp, honed to find the best, most graceful way around a problem.

On the other hand, he now had to deal with his sister, Dorothy, or Dottie as she'd called herself as a young girl. They'd been close as children, cemented together in the face of the strictures of their father, but Dottie had quickly stepped aside in quiet disdain when Amy entered the picture. Single and a loner, she would either be home or at the hospital, he thought, and if she picked up, cool but helpful.

"Dottie, it's Peter."

"Oh, hello, Peter. You're alive and well, I see," she said.

"Alive at least. You're doing fine?"

"Oh sure, except for this cough that I must have picked up in emerg. You?"

Bradley tapped into his conciliatory side. "Good, good. I'm calling for two reasons. The first is whether we can have dinner soon. Tuesday night, maybe? You still have Tuesdays off?"

After a pause, Dottie said, "Sure, I suppose we could. Can you call me in the afternoon to confirm?"

"Yes, I can. I'll come out your way. Pick a restaurant there."

"And the second thing?"

"You remember John Carver?"

"Of course," Dottie said, a bit too warmly, Bradley thought.

"He's here tonight — you remember he's chief strategic adviser to the premier now?"

"Vaguely, yes."

Bradley briefly explained the situation, careful to give the minimum information needed. Dottie was a quick study, faster than Bradley, as his father had ceaselessly reminded him.

"There are several rehabilitation centres in the city. Occasionally we're in contact with them at emerg once a patient dries out in detox. And I do know someone who is very good in the field, actually."

"I don't think the mother needs rehab." Bradley paused. "I'm less sure about the daughter. John says she's angry. She might need more intensive care, I think. She's only sixteen; she should get proper treatment."

"They'll make their own assessment. In any event, they have family counselling programs at several centres, on an outpatient basis. I could try to reach this person I know right now. I suppose I should be very discreet."

"Very. No indication of ties to the government. Just people with a public profile, that's how I'd put it. People who need the best professionals this week."

"All right, I'll call you back shortly."

Bradley hung up, happy with the result. After adding a few ounces of Scotch and an ice cube to his glass, he headed downstairs to the kitchen. He found Amy and Carver sitting at right angles at the end of a small dining table pushed up against a kitchen window. Leaning in closely, they were sharing a laugh. They each had a plateful of Thai food from aluminum trays in the centre of the table. Between them were a half empty bottle of Sauvignon Blanc and partially drained wine glasses.

Catching sight of Bradley, Carver leaned back and said, "Dottie helpful?"

Carver appeared flushed to Bradley. "Looks promising," Bradley said. "She knows a good professional in the rehab field. She's calling him now. He should know the right people for counselling."

Carver nodded. He was about to add a comment when his smartphone rang. He looked at the caller ID. "Duty calls. It's the premier. Can I take this in your study?"

"Sure."

"Going to brief him on our thoughts."

Our thoughts? "Absolutely," Bradley said.

Carver took large strides out the kitchen and up the stairs to the study. Before closing the study door, he answered the phone, taking control of the conversation with a confident, engaging voice.

Bradley sat at the dining table across from Amy. She didn't look at him, pretending to struggle with chopsticks. He hadn't eaten much all day and noticed how hungry he was. As he spooned food onto a plate, he searched for a conciliatory tone.

"How was your day?"

Amy glanced at him. "I was going to get some sun, but of course it's been raining all day. I asked Reggie over."

Bradley had thought he smelled dope when he got in the house. He instructed himself to resist all temptation to remind Amy that Reggie was a lost cause and a money sinkhole. *I am the peacemaker*, he repeated to himself three times. "How is he?"

"He got into a fight with a bouncer last night, if you really want to know. I know what you're thinking. Reggie is a loser. He is a bit, of course."

A bit? "I want to talk to you after John leaves," Bradley said, taking the offensive, brave with Scotch. Amy looked at him in distrustful surprise. He had guessed that would be her reaction; he couldn't remember the last time he had used similar words. Bradley poured himself a glass of wine and topped off Amy's glass. "I want things to be better between us," he added.

One of the chopsticks slipped from Amy's fingers and fell to her plate. "Ok," she said with a light, mocking laugh, cocking an eyebrow.

Bradley was cut off by the home phone ringing. Suspecting that Dottie was calling back, he hurried across the kitchen into the hallway where the phone sat on a side table. He hardly heard Amy say, "Good start."

Dottie spoke quickly and matter-of-factly. A few minutes into the call, Carver opened the study door and came down the stairs. Stopping in front of Bradley in the hallway, he gave a thumbs-up that his call with the premier had gone well. After Bradley nodded and motioned that he needed a few more minutes, Carver went back to the kitchen.

Near the end of their call, Dottie began to update Bradley on their father. In a long-term care facility with Alzheimer's disease for two years, he was too far gone for Bradley to see much point in visiting him. Amy and Carver laughed in the kitchen; Bradley felt his impatience with his sister building quickly. No longer paying attention to her update, he edged down the hallway.

Amy and Carver stood close together near the dining table, each with a glass of wine, too busy noticing each other to see Bradley. Amy laughed into her glass at Carver's humour, playfully batting him on the shoulder and mouthing, "You're bad!"

She turned away from Carver, bending over the dining table to pick up some aluminum trays. Her ass pushed up against Carver's thigh and she took inordinate time with the trays. Bradley's heart caught in his throat. A look of extreme concentration come over Carver's face, like a wolf setting eyes on its prey. Carver turned a hand, and overtop Amy's summer dress softly palmed one of her buttocks. Unopposed, he began hiking up one side of her dress.

Breathlessly, Bradley retreated down the hallway. "Dottie, I have to go," he said curtly, cutting his sister off in mid-sentence.

"But, Peter, I haven't finished about Father."

"Goddamn, Dottie, what's happening here is much more important. I'll call you Tuesday afternoon," he said and slammed down the phone.

CHAPTER 15

When Bradley walked into the kitchen, Amy and Carver had separated and were conversing with unconvincing nonchalance. To Bradley, each of their faces was wan with yearning.

"All good?" Carver asked breezily.

Bradley choked down his dismay. He decided to get Carver out of his house as soon as possible. Amy was the problem as far as he was concerned.

"I've written out the name and number of the doctor Dottie called and the name of the centre he works at," he said woodenly, handing Carver a piece of paper, then looking away. "They have family counselling programs. Dottie will give the doctor your name. As a favour to her, he'll take your call this evening. If the premier is onside, then all you need to do is convince Carol — and her daughter."

"That's great, Peter. Thanks so much. The premier is warming up to the idea. He'll come onside when I update him."

"Are you good to drive, John?" Bradley asked. He couldn't care less if Carver ran into the same cop who'd busted McLeavey.

"Not far to go. On my way, I guess. Goodbye, Amy. Thanks for dinner and the company."

Bradley hurried Carver out the door. Looking to compose himself, he walked into the living room and sat in a faux Chippendale chair. His mind and his gut were at war. He reasoned that what he had seen in the kitchen had been minor. Longer term, it was more important to soften the edges between Amy and him, to have her love him again, or at least have some affection for him. And the only way to get there was to look past the evening's transgression, and all the other ones, and try to connect — now.

But his gut convulsed with anger. Making her body available to Carver, even if briefly and partially, was a provocation that demanded action. For a second he wondered if in his middle age he had become too physically unattractive for his young wife, or too harsh. He batted the self-doubt aside, got up and walked toward the kitchen. One way or another, he knew, he had to bring Amy back onside.

She was finishing cleaning up the kitchen. The dining table had been cleared and wiped, and garbage tossed out. She stood in front of the sink, her hands lost in soapy water, prepping plates and cutlery for the dishwasher. To his surprise, without looking at him, she spoke first.

"Peter, I wasn't going to talk to you about this, but I need to do something with my life. I can't stand being stuck in this house all day, taking care of your every need. I need to accomplish something, take something on. You say you want things to be better between us. It would help for me to have something to do that gives me satisfaction. Something. Anything. Just not this."

He couldn't remember a single need — other than ordering dinner that evening — she took care of, but that didn't matter to him just then. She was bargaining with him, and he could work with that.

"What are you thinking of?" he asked a bit hoarsely.

Amy took her hands out of the sink and dried them. She looked at Bradley, both imploringly and with agitation. "It's a business — a small business — but I actually don't want to tell you more. I want you to have faith in me, to trust me that I know what I'm doing." She looked at Bradley, searching for some understanding. "What I need from you is the start-up capital. I hate asking for it, but you hold all the purse strings. You don't need to worry — I'll be responsible with it."

Some cash was probably a small price to pay for harmony, Bradley thought. He could see resolution.

"Ten thousand good to start you off?"

Amy laughed. "I need a hundred thousand."

"*A hundred thousand?*" Bradley blurted. "You're kidding, right?"

"No, I'm not," Amy said testily. "It's a business. I need a reasonable amount to start with."

Bradley was stunned. "What do you know about business? What business are you talking about?"

"I know much more than you give me credit for. And I told you I don't want to talk about what it is."

"For a hundred thousand, I'm your partner and I want to know the business."

"You're not my partner. This is my business, my idea." Amy paused and sighed. "For Christ's sake, I want to own an art gallery. Ok, there it is. I've told you. I'll train — maybe you can help me get a job somewhere for a while, just to learn. Then I'll start on my own. I've done a business plan — it takes a hundred thousand to start."

"Open your own gallery?"

"Yes, that's what I want to do."

Bradley went silent, trying to find a way forward.

After a few moments Amy said acidly, "I can see I'm not getting anywhere." She turned to face the sink again and began moving dishes into the dishwasher. As she inserted each dish, she turned and leaned over, and her summer dress strained against her ass. Breathlessly, Bradley watched. Visions of Carver's advance and imagined activities at Maximus floated before his eyes. An unexpected surge of lust, sharpened by stabbing jealousy, joined alongside his anger. He moved behind her and felt the outline of her waist and hips. Then, like Carver, he found the contour of one buttock and began to lift her dress.

Amy stiffened. Through the soapiness of the sink water, Bradley saw her left hand tighten on the handle of a large kitchen knife. "Don't, please," she hissed. Bradley backed off.

"So you just provide your ass for John? Anyone else I should know about?"

"What are you talking about?"

"Don't give me that shit. I saw you push your ass into Carver's hand, and you were happy to have him leave it there and lift your dress, at least until I got a little too close for comfort."

Amy gave Bradley a vile look.

"Please, I saw," Bradley said, lifting a hand in protest. "I was in the hallway — but that didn't bother you."

"You saw *nothing*. But if you did, you know what, it happens, Peter. Yes, it does happen. Other men make advances at me all the time. All the fucking time. Eye contact here, a smile there, a brush of the hand — whatever."

"So you notice this, do you?" Bradley felt himself enjoying the encounter. "Play with these guys' hearts and dicks all the time, is that right?"

"So this is how you want to make things better, is it?" Amy asked, seething, her hands trembling.

"Twenty-five thousand then."

"It's not a stupid negotiation, Peter. You're not in the office right now. You're with me, here in our home, listening to a dream I have."

"This is not your first dream. You've had lots of other dreams, and I've given them to you."

"Like what?"

"This house. The cottage. The clubs you belong to. There are many women who'd be envious of you. Very envious, Amy."

"And you get nothing? You *know* that's not true. Many men would be envious of you too, Peter. Many are."

"So I heard."

"What?"

"Amy, I think you're forgetting your roots."

"How can I?" she yelled. "You never let me!" Amy grabbed a fruit plate not far from the sink and raised it menacingly.

"Oh, you're going to throw that at me?" Bradley said. "Bit more drama here. The plate flying across the room? Smashing against the wall in a hundred pieces? Or maybe it catches my temple and I just die right here, on the kitchen floor? I got news for you — that little plate isn't going to make any difference. No difference at all, Amy."

She tried to get words out, but she was strangled by anger. She put the plate down hard on the quartz kitchen top, and it broke into three parts. Releasing a cry of frustration, she stormed out of the kitchen.

"And you know what else?" he yelled after her. "You better pay a bit more attention to *me*. Without me, you're going to end up right back where you came from. You and your sorry ass brother. You *need* me."

A few seconds later, the master bedroom door slammed. Bradley laughed, shaking his head, and poured a glass of wine. She was more pathetic now than when he'd found her.

CHAPTER 16

Am I really serious about this? Deadly so, I think, pardon the pun. I can't pinpoint when I transitioned from fantasy to real intention — but it seems to have happened in the last twenty-four hours. Maybe I'm wrong about that. I have to monitor myself, very closely.

I might be damning myself forever. Maybe I'm setting myself up for retribution, from another person, or from some otherworldly being, just like PB has. That is a very scary thought. I won't have achieved anything then, will I?

I need to do some planning.

CHAPTER 17

Late Sunday evening, when Anita and the baby were asleep, Anand sat in his home office and began drafting his email to Bradley. He couldn't even find a toehold. After an hour, the reason why dawned on him. Deep within him, Anand suspected Bradley would mindlessly dispute how Anand's lateral thinking had contributed to files. And that was little different than labelling him a liar and throwing his integrity into question. Then Anand would have to respond, and who knew where things would go from there.

Around 1:00 a.m., the baby had his first night cry. After Anita calmed the child, Anand talked to her about his fears, both to comfort himself and to warn her of what might lie ahead. He fell into a story about his father, a kind and tolerant man loved by Anita almost as much as Anand, and his decision years earlier to uproot his family from their home in East London.

Near Anand's seventh birthday, a sudden and unusual restlessness and despair developed in his father that even the young boy noticed. Eventually, his mother said they were emigrating again. That it was possible to lose his home shocked the boy. "Why must we go?" he finally asked his father. With a deep sigh, his father said, "Some people where I work have said that I've not told the truth. I can't be in a place where my honour is questioned."

Quietly and reluctantly, Anita nodded when Anand said he felt in a similar situation now. As he knew she would be, she was supportive. Her family, like his, would not tolerate obvious disrespect. Though an entirely different matter, there were vague rumours of honour killings in India years before. She simply said, "No one should impugn your character, Walter," and went back to bed.

The next morning, for a man who'd only slept two hours, Anand was alert. He went to work at 6:30 a.m. and reworked his draft email. Bradley arrived an hour later. Around eight, Anand felt the email was ready. Still, he read it one, two, three more times. It could unleash uncontrollable consequences and had to be perfect.

Done reviewing, Anand gulped hard and hit "Send".

CHAPTER 18

Bradley's laptop announced the arrival of an email. When he saw it was from Anand, he was inclined to disregard it and continue with the work in which he was immersed. Then it occurred to him that it might be an update on Oshwegan. Impatiently, he moved the cursor over the email and opened it.

"Peter, further to our discussion yesterday afternoon, I am summarizing files where I believe I've demonstrated 'lateral thinking' in the last year. My intention is for you to feel fully confident in supporting my partnership bid this year..."

The discussion of late Sunday afternoon crept back into Bradley's mind. He spent only a few seconds more on the email. Overnight, he'd lost any doubt that he could convince Collins and Abrams to decline Amato's approach to the firm. Anand's email was of no consequence. Even if it was filled with distortions, as it seemed on first glance to be, Bradley needed Anand for his strategy against Amato, and he might as well let Anand know that.

Bradley returned to McLeavey's press release. It followed the approach he had suggested to Carver almost exactly. Unfortunate incident; pressure at home and at work; all families encounter difficulties from time to time; she and other family members creating some time for counselling at the best clinic; back on the job full-time in two weeks. Bradley thought the release would be met with public understanding.

In his inbox, Bradley also had an email from John Carver thanking him for his help. Normally, Bradley would have called Carver to puff his chest a bit more, but he had no inclination to speak to him. He would tell Collins and Abrams, though; he needed to blow his horn more often.

A few minutes before ten, Bradley put down his pen. He sat still, composing himself, and ran through what he would say to Collins and Abrams. The plan was to hit them hard in the face: adding Amato to his team would be an enormous mistake. For one thing, he wouldn't be able to bring nearly as many clients to Collins, Shaw as the Management Committee imagined. Many would be ruled out by conflicts of interest, and others would stay at Bergheim's because they preferred that firm or had other legal work done there. For another thing, Bradley had the growth of the anti-trust group under control and well designed. Make Anand, not an outside person, the second partner in the group, and in each of the next three years hire a junior associate to cast into the group's mold.

And maybe most importantly, they didn't know Amato like he did. Acerbic, strident, always pushing the limits, Amato wouldn't fit into the collegial culture of Collins, Shaw or the tight-knit nature of Bradley's group. The discord from trying to accommodate Amato might even become apparent to the outside world and threaten the group's powerful flow of business. It wouldn't be Gretzky and Crosby, it would be Junior A. And, if after all that, Collins and Abrams didn't see things his way, he'd be forced to hint that he would consider leaving Collins, Shaw and taking *his* book elsewhere. It was the farthest thing from his wishes, but it would show how deadly serious he was.

Bradley was ready for action. Abrams had called him to say they were meeting in Collins' office two floors up. Bradley bolted into the hallway for the elevators. As he passed by Anand's office, he glanced in and caught an expectant look. Lurching to a stop, he said, "I looked at your email, Walter. It's well done. Don't worry about the partnership. I will support you."

A look of relief crossed Anand's face. He wanted to express his thanks, but Bradley held up his hand. "Important meeting," Bradley said. "Sorry, got to run. We'll talk later."

After Bradley strode away, Anand called his wife.

CHAPTER 19

Bradley was surprised to find Collins in his office alone. He was seated at his desk, banging at his keyboard, eyes trained on his computer screen. "Abrams late?" Bradley asked, taking one of the chairs across from Collins' desk.

Without looking away Collins said, "I asked him to hold off for a few minutes." Bradley immediately noted the red flush in Collins' face, leaping out in stark contrast to a full head of white hair. "Do you mind closing the door?"

Bradley did as asked. Having started together in 1988, Bradley knew that look on Collins' face, and he didn't like it at all. Taking his seat again, he decided to let Collins lead but was ready for a fight. Unlike Collins' career, which basically had been handed to him, Bradley had had to earn his — and he was here to protect it.

"I have a problem," Collins finally said with a sigh, turning his attention to Bradley as he sank back in his chair. "You know our night receptionist, Debbie?"

"Sure."

"She is the daughter of a good friend of mine. You don't know him. But she takes her job seriously. She does a great job, in fact. Did you know that late last year she was responsible for identifying some asshole petty thief who somehow got past security downstairs and was up here, walking the halls, lifting wallets?"

"No, I didn't."

Collins nodded. "Yeah. Takes her job *very* seriously. Actually, she's a pain in the ass sometimes. I'd say I get an email from her once a week describing one thing or another she's seen. But I've learned to pay attention. She's smart. She's going to do well."

Deep in his stomach, Bradley felt unwelcome stirrings of something like heartburn.

"Late Friday," Collins continued, "she sent me an email. I was still in Italy, actually —"

"How was your trip?"

"Doesn't matter. She tells me that two young ladies came to visit you quite late Friday evening." Collins looked hard at Bradley, and Bradley's face began to burn. "She also tells me that they were in your office for about an hour, then left again — and that she thinks they were hookers. She didn't use that word — quite. But that's what she meant."

Collins smirked. "Why does Debbie think they were hookers? They looked the part. And they said they were from 'the agency'. And they signed in as Bunny Smith and Raven Jones. When you came out to get them, you apparently told Debbie that they were friends of your wife, but they were about twenty, so that doesn't seem right. And Bunny and Raven?"

Collins took a deep breath, his face twisting in evident displeasure. "Debbie is smart — that's what I think. And sometimes you're not. In fact, not to put too fine a point on it, Peter, but you can be a loose cannon. Please tell me they weren't escorts."

Bradley shifted on his seat and swallowed hard. "Absolutely not, Ted. I don't know how Debbie dreamed this up. Maybe — well, you know women —"

"I don't, actually. Never understood them."

"Well, maybe these days this is a bit inappropriate, but you know, every other woman is a whore. These were friends of Amy dropping by for a visit. These women didn't look a thing like escorts and weren't. Actually, Ted, as I think about it, this is quite outrageous —"

Collins cut him off with a slicing motion. "Peter, I don't really buy your theory of women, and I don't buy your denial. You should know that I had the surveillance tapes pulled. Sure, the tapes are black and white and not HD, but these girls didn't look at all like friends of Amy to me and, quite frankly, I think they look like escorts — not that I know about these things, but you sure do. And they were there for an hour or so, then gone. I'm guessing they weren't there to discuss competition law."

Bradley's throat was getting dry. He was having trouble seeing a way out of this predicament.

"If I was dealing with any of my other partners, I *might* be convinced to let this go *if* it was the first time it happened and *if* I got a lot of assurances it wouldn't happen again. But, Peter, you have a history —"

"I know, but it's not —"

"A history that makes it almost impossible for me to look the other way."

"— like that this time."

"I have an idea, Peter. Why don't we refer this to the sexual harassment committee? Because Debbie happens to say in her email that she feels harassed by having to deal with hookers at reception on Friday evening. Not exactly what she signed up for. Then the committee can investigate. But, you know, if Amy can confirm to the committee that she has friends whose names are Bunny and Raven, well then, all will be good and done. What about that idea, Peter?"

"Ted, seriously, this is completely outrageous," Bradley said. He was trying to sound aggressive, but his voice was emerging hollow.

"Peter, I'm giving you *one* chance here. Come clean, and you can stay at the firm. It'll go on your record as a private and confidential matter. But if you fight me on this, I'll insist on the harassment committee, and if the wrong answer comes out, you're gone — and forget about working at another firm, at least in this country." Collins burned a hole in Bradley's face with his eyes. "Were those escorts, Peter?"

Bradley felt his entire body seize and sweat break out over his brow. He swiped a hand down his long face and said, "Yes."

"And you had sex with them in your office, is that right?"

Bradley turned to look out the windows in Collins' office. Sunday's bad weather had cleared. More than anything else, he wished he could sprout wings and fly off the thirty-first floor into the crisp, clear fall day. "Yes," he squeaked.

Collins' face was red like a swollen raspberry. "Are you fucking out of your mind? Goddamn it, Peter. Last time you brought them to the Christmas party. I don't care if it was eight years ago or whatever, people don't forget that kind of shit. This time right to your office. And you had sex with them. Seriously, you got to get help. You probably have the most beautiful wife in the damn world."

Collins shook his head so hard, his white hair bobbed. "Your personal life is not my issue. Except when it affects this firm — which it is now. I'm going to insist that you get help, understand me?"

"I got it, Ted."

"You get help. You come back to me with details about what you're doing. And you keep your nose *really* clean from now on."

"Yes, yes, I completely understand."

Collins shoved back from his desk, slumping further into his chair. "You're very lucky that we go back as far as we do, not to mention that you're such a fucking good lawyer. For your information, I haven't told Abrams any of this. I'm really going out on a limb for you here. You understand that? *Really* going out on a limb. I'm dead if you screw this up. So *don't*."

Bradley couldn't think of anything to do but let a few more awkward seconds pass. Somehow he needed to surface the issues about Amato. Finally, he said, "Is Leonard going to join us?"

Collins stared back. "What for?"

"We were going to talk about Tony Amato, weren't we?"

"There'll be an announcement Thursday morning that he's joined the firm as a partner. I settled the terms with him over the weekend. I'll call him when you leave. He wants to meet with you this afternoon."

Bradley sat stunned.

"Peter, you're a liability as much as an asset right now. I need a strong anti-trust group. If you do screw up again — and I'm not sure you won't — I don't want to be the one explaining to the Management Committee and our other partners why we turned Amato away. Make this work, don't screw up and everything will be fine. Got it?"

"I — I, ah —"

"Peter, if you think there's a choice, there's not. Do you doubt Tony is a good addition to the firm?"

Several seconds passed. Bradley tensed his jaw muscles, milling enamel off his molars. "No, I don't," he finally said.

"Right, then I suggest you go prepare for your meeting with Tony. Not a word about this to anyone until Amato is sitting in his new office Thursday morning. Thanks for your time."

Bradley could not remember finding his way back to his office.

CHAPTER 20

Deep breaths, Bradley told himself as he paced back and forth in his office with the door shut, *deep breaths*. Problems were everywhere, squeezing the life out of him like a boa constrictor. He swiped his right hand across his face. Amy was out of control and not speaking to him, and probably wouldn't for three or four days. Collins also was out of control, betraying Bradley with decisions that rightfully were Bradley's. And Amato — Bradley had no idea how he was going to conduct a civil conversation in mere hours.

Then there were the clients, the ones who paid the bills, clamouring for his attention. Pink message slips demanding return calls formed an ominous, neat stack in the centre of his desk. He should have used Sunday evening to prepare for the week, not succumb to the vanity of solving Carver's problems *pro bono*.

After a few minutes, Bradley dropped into the large leather chair behind his desk. He looked to Lake Ontario for composure. It was time for damage control mode. He would apply his full force and focus to isolating and solving the most pressing problem, then the next one, and so on, until enough breathing room developed for him to relax.

Though only a wall and cubicle separated Bradley from Margaret, he phoned her to come into his office in five minutes and help him sort out which clients needed attention most. He checked voicemails, emails and texts, and sorted pink message slips into urgent and almost urgent. On cue, Margaret joined him, her fleshy body facing him across from his desk. Usually a calming influence with a sixth sense for when to leave Bradley alone, she was more fidgety than usual. Bradley assumed she was affected by his nervous tension. She handed him a new message from Tony Amato's assistant, suggesting a three thirty meeting and asking for a location.

Within ten minutes Bradley had a road map for the rest of the day. Most pressing was the Oshwegan file. Bradley pulled Anand and Murphy into his office.

"Where are we on Oshwegan's submission?" he asked without anyone taking a seat.

"I spoke with Dave," Anand said. "He thinks he can get the customer onside with signing that letter — though it's still early on the West Coast."

"Ok, good."

"I checked all the formatting," Murphy added. "Walter has all the information he emailed me about yesterday."

"Let's meet at eleven for a final flip through. We can make any last minute changes today, then Dave can add the letter, sign everything up and courier it to the Bureau tomorrow."

As Anand and Murphy departed, Margaret cautiously stuck her head into Bradley's office.

"Tony Amato's assistant called again. She said that he thought it would be best if you met in Roaster's Blend at Bay and Temperance — not here."

Bradley cringed, hoping Anand hadn't heard anything from his office. He waved Margaret into his office and in a hushed voice said, "Sure, tell her that's fine. But the Amato thing is top secret. Keep your voice down about it." Though he knew he could trust Margaret, she looked surprised. "That's all I can say right now," he added and put on a deadpan expression.

Meeting Amato was Bradley's next most pressing problem. Collins had done an end run around him, deftly stripped him of his power over the Amato decision. And Collins and Abrams would be watching him closely, ensuring that he was treating Amato professionally and seizing the opportunity to affirm the anti-trust group's pre-eminence in the city. For the moment the only option he saw was to play along — at least until his mind cleared and he had more information from Amato. But he had no idea how he would contain his anger when he met Amato at three thirty. Wearing his heart on his sleeve would do him no good. Bradley needed a plan of containment, and soon.

Anand and Murphy duly showed at eleven, and they collected at the oval meeting table. The submission was in good shape. Bradley suggested only a few changes, which Murphy made on her laptop as they went along.

"I'll call Dave to say I'm emailing a fresh document once Carolyn finishes with the changes," Anand said. He was calm again, even light-hearted. It occurred to Bradley that he had another potential problem on his hands.

Anand left the office to make the client call, and Murphy typed busily. Bradley grabbed his smartphone and emailed Collins.

"Subject: New arrival

In light of Thursday's announcement, what is the plan with Anand's partnership? I told him this morning I would support it. Also, I should really give Carolyn and Walter some kind of indication before the announcement — as a matter of courtesy and inclusivity. OK?"

Waiting to see if Collins would respond quickly, Bradley leaned back in his chair. He glanced at Murphy. Less frumpy today, Bradley thought. Vaguely attractive even.

"How was your dinner last night?" he asked, surprising himself he remembered.

Murphy looked up from her laptop and eyed him coolly. "It was nice, actually. My parents go through a lot of trouble for these things."

"Good. Glad to hear."

A little hesitantly, Murphy added, "Thanks again for accommodating my plans yesterday."

"Sure. The submission looks good. Everything worked out fine," Bradley said. "I'm really not such a bad person, though not everyone agrees," he added with a laugh. Murphy didn't join in. After several seconds, Bradley continued. "Say, I have a question for you. You remember when you and I and one of the litigators met with the regulators a few months ago —"

"The Pillar file. June 26. The one Walter couldn't make?"

"Yes." Murphy had a better memory for dates than him, he thought. "Did it seem like I was irritable or angry during the meeting?"

Murphy hesitated. "Go ahead," Bradley said, motioning toward himself, "bring it on."

"Ok," Murphy said, a wry smile crossing her face. "It seemed you were first irritated on the way there, that Walter couldn't make the meeting. Their baby was sick, I think, and so was Anita. And I think there were flashes of anger from you during the meeting. It seemed to work with the regulators."

Bradley nodded. "Of course," he said. But in truth he was taken aback. He looked away, paused for several moments, then refocused on Murphy, who had started typing again. "I wonder what I should do to be less obvious," he said, letting his voice trail away.

Murphy looked up again and laughed. "Are you asking *me* for advice?"

Bradley shrugged. "I guess I am."

Murphy returned to her wry smile. "Can one do anything

about that — showing irritation or anger?"

"I'd like to think so. I always think it's possible to change. Don't you?"

"I suppose. I never really know the answer to that."

"Give it a try."

"I guess I would say separating the important from the unimportant would help. What's the point of being irritated with Walter for taking care of his baby?"

Within himself, Bradley reluctantly conceded that Murphy was right.

"As for being angry about issues that are important, I think there's a place for that, but you can also end up betraying yourself."

"Meaning?"

"For example, meeting with regulators. Maybe it's part of your strategy to show impatience or even anger occasionally, just to intimidate them. But if it's less controlled than that, you could also say things you regret, that hurt your cause. That, I think, is a strong incentive to control your anger as much as possible. The other side, whoever they are, may resent your emotions and refuse to be intimidated or, worse, try to take advantage of them. But you're the partner, and I'm just an associate, and I think I've said enough."

Murphy knew far more at her age than he had, Bradley thought. "You're right, I've always been aware of that," he said, covering the truth. "If I show my anger, I'm telegraphing my feelings — I know that. Frankly, you know, getting a little riled up, it's usually worked for me. But not always…"

Bradley felt he had shown enough vulnerability and diverted his attention to his smartphone. Murphy refocused on her laptop.

Collins had responded to Bradley's email, cc'ing Abrams.

"We can't have three partners in your group this year — too expensive. I like Anand a lot, but we will have to defer him another year. Talk to Anand — in the strictest confidence — after you meet with Amato, and tell him exactly what's happened. I am hopeful he will understand. We can significantly increase his associate's salary next year to ensure he doesn't leave. You can also tell Murphy that an important announcement regarding your group is coming, but I prefer if you don't use names with her."

Bradley cringed at the thought of speaking with Anand, then dismissed it as a problem for later.

"Do you have time for a drink Wednesday after work — maybe for an hour or so?" he asked Murphy, looking up from the email. "There are a few things I need to go over with you. Confidentially, they concern our group — best if you don't mention to Walter that we're getting together. Say five?"

Murphy looked surprised and cautious. "Wednesday I usually go to yoga, but I can move it to tomorrow night if necessary."

"Could you? I can't meet tomorrow evening — having dinner with my sister — and then the rest of the week is busy. I think I mentioned to Walter and you yesterday that I'm leaving early Friday to close the cottage."

"All right, I'll do that. I've made all the changes to the submission," Murphy said, closing her laptop. "When I get back to my office, I'll email it to Walter and you, and he can send it to the client."

Murphy packed up her things and headed for the door. Bradley walked to his desk and started grabbing at pink slips. Murphy paused. "It must be lovely at your cottage now. I remember last year, when you had Walter and Anita and me up for the weekend, the fall colours were already quite beautiful. How is Amy?"

Bradley stared blankly at Murphy. Her inquiry was out of character; they rarely chatted socially because it had always seemed her preference to maintain a cool, professional distance. At the cottage the year before it had been painful to engage her in any real conversation, and eventually he had spent most of his time with Walter and Anita.

"She's fine. Yes, the colours were nice," he said. "We should get that submission out."

For the next hour Bradley answered most of the urgent client calls. Throughout, the question of how to present himself to Amato gnawed at him. After the last call, he thought lunch would give him clarity.

Anand stepped out of his office as Bradley left his. "Oh, Peter," he said, walking alongside Bradley, "Dave has the submission. He said he'll review it as soon as he can."

"Good. Glad to get that out."

Anand dropped his voice. "Also, I didn't get a chance to thank you this morning."

"Thank me?"

"For your expression of support."

Bradley sucked in a deep breath. Eyeing a small meeting room, he said, "Let's step in here for a second."

He closed the door behind them. He was tired of Anand's pestering. At that moment, he couldn't care less if Anand stayed — and if he didn't, it would show Collins what happened when he interfered with Bradley's group. "Walter, I know partnership is very important to you. I just want to be sure you understand that the Management Committee has the final say. They insist on a business case, of course."

Anand scrutinized Bradley. "Yes, you've mentioned that several times. It was one of the reasons you gave for deferral last year. Do you think there is a problem?"

"I — I don't. But I don't always predict the MC's actions correctly. Let's have lunch tomorrow. There may be some changing dynamics for our group I'd like to talk to you about." Bradley edged out of the meeting room. "Lunch tomorrow, all right? Don't worry. Everything will work out. I'd prefer if you keep our plans for lunch private — especially from Carolyn." Bradley left before Anand could confirm he was available.

Bradley seldom took advice from others, but after grabbing a quick sandwich, with some indigestion he phoned John Carver. As he expected, Carver did not pick up, but after the previous evening, Bradley was sure Carver would quickly return his call. He did. Bradley gave a skewed summary of how the MC had hired Amato without his approval, even though Bradley had grave concerns how he would work out.

"Why would they do that?" Carver asked.

"They're thinking succession. And Ted Collins and I — we don't always see eye-to-eye."

Carver didn't take long to respond. "Unless this is so important that you want to risk all the goodwill you've accumulated at the firm on the issue — and be ready to jump firms — sounds like you have to deal with him. Is it that important?"

Bradley's jaw muscles seized up. "Probably not. I have to meet the guy at three thirty. We'll see. Thing is, I want to be ... welcoming."

"You'll need to be then. Don't show Amato any displeasure. This guy's ego will be as big as yours, no offence intended. Expecting you to be thrilled he's joining the team, et cetera. Presume you want the higher ups seeing you're doing your best."

"Right."

"So, sit back and figure out how you can work with this person."

"Right again."

"All of which you already know, so I'm not clear why you're calling me."

"I suppose — I suppose because it feels so political to me."

"Ah-hah. Peter Bradley sees a challenger. No longer master of his domain. Everything he's worked for at risk. You're probably a long way from accepting this, whatever your esteemed firm wants."

Bradley swiped his face and pondered.

"I will take silence as confirmation," Carver said after several moments. "Late for a meeting right now, but here's a thought to leave you with. Every good politician I know sees an emerging bright light as a possible friend or foe, someone who might be useful to them — or someone they may have to ruin. They won't put it that way, but that's the heart of it. And then they learn everything they can about the person to serve both purposes down the road. Maybe that's useful to you, Peter. Got to go. Great to see Amy and you last night. By the way, the press release seems to be working fine."

"Glad to hear," Bradley said, but Carver had already hung up.

Tony Amato: friend or foe. Be prepared to use him or ruin him. It was a perspective that interested Bradley. His quandary about Amato started lifting and his mind began processing. What interested him particularly was Amato's ruin — and Bradley's re-emergence as uncontested leader of the anti-trust group.

CHAPTER 21

Anand and Murphy sat in their respective offices, each considering why Bradley had asked for one-on-one time.

For Murphy, having a drink with Bradley was intriguing. She sensed that whatever he would reveal to her about the anti-trust group would bring her opportunity and advantage. At the very least it was a chance to get to know her boss a little better. It would be awkward if a drink was an excuse to hit on her, but her antennae didn't point in that direction.

Anand was in a valley of gloom, far from his morning's heights of happiness. Bradley's warning that the final partnership decision lay with the Management Committee made no sense to him. The warning was obvious unless Bradley was once again squirming out of supporting him and deflecting responsibility to others. He wanted to call Anita, but when she asked why he continued to trust Bradley, he knew that he would find the shame unbearable. It was a gut-wrenching game Bradley was playing with him, and the time had come to change the rules.

CHAPTER 22

It was early Monday afternoon before Reggie rolled out of his sofa bed. In the washroom, he spent several minutes in front of the mirror examining the area around his left eye. The swelling was down and he could see out of the eye, but the number of sickening colours had multiplied. His plan had been to call Faster Delivery for a job when he got out of the shower and then, with any luck, visit them the same day to fill out the paperwork. He decided to present himself the next day, hoping his face would look less revolting.

In the mirror Reggie also saw a new cut. It wasn't long or deep, but it was there, on the inside of his left arm. It began to throb, but he couldn't remember inflicting it on himself. It was always like this. His bouts of self-recrimination could be so deep, they left him exhausted, without recollection of what he'd done to himself until he saw it the next day. Then the pain would start. This cut, he guessed, would leave a scar to join the others up and down his arms. From under the washroom sink he took some antibiotic cream and applied it gently to the red, encrusted line.

After showering, Reggie brushed his teeth and combed out his longish hair, then re-applied the antibiotic and chose not to shave. He felt slow to the punch, emotionally hung over from talking himself down the night before. As he dressed, careful to pick out a long-sleeved shirt, he remembered Amy's text that Dominic would call. There wasn't a single message on his phone.

Reggie called Amy as her text had asked.

"Hi," she answered brusquely. She didn't allow Reggie to respond. "I want to do it today."

"What?"

"I want to get that fucking password of his so I can start my project."

Amy's voice was piercing. Reggie hadn't heard his sister so upset in weeks. "Ok, but what's going on?"

"Seriously, he is an asshole sometimes. A complete asshole."

"We know that part, sis."

"I just keep forgetting it. Or I don't want it to be true. I don't know. But there's this other side to him — it's *evil*."

"But what happened?"

"I'm not kidding. I want you to come over — now — and do whatever you have to do so I have access to his account."

"You know, I haven't really thought about it yet. I don't know if I can get it done this afternoon, you know what I mean?"

"Reggie, I need this done. Now. Do you understand?"

"Ok, ok," Reggie said testily. "I guess there are probably two passwords."

"Two?"

"One for his computer and one for the bank site. Check for the first — just turn his computer on."

"You're not going to believe it when I tell you how he pissed me off last night."

Amy's irritation seeped into Reggie, penetrating his stupor. "Are you going to tell me what happened?" he asked impatiently.

"I'll tell you when you come over. You need to get here soon. As far as I know, Peter will be home around six tonight."

"All right, I'll get there as soon as I can. Your text — it said you called Dominic."

Amy paused to remember. "Oh, yes, that. He said he's going

to call you about someone he knows. And of course then he'll deny that he knows this guy, but that's Dominic."

"He hasn't called yet."

"He sleeps late, Reggie." *Just like me*, Reggie thought, *except Dominic has a real occupation.* "He'll call — for me."

"Ok. I'll get there as soon as I can. I may have to buy some stuff for this."

"Buy what you need to, Reggie. I'll pay you back."

As Reggie put down his phone, he reflected how much of an asshole Peter Bradley was. He couldn't imagine any reason for treating his sister so poorly. The risk of his sister's marriage dissolving — and the threat to his supply of cash — looked to be compounding. Feeling a stab of panic, Reggie decided he needed a fallback. It took some time, but he got through to his former boss, Kevin Dychtwald at Faster Delivery.

"Reggie," Dychtwald said, condescendingly drawing out the name. "My employee who comes and goes as he pleases. One day he's here, the next he's not."

"Sorry about that, Kevin. Something came up."

"You mean you got busted. I heard. How did that work out for you?"

"All behind me. Is there any chance I could start again? I have a car I can use now."

"A car? Really?" Reggie could tell that Dychtwald was interested.

"I could start tomorrow or Wednesday."

Dychtwald sighed. "Oh for Christ's sake, I was looking forward to kicking your ass when you called back, but one of my drivers just quit. Your commercial license hasn't expired, has it?"

"No," Reggie said, without knowing.

"I guess you're no different than all the others. Come in tomorrow afternoon."

It may be a fallback, Reggie thought as he got off the phone, but it was not a great one. He doubted he could put up with Dychtwald and the insane demands of being a courier for long. He hadn't even been able to hold himself together the day before, promising himself to seize the day on the subway ride from Amy's house, then crashing unwillingly and miserably. He needed to act right away, before the dark clouds re-gathered and another stainless steel blade lured him. It was time to figure out how to get Peter Bradley's passwords.

He knew one option was to buy spyware online and email it as a disguised attachment to Bradley. He doubted Bradley had updated anti-spyware software on his home computer. And because the email and attachment were from Reggie, Bradley would likely open them so that, unbeknownst to Bradley, the spyware would load. What troubled Reggie was that it would be easy to trace the spyware back to him. He needed something better.

After doing some online research, he hopped the Yonge-University subway line to Eglinton Avenue. Nearby he located a store named SpyStory. He made up a compelling bit of fiction about why he needed to get someone's passwords. The bulky Asian man behind the counter didn't care about the background information but was animated about Reggie's options. One was an inconspicuous camera and surveillance system, but it was expensive, hard to install and might not give a clear enough picture. Another was installing software that would hide itself, and then email Bradley's keystrokes to Reggie's address. But that left the problem of uninstalling the software. The last option was the best: a connector that inserted between the keyboard cord and the CPU with four gigs of memory for keystrokes. It was discreet to install and uninstall and left no traces. Reggie feared his credit card would not take the charge, but it did.

A half hour later, Amy was close to the front door of her house when Reggie rang the doorbell, and she hastily let him in.

She looked at him intently, curling her long hair with two slender fingers, prancing from one foot to another.

"What did you get?" she asked. "It's already two thirty. We don't have much time."

"Relax, we have lots of time, sis," Reggie said, though he suspected he was more on edge than she.

Amy spotted the SpyStory bag and tore it out of Reggie's hand. "Hm — 'Keystrokelogger'. How does it work?"

Reggie explained. "Clever," Amy said in a hushed tone. "Nasty, but clever."

"And when Peter's done, you give it back to me and I'll read the file of keystrokes on my laptop. No problem to get his bank password and his computer password, if he has one. Did you check?"

"Yes, I was shocked. He has one."

Reggie swallowed hard. "We can install this thing right now," he offered.

Without saying more, they started walking up the stairs toward Bradley's study. Amy wrinkled her eyebrows, growing thoughtful. "So, somehow, I have to get Peter to go to his bank site."

"And then get this connector back to me."

In the study, Reggie crawled underneath Bradley's desk and had the connector inserted in less than a minute. Amy watched carefully. "Done," he said, half proud and half wary.

"Great," Amy said, lunging to give her brother a kiss on the cheek after he stood up. "Partners in crime again, huh?"

"Oh, please don't say that. What will Peter do if he finds out?"

"String us both up."

"Fucking awesome. And when does he use this computer?"

Amy wrinkled her eyebrows again. "Evenings, usually. I'll dream up some reason for him to use it tonight. He's having dinner with Dottie, the bitch, tomorrow, and then he's closing the cottage this weekend. Tonight — that's when it has to be. You should have dinner around here somewhere this evening." Reggie looked apprehensive. "Don't worry, I'll give you the cash. Then, when Peter's done in here, I'll text you and you can come over and get this thing. I'll sneak it to you out the back door."

"Ok," Reggie said, reaching behind the back of his head to release tension. "This whole thing seems kind of —"

"*Reggie, not again,*" Amy shrieked.

The cuff of Reggie's left arm sleeve had come undone as he struggled to insert the Keystrokelogger. With his arm outstretched behind him, the sleeve had fallen to his elbow, revealing his angry-looking cut.

"Why do you do this?" Amy continued anxiously. Stepping away, Reggie started pushing down the sleeve, but Amy caught his wrist and stopped him from doing up the cuff. "Show me. I want to see." Reluctantly, he let go of the sleeve and looked away as she fretfully examined the infliction. "Do I need to take you to the hospital?"

"Amy, it'll be fine," Reggie said impatiently. "This one's not deep. It'll heal. I put antibiotic cream on."

"Well, I'm putting gauze and a bandage on, and some more cream. I'll never understand this, Reggie, never." Amy left for the washroom and returned quickly with an array of medical supplies. As she dressed Reggie's wound, she scrutinized her brother's face. "If this gets infected, you have to go see the doctor. You were supposed to go to the doctor for your eye."

"And what about the fucking passwords, Amy?"

She ignored his question. "What was the trigger this time?"

"I don't remember."

"Seriously, what was it?"

He ignored her question.

"There, it's done. Listen to me," Amy said, peering into her brother's eyes. "*Stop* hating yourself so much. You're a great guy. You're going to find your way. *We* will find our way."

Reggie cursed himself for stretching his left arm behind his head. "I'm going. I'm gonna get a coffee before I have dinner."

Amy grabbed both his shoulders. "This is a new start today. Do you understand?"

"Sure," he said, and pulled himself away from his sister's grip. "I need the cash for dinner, though."

Saddened and maddened by his perpetual moods, Amy watched her downcast brother. "Two million," she said, finally.

"Two million what?"

"Two million life insurance. That's what Peter's taken out for me. I checked."

Reggie's eyes lit up. "I thought you told me once it was a million."

"That was a long time ago. Honestly, I thought it was more — maybe five."

"Two million is a *shitload* of money, Amy. Whenever you get it."

"Yes, whenever I get it. I'll be old and ugly."

"And what if you have children? Do you have to share?"

"I already have you," Amy said with a taunting smile. "No one else will share."

Reggie pressed his lips together at his sister's jab. "You can be proud of me about one thing, though."

"What's that?"

"I got my old job back."

"You see, a new start."

"I need your old car, though."

"Sure. It's filthy, though. You'll have to clean it up. I'm not going near that thing. I have to find the keys first. Oh, and you know what? I'm going to call Dominic again for you."

Amy went downstairs to the kitchen to find the car keys and her phone. Reggie trailed. She rummaged through various drawers in a vain search for the keys. Bored, Reggie stepped out onto the backyard deck, feeling the warm September sun. *Two million dollars*, he thought. He still could not fathom the sum.

"I found the keys!" Amy yelled from the bowels of the house.

Seconds later, Reggie heard Dominic's name. Amy jumped into animated discussion marked by bursts of laughter. Rather than having to listen, Reggie chose to inspect Amy's old car. He found the house entrance to the single-car garage, opened the door and switched on an overhanging bulb. It shone a dim light on a fourteen-year-old Corolla and a stack of boxes on the far wall. Reggie pushed through to the front garage door and forced it open. Sunlight caught dust in the garage floating in the air and covering the car's rust-spotted crimson body. Reggie used an old rag to wipe the front and back windshields clean.

Amy soon found her brother in the garage. "Here are the keys," she said. "And some cash. Try it out."

Reggie started the car. After one belch, it ran fine. He eased it out of the garage and stopped in the driveway, the brakes grinding away rust. Amy came around to the driver's side and motioned Reggie to roll down the window.

"Dominic is going to call you in an hour or so," she said. "He's found someone for you to interview."

Reggie nodded. "Thanks, sis."

"The only thing, Reggie, it's going to cost some money. And you have to be careful. You know what you're dealing with here, right?"

"What? It's only a guy who kills people for a living, know what I mean? Don't worry, Amy, I've thought it through."

"Seriously, with you, I never —" Amy started before pausing.

"Anyhow, meet in a public place, don't take too long, have all your questions ready —"

"Amy, I know."

"No dope, either."

"Shit, Amy, I know," Reggie said impatiently. "How often do you talk to Dominic anyway?"

"What do you mean?"

Reggie pretended to wipe the car's dash clean. "When I had coffee with him, he said he's in touch with you once in a while." He looked back at his sister and thought her face was red, but it was hard to be sure in the sunlight.

"I've had dinner or lunch with him a few times in the past few years. Nothing more than that."

"Why? He's a jerk."

"I just bumped into him one day. It was good to catch up."

"I don't fucking trust him, Amy."

"I didn't say I do, either. He's interesting sometimes. It's not like I'm flaunting myself."

"Ok, whatever," Reggie said, engaging the Corolla's reverse gear. "I'll see you later tonight."

"You will," Amy said. "Get ready to be a good spy."

Carefully, Reggie backed onto Gregory, then pulled forward to Whitehall Road and signalled left toward Mount Pleasant Road. In the rear-view mirror he saw his sister standing in the driveway, watching him. It occurred to him that she had never explained why her husband had irritated her so much. It hardly mattered. Stealing Bradley's passwords was now as much about him as it was about her — maybe only about him. He lifted his left arm out the side of the car and waved. Immediately, she waved back. She looked happy, a complete contrast to when he had arrived. For a moment it stirred envy, but he grabbed hold of her promise for a new start. Soon, with the money coming his way, he'd be a player in the game, every bit as content as his sister. Feeling a stab of confidence, he peeled the decrepit car through the left-hand turn.

CHAPTER 23

It seemed that Dominic could be trusted to call when he said he would. It hadn't taken Reggie long to locate a coffee shop near Amy's house. His cell vibrated ten minutes after he'd found a lonely seat in a back corner.

"Hey, little brother."

"Dude, I'm *not* your little brother."

Dominic paused at Reggie's aggressive tone. "Relax, ok? I'm calling because your sister asked me to."

"Well, actually, I also asked you to call me."

"Like I said, I'm calling because your sister asked me to. Do you want this favour from me or not?"

Reggie took a deep breath. "Yes, I do. How much is it gonna cost me?"

"Five."

"Five thousand? Are you fucking serious?"

"Reggie, I am *always* serious about business."

"And how much are you getting of that?"

Another pause. "Look, little brother, what I get or don't get out of this is my business, ok?" *Payoffs, payoffs, payoffs*, Reggie reflected. "Do you want to do this or not?"

"I said, yes. How is this gonna work?"

"Thursday afternoon. You got time?"

Reggie wondered how he would get time off in his first week

back at Faster Delivery, but he would find a way. "Yes. What time?"

"Two or so. I'll call you in the morning with details."

"I want it to be a public place."

Still another pause. "You're going to get what my contact is comfortable with. Bring the money — cash, obviously — with you."

"Will you be there?"

"Probably, just for the beginning. I don't know yet."

"And who am I meeting?"

"You will never know the answer to that. But he does what you're interested in. That's all I'm going to tell you."

"One other thing, Dominic."

"Yeah," Dominic said, exhaling a sigh of indifference.

"Please don't fuck my sister around, ok?"

A final pause. "Hey Reggie, what I do with anybody is none of your fucking business. Remember who you're talking to here, ok? Learn your place."

Dominic hung up. Staring at "Call Ended" on his cell phone screen, Reggie blurted, "What a complete asshole," and sent the phone rattling onto the table in front of him.

CHAPTER 24

The Roaster's Blend at Temperance Street was in a claustrophobic stretch of Bay between King and Queen Streets where bank towers blocked every ray of sunlight. The coffee shop's bright lighting counteracted the gloom, and along with comfortable seating and ceaseless wafts of overpriced coffee, it ensured a steady bustle of activity.

As Bradley hurried north along Bay, he digested Amato's choice of a meeting place that was closer to his office than Bradley's. A little after 3:30 p.m., he crowded through Roaster's Blend's front doors and stopped to scan for Amato. From a table in a back corner, Amato raised a hand. Bradley returned the gesture, got a coffee and worked his way to the table.

He greeted Amato and shook his hand, then sat directly across from him. To Bradley, Amato was a curlicue of a man, his slender, fit frame sartorially resplendent and his receding hairline and short beard perfectly coiffed. Bradley engaged him with a large smile; Amato responded in kind, but more guardedly.

"So what do you think about our little venture?" Bradley asked after a few seconds.

"Interesting. Very interesting."

"I think it's going to be incredibly exciting. It'll get noticed big time by the competition bar," Bradley said, leaning forward a bit.

"Maybe by the entire street," Amato added.

Amato's eyes strayed; he seemed quite tense. "It must be a big shock to you," Bradley said.

Amato looked back at Bradley, sardonically, Bradley thought. "As I'm sure Leonard told you, I approached your firm — my firm now, I guess, not the other way around. It was my idea to leave Bergheim's, so in that sense not too big a shock." Amato paused. "But the truth is, while I'm usually very sure of what I do, I'm still waking up in the middle of the night, screaming 'What the hell am I doing?'"

Bradley laughed. "We're lucky to get you. Very lucky."

"I don't know about that, but I'll take the compliment. I hope you know, I've always respected you — a lot."

"Thank you. And your wife is with you on this? It's important, you know."

Amato gave a curious pause and averted his eyes. "Yes," he said finally. "I think it'll be an amazing team," he added in a firmer tone, looking up again. "You must have been a bit surprised."

"I was," Bradley said, nodding slowly. "When Leonard first talked to me about it, I have to admit, I needed a few minutes to absorb it. But then I saw the potential. I know my clients will be thrilled."

"Mine as well. And I'm confident they'll follow me — most of them, anyway." Amato seemed to relax a bit. "I hope you don't mind that I didn't call you directly with the idea."

"Not a bit."

Leaning forward, Amato said, "You see, it was never a question for me that we would make a great team. And I didn't think I would have to sell you too hard on it. I felt I had to explain directly to Leonard and Ted why I wanted to leave Bergheim's, and what I can offer Collins, Shaw. That, I thought, was information that should go through as few hands as possible, straight to your executive. You don't just leave a firm you've been with for fifteen years. I didn't want Leonard or Ted to think I up and leave every time there's a little problem. Plus I knew Leonard a little in law school."

"Do you mind if I ask what the problem was with your old firm?"

"Well," Amato said, leaning back and grimacing a bit, "I don't want to go into too much detail. It's not my style to speak critically of others. But let's just say that there were two main things. Money — money was the first. It's always about money at some level, right?"

"Sure it is."

"My revenues went like this —" Amato said, motioning an upward trajectory, "but my partnership points never kept up. They refused to see the potential for our area. I was never as good as the big corporate guys. Drove me crazy. Whereas when I talked to Leonard — more Ted, really — he seemed to see the potential. And offered me a fair deal, I thought. You guys do well — better than us — I mean, them."

"The other reason?"

"Well, look, basically there was one of me doing this full-time and there are at least three of you. Walter and Carolyn are both very good lawyers; Walter I know better. I had more work than I cared for, and I said, over and over, 'You know, I think it's time that we hire someone to work with me.' But they wouldn't hire a junior for me, so I became a victim of my own success. All I got was a corporate associate with an interest in the area who worked part-time with me. Except every time he was on a deal, I lost him. Just no commitment to competition law. None of this will surprise the partners at Bergheim's at all."

Bradley listened and processed. After a few moments, he lowered his voice and said, "So, have you told them yet?"

Amato shook his head. "Wednesday afternoon is my plan.

Then the announcement goes out from Ted or Leonard Thursday. Spot in the paper Friday morning. I thought maybe you could do a draft of the firm and public announcements for everyone's review, and I'll do a draft of the bit for the newspaper and website under my mug shot."

"Sure. Let's trade drafts tomorrow morning. Then I'll get Ted and Leonard's input."

For ten minutes Bradley and Amato discussed logistics. Bradley exuded enthusiasm while Amato became increasingly animated.

"There is one other thing, Peter," Amato said near the end of their discussion. He eyeballed Bradley closely. "Oddly enough, Walter Anand sent me his résumé just an hour ago. To join Bergheim's. He must be due for partnership, isn't he?"

Bradley pursed his lips, trying not to look too surprised. He searched for the right words. "Walter was passed over for partnership last year. He's a solid lawyer but very technical. I thought he needed at least another year."

"Does my joining the firm complicate things for him?"

"We decided to defer him another year. Ted doesn't want three partners in the group."

Amato nodded. "I see. Does he know that?"

"Well, he hasn't heard it from me. I was going to tell him tomorrow. He must sense something's up. He's a funny guy. Very calm on the outside but can be seething with anger inside, and you wouldn't know it. He took the partnership deferral hard last year, but it took me three months to figure that out. Bit of a chip on his shoulder now." With a large smile, Bradley said, "I, on the other hand, have no trouble showing my irritability to the entire world — or so I'm told."

"I think I've been on the end of that once or twice."

Bradley forced a laugh. "I'll manage Walter. I guess I wasn't doing as good a job as I thought."

Amato shrugged. "If we lose him, we lose him. Won't be the end of the world. Carolyn Murphy seems like a good lawyer. No issues with her?"

"Not that she's told me. Very hard worker, ambitious, but keeps her distance. Smart for her age."

Amato got up and extended his hand to Bradley. "I have to get back. I'm looking forward to working with you, Peter. I'm sure you'll see I have a lot to offer."

Bradley took a last sip of coffee and heartily shook Amato's hand. "Likewise," he said. "We are definitely going to take advantage of you."

CHAPTER 25

In early July, Amy had dragged Bradley to the city's annual out-door art exhibition at Nathan Phillips Square. The weather was hot and muggy, and the multitude of artists and styles soon over-whelmed Bradley's ability to distinguish one piece of art from another, let alone appreciate any of them. As his face swelled with fatigue, he found watching art lovers divert their glances to his wife much more entertaining.

Near the end of their excursion, however, Bradley's attention was caught by one mixed media work. It was a close replication of one of the versions of *The Scream,* with a notable addition. The screamer had an identical twin standing next to him, his elbows leaning on the wooden railing, his head gently resting between his hands, contentedly appreciating the view of water flowing under the bridge. Bradley didn't know what to make of the piece and asked the young male artist to explain. With considerable animation, the artist said, "I guess it's what you want it to be. But for me, it says that a person's state at any one time is not made up of one emotion, but a confluence of them — a *conflicting* confluence of them." Despite the artist's heroic explanation of his piece, seeing Amy waiting impatiently several booths over, Bradley thanked him and moved on.

For no discernible reason, the piece had stuck with him and it returned to him now as he left Roaster's Blend. Part of him was content with the bravado enthusiasm he had just contrived for Amato. It had fully misled Amato, creating a sense of security in place of the apprehension that Amato, quite naturally, had brought to their meeting. Carolyn Murphy had been right; if Bradley had shown any hint of anger or dismay, Collins, Abrams or Amato would have used it, somehow, to Bradley's detriment. It was time to clam up, and Bradley had successfully faced down any untoward displays at the coffee shop.

But within him, the screamer screamed. What no one understood, not even the perceptive Carolyn Murphy, was that at some point the outrage had to be *released*, like steam out of a boiler. And there was plenty of outrage around. There was Amato's incursion into his territory, into what Bradley had painstakingly built over twenty years, and Amato's galling presumption that it would be an easy sell to Bradley. And Anand, the duplicitous prick, was jumping ship, after everything Bradley had done for him. But worst of all there was Ted Collins, the pampered member of the firm's lineage, in arms with Amato, displaying Brutus-like connivance and treachery.

Walking down Bay among a crowd of identical suits, the screamer in Bradley rose until he nearly gagged. It demanded to be given voice, right there, among his brethren. But even for Bradley, who, like his father, was often insensitive to social norms, screaming was outside the realm of acceptable behaviour. He had to find another way to release.

Five floors below Collins, Shaw in the Bay Wellington Tower, an elite fitness club thrived on unused membership fees paid by professional firms for their partners. For the first time in months Bradley found himself at the club's reception area. Once he'd remembered his way to his locker he found a leather gym bag, deposited some unknown time before, standing on end at the bottom of the locker with clean workout gear inside. Ten minutes later he was selecting a light setting on a recumbent bike positioned for a view of the lake.

His heart quickly started to pound, and sweat soon drenched his brow and rolled down his temples. But as the screamer screamed, power transferred to Bradley's legs and he pedalled on. The emotional debris in his mind began to settle, and he returned to his call with Carver less than four hours earlier. Use or ruin — that had been the outcome. Soon it was an internal chant, each word coupled with a thrust of a pedal: *use or ruin, use or ruin, use or ruin.* Thirty seconds later, the chant simplified, and as each foot rounded another turn on the bike, Bradley heard: *ruin, ruin, ruin.*

After fifteen minutes, his upper body soaked with perspiration, Bradley got up from the recumbent bike and towelled off his head. He massaged his scalp hard, and in doing so a gateway in his mind opened to designs of ruin. Discarding any notion of more exercise, he returned slowly and in deep thought to the locker room.

There would be presentations to clients of the anti-trust group to showcase Amato's arrival. Bradley could use those occasions to upstage Amato, drumming home his own pre-eminent reputation and deep experience. Or if Amato and he met together with regulators, he could ensure that he led the charge and relegated Amato to a junior role. He could even tell Anand and Murphy to make his work a priority. Bradley let out an involuntary snort as he dumped his sodden gear in front of the locker and entered the shower area. None of those ideas was more than an inconsequential inconvenience, not even close to ruin.

Bradley muddled his way to the shower room and found a shower in a corner where he could be alone. As he cranked open the faucet, unconsciously dodging cold spits before the water grew warm, a new design came to him. Amato would be covetous of the clients that he brought from Bergheim's, particularly the two large ones. Over time Bradley could insert himself in enough files to spark a transition of allegiance. That would show Collins who had the most clout in anti-trust law. But that would also take too much time; months, or years more likely. Steam from the shower rose around Bradley. He shook his head and continued pondering.

Maybe introducing a horrible mistake into a major deal document that Amato had drafted. Every lawyer's nightmare was revisiting one of his agreements and in a key provision finding a "not" where there wasn't supposed to be one. Bradley smiled at the shame Amato would feel when he told Collins — and the errors and omissions insurance company — of the surprising and gruesome reversal of intended effect. But as delightful as that scenario seemed to Bradley, he knew everyone would try to bury the problem from clients. And any that did find out might wonder as much about Bradley's anti-trust group as Amato.

Dousing his head under the hard, stinging stream, a more arresting design came to mind: an inexplicable accident befalling Amato. With a wry smile Bradley imagined Amato's astonished look just before he was victimized, and Collins' sour face on learning the next day that Amato was lost to the firm for months.

And then a bombshell of idea landed, making Bradley's eyes open wide in spite of the spray of water in his face. A gunshot, close to Amato's house, and Amato seized with terror as blood oozed from his chest and his consciousness faded. Bradley grinned as he imagined Collins' shock and helplessness in the face of a sure bet gone wrong. For the next ten minutes, Bradley stood stationary in the shower, letting the water wash away sweat and, at least temporarily, inhibitions. In the safety of clouds of steam, Bradley nodded to himself that such an event would indeed be Amato's ultimate ruin — and, amusingly, give unfettered access to Amato's book of business.

With a last snort, Bradley turned off the water. As he exited the shower area and re-entered the real world, he pushed aside his musings on ruin. Certainly, visiting the club had helped; within him, the screamer had grown quiet. But Bradley still detected him. Like an alligator in water he lay submerged and motionless, except for two probing eyes just above the surface.

CHAPTER 26

Waiting for Bradley to come home, Amy paced the house, often stopping to dance from one foot to the other, hardly able to suppress her excitement. Her first challenge was to re-open the lines of communication with her husband. She needed an authentic strategy. After the previous evening's argument, he would be expecting the traditional two or three days of remorseless silence until he bled forgiveness. Her second challenge was to induce him to access his bank site.

Around four thirty, she called Bradley's smartphone. It went straight to voicemail and she left a message. When she hadn't heard from him by five thirty, she called again. This time he picked up.

"You're avoiding my calls?" she asked as playfully as possible.

Bradley was surprised to hear from his wife. "I was at a meeting and then went to the club."

"The club? What for?"

"It was just time, that's all. Is there something wrong?"

"No. I was just wondering if you're coming home soon. I was going to make spaghetti and open a nice bottle of Chianti. How does that sound?"

Amy's call was surprising, but her offer of food was shocking. Bradley's overtired brain tried to make sense of the situation.

"What's going on, Amy? I don't understand."

"Nothing's going on, Peter. Consider it an olive branch. I'm tired of fighting."

Amy conciliatory? Highly unlikely, but conceivable — by a hair. Bradley decided to clutch the branch if he could carve out time later in the evening to think more about Amato. "I have to work after dinner. Otherwise, it's fine."

"Come home soon," Amy said and ended the call.

When Bradley got home, Amy greeted him at the door with insouciant attentiveness and relieved him of his briefcase. She had put on a bit of makeup and a long, flouncy dress that always caught eyes. She hoped he understood her signal of détente without interest in sex. Guardedly, Bradley eyeballed the first floor rooms and dinner spread in the kitchen.

After a glass of wine, some small talk and the first mouthfuls of spaghetti, it seemed to Amy that her husband was slowly beginning to trust the situation. He remained preoccupied and distant, however, and she was forced to lead the chat. Though he dutifully responded, in another circumstance their misfiring connection would have irritated her.

At the end of dinner Bradley finished off his second glass of wine and sat back in his chair. Amy went to the refrigerator and returned to the table with a key lime pie.

"Your favourite," she said in a measured tone, trying not to seem obsequious.

A bent smile of wonderment crossed Bradley's face. Amy looked for cynicism but judged it genuine. As she cut the pie she said as casually as possible, "You know, my usual amount didn't go through this month."

For once during the dinner, Bradley looked directly at his wife. His eyelids were heavy from the wine, often a precursor to annoyed ramblings. Berating herself for having poured the second glass of wine, she worried that he would lock onto some wrong that needed righting instead of going to his study.

But Bradley was happy for the dinner and peace. "I'll check on it tonight when I'm on the computer," he said simply and dove into the pie.

Within a half hour Bradley announced he had work to do. After Amy heard the study door shut, she grabbed her smartphone and called Reggie. "He's in his study. Where are you? He should be going to the bank site sometime soon."

"I'm eating at a pub on Yonge."

"You're not drunk, are you?"

"No, you didn't give me enough cash for that."

"Seriously?"

"Seriously, I'm sober as hell."

"Ok. I'll call you when he falls asleep. Then I'll get that Keylogger thing and you can meet me at the back door. Park the Corolla down the street. I don't want the neighbours to get suspicious."

"Yes, sis."

"Got to go."

Returning to his nachos and second beer, Reggie repeatedly shook his head, wondering what he'd gotten himself into.

CHAPTER 27

Bradley threw his briefcase on the couch in his study then fell into the chair behind his desk. He punched the power button on the CPU of the desktop computer that sat under the desk's right side. When the pop-up box for a password opened on the screen on his desk, Bradley exercised his single-finger typing skills. Eventually, the blue desktop screen flickered into view.

But Bradley's hands stayed still. On the drive home, tapes of his meetings with Collins and Amato had played in his head. In response, the screamer's head had started to rise above the surface and, uncomfortably, Bradley had forced him back down. But now, alone and in the quiet of his study, he gave him some airtime. The screamer took full advantage, soon standing tall and strong, convincing Bradley that a reckoning was due. The only real question was in what form.

The designs of ruin Bradley had toyed with in the shower after working out clipped through his mind like a series of movie stills. When the still of a handgun came up in lights, his mouth dried, and despite the wine, a swell of shock rolled from top to bottom through his body.

Bradley recoiled and substituted a new design of ruin. He imagined trapping Amato in a crime and instigating his incarceration. It obviously would ruin Amato professionally and settle Bradley's score with Collins. As he thought about it, Bradley could even make a case that a long time in jail, trying to piece together what had happened, might be a worse hell for Amato than death. But framing Amato would be complicated, and he would scream his innocence forever. As shocking as it was, pulling the trigger was cleaner and simpler. Bradley wiped a hand the length of his face. His familiar sense of self-confidence joined the screamer.

Whatever the path, it all started with research — and being careful. He got up and double-checked that the study door was closed and locked. Using the browser's private setting, he searched Tony Amato online and began to find facts of interest. A Word document with extensive notes developed quickly, and after half an hour he saved the document in a folder. The only code name he could think of was "Project Pizza".

After his search, Bradley moved on to Facebook. It took him half an hour to retrieve his user ID and password, but he was delighted with what he found. Amato had posted several pictures of his family for the entire world to see, and one was in front of a house in a bucolic neighbourhood that Bradley guessed was close to his own. Amato's churlish grin as he stood with his arms around his wife on one side and his two children on the other made the hair on Bradley's neck stand. He chuckled as he imagined a gunshot ringing out, replacing the neighbourhood's calm with ghetto tension.

Around ten, Bradley emerged from the study. After going to the washroom, he joined Amy in the master bedroom. She pretended to read in bed. The question echoing in her head was quickly answered.

"The transfer looked fine to me, Amy," Bradley said absent-mindedly. "It's in the joint account. Anyway, I sent it again to be sure."

Once Bradley had heaved himself into bed, Amy leaned across, and making sure their bodies didn't touch, gave him a light kiss on the cheek. "You're a sweetheart," she said. Bradley had already turned off the lamp on his side of the bed and shut his eyes. Increasingly heavy breathing told of early sleep.

Amy lay still as Bradley's slumber deepened. Hearing her husband had re-sent the transfer, she felt a punch of guilt. But his never-ending counterplay of good and bad had become too exhausting, and she repeated her mantra: *I deserve better*.

Five minutes later Amy slipped out of bed and tiptoed out of the master bedroom, gently closing the door behind her. In the study, on her hands and knees in silk pajamas, she had little difficulty disconnecting the device Reggie had bought. Shortly after, she was in the kitchen, grabbing her phone, which she had purposely left on the kitchen island.

"Come and get it," was all she said.

A long fifteen minutes passed before Reggie's spindly figure skulked up to the kitchen back door.

"God, I thought you'd never call," he said disgustedly after Amy opened the door.

"Are you drunk?"

"Hell, no," Reggie said.

"Shall we look at it here?" Amy asked, curling a loose strand of hair.

"No, no," he said. "I'll take it home and call you in a little while."

"Let me call you," Amy said. "At midnight, ok? You have to go now."

Amy's call was right on time. Reggie sat in the swivel chair in front of his laptop and digital audio workstation amidst the bedlam of his condo.

"How does 200760 sound for his computer password?" Reggie asked.

Amy thought it over for a second. "That's his date of birth — July 20, 1960."

"That's what I thought. He spent a lot of time on Google and Facebook. Searching for Tony somebody —"

"Another time, Reggie. I know he went to the bank site."

"How does 200760PB sound?"

Amy giggled. "Very original. I'll check it out tomorrow. I have to go back upstairs now. Bye and thank you, thank you, thank you."

"Amy..."

Reggie wanted to tell her that by Thursday morning he needed five thousand dollars for his venture with Dominic, but she had already hung up.

CHAPTER 28

Last entry, I said that I need to do some planning. I've started.

Three Plans

PLAN A

Key Steps:

1. *Find PB at Café Sorrento, his usual Saturday morning spot. Disguise myself enough so other patrons can't identify me.*

2. *Join him; administer date rape drug.*

3. *When drug takes effect, pay bill (cash; watch for prints) and help him away.*

4. *Take him to car parked in alleyway behind Café Sorrento, get him in passenger seat. Use spiked bottle of water in car (if needed) to make him unconscious.*

5. *Drive to abandoned farm property north of city.*

6. *Dolly him to house. Tie him to chair.*

7. *After deed is done, dolly him to pond. Add weights to clothing. Dump everything.*

To Do:

1. *Locate abandoned farm property north of city — done. House*

> boarded, but back door broken down. Pond a few hundred
> yards at back.
>
> 2. Investigate trunk size of car — seems enough, especially if back
> seat folds down. Confirm back seat folds.
>
> 3. Choose/purchase disguise; dolly; chair and rope; weights;
> broom (to cover up tracks from moving body into house or out
> to pond); knife.
>
> 4. Deface tread on old boots.
>
> 5. Complete investigation of date rape drug. Purchase.
>
> 6. Confirm alleyway is large enough to park car.
>
> 7. Check for surveillance cameras around Café Sorrento.

Weaknesses: Overall, seems like too much risk??? I will be seen at Café Sorrento, arriving, eating and leaving with him (after drug takes effect). In other words, there will be witnesses to say that I was last person with him — unless my "disguise" is really effective and I also have an alibi (and what is that?). Will I get a chance to administer the drug? Can I get him to car, to farmhouse, to chair? What do I wear to avoid blood on clothing? What about a trail of blood? I want him to regain consciousness so he can witness his death. How long till drug wears off? And will he be in any shape to understand what is happening?

PLAN B

> *Key Steps:*
>
> 1. Contact him when he is at home with fake nearby car trouble.
> Tell him I'm close to Rosedale Park, at (Edgar?).
>
> 2. When he arrives, direct him to trunk to get tools out.
>
> 3. Bludgeon him so he falls into trunk (trunk must be covered
> with tarpaulin).

4. *Follow steps 5–7 in Plan A.*

5. *Dispose of tarpaulin.*

To Do:

1. *To do items 1–4 in Plan A (except disguise).*

2. *Scout Edgar. Find spot where houses have no view.*

3. *Use baseball bat for bludgeoning?*

Weaknesses: *Can I get him into trunk? To farmhouse and into chair? What do I wear at farm to avoid blood on clothing? And, again, I want him to regain consciousness in farmhouse — how hard to hit him? What is my alibi?*

PLAN C

Key Steps:

1. *Hire a "professional" to get him and bring him to farmhouse.*

2. *Then follow steps 5–7 in Plan A.*

3. *Then I can perform the deed — or watch???*

To Do:

1. *To do items 1–4 in Plan A (except disguise).*

Weaknesses: Do I have nerve to meet possible hire? How much will he charge? Alibi?

Time frame for all three plans: complete October 15 (3 weeks).
Organizing PB's end without implicating myself is much harder than I thought. This is going to require a lot of careful effort. But I think I can do it. Yes, my confidence is growing that I can pull this off. My thirst for

revenge surprises me, but I'm going to tap into it. Every time I remind myself how he has mistreated me, well, let's just say I'm not the only one who would take matters into their own hands.

Another thing is worrying me: after I've killed him, will I be able to live with myself? The act might consume me, cause me to relive it constantly, until I exhaust myself and simply die. Or maybe I'll isolate in fear of events catching up to me until I become a recluse and completely step outside of normal living. I already feel isolated sometimes — this could drive me underground.

I can't get caught. I need to think through every little detail. I need an airtight alibi.

If I don't get caught, no one will miss him. In fact, if they knew I was the one responsible for his death, they'd congratulate me. That's the answer to my worries. Everyone will understand — or just not care. He's pushed me to this, and we'll all live better without him.

CHAPTER 29

Tuesday morning, Bradley had no choice but to concentrate on client matters. Monday's intended accomplishments had been swamped by his plunge into fitness, rumination and research. Timelines on more than one file had passed, and clients were showing exasperation in repeated emails and voicemails. When Margaret arrived a little after nine, Bradley met with her, as he had Monday, to be sure nothing was falling between the cracks.

"And you have 'WA' marked in for lunch. Is that Walter?" she asked.

"Jeez, yes," Bradley said, running a hand across his face. "Could you talk to him for me? Just tell him I need to defer till tomorrow."

Margaret nodded. "One last thing," she said hesitantly. "Could I talk to you sometime today — about a personal matter?"

Bradley became nervous. "You're not quitting, are you?"

"No," she said with a quick shake of her head. "Something else."

Bradley had benefited from Margaret's down-to-earth, compliant nature for fifteen years. He was one of the few lawyers who still had a dedicated assistant, mostly because he threatened holy war every time the firm suggested sharing Margaret with another lawyer. It wasn't like her to bring her outside life into his practice, and he knew surprisingly little about it. He was aware of an erstwhile husband who had left her years before, and occasionally she spoke of her daughter, Kaley, whose full care she had assumed.

Bradley looked at his watch; he desperately needed time for his clients. *They pay the bills*, he reminded himself. "Can we talk after lunch? Then I can get through the worst stuff here."

"Sure."

Bradley knocked off one client issue after another. Around eleven, he phoned Anand to make sure Dave Gryzbowski was couriering Oshwegan's submission to the Bureau later that day. If Anand was peeved because Bradley had delayed their lunch by a day, it was hard to tell.

It was well after lunch when Margaret stuck her head in Bradley's office. Bradley instantly remembered that he had promised her his attention.

"Come in, come in. I'm sorry — just got caught up in things."

Margaret took a few steps in. "I know you're busy," she said, attuning herself, as always, to Bradley's mood.

"What's going on? Pull up a seat."

With one of her thick arms Margaret dragged the closest chair from the oval meeting table to sit across from Bradley. In her pudgy face beneath clipped pepper hair he saw lines of anguish. He had never seen this type of emotion from her, and it set him on edge. "It's about Kaley," she began, immediately tearing up and pushing back a few sobs. "She may have multiple sclerosis."

"Oh dear," Bradley said quietly, watching Margaret dab her nose with a crumpled facial tissue that emerged from the fist of her right hand. "What do you mean 'may'?"

"They don't know yet. She's had this tingling in her hands and feet for months. We didn't think anything of it. But then she started getting some muscle weakness and couldn't see right, so we went to the GP in May and finally got an appointment with a neurologist last Friday afternoon."

"I remember. But you didn't tell me anything about this."

"You're so busy. And the GP said it could be any number of things, so Kaley and I didn't want to think about it. But the symptoms are getting worse, and the neurologist was pretty clear it could be MS."

Bradley recalled Margaret's obvious agitation when they had met Monday. "When will you know?"

"The doctor said it can take a long time to know for sure. But he tested her movements and asked her all kinds of questions. And they took some blood. Now he wants to wait until she has an MRI. It's *so* stressful, Peter."

"And she's so young."

"She's twenty now. That's when it can hit."

"Twenty — really?" Bradley said. "Do you need some time off?"

Margaret shook her head. "No. It's better to be here, and Kaley's at community college anyway. But the reason I'm mentioning this — I may have to leave for doctors' appointments."

"Of course, of course. There's no issue there. Just let me know when you go." Bradley paused. "By the way, what's the name of the neurologist?"

"Dr. Shapiro. Bob Shapiro."

"You know, I'll ask Dottie about him. I'm having dinner with her tonight. Just to see if she knows him — what his reputation is."

"His online reviews are not that great, to be honest."

"Ok. Let me know what happens. Take as much time as you need." Bradley felt at a loss what to say next. "I'll help you as much as I can," he said finally.

"Thanks," Margaret said. Noiselessly, she got up and left Bradley's office.

Before attacking the next file Bradley paused to look out at the lake and shake his head at the way of the world.

CHAPTER 30

It was midafternoon before Bradley called his sister about dinner that evening. As the day had drawn on and he had conquered the most immediate client problems, he hadn't relaxed but again fallen into the grip of what to do about Tony Amato. He hoped Dottie would cancel. Instead, she offered to prepare a meal rather than go to a restaurant. Bradley felt obligated to accept in order to repay her for helping him with Carver's problem Sunday evening. More rumination about Amato would have to wait.

Dottie's house was in Greater Toronto's west end near Royal York Road and Bloor Street, driving distance from the hospital where she worked. As usual, traffic out of downtown was heavy. The stick shift in Bradley's BMW M3, which he had just leased in August, made the drive especially hard going. He arrived a little after six, only slightly late. Dottie had bought her home more than twenty years before, two years after earning her specialty in emergency care. Though a small, late-fifties design, it was welcoming. As he walked up the short stone path to the front door, Bradley surveyed the early fall blooms of his sister's careful planting and the manicured grass.

Dottie answered quickly after he knocked. Her slim face, framed by short grey hair, peered around the front door; her long, slim figure stayed hidden behind. Crowding into the small front hall, Bradley gave his sister a quick peck on the cheek and waited expectantly for her to notice his new car in front. She didn't.

"Let's sit in the living room," Dottie suggested. "The roast beef will be done soon. My goodness, you look awful."

Bradley knew she was right. In contrast, Dottie looked rested and tanned. He took a seat on a short couch while his sister sat across in a matching chair.

"Everything looks just like it always has," Bradley said, glancing around the compact room. Dottie waited for more information, and when none came, she shrugged dismissively. "Before I forget — sad news from Margaret today," Bradley continued. "Her daughter, Kaley, may have MS. She has to do an MRI."

Dottie put a hand to her mouth. "Oh, that's awful. I hope that's not the diagnosis."

"Do you know a Bob Shapiro? He's the neurologist treating Kaley."

Dottie took a moment to reflect. "No, I don't."

"Could you find out if he's any good?"

"Probably."

"I'll let you know." Bradley didn't know what to say next. Again he surveyed the living room. "What about some new furniture, Dottie?"

"Why?" she said. "Why change anything? I'm comfortable. Although I do have some new pictures." She walked over to a small brick fireplace. On the wooden mantle was an array of framed family pictures from which she picked one. Handing it to Bradley, she said, "I think you were eight and I was six. About that."

A smile emerged on Bradley's face as he absorbed a scene more than forty years old: he and his sister standing at the side of a pool on a hot summer day, both dripping wet with plastered hair, his arm pulling her reluctant smaller frame toward him.

"I remember that," he said with a laugh. "Mom made me put

my arm around you. I didn't really like you that much then."

"The feeling was mutual. That was at Sunnyside Pool — do you remember? Mom used to take us there all the time when it was hot."

"I haven't thought about that in years. The best thing was that the old man wasn't there. We actually look like we're having fun."

Dottie nodded. "Speaking of which, I have to update you on Father. You didn't let me finish Sunday evening."

"Later, later," Bradley said with a wave. "Or maybe not at all. When is dinner?"

"No, I have to." Dottie stood up and began walking to the kitchen. "I'll check the food."

Bradley pushed himself up from the couch and replaced the picture on the mantle. Twenty or so other framed family pictures stood in front of him. There was nothing similar in his house, though there were a few wedding pictures in the master bedroom. With some trepidation Bradley walked slowly along the mantle. Quickly, he grasped Dottie's chronological ordering. The first picture was a black-and-white of their parents at their wedding. Then there were images of Peter and Dottie as babies and, in later years, posing with one or both parents, or at graduations. The last picture was of their mother shortly before she died in 2007.

Dottie walked into the neighbouring dining room with a white serving plate of steaming roast beef cut into thin slices. She returned with a large tray jammed with a white porcelain gravy boat and three matching plates heaped with potatoes, carrots and salad.

"Help yourself," she said simply as Bradley took a seat at the table.

"This looks great —"

Bradley was interrupted by the ring of Dottie's landline. As Dottie took the call in the kitchen, he served himself, listening in with mischievous pleasure. "I can't talk right now, my brother's here ... Yes, can I call you back later? ... Sure, this weekend would be fine..."

When the call ended and his sister took her seat, Bradley couldn't resist. "Dottie, are you dating someone?"

The face of the usually equanimous Dottie flushed. She smiled furtively as she sat down and began to arrange small portions of food on her plate.

"You are," he said gleefully. "Why didn't you tell me about this?"

"I haven't heard from you in months. And I don't like calling your house, because then I have to have a torturously civil conversation with Amy when we both can't stand the sight of each other. And it's casual." Finished serving herself, Dottie looked at her brother. "Why do you have that grin on your face?"

Bradley tried but couldn't shake his expression. Finally, he just laughed. "I'm not used to my sister dating, I guess. Not that you shouldn't be. You're obviously very smart and good-looking —"

"Please stop. This is worse than talking to Amy."

With a final snicker, Bradley successfully wiped away the grin. Digging into the food on his plate, he asked, "And who is the guy? Another doctor?"

"Yes, she's a doctor," Dottie said, casually assessing her food.

It was Bradley's turn to redden. "She? I see — I didn't know," he sputtered, cursing his uncontrolled response.

"You need to pay more attention to your family members," Dottie said matter-of-factly. "Anyway, it just happened — sort of."

Bradley couldn't imagine that anything in his sister's controlled, methodical life "just happened", but he felt pleasure for her.

"That's great news, Dottie," he said. She measured his face for sincerity. "When do we meet her?"

"It's far too early for that, Peter. I wouldn't have told you for weeks if you hadn't been snooping."

"The phone is right around the corner."

"You were snooping. Your eyes and ears always go where they shouldn't. Anyhow, it will be a long time till I visit Casa Bradley and the lovely Amy, alone or with anyone else."

"Why do you dislike her so much?"

"Amy? Other than being a self-centred, superficial flirt con-sumed by a sense of entitlement, she's wonderful. I really like her."

"She told me Sunday night that she wants to own an art gal-lery."

"Hah! What does she know about art and business? Zero."

"She does have a Master in Fine Arts. And she wants me to get her a job at a gallery first — which I probably could do."

"I repeat, zero."

"Well, truthfully, that's my view, too. But you know, she's been difficult recently." For a moment, Bradley's mind travelled to Maximus and his friend John Carver, and his jaw muscles tightened involuntarily. "Difficult is an understatement. Maybe I should just give her what she wants. Just to solve the problems."

Dottie eyed her brother. "That's exactly what she wants, of course. That's how she's working you."

"She's not *that* bad. Not usually —"

"Oh, please. Give her an art gallery so she's nice to you? Clare was better for you." Bradley grimaced. "She was. You know that. She had compassion and a — and a tranquillity about her."

"She died, Dottie."

"Obviously I know that."

"It was a very long time ago."

"I'm just saying that what happened to Clare — and to you — not even to mention Ann — was a terrible shame. Clare had character. And then you ended up with Amy. You were single so long. You should have stayed that way."

"That's a little rich coming from you right now."

"I've been happy without anyone for a long time. This relationship — I can't believe I'm using that word — could end tomorrow, and I wouldn't care."

"Really?" Bradley said, a skeptical smile darting across his face. "You wouldn't care? Not at all?"

"Hardly at all."

"Clare had her challenges, too."

"You're just thinking of the last months."

"Not just that. We were both twenty — no idea what we were doing, really."

"And that mix-up with medication at the end. I still don't understand how that could have happened."

"It made no difference," Bradley said, feeling some irritation rise. "It just made things go a little faster, that's all."

Dottie reached for another helping of salad. "Don't you think of Ann from time to time?" she asked after a few seconds. "I do."

"Yes, I know you do," Bradley said. His irritation worsened.

"I do. She was a sweet little girl. I have a few pictures of the three of you — there should be one up there," Dottie said, flicking her head in the direction of the mantle, "but I don't want to ruffle your feathers, not that you're ever here."

"Well, I don't think of her except when you remind me. She's not part of my life."

"You married your profession."

"It wasn't as thoughtless as that, Dottie."

"Maybe I should have taken her after all. I was just too young."

"It was a hard decision."

"I have to say, Peter, it didn't seem that hard for you at the time."

"This is why I don't come over so often. This old chestnut of yours. You know I did what I had to do after Clare died. Ann wasn't even five. She still had time to become part of a good family, and I found her one. It was best for her."

"Your family lawyer found her one."

Bradley sniffed a bit derisively. "Whatever."

"Haven't you *once* thought about looking her up?"

"No, as a matter of fact. I wouldn't even know where to start. Once the lawyer had the family, I just signed the private adoption papers and made sure she got a few things from Clare. I hope I don't have to remind you, Dottie, it's my life."

Dottie stayed quiet. After a few seconds, Bradley cleared his throat. "All right, so let me guess, the old man is not getting any better."

Dottie shifted on her seat. "The Alzheimer's is getting much worse. He doesn't recognize me half the time."

"I guess we knew this was going to happen."

"What I'm saying, Peter, is that if you want to say your good-byes to him, when there's a chance he might understand you, now's the time. In a few months he won't get it and in a few months after that, I think he'll be dead."

Bradley paused. "I really don't know what I'd say to him."

"That you love him and wish him the best. Nothing more than that."

"But, Dottie, it's not true. I don't think I could get the words out."

"Peter," Dottie said with a noticeable sigh, "what's done is done. We can't turn back the clock. But we can reconcile a bit now."

171

Bradley's irritability turned to incipient anger. "I don't want to reconcile with him. What he did to me was inhuman, as simple as that."

"I understand that, but for family peace —"

"He didn't pound the crap out of *you* repeatedly. He just told you to look at me after he was finished, to make sure you knew what *could* happen to you if you crossed him."

"Maybe looking at you was harder."

"I'm sure it was hard. It was a lot harder for me just standing there taking it — as if I had a choice — and explaining it the next morning to my friends."

"It was what he knew, what had been done to him."

"It was what the Scotch told him to do. Are you seriously defending him?"

Looking at her brother, Dottie reached across the small table and took his hand. "No. It was wrong. Dreadfully wrong — for both of us. But if there's anything you want to say to him, now's the time."

"What I want to tell him is that he's the reason I left the house so early, and that I married when I was all of twenty. That being a lawyer is every bit as good as a doctor. That he failed as a father. That's what I *want* to tell him. And that he practically killed our mother with his temper."

Dottie pulled her hand away. "I thought you loved Clare."

"Dottie, yes I did, but I wanted to escape, too. And — and she was there. It all made sense at the time."

"I told him that I wished him well, that he'd been far from the world's best father, but that I knew he had tried his best."

"That's bullshit. He didn't try his best. He was too busy being angry at the world and whatever happened to him when he was kid. *None* of that was our fault. It wasn't our fault that he grew up in the war, that his parents never had money. We never even met them."

"I know all that, Peter."

"So did he understand you?"

Dottie pressed her lips together. "I really don't know."

"What's the point then?" Bradley said defiantly. "It's a waste of my time and his."

"I'll leave it alone then, Peter," Dottie said with a heavy sigh. "What do you think of the roast beef?"

CHAPTER 31

Each weekday around 6:00 p.m. he came home from his mid-level engineering job, and after making himself a Scotch on the rocks dropped himself in his usual chair at the table in the cramped kitchen. He catalogued to his wife the day's inequities and falsehoods, and based on their relative injustice took larger or smaller sips of his drink. Wearing an ancient, heavy apron, his wife finished dinner preparations, keeping a wary eye on him and depositing "Yes, dear" as necessary. He didn't get up from the table before dinner unless it was for a second Scotch.

After their mother called through the small house that dinner was ready, the children arrived at the table at the last possible moment. He controlled the dinner conversation, growling at this in politics or that in the class system, and if he didn't speak, the table fell silent. But everyone was paying attention to whether he would have a third Scotch. They employed tricks to distract him from the thought. Each child was instructed to have one story of the day, something amusing or funny, to offer if the silence became too long. The mother might recall a comedy show on television the night before. And if he engaged and stayed at the table, the evening could be relaxed, even fun.

However, more often than not, some event bore down on him so hard that more Scotch was inevitable. No one had the courage to say anything when he got up for the third, and they kept their heads down, guardedly watching him from the corners of their eyes. The remaining hope was to lay low and keep quiet. But if the berating started — what mother had cooked, what she was wearing, whom she had smiled at — tension grew. Then dinner was finished hurriedly, dessert often skipped, and the children bolted for their rooms upstairs as the mother cleaned up and listened to the recriminations. On one occasion she had offered him a fourth and a fifth to knock him out, but it had only made him more venomous. Instead she had come to know that the only way through was to let him verbally hunt and kill the demons until she could coax him in front of the TV, where eventually he would doze off.

But if he got it into his head that the children did not understand how good they had things, all bets were off. They all dreaded the sound of his heavy feet plodding upstairs. He opened their bedroom doors, shoving aside anything that they'd used to block his entrance. And for the nth time, standing in the hallway outside their bedrooms, he recounted to the children the hardships and injuries life had picked out for him, and how they needed to learn from them.

In his mind neither the girl nor the boy was listening, but especially the boy. "Why don't you listen?" he screamed at him, entering his bedroom. "Maybe this will get your attention," and an open-handed swat followed across the back of the boy's head. "Another? Is that what you need?" And another came.

The father made the boy stand in front him, hands at his side. He quivered, expecting his father's worst trick: mindless yelling from inches away that the boy was no good, and then a quick fist to the face. The mother would race into the boy's room — always too late — hugging the bent-over boy and pleading with the father to stop. The boy made sure he stood up straight again, resiliently snapping to attention like his wind-up toy monkey after playing the drum. And expressionlessly he would carry out his father's last instruction: "Go show your sister what a no-good son and brother looks like. Go show her your face."

As Bradley drove home along the Gardiner Expressway, he could only imagine that Dottie had boxed out those memories of their childhood. The tape must not run in her head as it still did in his, frequently, each time provoking acute indignation.

There was no way he would visit his old man to communicate false love or hope. He could rot in hell. Bradley had long ago sent the only message of any import: he was a far greater success than his old man had ever been, or ever predicted. For several moments Bradley revelled in his old man's failure to neuter his son. It was a thought that Bradley turned to often, especially when under attack. If his father couldn't get him down, no one could. He might not have become a doctor like his sister, but he had every other success, and nothing was going to take that away from him, nothing. No premature death, no pathetic bout of Alzheimer's, no Ted Collins, no Tony Amato.

Bradley took the Jarvis Street exit off the Gardiner. At that moment, rather coolly, he embraced the most extreme option for Amato's ruin. With a crooked smile he imagined applying the skills for planning and care that his legal practice had taught him. His plan would involve acquiring a gun, and he knew where he could get one. And it was time to start covering all his tracks. Before the evening was out, Bradley would email Amato his comments on Amato's draft announcements about joining Collins, Shaw, with cc's to Collins and Abrams. Then he would send Collins and Abrams another email, telling them that after meeting Amato he fully endorsed Amato's addition to his group. For good measure, he would suggest a Thursday afternoon, firm-wide "Meet Tony Amato" event.

Bradley followed Jarvis as it flowed right onto Mount Pleasant. As his exit to Whitehall came into view five minutes later, Bradley reminded himself also to email Margaret that evening, telling her that his sister could get more information about Kaley's doctor if she wanted it. He was certain he would forget to tell Margaret the next day and, if anyone deserved better, it was her.

CHAPTER 32

I've thought of a new plan. There is a big catch, though — IT HAS TO BE DONE THIS WEEKEND.

PLAN D

   Key Steps:

1. *Drive late Saturday afternoon to Otter Lake; PB is closing cottage.*

2. *Arrive when sun sets (7:00 p.m.); park car on left fork of Prior Lane, just after split in road.*

3. *Walk along right fork of Prior Lane to cottage.*

4. *From outside cottage, watch his movements inside. Enter from lakeside deck (always unlocked).*

5. *Bludgeon him from behind.*

6. *Tie him up to chair. Stuff his mouth so he can't scream (neighbours around?).*

7. *After deed is done, drag him down to lake, add weights, and dump him into lake off dock.*

   To Do:

1. *Fill car with gas.*

2. *Deface tread on old boots.*

3. Make sure no one sees me leaving or returning.

4. Purchase clothing; rope; weights; broom (to cover up car and boot tracks); knife.

5. Use baseball bat to bludgeon him?

Weaknesses: Again, I want him to regain consciousness so he can witness his death. How hard to hit him? Maybe simpler just to bludgeon him when he is asleep in bed? Also, much easier to find the body in the lake than at the swamp behind farm property (Plans A-C). How can I move body farther into lake? What about another lake? Alibi???

    I've realized that all my plans are complicated because I want him to know that I'm his assailant; that I'm the one inflicting the pain on him before he dies; to feel that pain from me, as he contemplates his end. All of that would be extraordinarily satisfying, but it also exponentially increases the risks of being found out. And I haven't figured out an air-tight alibi.

    He won't be taking his final memories of me anywhere. Maybe I should simply kill him gangland style. Drive-by shooting maybe. Just snuffing out his life could be enough to release me from his bondage.

    "Forgive and forget," that's what I hear people say. That doesn't always work, and it's not working for me now. I need some retribution and some control over my life. That is what I need and, frankly, what I deserve. Death is what he deserves, and maybe that's all I should care about.

CHAPTER 33

In bed late Tuesday evening, wary about his lunch the next day with Bradley, Anand vaguely heard another of Anita's entreaties.

"What is *wrong*, Walter?" she asked without looking at him.

The baby was finally asleep, at least for a few hours. His wife looked tired.

"Why should something be wrong?"

"I can tell."

"I thought you said you never can tell what is happening with me."

"I can tell *something* is wrong. Aside from the occasional blow up, with you it's always a question of how quiet you are. And you have been *very* quiet the last two evenings."

Looking straight ahead, Anand summoned energy. "Things are spinning out of control, Anita. It's all happening so fast."

"What things?"

"My career. It's falling apart before my eyes."

Anita shook her head in astonishment. "You told me Monday morning that everything was going to be fine."

"I didn't have the courage to finish the story." And then he did. He told his wife of Peter Bradley's sudden tentativeness only hours after his clear expression of support, and the unexpected, foreboding suggestion of lunch, deferred a day.

"Maybe there is no problem at all, Walter. This could all be in your mind."

"I wish it were."

"Or maybe the Management Committee has some problem, like Bradley says."

Walter looked pityingly at his wife. "I know the Management Committee has final say. He doesn't have to tell me that. The problem is with Bradley. I have a sixth sense about him. Which I should have listened to a long time ago. There is a problem and I am in deep trouble."

"Only women have a sixth sense."

"Occasionally, very occasionally, men do too."

"Go have your lunch first. Then we will decide. Anyhow, what difference does it make if you work with Peter Bradley at his stupid firm? He is slowly driving both of us nuts. Work somewhere else if you have to, Walter."

"It makes a lot of difference, Anita. He is the best, the acknowledged best. I don't know if I can work elsewhere."

"There must be people just as good at other firms. These are lawyers, not gods."

"It's not as simple as that. You don't just start over, with everything I've invested there."

Anand saw the growing irritability on his wife's face. Rather than disclose to her that early Monday afternoon he'd sent his résumé to two local and two English law firms, he got back out of bed, dressed and excused himself for a long walk in the cool night. Instead of relaxing him, the walk left him more apprehensive, convinced that Bradley was about to betray and dishonour him.

CHAPTER 34

Anand's sixth sense was going off like citywide fireworks. Seated with Bradley at a window table for two at Fortuna, looking over the intersection of King and Simcoe, conversation was hard and humourless. Repeatedly Bradley looked out at passersby or repositioned his cutlery. Anand guessed Bradley would rather have a root canal and colonoscopy than lunch with him.

"Well, here's the thing," Bradley said just after their pizzas arrived. "We're going to have to defer you one more year. But because you're such a valuable associate, we're going to raise your salary significantly. You'll be way above others in your year."

The anxiety in Anand staggered into horror, and his face contorted involuntarily. "That's not satisfactory," he croaked, surprising himself with his own audacity.

"Walter, just listen to me," Bradley said tersely. "As I said Monday, I understand how important this is to you. It was to me, too. It is to everybody." Bradley was tired of having to stroke Anand's ego, and there was so much else to do. But he needed Anand if the future was going to pan out as he hoped. "There's going to be a change — a very significant change — for the anti-trust group. It's going to be announced tomorrow."

"Peter, I don't care —"

"You need to care. It's why we're deferring you, but it's also a great opportunity for you, long-term." Bradley wondered how his pitch about Amato's arrival would sound credible if he didn't believe it himself. "A senior guy in our field — a very well-known guy — is going to join our group as partner. You'll be impressed."

Anand looked at Bradley uncomprehendingly. "How does that help me?"

"It's Tony Amato." Anand blanched. "And yes, I'm aware that you sent him your résumé — which I really wish you hadn't done. It was too early."

As Bradley had hoped, Anand felt caught out. But nervously Anand pushed back feelings of intimidation.

"Peter, I really had no choice. I have to protect myself. There are too many mixed messages."

"Mixed messages? There is only one message that's important: the one from the Management Committee. You didn't show good judgment there."

"There is no point in waiting for the Management Committee if you don't support me."

"I told you that I support you."

"Really, Peter, that's not true," Anand said, feeling bolder. "Sunday, you said you are only *inclined* to support me, and that I need to show more out-of-the-box thinking. Monday you told me that you support me, then, hours later, tell me that the MC has the final decision."

"There has to be a business case," Bradley said.

"I mean, for goodness' sake, Peter, it's *your* group," Anand said. "I assume they'll do what you tell them is right." Deep inside, Bradley understood Anand; the MC *should* be doing what he told them. "No, it's quite clear to me. I'm simply not getting the required vote of confidence from you. Like last year."

"Look, Walter, this idea with Amato came up very quickly. Everything was settled Sunday night. He's a great lawyer, and he's bringing a great book of clients. My view is that this is a great opportunity for our group, and as I said, especially for you. Just think of the new clients and work you'll have access to. We just can't have three partners in the group this year — it'll look top-heavy and expensive to clients." Bradley sighed. "And I promise you, unless you really, truly screw up, I'll move heaven and earth to get you partnership next year."

Anand thought for a moment. "Peter, I have a wife and young child at home. I want security, for them and for me. I can't live with this erratic behaviour. I don't even know how I will explain this to Anita. How do I explain to her that this is a good thing? That some lawyer from another firm is taking the place that should have gone to me, and I get to wait another year. It's — it's humiliating, really."

"You need to explain to her that Tony Amato is not 'some lawyer'. He's — he's probably number two on the street, at least in this city. A firm doesn't get this kind of opportunity very often. It's like getting Gretzky and Crosby on the same line."

"Gretzky and who?"

"Goddamn, Walter, it's like bringing the number one and two cricket players in the world together."

"Why do you assume I follow cricket, Peter?"

"Movies?"

"Bollywood."

"Whatever, this is an extraordinary deal. It's once in a life-time. That's what Anita has to understand." Bradley cringed at his own words.

Again, Anand grew thoughtful and Bradley felt tetchiness. After a few moments Anand leaned in a bit toward Bradley.

"Peter, have you ever had to explain something to your father that — that you're ashamed of?"

"Not really. I pretty much kept things to myself. And this is nothing to feel ashamed of, Walter."

"*He* won't see it that way. For him these kinds of things are a question of honour."

"Walter, how is it a question of honour? This is a partnership. There are no guarantees you get in. Even if you're the best young lawyer in the world, with the best judgment — which you have me wondering about a bit here — there are no guarantees."

Anand could see things unravelling quickly. He wished he hadn't been so direct with Bradley. "It just is, Peter. After a certain amount of time, associates are made partner if they work hard enough and do a good job. That is what he understands."

Bradley was stupefied. "Once upon a time, maybe. You know that's not true now. Now it's a business through and through. If you care that much what your father thinks, he should be proud that you're part of the best team in the city. The best."

Anand's throat was parched. He took a sip of water, glanced at his cold, sodden pizza, and then looked at Bradley. "Can I ask — when did this idea of Amato joining the firm come up?"

Bradley didn't understand why Anand was interested. "It was raised with me last Friday."

"So, Sunday, when I asked you if you would support me for partnership this year, is that why you were asking me about Amato?"

Bradley paused. "I was just making sure your experiences aligned with mine. Why?"

"Your concern about my lateral thinking — was it real, or were you hedging your bets until things were decided with Amato?"

How insightful of you, Bradley thought. He was aware that he was squinting, and he wondered if Anand had seen. "It was real. All part of the mix, Walter."

Anand sighed, his doubts about Bradley and lateral thinking not dispelled. "I will let you know Monday if I am resigning. Let's just leave it at that."

Bradley stared irately. "Judgment, Walter. Show me judgment."

CHAPTER 35

An hour after returning from his fruitless lunch with Anand, Bradley went down the hall to the small meeting room. He made sure that the door was firmly shut then picked an extension on the landline and dialled the number.

When the familiar voice answered, he launched right in. "Peter Bradley. Two things. First, the receptionist Friday night figured out that the girls you sent were escorts. And reported it to the Chair of the firm. I'm in deep shit here."

"That's why I never send girls to businesses. I make an exception for you — now you see how it turns out. Too much risk."

"Do you want to know what the problem was? The problem was that one of the girls said she was from the agency. *From the agency*, for Christ's sake. A lot more discretion, please, especially for what I pay you."

"Just use a hotel, like you usually do, not where you work."

Bradley scowled at the condescending tone. "It's only been a handful of times here. Thanks for the goddamn helpful advice," he said. "Anyway, the second thing. I need a gun. A handgun — for tomorrow or Friday."

There was a pause at the other end of the line. "I didn't hear what you said. There's a bad connection. Let me call you back."

"The Pearson Room."

Moments later, a call came through from a number Bradley didn't recognize. "Be more discreet, ok? What's it for anyway?"

"What difference does it make to you?"

"Don't want to get involved in some problem."

"I'm closing the cottage this weekend. There have been a lot of bear sightings."

A second pause followed. "Call me tomorrow, in the evening, at this number."

"Ok." Bradley quickly wrote down the number. He was about to put the phone down when he heard, "Hey."

"What?"

"This is not for Amy, is it?"

Bradley pressed his lips together in disgust. "No, Dominic. It's for bears," he said and hung up.

Bradley walked over to the closed door of the meeting room. "What the fuck did Amy ever see in him?" he muttered. Then, before pulling on the door handle, he paused and imagined a gun in his possession. A tingle of exhilaration flashed through him, and he whispered under his breath, "I am about to cross the Rubicon."

CHAPTER 36

Not long after, Carolyn Murphy knocked on Bradley's door. "Cancelling drinks this evening?" he asked hopefully as she remained at the threshold of his office.

"Not at all. Robert Platz has been trying to reach you. He also tried Walter, but he's not around, so he tried me. It's about a new deal. I said I would try to track you down."

"Too much going on," Bradley muttered, letting a document he'd been reviewing flip shut as he looked at his laptop screen. "Yeah, there are a few emails from him I haven't opened. Some of those voicemails are probably his, too. I'll call him. Where is Walter, anyway?"

"I don't know. He said he had to step out." Bradley ran a hand across his face then threw his hands in the air, palms open, evidencing surprise. "I know," Murphy added, "the clients pay the bills."

"Exactly."

Murphy became aware that Margaret was crowding in behind her, also looking for Bradley. "I'll wait for your call for drinks. Let me know if I can help," Murphy said and left.

Margaret grabbed her opportunity and stepped farther into Bradley's office. "I just wanted to let you know that I'll be in late tomorrow. There's a cancellation at 8:00 a.m. for an MRI. We're going to take it."

Bradley felt pressed to call Platz, but knew he should give

Margaret a few seconds of his time.

"I'm sorry, Margaret. I meant to ask you earlier how things are going. Come in and have a seat for a second. You got my email from last night?"

"I'm not going to bother you — I've got work to do. Yes, I got the email — thanks. You probably haven't seen my response. Dottie doesn't need to make any inquiries. We're into it with Bob Shapiro, for better or worse."

"So when do you get the details?"

"I don't know. Soon. I won't get a wink of sleep tonight."

"Let me know how it goes," Bradley said, slowly reaching for his landline, signalling he needed to move on.

"I will," Margaret said and left.

Platz wasn't a senior partner at Collins, Shaw for his legal skills. His forte was networking, bringing in deals, and finding other lawyers in the firm who could give the right advice. Because he brought so much revenue to Collins, Shaw, Platz had nearly as much power as Collins, and acted like it. When Bradley finally got hold of him, Platz brusquely told him that it was too hard to track down members of his group. Bradley assured him his team was on the deal and would work the weekend if necessary. After telling Bradley he assumed as much, Platz proceeded to describe the acquisition in exhaustive detail, and followed with an email of background material.

Close to five, Bradley realized how tired he was. The next morning, in all his pride and glory, Tony Amato would assume residence in his new office at Collins, Shaw. Late Thursday afternoon, Bradley would need to muster enough enthusiasm at the "Meet Tony Amato" event to deceive many of the hundred lawyers or so who would drop by for a drink. In the meantime Anand was missing in action with a meltdown, and Bradley had to sound more convincing with Murphy at drinks than he had with Anand. And then there was the client work, where he was falling woefully behind. And Amy. And the Rubicon.

Bradley called Murphy to tell her that he would be by in five minutes. He walked over to the bookcase on the far side of his office and opened one of three small cabinets along the bottom. In it he looked at his accoutrements for celebrating the closing of a deal or winning a tough piece of litigation: a selection of forty-year old malt whiskies and six sparkling glasses on a tray. Bradley chose his favourite bottle and poured a generous portion into one of the glasses. Toasting its salutary qualities, he drank the whiskey in a few affectionate gulps.

Finding Murphy waiting for him in her office, Bradley suggested a favourite Collins, Shaw haunt, the Embassy Pub at Yonge and Wellington. At street level they were enveloped by a summery swan song of bright sun and breezy, humid air. As they walked the half block to the pub, Bradley found Murphy's company oddly comforting. She seemed more elegant than usual in a well-fitting grey pantsuit and heels.

The pub was in a nineteenth century former bank building. They walked up expansive steps, past colonnades either side, and through a glass-doored entrance. At the top was a brightly lit cupola. Bradley scanned the pub for private seating and spied two empty stools at the far end of the bar.

Murphy was unusually bubbly. Her spirit, together with the whiskey, gave Bradley a lift. After each ordering a drink, she said, "Ok, what's the news? Time to spill your guts."

"You seem to be assuming it's good."

"I didn't say that. But it's got to be interesting. This is the first time you've taken me out for drinks. Although I'm a little worried that Walter has gone AWOL. I assume you've talked to him. And I'm a little worried you're firing me."

Bradley laughed and drained half of his Scotch on the rocks.

"No, you're not being fired. Your work is great. Yes, I told Walter at lunch. Complicated person sometimes, don't you find?"

Murphy took a sip of her Chardonnay, watching Bradley closely. He seemed quite distracted to her. "I enjoy working with him as a lawyer. He's very closed in, though — all business. Frankly, I feel I know you better than him — and I really don't know you at all. He didn't like what he heard?"

"There was a lot of other stuff that we had to talk about," Bradley said with a wave.

"Ah, partnership stuff." She caught Bradley off-guard. "He's mentioned it a few times to me, that's all," she added with a shrug.

Bradley had no interest in dwelling further on Anand. "Let me get to the reason for our drinks," he said after a moment. He finished his Scotch, pointed at the empty glass for a second and proceeded to talk about Tony Amato with as much zeal as he could manufacture. Once he was done, seeing the surprise on Murphy's face, Bradley asked, "So what do you think?"

"Honestly?"

"Of course."

"It will be a killer team, no doubt. You number one, Tony number two. From an associate's perspective —"

"Here we go."

"I don't know if it's good or bad for me. And frankly, I understand Walter's reaction — if he didn't like it, I mean."

"Don't worry about Walter. It's good for you. It's more clients, different work. Lots of chances to continue to prove yourself."

A large hand came from nowhere and loudly slapped Bradley's back. "So this is what the anti-trust lawyers do — drink themselves under the table. No wonder they're so hard to reach on the phone." Robert Platz, with Ted Collins and a third lawyer standing behind, came crashing in between Bradley and Murphy.

"Thought you could avoid us by hiding off in the corner here?"

It seemed to Murphy that the triumvirate was a few drinks ahead of Bradley and her — or at least her. For five minutes or so the laughter was loud and the jokes flew, and the four alpha males cavorted like college kids.

"Come on," Collins finally said with a sly smile. "Let's leave Peter and Carolyn alone. They have stuff to talk about. By the way, Peter, really good to see your support."

"Everything's going to work out really well," Bradley said with a large smile, clinking Collins' glass. Bradley's keenness felt fabricated to Murphy.

"What are you talking about?" Platz said loudly. "There's something I don't know about here. Let me in on the secret."

"Does Carolyn know?" Collins asked, looking back and forth between Murphy and Bradley. "Does she, Peter?"

"I think I do," Murphy said, giving a cautious smile then finding refuge in a small sip of her Chardonnay.

"What the hell?" Platz interjected. "I should *not* be out of the loop."

"Big changes coming for the group, right, Peter? Good work. Now, let's kill our competitors out there." Collins began to pull his compatriots away. "Come on, I'll tell you what's going on. Let's go."

The three lawyers walked away, Platz continuing to protest his exclusion from firm confidences.

"Big changes, my ass. He is such a dick."

Murphy turned back to Bradley and was startled. He was slumped over his drink, lost in his world, his face glowering and bitter.

"Who's a dick?" she asked.

"Collins, Amato, they're all dicks," he said.

The pub had filled completely and the noise was engulfing.

Murphy was not sure she had heard correctly. "Pardon me?" she said.

Bradley turned to look at her, seeming to take a second to register her presence. "Platz is a dick. He expects us to work this weekend for his deal. That guy noses into everything."

Murphy paused, sorting out Bradley's words. "The client pays —" she finally ventured.

"I know, Carolyn. Blah, blah, blah. Do you want another drink? I'm going to have one."

"No, I'm still working on this one." An awkward silence fell between them until the bartender brought Bradley his third Scotch. "Anyway, I'm sure things will work out very well with Tony."

"You know what, I'm a little tired of talking about Tony. That's all that's been on my mind for the last few days. Let's talk about you. What's going on in your life? Are you happy with us at Collins, Shaw?"

Murphy was taken aback. Other than for performance re-views, it was the first time she could remember Bradley taking an interest in her. "I am. A lot of work, of course. A lot of *weekend* work," she said, giving Bradley a fake jab to the arm.

"It's Platz's fault, not mine," he said, dropping a bit of his sullenness.

"But I like it. I learn a ton from you and Walter — especially you."

"You seem to watch what I do carefully. That's my impression anyway."

Murphy decided to be bold. "I do. You know why?"

"Because you're ambitious as hell?"

"Exactly. Maybe more than you," she added with a forced laugh.

"I doubt that."

"May I ask you a question?"

"Let me ask you another first. How are things with your boy-friend?"

Murphy felt a bit uncomfortable. "I'm dumping him tomor-row evening, if you really want to know."

Bradley looked up with surprise, even an element of sympa-thy, Murphy thought. "Really? I'm sorry to hear that. I'm not hitting on you, by the way — just to be very clear. None of that stuff in the firm — ever."

"Well, with the world's most beautiful wife."

"The world's most difficult too," Bradley said acidly. "Jeez, she's out of control sometimes."

"I don't know her well."

"She's very willful, let's just say that."

"I did talk to her a lot at your cottage last year. I thought she was incredibly funny, actually."

Bradley stumbled over Murphy's comment. He couldn't re-member Amy and Murphy hitting it off at the group getaway the previous year. His only memory was Murphy keeping to herself, a spectator more than a participant.

Watching Bradley lightly sway on his barstool, beginning to slur, Murphy felt a desire to provoke. "You probably don't re-member. You were talking quite a bit to Walter and Anita. I think you were trying to get Walter to relax. He was so nervous about last year's partnership decision."

"Don't remind me."

"So Amy and I snuck off into the kitchen. We pretty much finished off a bottle of wine together. She told me some *really* interesting stuff."

Bradley shifted uneasily on the barstool. "Such as?"

"Girl stuff mostly. Never to be repeated."

"No, seriously," Bradley said, a bit aggressively.

"She talked about how hard you work. About your house — which you say you bought for her."

"I did. Cost me a fortune."

"How you met."

"She talked about *that?*"

Murphy had Bradley's full attention. "A bit, yes. She was working at the gift shop in the art gallery, something like that. You basically picked her up on a Saturday afternoon when you were being cultural."

Bradley looked a little relieved. "I've been a member of the Art Gallery of Ontario for years. Amy did a Master in Fine Arts — that's her world. I hardly get to the gallery."

"She talked a bit about her brother, too, and his problems. I mean, I don't know if they are problems —"

"They are *big* problems. I think he's bipolar but no one does anything about it. I get nervous around him, actually. Very unpredictable guy. And a money sucker."

"Well, she talked about her parents dying in that horrific car crash, and how she basically had to raise her brother. And she mentioned that you were married once before. That's it, Peter. My lips are sealed. Not a word has gone to anyone — except back to you this evening."

"That's far too much information," Bradley said with a snort, finishing off his third Scotch. "Are you sure you don't want another glass of wine?"

"I'm fine."

"So what's the story with your boyfriend — your ex-boyfriend?"

Murphy looked down at her glass of wine. "I'm not sure I'm comfortable talking about that."

"Come on, come on. You know my life history. Something has to come back this way. It's only fair."

"I mean, *he* doesn't even know yet."

"Ok, whatever," Bradley said with a shrug.

"You already know that I'm very ambitious. There is a lot I want to achieve. Kyle — Kyle is more of a *drag* than a help, if you know what I mean. I'd rather be single than have someone holding me back. But I'll be much more diplomatic than that with him."

"How about 'it's me, not you'?"

Murphy laughed. "Has that ever worked for you?"

"I was single for years. Worked out fine."

"That was what I was going to ask you, by the way."

"Why I was single?"

"No, no — why are *you* so ambitious?"

A crooked smile landed on Bradley's face and he circled the rim of the empty glass in front of him with a finger. "I needed to prove something, I guess."

"But what? That you're smart as hell?"

Round and round Bradley's finger went. "I needed to prove to my father that I was ok. He made it his mission in life to prove to me I wasn't, so I made it mine to prove I was. Probably hard to understand, right? I have this concept in my head that you grew up in a *Leave It to Beaver* home. Am I right?"

"A leave it to what?"

"Before your time — don't worry about it. An idyllic home is what I mean."

"Hardly," Murphy said with a splutter. "My parents have been wonderful to me, but honestly, I never really felt part of their lives. For one, they're older than most of my friends' parents."

"Brothers or sisters?"

"None."

"Oh jeez, an only child. If I'd known that, I wouldn't have hired you."

Murphy laughed. "You — oh, you have a sister, don't you?"

"I'm beginning to wonder what you don't know about me."

"As a matter of fact —"

"Yes, Dottie. The sister who can do no wrong. In my father's world, anything short of being a doctor was a failure. Dottie escaped his wrath by becoming a highly respected emergency care doctor. Anyway, ancient history. My gut tells me your parents are proud of you."

"Mostly they remember the tuition fees. Joking aside, they are, actually."

Bradley looked at his watch and stumbled off his stool. "Time to go. Must prepare for the great Tony Amato."

"Are you ok to drive?"

"Oh, sure."

"No, seriously, Peter. Take a cab. I mean, I'm not your mother or wife, but we've had quite a few drinks."

"*I've* had quite a few. You haven't. Amy wouldn't care — but maybe you're right."

"She would care, I think. You don't want to hurt anyone."

When he got up from his bar stool, Bradley found his legs unsteady. "Ok, ok. I'll take a cab." He patted the front of his jacket, checking for his wallet. Then he raised the forefinger of his right hand in the air as if he had just remembered something. "You know what I recently thought about? Say I did drive now, and say, also, something awful happened — I don't know, something very bad. I know, I hit another car head-on and kill a person. And then society would punish me — justifiably. The question is, would it be better for me to die at the accident scene or to go to jail for a long time? For me personally, I mean, not for society."

Murphy snapped back on her bar stool. "Peter, what a terrible thought. Why would you ever ask this?"

"No, listen, I'm serious. As I said, this recently crossed my mind. It's come back to me because you're so worried about me driving. Don't you think that at some point it's a worse fate to be incarcerated for a long time than to die? I don't know what period of time in jail I'm talking about — I'm sure it would be different for everyone. What would it be for you?"

"I've — I've never thought about it. Peter, you should get home."

"I think for me, it's about twenty years. But maybe it's different when you're really faced with the situation. I don't know. Either way, it's total shit."

"Do you want me to help you find a cab?"

"Ok, well, I can see you're no fun at all. No, no, I'm totally fine. I'll see you tomorrow." Bewildered, Murphy watched Bradley sidestep his way out the pub. She realized that he had left her with the bill.

A few minutes later, she was back at the office. She wrote a note to herself to charge the bar expense to the firm, then put sunglasses she'd left in her office into her purse. After making sure she hadn't forgotten anything else, she stepped out of her office, closing the door behind her. She looked down the long hall toward reception, and then in the opposite direction toward Bradley's office. When she didn't see anyone, she scurried to Bradley's office, opened the door and quickly shut it behind her.

His laptop sat to one side of his desk. She powered it up and let the operating system load. When it asked for a password, she typed in "072060PB124". To her alarm, an error message was returned. Then she remembered that the next monthly password reset was Monday and guessed that Bradley had already reset his. She typed in "072060PB125" and in seconds the desktop appeared. For the next ten minutes, with great interest, Murphy read each of Bradley's opened emails about Tony Amato.

CHAPTER 37

Early every morning Sunil Anand drew up a makeshift schedule of appointments and tasks for the day. He tackled them diligently because, with sleight of hand, he convinced himself that they were important. Like other recent days, however, Wednesday's schedule had dwindled to nothing by midafternoon and he warily foresaw another evening of circular rumination and despondency. He was heartened then when his wife told him their eldest son was visiting late afternoon, though both puzzled why he was coming alone and not staying for dinner.

Anand was smothered by his mother when he walked through the front door.

"How is Daddy?" he asked.

"Impossible, just impossible," she said, vigorously shaking her head. "He mopes around all day and gets in my way all the time. This can't go on much longer."

Anand heard his father's footsteps coming from his upstairs bedroom.

"No luck with a job?" Anand asked quickly.

"He had an interview yesterday but he said it didn't go well. Shhh, I can hear him coming." Anand's mother stepped back and called upstairs. "Sunil, Walter is here."

Distantly, Anand's father said, "Yes, I know, I'm on my way."

"It's a good thing you're here," Anand's mother said, patting her son lightly on the chest. "Shall I make dinner? And how is my grandchild?"

Anand's father emerged at the top of the stairs of their sub-urban home and walked stiffly down the stairs. His hair seemed greyer and the bags under his eyes heavier since the last time Anand had visited.

"The baby is growing a lot," Anand said, keeping his eyes on his father. "We'll come by in the next few weeks. Or maybe Sat-urday — except I probably have to work. No dinner, I just want to talk to Daddy about something."

His mother gave him a slightly worried glance. "Is everything ok?"

"Yes, everything is fine. Hi, Daddy, how are you?" Anand said.

"Drop Anita and the child off here Saturday," Anand's mother said. "They can stay the night." She saw her son's attention had passed to his father. "Well, let me know," she added and disap-peared into the kitchen.

"I'm fine, Walter." Anand's father smiled broadly and reached a welcoming hand to his son's shoulder. "Are you joining me for my afternoon walk?"

Anand glanced at his watch. "It's 5:15, Daddy," he said with a chuckle. "Isn't it a bit late?"

Anand's father leaned toward his son and whispered, "I have no choice, really. Your mother will shoot me if I'm in the house while she prepares dinner. Come on, let's go."

Anand followed his father into his parents' neighbourhood. It was like every other box-house subdivision in Brampton, north-west of Toronto. As meaningless talk flowed, Anand observed his father turning street corners and negotiating intersections with-out any thought, each step memorized from repetition.

At some length, Anand's father said, "You are not here to lis-ten to me jabber. What is on your mind, Walter?"

He heard his son take a deep breath and caught an involuntary tremor in his voice. He listened closely as, quietly and carefully, his son spoke of his chances for partnership and the arrival of a new partner. Then he thought for a few moments.

"That Peter Bradley is not to be trusted."

"No, I know. I'm sorry. You told me that last year, and I didn't listen."

"Six months ago, Walter, I would have told you to leave — but I see things a little differently now."

"What do you mean?"

"What is that saying? 'Keep your friends close but your —'"

"Enemies closer."

Nodding, Anand's father said, "Exactly."

"I don't follow," Anand said patiently, long familiar with his father's tendency to make a point indirectly and laboriously.

"I haven't spoken to anyone about this, but for you, now, it seems relevant. In March, when Tyrell Industries invited me to pursue my career elsewhere, there were four of us in the accounting group. I was by far the most senior person. Imagine, more than thirty years in the company, England and here. When they downsized, it never occurred to me that I might be on the list. In fact, I assumed that as the senior accountant I would *see* the list. But I was wrong, and why? Well, I don't know on what basis, but the CFO came to have mixed views of me. And while I'm not a hundred per cent certain, the only thing that makes sense is that, when the CEO asked whom to let go, the CFO gave my name for the accounting group. My point, Walter, is that I knew the CFO didn't care for me much, but in my typical way I occasionally tried to ingratiate myself toward him and otherwise kept my distance. In a sense he was my enemy. I should have stayed closer to him, as they say, to make myself indispensable, to show him why he was wrong about me, to *control* him as best I could. I know I could have done it. But I just laid low."

"I've never thought of Peter Bradley as my enemy," Anand said in a confused tone. "I've had many appalling thoughts about him — that he's not a man of his word, that he's only motivated by self-interest — but not that he's my enemy."

"Given his slippery ways, I think he is. And make no mistake, Walter, if you resign, he certainly will be your enemy. And the new fellow as well, perhaps. Wherever you go, he will disparage you, perhaps subtly, but enough for people to draw the wrong conclusion."

"Then Anita and I and the baby will go to England. I'm sure a law firm there will take me."

"And start all over again? And leave your family behind?" Anand looked to the sidewalk. "Walter, you're almost damned if you stay and damned if you go. He has promised you that you will make partner next year. If you can't trust him, why not get that in writing, as you lawyers say, and stay? And once you are partner, you can build up your own clients."

"Daddy, how can I work with this man? It's almost humiliating. And I've never heard of a management committee putting a promise of partnership in *writing*. That will look poorly on me."

"You make your own judgment on how to do it. What I am suggesting is that you work with him by acknowledging within yourself that he is your adversary. Stay close to him, pick up his crumbs and make him feel comfortable with you. People like him fall one day — that's a belief I still hang on to — and then you'll be there to take over. Sooner than you might imagine."

"Well, the new fellow and me."

"That might be better! Not everyone is a Peter Bradley, thank goodness." Anand's father slowed his pace. "Walter, let me ask you this. Do you somehow need my approval for your way forward?"

"No," Anand said then paused. "Well, in a way, if I'm honest

— yes."

"You don't," Anand's father said, coming to a full stop. "It's your life. Take my guidance, then leave me out of it."

"But when Peter Bradley pretends my work is his, when he plays me by saying I don't think out-of-the-box, my honour, our family's honour is being disregarded. You wouldn't tolerate that. Would you?" Anand observed his father remaining quiet and continued. "Isn't that why you had us leave England, because someone said you were lying, and you wouldn't tolerate that?"

"That's why we left England — yes." They started to walk again, near the end of their loop. "But I'll tell you, Walter, it wasn't a direct accusation that I lied, it was an implication. And while we've had a good life here — I would never have imagined a house like this and all three of my sons with good opportunities — I wonder now if I made the right decision."

"You're feeling beaten down because you lost your job. You'll get another one, Daddy."

"Maybe I will. No, more because I might have been too prideful. That's a flaw I have. We all do. Things might have been even better if we'd stayed in England. But I'll never know."

Anand saw his mother standing impatiently in the doorway of their house. "Imagine," he said, "both of us looking for work at the same time."

"Oh my, just don't tell your mother."

Anand stopped on the sidewalk in front of his parents' house and his father did the same. "Everything seems out of order and control; *nothing* has worked out as it should. Poor Anita — I'm worrying her sick. I keep asking myself, what's going to happen, what should I do? All these ideas — crazy ideas — are going through my head. Do you understand what I'm saying?"

"Of course I do. I've thought of everything, and at my darkest moments, the very worst. But you can't control everything, Walter. Stay with the simple things. Besides, you have to be careful about bad karma. I don't want you to be reincarnated as a toad or some such beast."

Anand and his father shared a laugh. "You don't really believe in that, do you?" Anand asked.

His father smiled. "Maybe a bit more than you think. Say a prayer at our little temple on the way to the kitchen."

As Anand and his father walked up the black asphalt driveway to the front door of the house, Anand's mother blurted, "Where have you been? Hm?" She started back into the house but stopped in her tracks and turned to face them again. "If you think things can keep going on like this, they can't, you know. They can't," she said and left for the kitchen.

CHAPTER 38

It's been a treacherous day. I can't get a hold of myself.

Three parts of me are at war, and together they're exhausting the whole of me.

There is one part that wants so badly to exact revenge and set my life straight. It's not a rational or practical part — it's all emotional. It doesn't talk to me, it runs movies in my head, creating a fantasy world of variations on a theme, namely PB's tormented death at my hands. One day, the movie has me shooting a gun. Another day, there's a knife I use for surgical cuts. And yet another day, I have a thin nylon rope with which I strangle him. It motivates me, this part, but it also wants to control me — and that is dangerous.

This gets me to the second part: the fear. Really, there are two forms of it.

The first is basic: that I make a mistake. I don't execute properly and end up destroying my own life. If that happens, it will be because the first part of me that wants revenge has won. The fear is fighting my vengeance, usually through my dream world. Like last night. I've tied PB up, he's suffered his agonies, he's gone — and some stranger walks in, and I'm caught. Doesn't really matter who catches me, the point is, I've been snared because emotion has taken over, and I haven't planned right. And if that happens, I know this: the first part of me will vanish; the movies will stop running in my head, taking with them whatever strength they give me; and the whole thing will seem like an utterly horrible mistake.

What gnaws at me more, though, is the fear of what this act will make me. I know I keep talking about this, but in all truth, what does it make me just to think about this, or plan it? What am I? An animal without any sense of right or wrong? An extremely ill person? A candidate for some kind of eternal punishment? Am I just different?

But though he may have no sense why, he's harmed me, there's no denying that. And he keeps harming me, and no one will protect me unless I do. In the end, this is what I keep coming back to, and what I think life sometimes calls us to do.

At least there's the third part of me. Convinced, cold-hearted and calculating. I wish it were all of me; everything would be easier. It's the part that says hire a contract killer and let him do all the work. The part that realizes that, in taking things into my own hands, I'll make the mistakes of an amateur. That's how I'll really get in trouble. I can't underestimate how persistent the police will be. I have to bury the connection and motive.

Forget about Plans A to D. Forget about inflicting pain myself. I've done my homework. My meeting is set up. Shortly, I'll meet this person, and he can take over. What do I really care about how the act will be done or who does it? A contract killing will be just as sweet. A contract killing that looks like an accident. That will be the safest. The point is that he will be dead and will have suffered the ultimate consequence for his actions. That's enough for me.

CHAPTER 39

On Thursday morning Amy finally worked up the courage. She had spent long hours Tuesday and Wednesday nervously walking around her husband's study, often stopping and rapidly shifting weight from one foot to the other, wondering if she was doing the right thing. She was tired of her indecision. And she was tired of her brother's repeated calls, reminding her, each time more shrilly, that he needed five thousand dollars.

Sitting down in the voluminous leather chair behind Bradley's study desk, Amy wiped her clammy hands on her jeans and moved the chair close to the desk. She powered up the old desktop computer and uneasily watched it grind to life. When the ancient operating system finally appeared and requested a password, Amy held her breath and with the beautifully manicured long forefinger of her right hand carefully pecked "072060". A wave of relief rolled through her body when the computer flipped through several screens before landing on the desktop.

She pulled a piece of paper out of one of her jeans pockets. On it she had written the URL of Bradley's bank site and his bank card number, which she had secured from his wallet after he came home from dinner with his sister Tuesday night. She opened the browser, typed in the URL and waited for connection. Eventually, the page requesting a bank card number and password to enter accounts emerged. Bradley had saved the bank card number. Amy pecked again, this time "072060PB". A few moments later, when her husband's accounts appeared, she felt a second surge of relief.

Much as with school exams, she became calm and focused. There were more accounts than she'd anticipated, but true to the complaints of Bradley's financial adviser, two of them dominated. One was a chequing account with over a hundred thousand dollars and the second was a savings account with nearly one and a quarter million.

Amy opened the chequing account and looked at the activity in July, August and September to date. She gasped at the size of the direct deposits from Collins, Shaw. In the middle of each month were equally startling payments for mortgages on the house and the cottage as well as disbursements for hydro, water and gas. Credit card payments came out toward the end of each month, the same time as the automatic transfers of her monthly allowance into a joint account. There also were fairly regular large cash withdrawals. For a moment she speculated what they might be for, but without a quick answer, she didn't dwell on it.

Amy closed the chequing account and opened the savings account. The activity was dead simple: in the entire three months, other than interest, there had only been one transaction, a transfer in from the chequing account.

Amy considered her idea, and it seemed to work. Her husband rarely checked his accounts, but if he did she was sure he would gloss over payments to the joint account if they matched mortgage payments for the house and cottage. She made a quick calculation: it would take only seven months for her to have a hundred thousand, with five thousand for Reggie.

She curled a strand of her long hair around a finger then took a deep breath and completed two transfers to the joint account. She smiled at the irony of her husband's paternalism backfiring on him, insisting as he had on a joint account for her monthly allowance. When that was done, she ran to the master bedroom where her laptop was and transferred the money from the joint account to a personal account. She felt equal doses of exhilaration and fear. *What's done is done*, she told herself. Then she returned to the study and looked at the new entries in Bradley's chequing account. Satisfied that they melted into the morass of other entries, she shut down the computer.

An hour later, Amy had gotten a five-thousand-dollar money order for Reggie and called him with her success. She told him to hurry over and get it. What she really wanted to do was spend the afternoon shopping for a new pair of shoes.

CHAPTER 40

Two weeks earlier, for four days straight, Reggie had exempt-ed himself from life. The entire time he ignored visits, calls and texts. Each day, as morning lightness filtered into the condo, he hung old sheets across windows to regain darkness and retreat-ed to the sofa bed, covering himself with stale blankets. Around 9:00 p.m., he emerged for some food then spent the night play-ing online games and watching illegally downloaded movies and TV shows.

His mood had finally been dislocated by an episode of a re-ality TV program, *Perpetual Crime*. It depicted the operation in the 1990s of a South Boston crime organization with a penchant for selling crack. Most of the excerpt seemed mundane to Reg-gie, covering ground he'd already seen three or four times, in one form or another, during his four-day funk. What grabbed Reg-gie's attention, however, was a series of brief interviews with a gang member who'd been responsible for "strategically minimiz-ing the competition".

He could have been talking about energy drink companies or hockey teams, but without saying it he was discussing kill-ings. The gang member's unaffected distance from the personal consequences of his work fascinated Reggie; he replayed the in-terviews five or six times. The face on the screen was darkened and the voice altered, but well-dressed and articulate, the gang member exuded a confident calm. In fact, he seemed proud.

Like an unruly vine, the interviews had taken seed in Reggie's mind, growing into a scheme to Q-and-A and write about a professional assassin. The project, he was sure, would grab attention and put him on the road to independence from the man who'd stolen his sister from him. Eventually, he'd summoned the will to ask Dominic for coffee.

Now, as he stood in line at his bank waiting to cash his sister's money order, he felt creeping excitement at the thought of his self-redeeming project coming to realization. Since Tuesday he'd been prepared with a list of questions, a cheap recording device and full battery power in his laptop. Waiting for Amy to get the money to him had been almost unbearable, at one point shaking him with doubt that his project would ever see the light of day. The work at Faster Delivery had been a surprising relief, helping him stay away from useless rumination; he even happily worked an extra shift to have Thursday afternoon off. But this close to the cash the doubt was dissolving, and the next step was to hear from Dominic.

When Reggie presented the money order for cash, the teller, a young Asian woman, looked at him skeptically. He was reasonably certain he looked presentable. The swelling around his eye was gone and the colouring below it mostly washed away. He'd even shaved and properly combed his stringy hair. In a rush of words, he told her he had two accounts at the branch. Without explanation, she locked up the cash till and excused herself for more than a minute. His heart began to bulge into his throat. But when she returned, she coolly explained that she'd needed to check if they had enough cash on hand. A half hour later, after the teller put her hands on most of the hundred dollar bills in the branch, Reggie walked out with the biggest wad of cash he'd ever had in his pocket.

Dominic called him around noon. He sounded groggy and Reggie presumed his day was just starting. Dominic's first question was whether Reggie had the money. Then he asked him where he lived and said he would pick him up in front of his building around one thirty. "When it's done, I'll drop you off downtown somewhere," Dominic added and hung up.

The half hour that Reggie had to wait crawled along. Irresistibly, his mind went to imagining how events would unfold. He saw Dominic pulling up in front of his condo in a Benz sports coupe with twenty-thousand-dollar rims and a pounding bass rattling nearby windows. He guessed they would end up on a patio in Little Italy, sequestered at a reserved corner table. Dominic's connection would be swarthy and stocky, wearing a suit from Milan and five-hundred-dollar sunglasses. Over several premium beers, a bond of trust would cautiously develop. Eventually, the connection would talk, hypothetically, about the ways and customs of the underworld, about the jobs somebody had to do for order to be maintained, about his reconciliation with his sordid past.

At one thirty, Dominic drove into the semi-circle driveway of Reggie's condo in a dark blue Civic. The passenger side had a long scrape from a recent sideswipe, and Reggie, carrying a knapsack with his laptop, struggled to open and close the door. The local AM traffic and weather station squawked through the factory stereo system. After giving Reggie half a glance, Dominic lowered the volume. He slumped back into his seat, leaving the palm of one hand on the top of the steering wheel, and drove a short distance along the driveway before stopping again. Reaching for a plastic shopping bag in the back of the car, he pulled out a baseball cap and dark goggles and put them on his lap. "What's in the knapsack?" he asked.

"My stuff for the interview. Speech recorder. Laptop."

"Are you serious?"

"Yes," Reggie said with a shrug. "What's that for?" he asked, pointing at the baseball cap and goggles.

"You got the money?"

"I told you I do."

"So let's have it."

"What, now?"

"We're not going anywhere if I don't have the money."

Reggie reached inside his jeans pocket, pulled out the wad of cash and hesitantly handed it over to Dominic. After counting the money, Dominic put the cash in his jacket pocket. Then he handed the cap and goggles to Reggie. "Ok, put this shit on."

"What for?"

"The goggles are so you don't know where we're going. The baseball cap is so you don't look like a complete idiot, little brother."

"I told you I'm not —"

"Yeah, yeah, I know. Just put that stuff on."

Reggie did as instructed. The goggles wrapped completely around his eyes, enveloping him in darkness. He put on the baseball cap, not knowing if it sat properly. Dominic pounded the gas pedal, snapping Reggie's head back, and noodled the car onto Spadina. Reggie was sure he looked like a fool.

Quickly they were on a highway; Reggie presumed it was the Gardiner Expressway. He guessed that they were heading east but in the darkness it was hard to be sure. After a while they took an exit ramp and re-engaged with city traffic. Nothing was said for the entire time. After what Reggie estimated was forty-five minutes, the car veered right, crossing heavily over a sidewalk ramp and came to a lurching stop.

"Stay here. Don't touch the goggles," Dominic said. Reggie did not have the courage to sneak a peek as he waited for Dominic to return. Several minutes later the passenger-side door opened without warning and Dominic grabbed Reggie's right arm. "Ok, let's go. And leave the knapsack. Don't worry, it'll be safe."

The blindness and lengthy car ride had made Reggie increasingly anxious. As Dominic led him to an unknown destination, Reggie's stomach started cramping and an urge to take flight became overwhelming. He had little trust in Dominic, but had it been anyone else, Reggie would have torn off the goggles and run like hell. He held it together with the thought that, for Amy's sake, Dominic would ensure his safety.

Dominic brusquely brought Reggie to a stop. A door opened and Reggie felt one of Dominic's hands on his back, pushing him through. The door closed behind him and the chain lock was inserted. A smell of cheap air freshener and underlying dankness rose to Reggie's nose, and an HVAC rattled loudly in the background.

"You're going to sit here," Dominic said. He turned Reggie a hundred and eighty degrees then pushed him back a few steps until an edge caught the back of Reggie's knees. Unceremoniously, Dominic shoved one more time and Reggie plopped into an uncomfortable chair. "Ok, ask away."

Reggie sat bewildered, trying to process the situation he'd gotten himself into. Finally, he said, "Dude, you can't be serious. I need to see. I need to record the conversation. I need my laptop for my questions."

"No, *you* can't be serious," Dominic replied forcefully. "This is not Larry King or Piers Morgan. Why would you even expect to be able to see? All you need to do is hear."

"Dominic, please, for five thousand bucks, I thought I'd have three interviews, face-to-face, you know what I mean?"

Dominic laughed. There was another voice, thick with a Russian accent.

"What he say?"

Dominic repeated Reggie's protestation, and the Russian

joined in with a slow, sniggering laugh.

"You're a fucking idiot, you know that? I don't get how a woman as smart as Amy could have such a dipshit brother. Really."

Reggie's mouth had gone dry. He gambled. "Amy wouldn't think this is worth five thousand dollars either." He imagined he could feel the heat of Dominic's anger and braced himself for a shot to the mouth.

"You little dick," Dominic said. The Russian interrupted, and there was an exchange of whispers. Eventually, Reggie caught Dominic saying, "You sure?"

"Sure, ya, it's ok."

Reggie sensed Dominic come closer. "Here's what we're going to do, little brother. I'm going to get your laptop. You can read your questions and type in answers — no recording device. Needless to say, my friend does not want his voice taped. Then I'm going to take you into the washroom and you can ask your questions from there."

"And where is your friend gonna be?"

There was a brief intake of breath. "In the bathtub," Dominic answered mockingly. "In here, of course, you dumb fuck. Seriously, Reggie, are you actually related to Amy? Or did you come from an orphanage for idiots? Oh, and by the way, this is the interview. No more after this."

Reggie's anger rose against the tirade of insults, but he understood his vulnerability. "Ok," he said tersely.

"Don't move."

Dominic left the room and returned seconds later. Grabbing Reggie's arm again, he pulled Reggie out of the chair and led him across the room. Then Dominic pushed a shoulder against the washroom door until it groaned open.

Pulled into the small room, Reggie was jammed between

Dominic and a bathtub with a plastic shower curtain. The toilet seat dropped and he was whirled around then shoved onto the seat. A second later Dominic rammed the laptop into his hands.

"I'm going to leave now," Dominic said, "and I'm going to close this door behind me. I'll tell you from the other side when you can take that stuff off your head. Whatever you do, little brother, don't open this door. Just ask your questions, tell us when you're done, and I'll come and get you when it works for my friend and me. Got it?"

"Yes."

"And don't ask too many questions. Seriously, we don't have all day."

The door ground shut and a few moments later chairs in the main room were drawn up to the washroom. "Ok, one more time, ask away," Dominic finally said.

Reggie removed the baseball cap and goggles. The only light in the washroom was from a glazed window high above the toilet, but it still hurt his eyes and made him blink.

After allowing his eyes to adjust, Reggie announced, "I'm starting up my laptop." As he located his file with questions, Dominic and the Russian talked and occasionally chuckled. "Ok, here we go," Reggie squeaked, trying to get their attention. "First question. How old were you when you first killed a man?"

There was a brief, stony silence, then loud, mocking laughter. Reggie didn't understand the response. "I said, how old were you when you first killed a man?"

"Nineteen." Reggie typed in the answer as best as he could, awkwardly perched on the toilet seat.

"And where was this?"

"Chechnya. You know Chechnya?"

Reggie had only the vaguest idea. "A little. And what were you doing there?"

"Russian army. Second Chechen war."

"Oh, so that wasn't a hit?"

"A what?"

"A contract killing."

Reggie thought he heard Dominic explain.

"No, it was army. War."

"And what year was this?"

"Ninety-nine, I think — yes."

"And did you like it?"

"*Like* it? What kind question is that? No, of course not. But we had orders — kill Chechen rebels. So I did. Otherwise, army kill me, you understand?"

"Yes, I guess I do. And it was one man?"

"First time?"

"Yes."

"And a woman."

"A woman? His wife?"

"How do I know? She was there. I had no choice."

"How did you feel — I mean after you shot them?"

"What you mean, how do I *feel*? Awful, ok, awful. But it's war. Awful shit happen every day."

"And in the army, how many others did you kill?"

"Well, you never know, right? You just shoot half the time."

"But others died?"

"From me, you mean?"

"Yes."

"Sure."

"And did it become easier for you over time?"

"Look, never easy. It's war, though. Understand? Maybe you don't. You been in war?"

"No."

"Well, whole thing sucks. Every day, every hour, every minute, sucks. Of course, you much rather be at beach, or drinking, or with girls, but you got no choice. Nothing easy."

"Ok, let's move past the army thing," Dominic interrupted. "You got enough there."

"And you emigrated after that?"

"Four or five years later."

"Can I ask why?"

"Hated army. Had family. Needed job. So much corruption in Russia. I thought better opportunity here."

"And what do you do here? Your regular job, I mean."

"Construction."

For the first time, Reggie noticed that Dominic had not fully shut the washroom door. It was dirty white, with scuffmarks along the bottom, and from the widening gap between the door and the hinge-side frame, it was clear the door was off-kilter. It was jammed on the other side, near the top of the frame.

"When did you start doing contract killings?"

"Can't answer that question."

"Why not?"

"Because, dumb fuck, he doesn't want you to know which ones they were, obviously," Dominic said loudly. "Move on, Reggie."

Reggie shook his head in frustration. The answers he was getting were so cursory that they were next to useless. And he couldn't see the Russian. He realized how much he'd counted on physical appearance and movements to inform the interview. He wondered if he could reach the bottom of the door with a foot from his perch on the toilet. With a gradual stretch of his left leg, he found he could.

"You there?" Dominic asked.

Quickly withdrawing his foot, Reggie said, "Yes, just finding another question. So how many killings have you done?"

"You mean, like contract?"

"Yes."

"Five."

"Can I ask you about the first one?"

"Sure."

"How did you get the idea?"

"Not my idea. Guy I worked for, we drank lots of vodka one night, and he said he owed guy lots of money, and he asked, like, how much to take care of this guy."

"And you killed him?"

"That's why we're here, right?"

"How?"

"Well, can't tell you details, but I shot him."

Again, no details, Reggie thought indignantly. On the other side of the sink next to the toilet, a shaving mirror on an expandable metal arm hung from the wall. Angled correctly and with the door slightly ajar, Reggie realized he could probably see a bit of the Russian in the mirror.

"And how did you feel after you'd done it?"

"Well, terrible. Really shook me up."

"Then why did you do it?"

"What do you mean, why did I do it? For money, of course. Got young family, hard to get job sometimes, hard to pay bills."

"Does your wife know you do this?"

"Like, what kind questions are these? Of course not."

"What would she think of you, if she did know?"

"Hate me, I'm sure."

"All this feeling stuff drives me crazy," Dominic pronounced. "I'm going to have a coffee. I'll be back in half an hour and we're done, ok? Lock the door behind me, Vlad."

Reggie waited for the Russian to rebuke Dominic for using his name, but nothing was said. As he heard them stand, it seemed to Reggie that Dominic and his friend weren't professional at all. From under the washroom door he could see lights on in the main room. With the washroom unlit, Reggie judged the Russian wouldn't notice a new crack in the door. Here was his chance, he thought breathlessly.

As quickly as possible, Reggie put the laptop on the ground and angled the shaving mirror so he could see the left side of the door. Then he tugged at the door; with a soft groan, it gave way. Leaving it open a crack, Reggie sat down again and grabbed his laptop. His heart pounded, wondering if Dominic or the Russian had heard anything above the rattling of the HVAC. Instead the chain lock of the front door was re-inserted, and the Russian threw himself into his seat.

"Ok, let's go," he said.

"So how much were you paid for your first killing?"

"Twenty thousand. Bargain."

"Did you think about it a lot afterwards?"

"I tried not to."

"Did you feel guilt?"

"Sure, a little. But, you know, somebody was going to do it."

Reggie shifted slightly on the toilet seat and shot a glance at the shaving mirror. He could see the lower half of the Russian's legs, crossed with the top foot kicking nervously. The track shoes he wore were soiled and ragged.

"What about the other killings? How did you get that work?"

"This guy, you know, he was in construction, too. Lots of crap there, lots of bullshit goes on. He had friend who needed help, and now a few people know about me. So, that's how it goes."

"Aren't you afraid of getting caught?"

Swallowing hard, Reggie shifted enough on the seat so that, momentarily, he could see all of the Russian in the shaving mirror. He was bulky, squeezed into an orange lounge chair. He had uncrossed his legs and bounced them as he nervously looked around his room, scratching an arm. Short, oily, unkempt hair gave way to a puffy, acne-scarred face. Reggie pulled back.

"I make sure I know enough about who pays me that they will stay quiet. And I do good job."

"When you kill someone, do they have fear in their eyes? Do they plead for mercy?"

"Sometimes."

"And do you feel shaken up afterwards? Are you upset? Trembling?" Reggie wanted to see the Russian's expression as he answered that question. He shifted and looked in the mirror as the Russian raised his head from watching his thumbs twirl in his lap.

"You keep asking that —"

Their eyes met in mutual disbelief. For a large man, the Russian moved adeptly. He kicked open the washroom door, breaking it off the bottom hinge and nearly hitting Reggie. He stood threateningly in front of Reggie, centred by the door frame.

"You fucking around with me, huh?" he barked.

"No, no," Reggie squealed. "The door just opened by itself — I didn't know."

The Russian used a thick hand to swat the laptop off Reggie's lap onto the ground. Moments later, Reggie's wiry frame was a foot in the air, the Russian's dull brown eyes and foul breath filling Reggie's face.

"You pick wrong guy. You really stupid fuck, you know. I think I kill you."

"Oh, god no, please. I'm sorry — I really am. Please let me go. I won't say anything to anyone."

"You better not say anything to anyone — unless you want to die. What money you got?"

"I don't have anything. But take the laptop. It's new, it's good.

Just take it."

The Russian glanced at the laptop, as if seeing whether it was in one piece. Then he slammed Reggie to the ground, maintaining a grip on Reggie's arms that cut off the blood to his hands. "Don't need fucking laptop — already got three. Dominic tell me where you live. See, that's how I protect myself. If I see your face again, I kill you, and maybe everyone in family too. Understand? In fact, maybe I just come and do it anyway."

"I won't bother you again. I fucking promise."

"How I know that? Maybe you talk to police?"

"No, no, I promise. Please, leave everyone alone."

"I got friends, you know. They help me take care of your family if I'm not around. Got it?"

"Oh, jeez, yes."

"Get in bathtub. Get on hands and knees."

Reggie did as he was told, whimpering. The Russian tore the cheap plastic shower curtain from its rings, ripped it in half, and made two long rolls. Pushing Reggie's face down to the tub surface, he roughly pulled each of Reggie's hands behind his back and tied them together with one roll. Then he knotted the other roll around Reggie's ankles, so tightly his feet began to swell.

"Open your mouth," the Russian said gruffly. He took an old grey washcloth that hung above the sink and stuffed it behind Reggie's teeth until Reggie gagged. Struggling for air and feeling the pain of constriction in his hands and feet, Reggie didn't notice the Russian leave the washroom. But he did hear Dominic knock on the front door, back from coffee, and the Russian unlock and open the door.

"You done?" Dominic asked.

"Sure."

"Where's Reggie?"

"I let him leave."

"You let him leave? Weren't you worried about him seeing you?"

"I scared shit out of him. He won't bother me. Let's go."

"He is such a loser, that guy," Dominic said, sharing a laugh with the Russian. The main room's light switch snapped and in a fainter voice, Dominic added, "A complete dumb fuck loser." The front door shut. It was quiet and dim, just like when Reggie signed off from life two weeks earlier.

CHAPTER 41

Nicki Byrne was overbearing, overwrought and overweight, but Thursday morning, especially with Margaret late, Bradley blessed her existence every minute that passed.

As the point person for public relations and social functions at Collins, Shaw, Byrne used her perpetual energy to give her all to her job. With Abrams' blessing, Bradley had called her in Wednesday morning to talk about Tony Amato's arrival the next day. They covered all the bases: when Amato would arrive Thursday; the internal email and firm meet-and-greet that day; and client notifications, press releases and newspaper announcements. Meekly blaming work pressures, Bradley asked if he could count on her to run the show. "Absolutely," she enthused, jumping out of the chair she'd pulled up to Bradley's desk like a sprinter leaving starting gates. And true to form, other than for a bit of drafting and requests for approval, Byrne had taken everything off his plate.

As a result, to stay calm before Amato's arrival, Bradley could distract himself with the relatively mindless task of signing off client accounts. But at 10:55, he even gave that up. He put down his pen, placed his right hand at the ready close to the phone and began watching time tick by.

At eleven on the dot, Amato arrived at reception on the twenty-ninth floor, a light leather briefcase in his hand, and asked for Bradley. When the receptionist's call came, Bradley did what he'd told himself he would not: he jumped into the call late, as if he'd been with another caller. Then he told the receptionist he was on an emergency call and would be out in five minutes.

While Bradley paced in his office, Amato, seated on one of several austere black leather couches amidst the dark wood and mottled marble of reception, breezed through a newspaper. After six minutes, Bradley began the walk down the hallway to reception. As he turned the final corner, Bradley and Amato immediately caught sight of each other.

Offering his hand, Bradley said, "Tony, great to see you. An exciting day!"

Amato put down the newspaper and slowly got up. Bradley thought he seemed a bit peeved and momentarily savoured his delay tactic.

"Great to see you, too, Peter," Amato said quietly, shaking Bradley's hand.

"Let me show you to your office first, so you can start settling in. It's down this way," Bradley said. He extended a hand toward the hallway from which he'd emerged and let Amato lead the way. Bradley followed, scornfully thinking that Amato's silly gait resembled that of Charlie Chaplin's tramp character. Bradley was pleased that he was wearing his best Armani suit.

"Right over here," Bradley said, pointing to the next office. "It was the closest we could get you to the group. Actually, we were lucky that there was a partner's office free on this floor at all."

Amato and Bradley peered in. Bradley thought the office looked amazing given the short notice.

"This'll do, I guess," Amato said after a pause. He walked in, absorbing his new surroundings, and after putting down his briefcase, he wiped a few specks of dust from the desk and accompanying chair.

On cue, Collins arrived with Abrams in tow.

"Well, he's here. We got him," Collins said with a loud laugh. "No escaping now."

Amato laughed along and shook both their hands.

"So, how did your old partners take it?" Collins asked.

"Ah, they were not happy," Amato said. "Actually, they were really quite pissed. One of the hardest things I've ever done, actually. You make a lot of good friends over the years, and there's this idea of betrayal in the air, even though I don't buy it."

"I can imagine it was hard," Abrams said.

"And so, did the inevitable counter-offer come?" Collins asked.

"Well, there was talk of it," Amato said slowly with a grudging smile. "But as you and I talked about, Ted, it wasn't so much about the money." *The bullshit is starting again*, Bradley thought. "It was about their commitment to the practice area. And I let them know that a long time ago, so there weren't any long discussions."

Abrams looked at Bradley. "So Nicki can send out the firm announcement?"

"Yes, she's on standby. I just emailed her to go ahead. Yup — here it is, actually," Bradley said, looking at his smartphone. "And you guys will be there for the meet-and-greet at four?"

"Absolutely," Collins said.

"Do I have an assistant who can help me?" Amato asked. "There are a couple of clients I need to contact as soon as possible, although a few of them know something is up. I just want to make sure my phone and email are set up."

"I think Margaret — my assistant — made sure all that is taken care of," Bradley said. "But Chris down the hall will help you. I'll introduce you in a second."

"Peter, I thought you and I could call some of my clients together, either later today or tomorrow. They should hear directly from you about your accomplishments. I need to cement their comfort level about coming over to Collins, Shaw."

"Whenever you like," Bradley said.

"Yes, let's get those clients on board right away," Abrams said.

"Ok, well, settle in, and then you guys do what you have to," Collins said. "Welcome again to Collins, Shaw," he added with a large smile and another shake of Amato's hand. "Peter, can I talk to you for a second?"

"Of course," Bradley said hesitantly.

After introducing Amato to his new assistant, Bradley made his way to his office, followed by Collins. Margaret had arrived from the doctor's appointment, but when she saw Collins she remained hidden in her cubicle. Collins closed Bradley's office door, and they took seats at the oval meeting table. Collins cleared his throat.

"I am a hundred percent convinced that having Tony join is the best thing for your group and for the firm. But I know that competitive side of yours — lethally competitive, I would say, and for the most part I really like it. I think that's what makes you a great lawyer. So, I'm guessing that seeing Tony here must get under your skin a bit. Especially since I didn't give you a choice. Have I got that sized up correctly?"

Bradley looked to the safe harbour of Lake Ontario. He kept every voluntary muscle as still as possible. "Maybe a bit when Leonard first spoke to me about the idea at lunch Friday. I don't know about you, Ted, but I'm starting to feel my age. I can't battle any more like I used to. When I thought about it over the weekend, my gut told me it was a good idea. An excellent idea, in fact."

Collins buried a hand in the back of his white hair then took in his bulging midsection. "I hear you on that age thing. You

THE CASE FOR KILLING

know, I still work out three times week, but it just doesn't make any difference any more. Not to the eye, anyway."

Bradley glanced back at Collins. "What I do now, before I even think about going into battle, is ask myself — is this really necessary? That's what us old farts learn to do — pick our battles."

"And where does Amato fit in?"

"Like I said, when I thought about it, it seemed fine. Ten years ago, maybe then, I would have fought you to the bone, no matter what. Even for no good reason. You know, just to kick your ass. I like to do that once in a while, Ted, kick your ass."

"The feeling is mutual."

"But this is a good move. We're already the best in the city — we're going to be unassailable. My view is that I've got ten, maybe fifteen more years of practicing law, then Tony can take over. It works well. I'd have done the same thing in your shoes. I promise you, we'll make the most of it."

Collins scrutinized Bradley. After a few seconds he said, "Well, I'm glad to hear that. That's the main reason I wanted to stop by. I meant what I said at the pub last night — nice to see you come around. You have no idea the competitive pressures these days. We've got to get out west, and maybe international, fast, and having fantastic lawyers gives us so many more options. Even Tony pressed me on it. Anyway, Leonard and I both sensed you were working with us. That's good — we appreciate it."

"Sure, thanks," Bradley said. "I was never that concerned by it, you know."

"Ok." Collins leaned forward, still staring at Bradley. "Peter, there's one other thing I need to make sure you understand. You *have* to keep that sick part of you under control."

"My sick part? Ted, we don't really need to talk about this. Everything *is* under control."

"Is it? Have you arranged for the help I asked you to get?"

Bradley dragged a hand across his face. "It's been busy, Ted."

"Let me say this loud and clear. Three strikes and you're out. And you know you've got two against you now, right?" Bradley paled. "Peter, in case you haven't noticed, clients have changed. When we were young lawyers, all that mattered was that they thought we were smart and that we would take care of them. These days, probably because our fees have gone up so much year after year, they assume one law firm is as good as the next. So now it's about reputation. Lawyer reputation, firm reputation, all of it."

Collins sighed heavily. "I need everybody here to be *normal*. I won't be tolerant of eccentricities or stupidity, even outside the firm, if it's going to hurt our reputation. That's why I didn't give you any say about Tony coming here. I could have pretended you had a say, and pandered to you, and got you onside."

"I got it Ted. I'm onside."

"I made the decision to hire Tony on my own and rammed it down the Management Committee's throat, to put a rod up your ass and tell you to stay in line." Collins got up slowly from his chair and stood in front of Bradley, close, like his father used to. "Get rid of your peccadillos or bury them ten feet under. Don't bring them here. Remember, we're *professionals*. That's the last I'm going to say on it."

Rage began to build in Bradley's core. It wasn't so much the content of Collins' harangue; it was its reminiscent tone. Bradley stood and straightened up, ready to face another punch from Collins. But Collins turned away and walked over to the closed office door. Before opening it, he half turned back to Bradley, and said, "There is one other thing. The receptionist from last Friday night. Debbie?"

"Yes?"

"I took care of that. She won't say anything to anybody."

"Thanks, Ted."

Collins looked at Bradley, his face drawn with fatigue. "Do you ever apologize, Peter?"

Bradley smiled faintly. "I try to avoid it," he said. After a moment, he added, "But I am truly sorry for Friday. It won't happen again."

Collins cast a final, slightly disbelieving glance at him. "I sure hope not," he said and left.

CHAPTER 42

Calls and emails about Amato cascaded in from Collins, Shaw lawyers. Several partners asked for introductions. Others, like Robert Platz, made it their business to get to know Amato directly and drop by Bradley's office after. Bradley was the model of keenness, sharing his plans for client events and the group's expansion. Where it was offered, he accepted congratulations for the foresight in landing Amato.

It was not until midafternoon that Bradley got a breather. He finally noticed a sandwich that Margaret had snuck into his office an hour earlier. After the first bite of the wilted BLT, he recalled Margaret's anxious face. Still chewing, he walked outside his office and found her at her desk.

"Thanks for the sandwich," he said. Margaret looked up, worry criss-crossing her face. "Come in. I want to hear about the appointment."

They stood either side of Bradley's desk. Margaret looked at the floor and restlessly wrung her hands.

"The MRI went fine. I mean, it was kind of scary but she did fine. But now we have to wait for the results."

Bradley was lost for words. "That can be the hardest part, the waiting," he finally offered.

"You're right. Kaley is so calm. She keeps telling me that everything will be ok." Margaret looked up at Bradley. "But what if she's not? What happens then? I don't even want to think about it."

Bradley sat. "You know what, Margaret, I'm going to call Dottie tonight. She should find out about this Shapiro guy."

Margaret unwound her hands and threw them up in the air. "I don't know. I guess. To think we have to wait days or weeks."

Leaning forward and putting his elbows on his desk, Bradley said, "Margaret, look, if this guy's not the best, I'm going to make sure Kaley *does* get the best, even if he or she's in the U.S. Don't worry about the expense — I'll take care of that. You do some research this afternoon. I bet Dottie will know which neurology clinic in town is the best. I'll ask her."

"Are you sure? I can pay you back — over time."

"Don't be silly. It's done."

"Thanks, Peter," Margaret said. "I'm trying to be as attentive as I can today. I know it's a big day for you."

Even Margaret has to be fooled, Bradley said to himself. "Kaley's more important," he said. "Go do your research."

CHAPTER 43

Collins, Shaw's largest boardroom doubled as a gathering venue. When it was full of milling lawyers, it was easy to step into a corner and get lost. Bradley had picked the darkest one, and with a drink in his hand he took a break from the ceaseless and annoying confab about the morning's announcement. Tiredly, he scanned the gathering, still well-attended close to five thirty, an hour and a half after it had started.

For a moment, he had the impression of viewing a penguin colony. A few male lawyers had risked brown or beige suits, but most were in dark blues or greys with black leather shoes. There was more diversity among the female lawyers, but their dress was toned down and bland so there was a similar effect of blending together. They probably think their shoes are defining statements but only a few of the other catty female lawyers care, Bradley thought.

Everywhere, the usual cliques had formed. Collins, Platz, and a few Management Committee members held court among the corporate department elite, provoking regular, uproarious laughter from their suitors. The more eccentric litigators found lawyers they liked, maintaining others at a safe distance. And the loners searched each other out, awkwardly trying to connect.

Walter Anand stood near the other end of the room, immersed in serious discussion with several other lawyers of his vintage. Bradley guessed Anand was engaged in subtle, or not-so-subtle, subterfuge against him. Off to a side not far from Bradley was a semi-circle of partners and associates. Carolyn Murphy stood on the periphery, half-heartedly trying to make an impression in a dumpy blue-pinstripe jacket and skirt. And in the centre of the room, in the middle of a surprisingly large group, Tony Amato was telling a story that had its listeners in rapt attention. Seconds later he delivered the punch line and the din in the meeting room surged with laughter and guffaws.

Murphy caught Bradley's eye and gave him a cool smile. He tipped his drink back. She sidled up beside him, following his intent gaze toward Amato, and said, "It's so unlike you just to watch."

He looked at her, modestly taken by surprise. "I am exactly where I want to be," he said with a strained laugh. He retrained his sights on Amato.

"Your new counterpart has the gift of the gab," she said.

Counterpart? An odd choice of words, Bradley thought. His eyes did not waver. "He certainly does," he acknowledged after a few seconds. Again, he imagined Charlie Chaplin, though he wasn't sure if it was as tramp or dictator.

Bradley and Murphy stood together in silence, watching Amato command his group. "Shouldn't we be over there?" Murphy finally blurted.

Bradley took the hint. "That I should," he said forcefully and strode over before Murphy could say anything else.

For the next while Bradley stood next to Amato, imposing his size on his new colleague's diminutive frame. Murphy edged into the other side of the group. Whenever Amato launched his repartee, Bradley interjected or forced the conversation back his way. At one point he waved Anand over to the gathering then planted questions to Murphy and Anand at Amato's expense. Near six, as the boardroom crowd melted away, Bradley claimed dominance.

"Well, I thought that went well," he said to Amato as Murphy and Anand hovered awkwardly at the side.

"A good start," Amato said quite quietly. "I'm exhausted, though. And I still have to get my run in tonight. Time to head home."

"Can I give you a ride?" Bradley offered with his most ingratiating smile. "I don't know what part of town you're in."

"Leaside. No thanks, I drove. I just parked downstairs in visitor's parking for the day. Chris gave me my parking pass for tomorrow."

"Ok, not far from us. I have to get my briefcase from my office. We can take the elevators down to parking together, if you like."

"Sure. I have to go back to my office, too. Walter and Carolyn — see you tomorrow."

Ten minutes later Bradley found Amato in his new office. As they talked about client calls the next day, they took the elevator to street level then walked over to the neighbouring parking elevator.

Waiting for its arrival, Bradley said, "My wife and I looked at Leaside. Really nice part of town. Where are you exactly?"

"Rolph and Airdrie. Do you know it?"

"Approximately. She made me buy in Rosedale. I'll never pay off that mortgage."

"Well, if you got into the Toronto market when you joined the firm, at least you rode it all the way up. You're not going to get a lot of sympathy from me."

"More or less." Bradley disguised his pleasure. "You look like a regular runner. I went to the club for the first time in a long while yesterday — can hardly walk today."

"You know what my secret is? Same route, every night, except when there's too much snow. At this time of year, seven o'clock, unless it's crucial to be at the office. Even weekends."

"Through Leaside?"

"Down Bayview, into Crothers Woods, where I do some loops, and then out the other side at Millwood."

"Crothers Woods?" The parking elevator arrived and they entered.

"That large wooded area around the Don River, south of Leaside. Good cross-country running through there. I'm a creature of habit — keeps me honest."

"I don't know how you do it."

"Just part of my life. Gives me energy. Keeps me going on a tough deal."

"My wife would shoot me."

Amato laughed. "Maria tolerates it. She knows how irritable I get otherwise. And it's just a half-hour run."

The elevator pinged at P1.

"This must be you," Amato said. "I had to go to P3 to get a spot."

"See you tomorrow, Tony." Bradley shook Amato's hand and exited the elevator.

He walked quickly to his red M3, located near the exit in one of the best parking spots in the building. Stuffing himself behind the steering wheel, Bradley heard several cars emerging from lower levels. Every other day, he would have made it his business to bring his car's throaty roar to life and quickly maneuver to the head of the queue. This time he held off and lay in wait, watching out the rear-view mirror.

CHAPTER 44

A series of high-end cars exited the Bay Wellington Tower. In less than a minute, Bradley spied Amato in a new dark blue Audi A6. Bradley waited a few more seconds, enough time, he judged, for Amato to pay for a day's parking. Then he started his car and backed out slowly, in time to see Amato choose the quarter-turn ramp to Front Street.

Crunching the gearshift into first, Bradley flung the M3 toward an open exit lane and flashed his parking pass. He drummed his fingers on the steering wheel waiting for the barrier to lift, then catapulted the M3 up to Front. Ignoring the mess of construction for Union Station's refurbishment, he turned left toward Yonge Street. Instantly he caught sight of the taillights of Amato's car turning south on Yonge.

Amato had snuck into traffic just before the Front Street traffic light turned red. By the time Bradley got there, he had to wait. Losing patience, he forced his car between two others, eliciting an angry honk from behind. As usual, rush-hour traffic was dense, but not far ahead Bradley made out Amato's car. He hung back a short distance, his heart grabbing extra beats from the stir of a chase.

Using Queen's Quay East and the Jarvis Street on-ramp, Amato worked his way onto the Gardiner Expressway east and then the Don Valley Parkway north. He drove in the fast lane as quickly as traffic would allow, but it was child's play for Bradley to keep up. He delighted in his M3's power and agility and his decision to thwart the car dealer's irritating presumption in August that he would lease another five-series.

Bradley followed as Amato exited north on Bayview Avenue. Driving up the Bayview hill Bradley saw the expanse of Crothers Woods develop to his right then end at busy dual railway tracks that dissected the city. Traffic came to a stop at a red light at Nesbitt Drive before Bayview went under a bridge for the tracks. As traffic moved again, he followed Amato under the bridge and up a large S-curve before crossing Moore Avenue. A few streets farther north, Amato turned right at Airdrie Road into Leaside.

Several stop signs later, at Rolph Road, Amato turned right. Bradley eased his car to the intersection. Amato's car curled left into a garage on the other side of the corner house. Bradley turned onto Rolph in the opposite direction, made a U-turn and parked his car with a view of Amato's house across the intersection. Even with the light fading close to sunset, he recognized the house from Amato's Facebook page and the spot on the front lawn where Amato had stood with his arms around his family.

Bradley studied the house. It was an imposing two-storey red brick structure with the front door facing Rolph. The windows were trimmed in white and flanked by black shutters. A low hedge had been planted along the perimeter of the lawn on Rolph and Airdrie.

The Bluetooth in his car startled Bradley. Amy was calling.

"Where are you?" she asked impatiently.

"Nearly home," he said. "Had to work late."

Amy paused. "I'm getting hungry — should I start eating?"

"I'll be there soon," Bradley said, continuing to survey Amato's front yard.

"It's awful quiet there."

"I'm just stopped in traffic." The porch light at the front of

Amato's house burned to life and the rectangular grey wooden door burst open. In running gear, Amato jumped out onto the stone steps in front of the door and started a few stretches. "Actually, I just remembered I have to get some cash from the bank. I should be home in half an hour or so. Go ahead and start without me, ok? Bye." He ended the call before Amy could respond.

Amato ended stretching with some stationary high-steps then launched himself across his front lawn and over the hedge, onto Airdrie. Despite the failing light, Bradley's chest seized with anxiety at being seen. He slid down the driver's seat, cursing the car's small confines. Amato, intent only on the sidewalk in front of him, was out of sight in seconds, heading west back toward Bayview.

After waiting fifteen seconds, Bradley engaged first gear and eased his car onto Airdrie. Amato wore a running top with a neon strip across the shoulders; he was easy to spot in the distance. Staying well back, Bradley watched him negotiate several intersections before reaching Bayview. There he crossed and turned left, running on the west sidewalk, southbound beside Mount Pleasant Cemetery. With nothing more than a blind belief that it would somehow benefit him, Bradley made a similar turn and continued to follow. He kept the M3 purring in third gear, irritating drivers behind him with his slow pace. Twice Bradley got too close to Amato, and pulled into a parking spot to let him bound ahead.

Amato crossed Moore and began curling down the S-curve on Bayview that he'd driven up fifteen minutes before. Close behind, Bradley sensed that his game was coming to an end. The curve, stretching over several hundred yards and ending at the train bridge, descended steeply, and trees and thick brush took over from a strip mall on one side and housing on the other. In the rush of traffic down the curve, Bradley would catch up to Amato in no time and have nowhere to pull over.

Turning into the last side street, Bradley made a U-turn and watched Amato recede down the curve. It didn't much matter, he told himself. Shortly, Amato would be heading into Crothers Woods and it would be impossible to follow him there anyway. Reluctantly, Bradley pulled back into Bayview traffic. After the train bridge he would turn right onto Nesbitt and use Summerhill to traverse north Rosedale to his home.

Bradley pulled back into traffic. After the first part of the S-curve, in the midst of a large convoy of trucks and cars, he saw Amato again, running quite far ahead, about to pass under the train bridge. For the first time he puzzled why Amato ran on the west side of Bayview instead of the east side where the walk-in entrance to Crothers Woods appeared after the bridge. Close to Nesbitt, at the bridge, Bradley signalled right. He had the amusing thought of cutting off Amato as he turned. But to Bradley's astonishment Amato also went right.

Completing his turn, Bradley immediately pulled his car over to avoid Amato's attention. Twenty bounds later, Amato checked traffic both ways and slipped across Nesbitt. Once again, to avoid detection, Bradley slid hard down the driver's seat.

When he dared look up, he strained to see past parked cars down Nesbitt. Amato was nowhere to be seen. Slowly, Bradley pulled his car ahead. On his left was a patch of heavy forest, then a turn onto True Davidson Drive and a playground. Bradley couldn't understand how Amato had disappeared. Then he passed True Davidson where he glimpsed Amato running toward another bridge that crossed into a recent, Versailles-like subdivision. Without warning, Amato darted left and pushed headlong into the dense forest.

Bradley found a parking spot on Nesbitt across from the playground. The car clock flipped to 7:06; twilight was settling in. A series of ornate street lamps on True Davidson buzzed, then came to life. For several minutes Bradley kept an eye out for

Amato in the side-view mirror but he didn't re-emerge from the forest. Bradley went to his car's navigation system and turned a central control knob enough different directions to find a close-up map of the area. It was hard to tell, but it seemed Amato could access Crothers Woods through the forest where he'd disappeared.

Bradley thought he had enough light for a bit more exploration. He got out of his car, crossed Nesbitt, and walked down the east side of True Davidson. As casually as possible, he looked for the spot in the forest where Amato had vanished. Not far from the bridge, between two young blue spruces, he spied the outline of an unmarked, inconspicuous path. Bradley felt exposed by the glowing street lamps. Hurriedly, he ventured onto the path, parting tall, thick grasses either side and pushing his way between the spruces.

Ahead there was a fairly steep drop with six rudimentary steps. Bradley carefully negotiated the steps and continued onto a winding dirt path that declined over a series of undulations. Trees of varying height and green ground cover surrounded him. The air grew heavier, filled with an earthy smell, and except for the rush of traffic from nearby Bayview, the forest was quiet. After less than a minute, he walked heavily down the final dip in the path. He found himself on a single railway track.

Bradley stepped onto the track and looked both ways. To the west it ran under the True Davidson Drive bridge. To the east, with the upper reach of Crothers Woods to the south, it curled and merged after several hundred yards alongside the busy dual midtown tracks to the north. Bradley heard the sound of an oncoming train. His heart leapt but he quickly realized that the train was on the midtown tracks.

As he studied the single track, he realized it was abandoned. Not far from where he stood several dead trees had fallen across and tall weeds grew between ties. Hikers and runners had worn a narrow path along the southern rail. Glancing at some house lights in the subdivision across the bridge, Bradley held his breath as the train engine above roared by. On the track in the dusk air, surrounded by trees and the clatter of train cars, he felt eerily alone.

He waited a few minutes more. No one else came along the path or railway track. Amato was probably out the other side of Crothers Woods and running home along Millwood. With darkness rapidly closing in, Bradley worked his way back up the path and steps to True Davidson and checked all around whether anyone had seen him.

From Nesbitt he drove along Summerhill Avenue, immediately south of the midtown railway tracks, toward Gregory. On the way, he stopped in at a small fruit market. There he found an ATM and a rarity — a functioning pay phone.

Flush with a few hundred dollars, Bradley entered the decaying phone booth and slid in a credit card. After many rings, Dominic picked up then put Bradley on hold. A few minutes later, with Bradley's patience at an end, Dominic jumped back on the line. Without any greeting, he gave instructions. Bradley was to ask for the manager of a pizza shop near Yonge and Lawrence, Friday at 6:00 p.m. Twenty-five hundred cash for a handgun left a bitter taste in Bradley's mouth, but he saw no options.

When he got home, he gave one more performance, a compelling display of interest in the events of Amy's Thursday. But she was distracted, repeatedly checking her smartphone for a call or text from Reggie. When he finally did call, Bradley stole away to his study.

On the desktop computer he pulled up a map of the Nesbitt Drive area. On it he located the abandoned railway track. It ran more northeast than east, but as he had seen, it met up with Crothers Woods' northern perimeter. After thirty frustrating minutes Bradley figured out how to copy the map into a Word document. Then, underneath, he wrote out the parts of Amato's running route that he knew.

Bradley completed the document with a short "to do" list.

1. Get money for gun

2. Pick up gun Friday night

3. Practice shots?

4. When to shoot A.? Where?

5. Can I carry A.? Where to dispose?

6. Make sure all tracks are covered

7. Move Project Pizza off this computer!

In the Project Pizza folder, Bradley saved the document alongside the earlier document with general research about Amato. After a few drinks in the study, quite proud of the day's end, Bradley joined Amy in bed. He fell asleep before he could ask why she seemed so restless.

CHAPTER 45

Even before she sat down, Amy asked, "How could you let that happen?"

He had no idea what she was talking about. He preferred to remain focused on the flow of her blond hair over her shoulders and the top of a low-cut, form-fitting white dress. But her eyes had a wateriness that often foretold upset, and he recalled the edge in the voicemail she'd left him late the previous evening, saying they had to get together.

"Nice to see you, too," Dominic said. "Of course I didn't mind waiting. Wanted to make sure you and I got a good table — you know, Friday lunch can be so busy here. But it's worth it — still my favourite patio in Little Italy. Especially on a sunny September day."

As she sat down, Amy gave Dominic an icy look. He was spared her retort by the arrival of the waiter.

"I'll have a glass of whatever Chardonnay you have," she said. When the waiter left, her eyes bore into Dominic. "You don't know what happened to Reggie?"

Dominic felt deflated. A few previous lunches with hints of her husband's neglect; requests to help her brother; an unexpected voicemail, however edgy, asking for another lunch. He'd hoped Amy was looking for him to re-enter her life and help her overcome the boredom of her daily routine. She should have been noticing the cut and fabric of his suit and the style of his shoes.

But there was no hint of interest in that. Dejectedly shrugging, he said, "He did his interview. That's what I know."

Amy looked at Dominic incredulously. "I can't believe that Russian — Russian *thug* didn't tell you."

"About what, Amy?" Dominic asked impatiently, lifting his sunglasses in the hope of greater understanding.

"About the *bathtub*?"

"I have no idea what you're talking about. He was sitting on the toilet, doing his interview. He wasn't in the bathtub." Dominic looked around the patio. "Beautiful day. Kind of humid."

"Oh, for Christ's sake," Amy said, looking away. "Reggie actually was right. You don't know."

Dominic let the sunglasses drop and slouched further into his seat. His face was half-cocked to one side and he pressed his fingertips together above his chest. Dispassionately, he listened as Amy recounted how Reggie, tied up and stuffed, had flailed for hours in the tub before a neighbour complained about the incessant banging from the next-door washroom. "Honestly, how could you let that happen? He could have *died* in there."

The waiter returned with Amy's glass of wine. It was the tone implying Dominic's incompetence that irritated him. As Amy stared at him, he let several seconds pass without flinching from his pose.

"I told him not to open the door," Dominic finally said, slowly and deliberately. "He opened the door. You don't open the door with a guy like that. Probably even Reggie should understand that."

The waiter reappeared to ask if they wanted to order.

"Give us ten," Dominic said and waved him off.

Amy leaned forward, the outline of her breasts more distinct as her dress pressed against the edge of the table. Dominic fought the urge to stare. "You shouldn't have left the two of them alone," she said with a suppressed hiss so neighbouring tables wouldn't hear. "*That's* my point."

"Look, Amy, I don't control that guy. I set up a meeting; I introduced them. None of this would have happened if Reggie had an ounce of common sense. Am I right?"

"Leave my brother alone," Amy said as her phone rang. She dug the phone out of her handbag and looked at the caller ID. "It's Peter," she said and answered.

Dominic made out Bradley's voice but not his words. "I'm at lunch with a friend. Why? ... Café Rex. ... No, I don't know where your belt is. You had it yesterday. ... Yes, I'll be home before you leave for the cottage. I have to go ... bye."

Amy put the phone down on the table with a sigh of disgust. "My master and ruler. He needs to know everything I do."

Dominic pretended not to be interested and waved the waiter over. "Let me treat you to a nice lunch, Amy," he said, garnering a half-smile of appreciation. "The pasta here is the best."

After ordering, Amy again looked at Dominic. "You know I'm not done with you on this."

"I had a feeling."

"You should get another guy for Reggie to interview, or give him his money back. That would be the right thing to do. Five thousand dollars — that's ridiculous anyway."

Dominic laughed mockingly. "Are you serious?"

"Absolutely."

"That's crazy."

"It's not. You guys had a deal and you didn't live up to your end of the bargain."

"Amy, you're pissing me off like you always do."

"I don't care."

"Anyone else, I would say take a hike."

"I'm not anyone else."

The surface of the patio table was lightly undulating patterned glass. Around plates, cutlery and glassware, the sun filtered through. Dominic glimpsed down, momentarily catching his breath as he saw Amy's long, crossed legs revealed to mid-thigh by a deep slit in the front of her dress.

"No, you're not," he said as salads arrived, stealing his view. "I'll think about it."

"I want to know this afternoon," Amy said. "And it better be the right answer."

Dominic smirked and tried to change the subject. "What is the deal with your brother anyway?"

"What do you mean?" Amy asked nonchalantly, examining the contents of her salad.

It was Dominic's turn to look incredulous. "I told you a hundred times, there's something not right with him." He tapped his right temple, still holding his fork. "Up here."

"I'm tired of hearing that from you. I don't know what you're talking about."

"Sure you do. He's — he's completely unpredictable. He's high, he's low. He makes stupid decisions. You never know what you get with him. I think he's a little crazy, actually."

Amy gave Dominic a fierce stare. "You don't know what it was like, Dominic."

"I *do* know. I was there." Dominic crunched into his salad.

"That is *crap*. Only for some of it. Seriously, you didn't *live* it, Dominic," Amy said. "It was worse for Reggie. I was older. I had my school, which at least I was good in. If I needed something, I knew how to get it. Reggie was only nine when Mom and Dad died. And he was just so awkward around people. Do you know how many times he was beat up as a kid? I just held my breath when I went to get him at school. And the schools did nothing."

"He wasn't the only kid getting beat up in the schoolyard,

Amy. You just got to learn how to take care of yourself."

"You were good at that. You were strong, and that's cool about you, I guess. But Reggie wasn't like that. If someone gave him a hard time, he would hide in a corner somewhere and do nothing. Seriously, I was his lifeline."

"He needs to find something to do. So he gets off your back — gets his own money."

"*I* have to find something to do. Get *my* own money."

Finishing his salad, Dominic put down his fork. "You're married to a rich guy, Amy. What are you talking about?"

Amy laughed derisively. "Probably not as well off as you. And I never see any of it."

Dominic wiped his mouth with his napkin, leaned forward and said quietly, "Why don't you escort again? I'll set you up with my best clients, like when you were in university — no risks. Easy money and lots of it. Very discreet, of course."

He wondered if she would pretend to be insulted, but instead she pushed her salad aside and curled some hair between two fingers. "I'm old, Dominic," she said finally.

"Trust me," he said. "For someone like you, age is not an issue — not for a while anyway. What do you think? A few hours a week."

Amy looked away. "I have other plans, actually."

Dominic nodded. After a few moments, he said, "Well, let me know if you change your mind. I'll take good care of you."

"I have no doubt that you would," Amy said as the waiter arrived with the pasta.

CHAPTER 46

The morning had been a series of meddlesome, unsettling distractions for Bradley.

On being jarred awake by the alarm clock, Bradley carried the vestiges of a dream into the shower. Amy was at Maximus, lying naked on a bed in a small, well-appointed room, similar to one at an Amsterdam brothel Bradley had visited years earlier. She was motioning an aroused man standing next to the bed to make love to her. Behind him stood a lineup of similar men, each looking longingly at Amy, waiting their turn. Bradley stood in a corner, an excited voyeur and a horrified husband. His clammy, shaky right hand held a gun, and he was pointing it, ready to fire, if the man beside Amy's bed accepted her invitation. Unexpectedly, the man turned his head toward Bradley, and Bradley felt a stir of recognition. "Come on, Tony," Amy said, reaching an arm out, "ignore him." Then Bradley's father, young again, and now only a few inches from Bradley, whispered mockingly, "Really, Peter, is that the *best* you can do?"

Bradley, who never saw hidden meanings, nonetheless wondered if the dream was a cautionary tale. Tuesday night, to protect what he had built and to answer Collins' treachery, he had embraced even the most extreme option to ruin Tony Amato. Perhaps, in the dream, when Bradley's father derided him for failing to shoot, it was an admonishment for Bradley to follow through on his plan. Or maybe his father was warning that careful planning was necessary for Bradley to avoid an impulsive, self-made trap. In the end, all Bradley concluded was that a dream in which he turned the gun on his father would have made more sense.

Then, soon after Bradley arrived at the office, Amato unexpectedly pushed open his door and stuck his head in. "Can you join a call right away?" he asked. "This client is really hard to get a hold of."

Amato didn't wait for an answer, rushing back to his office and assuming Bradley would follow. *Already running the show*, Bradley said to himself as he hurried down the hall after Amato. *Assuming I'm at* his *disposal*. And on the call Bradley performed poorly, his edge lost in the murky residue of his dream. He hardly got two words in, failing miserably to take charge and assert his reputation.

And finally, later in the morning, there was the scrawny, ill-dressed personal banking officer who accosted Bradley every time he visited the main branch of his bank.

"Can I help you with anything, Mr. Bradley?" he asked soon after Bradley joined the long teller line.

"I need twenty-five hundred cash."

"Sure, come on into my office."

"I don't need a loan."

"No worries. Just helping you with this lineup."

Predictably, the banking officer tried a bit of marketing.

"The cash balance in your chequing account is very high."

"I don't need mutual funds, either. I got burned in 2008. My gut is telling me to stay out of the markets."

"And I see you've made quite a few withdrawals recently, so maybe you need the cash on hand."

"What do you mean?" Bradley asked, and the banking officer turned the screen to show him. After staring for a few moments,

Bradley muttered, "I don't recognize those last transfers."

The banking officer paused. "Does someone else have access to your accounts?"

Bradley didn't want to continue the discussion without further thought on his own. "You know, I'm sure it's all right. Let's just take care of the cash."

After returning from the bank, Bradley tried to work, but to no avail. Muggy outside air infiltrating his office caused sweat to fill the creases in his brow. He checked his laptop screen again. Yes, there'd been three transfers from his chequing account into his joint account with Amy that made no sense, two the previous day and one for sixty thousand that morning. Clicking through to the joint account, he saw the first two transfers withdrawn to an account he didn't recognize. He knew he hadn't made any of the transfers. How she'd gotten his passwords, he didn't know, but he was sure it was Amy and her crazy art gallery idea.

An hour and a half later, in the middle of his sandwich lunch at his desk, it struck Bradley that the money transfers were more than a meddlesome distraction. Like a match being struck, his anger flared. Just when he needed control and certainty in every aspect of his life, his wife had become a loose cannon, throwing his trust away like snot-filled facial tissue. She must be accessing his desktop computer at home and, if that was the case, she might also find the Project Pizza folder. However remote the possibility, it left him alternately feverish and chilled. He had to get home and remove the folder. But first he wanted to know if she would be home when he arrived, and called her on his smartphone.

Two minutes later, he signed off on his quick call with her, his body quivering with rage. Having lunch at Café Rex, was she? How cushy. Bradley got up from his chair and stood for several moments. He dragged a hand over his face and finished with a swipe across his brow. When he thought his anger had ebbed, he went to find Margaret. She was at her desk, typing ferociously, her face rigid and tense.

"I'm leaving for the cottage now," Bradley said.

Margaret looked at him, surprised. "Don't you have some calls with Tony shortly?"

"Just — just move them to Monday."

"Ok," Margaret said hesitantly. "Won't they be upset? You could do them in the car."

"I know how to deal with clients well enough, Margaret," Bradley said hurriedly. "Just tell Tony to move them to Monday."

Bradley started to leave, but Margaret spoke again. "Did you, by chance, speak to Dottie — about clinics? I've been doing some research."

Bradley's heart sank at his oversight. "I — I tried to call her, but she didn't get back to me. She's probably on a shift at emerg. I'll let you know as soon as she talks to me. Have a good weekend." He skulked away, hoping the emptiness of his lies wasn't as apparent to Margaret as it was to him.

In his office, Bradley turned off and unplugged his laptop. He stuffed it into his capacious legal briefcase then added the laptop's electrical cord. With a struggle, he found room for documents and a binder of background materials that Platz had sent him for the new transaction.

For a Friday afternoon, traffic home along Jarvis and Mount Pleasant was lighter than Bradley had expected. His brain was free to run in overdrive. Initially, he reasoned it was a good thing Amy was out with a friend. He could deal with the Project Pizza folder without getting sidetracked by a compulsion to confront her. But like maggots crawling into dying flesh, suspicions began to intrude. With whom, exactly, was Amy having lunch? She had no female friends, and if she'd had a luncheon date with a woman, she would have proudly told him. It had to be a man. John

Carver took hold of his mind. He imagined Amy and Carver at a long, boozy lunch, followed by a ride on Bradley's bed, safe knowing that Bradley was on his way to the cottage. Or maybe she was with a new acquaintance from Maximus. Bradley barked at himself: when he finished with Tony Amato, his next order of business was to get his wife back under his influence.

At home in his study he turned on the desktop computer. As it booted up he went to Amy's desk in the master bedroom and found a USB stick. Only weeks before, she'd shown him how they were used. With the stick inserted in the desktop, he went into Explorer and transferred the Project Pizza folder to the stick. He double-checked that the folder was gone from the C: drive, making a mental note to ask an IT person at work if there'd be any residual traces. His last step was to change the passwords to his computer and bank accounts.

When he was done, Bradley tried to focus on what he needed to close the cottage. But the image of his wife flirting with Carver at a surreptitious lunch chewed at him. He ruminated whether Amy would have mentioned Café Rex if she really was with Carver. It wasn't sloppy, he concluded; it was bold and sly. "This is all bullshit," Bradley blurted. "Time to catch her out."

CHAPTER 47

Bradley charged downstairs. From the side table in the hallway, he grabbed the keys to his car. Then he slammed the front door behind him and cut across the lawn to the other side of Gregory where he'd parked the M3. It was one hot-looking car, he said to himself, even if it was a little small. Perfect for Little Italy.

He arrived less than a half hour later. After crawling in traffic along College Street, he turned north on Clinton Street, directly past Café Rex's patio. In the overflow crowd beneath a swirl of open umbrellas, he failed to glimpse his wife or her companion.

Bradley found a parking spot a lengthy half block along Clinton. At first he walked hurriedly toward the restaurant. But as he grew closer and could hear the din of the outside crowd, he slowed and finally stopped behind the cover of a thick tree trunk. By his calculation, Amy would either be late in her lunch or already done. Trying to look inconspicuous by a feigned search for his wallet, Bradley peered from behind the tree trunk and studied the patio. He still did not see Amy. Just as he pondered walking into the restaurant and openly confronting her, she exited. A second later, Bradley recognized Dominic's sleazy saunter. "That prick," he hissed.

When Dominic caught up to Amy, she drew close to him and slipped an arm around one of his elbows. They began a slow walk, crossing Clinton and continuing west along the north side of traffic-choked College. When he was sure they hadn't seen him,

Bradley followed, staying well back in the stream of pedestrians.

A block later, at Grace Street, Amy and Dominic stopped, and after Dominic landed a kiss on both her cheeks, they parted ways. Amy looked relaxed and content. Bradley decided he would deal with her at home; it was Dominic who called for his attention. After Amy went into a store famous for its selection of international fashion magazines, Dominic crossed College, dodging a streetcar and several vehicles. Once across, he resumed his saunter and went south on Grace. Bradley hurried across College then broke into a hard walk and steadily caught up. Slowing at an older BMW three series with outrageous after-market rims, Dominic walked onto the street to the driver's side and unlocked the car.

"Hey, Dominic," Bradley said breathlessly. "How's it going?"

Dominic hung beside the open door of his car, trying to discern who it was.

Bradley walked behind the car and held out his hand. "Peter Bradley," he said.

Scowling, Dominic reluctantly shook his hand. "Get inside the fucking car," he said, dropping into the driver's seat.

Bradley scurried back to the passenger side of the car and shoved himself into a black bucket seat.

"What the hell are you doing here?" Dominic asked.

"Actually, I saw you and Amy having a nice lunch together, and I just wanted to find out — are you fucking my wife again? I don't really care what happened between the two of you before I met her, but I do now."

Dominic looked at Bradley disbelievingly. "You are the most screwed-up family I've ever met. And I thought my family was crazy."

"Could you answer the question?"

"Man, your tone is all wrong. What are you accusing me of?"

"I thought I was very clear. I want to know if you're having sex with my wife."

"Get out."

"Are you?"

"Has it ever occurred to you that once an escort, always an escort? Remember, that's how you met her."

Rage burned in Bradley's eye sockets. "So you are?"

Dominic smiled devilishly. "I wish I was — but I'm not. Now get out."

Bradley looked at Dominic, yearning to see behind his sunglasses. "I'm going to be watching more closely in the future. Don't tell her about the gun. I'll bury you if you do."

A sardonic laugh escaped Dominic's lips. "Are you serious? Do you have any fucking idea who you're dealing with here?"

Bradley attempted a similar laugh in return. "I think I do. I don't impress easily, just so you know."

Dominic pressed his lips together, curling them slightly to one side. "Listen, asshole, I'll take your escort business, but if you even come close to me again, you'll find out what burying really means. I got so many different ways I can do it, you'll never know what hit you. Now, last time — get out of my fucking car and go home to your nutso family."

Bradley thought hard about continuing the discussion but decided, a bit reluctantly, that he had made his point. Slowly, he pushed himself out of Dominic's car. He was still closing the passenger door when Dominic spun the back tires, spitting tiny stones at Bradley's ankles, and tore off.

Walking back toward College, Bradley felt at once shaken and exhilarated. He did not fool himself. If Dominic wanted to, he could take care of Bradley in whatever brutal fashion he wished — or knew someone who would for a modest sum. But more importantly, after a sickly morning, Bradley was taking control again. In fact, as he thought about it, his oft-rued anger and impulsiveness had served him well. He doubted whether Dominic would bother with Amy again.

At College, Bradley looked both ways. Just west, at the corner of Beatrice, was another café, Pompey. He walked there and found a patio seat. After a glance at the menu, he ordered a cup of mixed raspberry and lemon gelato. It felt good to be on the patio, cooling off after his encounter with Dominic, the late September sun dancing around him. When the waitress arrived with his order, he asked her to bring a double espresso as well. Bradley felt his swagger returning. It was time to make some decisions.

He curled a plastic spoon through the gelato, aiming for equal portions of raspberry and lemon, and thought hard. As for Amy, it was only a question of bringing her under control — and though she didn't know it, he had just started. What really mattered now was taking care of Amato. For more than half a minute he held the plastic spoon with a dollop of gelato in mid-air. Later that day, he would have a gun, and in Amato's running route there were some intriguing possibilities. He needed to take action soon. The longer he waited, the more Amato and he would be seen as established work colleagues, and the more he would risk becoming a suspect.

Bradley licked the gelato from the spoon and the waitress returned with his espresso. Sunday evening. *Why not then*, he asked himself. Though he would have to act fast, he was a rapid thinker, and since he would be alone at the cottage, he had enough time to strategize. At work in the afternoon on Sunday, then at home in the evening with Amy — excellent alibis, if he could sneak out unnoticed shortly before 7:00 p.m., when Amato ran.

Bradley's train of thought was interrupted by a scream of dismay from a little girl in a high chair at the next table. Mashing her face into an ice cream cone, she had accidentally pushed the top scoop of ice cream onto the table below. She looked in anguish at her lost treat.

"I *told* you to be careful," the mother said with exasperation. "Now look what you've done. Really, you're such trouble some times."

The little girl saw the irritation in her mother's face, and after a glimpse at her mother starting to clean up the mess launched into an outburst twice as loud. Bradley, who first was shocked into remembering how short-tempered small children could be, seized on something else. He needed to lay down the law with Amy that afternoon, not just to bring her under his thumb, but as a provocation, like the mother's tone with her daughter. Amy was sure to take it up, and then by Sunday Bradley would retake the role of determined peacemaker. Yes, at home with Amy Sunday evening, perhaps at a get together with friends, obviously intent on patching things up. No person would think him capable of premeditated murder in the midst of trying to resolve a bitter, prolonged row with his dodgy wife.

Bradley drained his double espresso, deposited some money on the table and left the crying child behind. A few minutes later he was in his car, fighting with the browser on his smartphone to find the address for Maximus. It was only two thirty, and he doubted whether the club would be open, but it was not far away. Bradley decided it was time to make an impression.

CHAPTER 48

A short while later Bradley parked his car on Fennings Street. He walked south and turned the corner at Queen. In front of a 1950s low-rise commercial building, Maximus' vertical neon sign hung unlit and forlorn. As casually as possible, he tested the smoke-coloured glass front door. To his mild surprise, it was unlocked.

His eyes took several seconds to adjust to the darkness of the inner foyer. It was empty, and no one came to see him. Bradley stepped through to the other end, and moving one of the blue velvet curtains aside, he cautiously stepped into the first room. A bartender wiped down the granite surface of the bar and a man and a woman conversed on stools. After a moment they spied Bradley. The woman slipped down from her perch and came over to greet him.

"Can I help you?" she asked. Bradley guessed that she was Amy's age. Her long, dark hair settled invitingly around a pretty face, and her voluptuous body strained against a black knit dress.

"Yes," Bradley said, clearing his throat. "I'd like to talk to the owner."

The woman's face registered caution. "Carl and I are the owners," she said, pointing vaguely toward her companion at the bar. "We're closed actually, until 9:00 p.m. What is this about?" she asked.

"I — I just wanted to understand how things work here."

"Are you from city hall? Somebody was here last week. We

comply with all the by-laws."

"No, I have nothing to do with that. I mean — can anyone come here?"

"We're a club. You have to be a member."

"I see. And what are the activities?"

"We cater to couples with open relationships. Consensual, safe, loving. Of course, you can get drinks and some food too, here, in the first room."

Bradley felt the woman stare at him hard, still questioning his presence. "And how do I join?"

"Well, we have an application form, and we do a few background checks. You have to agree to our rules and pay the membership fee. Some nights there are restrictions. Saturday nights there's an extra fee to get in, and single men aren't allowed."

Bradley smiled dismissively. "Why is that?"

"Things just seem to work out better that way."

"I see. My wife is a member here, actually."

"Oh, all right, if you're a couple — that's fine. The application form is online."

"You don't have an application form here?"

"We might," she said and began walking to the bar. Bradley followed. "Carl, can you hand me an application form?"

Carl reached in behind the bar and came up with three white sheets stapled together. "Shall I take over?" he asked.

"Certainly," the woman said and resumed her place on the stool, studying a tablet.

Carl, already in all black, handed Bradley the form, and Bradley began flipping through the pages. On the second page his eyes landed on "Preferences". There was no asterisk to indicate that part of the form was compulsory.

"May I ask," Carl said, "what is your wife's name?"

"Amy Bradley."

A puzzled look came over Carl's face. "Amy Bradley. I — I don't remember that name. Let me check."

"Can *I* ask a question?" Bradley said.

"Certainly," Carl responded, his face glued to his tablet as he checked the members' list.

"Under 'Preferences', there's nothing about dominance here."

Carl looked at Bradley, then back at his tablet. "You can put that under 'Other'. Oh, I see, yes, Amy Klein."

"Amy Klein?"

"Some members use pseudonyms in the club, and after a short time that's how I remember them. Then you're —"

"Peter Bradley. Can I see my wife's application form?"

"Ah, we don't usually share that — with anyone."

"Ok, I understand." Bradley paused. "And the dominance — how extreme is permitted?"

"How extreme?" Carl asked, his face puzzled again.

"Yes, say I want to fuck your partner there, Carl, can I, you know, tie her up?" The woman looked up. "Pretend I'm having my way with her."

Carl paused. "Everything is usually allowed, as long as it's consensual."

Bradley put down the application form and walked closer to Carl. "And if I just want to fuck her now, can I? Or do I have to become a member, and then I get to fuck her?"

Carl's face lost all form of ingratiation. "What are you saying?"

"I don't know why nobody understands me today. I want to fuck her, right here, right now. Can I?"

"I think you should go," the woman said.

"Oh, I see, it's a little uncomfortable now, is it? Shoe's on the other foot? Does my question bother you? Now you know what it's like when you're at this end."

"Listen, Mr. Bradley, we're just a club for consenting couples," the woman said. "I understand that if your wife was here alone, you might feel jealous, but that's not our issue."

"I'm not jealous. I'm fucking angry."

"I agree," Carl said. "I think you should go."

"You're screwing with my marriage. I won't have it. Take my wife off your list."

"I think she's entitled to make her own decisions. Now please go." Carl attempted to show Bradley to the entrance.

"Take her off the fucking list."

"Listen, I'll mention you were here when she comes again. How about that?"

"She's not coming back here."

Carl paused. "Whatever you say. It's time to go."

"You know, as far as I'm concerned, the Supreme Court of Canada should have ruled against these kinds of places."

"You're entitled to your views, but that was 2005. Long time ago. Will you go now, please?"

Bradley scowled, but as with Dominic, he felt he'd made his point. He walked over to the curtains. Before he went through, the woman said contemptuously, "Perhaps a little jealousy wouldn't be so bad."

CHAPTER 49

When Bradley got home, he was surprised to find the house empty. Eventually, from inside the kitchen he spied Amy on the back deck, lying on a patio chaise lounge, sunning herself. She wore a scanty black bikini and sunglasses, and she had collected her hair in a bun. Bradley admired the near perfect curves of her body. He thought of her with Dominic and felt both surging hatred and arousal. Then he labelled the thoughts a distraction and shoved them aside. He opened the patio door, walked to where Amy lay, pulled an accompanying patio chair next to her and sat down.

"You're home early," she said. He hadn't seen her move and wondered how she knew it was him. "Early start to the cottage?"

He paused. "I know about the transfers of money to your account, Amy." She didn't flinch, but he imagined he heard her suck in a breath.

"What are you talking about?"

"And about your lunch today with Dominic."

"You know I have lunch with him once in a while."

"I don't know anything of the kind."

"You're in denial then. Of course I told you."

Bradley smiled at the red flush growing on Amy's face. "Are you having sex with him?"

Finally, Amy moved, tilting her head toward Bradley and dropping her sunglasses down her nose to eye him. Bradley stared back, holding his smile as he took in a face crinkled with wrath.

"What are you suggesting?"

"What word in that sentence did you not understand?"

"This is crap. I don't need to take this." Amy rose from the chaise, and, grabbing her towel, walked toward the patio door.

"Oh, one other thing, Amy. I stopped in at Maximus on the way over," Bradley said loudly, not caring if a neighbour heard. "That's right, I know about that, too. You're not welcome there anymore, Amy Klein. Date's off for tonight."

Amy walked on, ignoring him, and slammed the patio door behind her. Unperturbed, even a bit amused, Bradley decided to follow. He got to the patio door and through the kitchen quickly. Chasing down the hallway to the front of the house, he found Amy walking up the stairs. The curves of her ass, the rock of her hips, the revealing bikini riding high — he didn't permit them to seduce him as a weaker man might have.

"What's the money for, Amy? You get plenty from me. I mean, sixty thousand alone this morning. You're going to be a great art gallery owner, is that it?"

Amy turned around violently at the top step. "I don't know anything about that. Fucking leave me alone."

Bradley continued to follow her into the master bedroom. "And how did you get into my bank accounts, anyway? You know that's a criminal offence, right? Oh, wait a minute. Your loser brother — he's pretty good with computers. Sometimes he can be a bit useful, right?"

At the far end of the master bedroom, close to the ensuite, Amy yelled behind her, "I said leave me alone! You're scaring me." She hurried into the ensuite, locking the door behind her.

Bradley walked up to within spitting distance of the door. "I changed the passwords, Amy," he yelled. "And I'll be watching. Keep the fucking money, but I'll be watching. And if there is any more shit from you — any at all — I'll see you in divorce court. And I'll make your life hell, you hear me? Utter hell." The shower water came on. "And then you can have sex with other men for a living again. Except at your age, could be slim pickings."

When he perceived sobs, Bradley stopped shouting. But he had one provocation left. Picking up his smartphone, he searched his contacts for the number he wanted, then dialled it. To his surprise, Reggie's dozy voice came on the line.

"Reggie, Peter Bradley," he said, loudly enough for Amy to hear. "There've been some unauthorized transfers from my personal bank account. I may not be able to prove it, but I am deeply suspicious that you're involved in this somehow. I wouldn't be surprised if some of the money has come your way. Anyway, buddy, you are cut off. I'm going to make sure none of my money gets to you ever again. You're done. Go get a job. Be a useful contributor to society." Bradley hung up before Reggie could say anything.

Bradley packed a few things for the cottage. When he was done, he returned to the ensuite door. The shower had stopped running.

"Honey, I'm going to the cottage now. I'll see you soon. Don't miss me too much," he said.

"Fuck off," Amy screamed from the ensuite.

Bradley chuckled all the way out the front door.

CHAPTER 50

Bradley decided to lay a careful trail of his whereabouts over the next sixty hours or so. He had time to spare before he would get the gun. At a hardware store he used his credit card to buy some gear for closing the cottage. Then he went to a large sporting shop and purchased two new paddles for the canoe, which were hard to fit into the M3. Around 5:45 p.m., he located the Pizza Town at Yonge and Fairlawn where Dominic had told him to ask for the manager. Bradley didn't think it was a good idea to buy food there. After emptying his legal briefcase in the trunk of his car, he walked with it to a patisserie on the other side of Fairlawn and had a coffee.

A few minutes after six, Bradley walked into Pizza Town. He wore a T-shirt, jeans and sunglasses; only the briefcase distinguished him from other patrons. When he asked for the manager, a short, slouching man with dishevelled hair and a day-old beard came forward.

"My friend Dominic told me to ask for you."

"Come on into the back," the manager said, not skipping a beat.

They crammed into a tiny office. Reaching into his pocket, the manager found a key and opened the bottom drawer of a small filing cabinet. From deep in the back he carefully withdrew a dirty green towel and casually unwrapped its contents.

"It's a Glock 22, Gen 4, ok?" the manager said. "Nearly new,

looks like. Chambered for the .40 S&W cartridges. Fifteen cartridges right here, ok? You need more, it costs more." He seemed
to recognize that Bradley could have been looking at a water gun.
"It's the gun the cops use," he added.

Bradley swiped his face and licked his lips. "Can you show me
how to load it?"

The manager gave Bradley a surprised look. "I don't really
give lessons, man," he said with a disdainful laugh. "But anyway,
you've got to rotate the gun left or right like so, otherwise the
magazine won't loosen. Press the catch at the bottom of the grip,
then you can pull out the magazine. And then you just press
down the spring loader here and keeping adding bullets until it's
full, then push the magazine up the butt of the grip until you
hear a click. If you want to unload the magazine, do the reverse."

"And to shoot it?"

The manager started to look irritated. "Once you got cartridges in the magazine, hold the gun with one hand, slide the
rail with the other hand, like so, and let it go. You'll hear the first
cartridge load. Then it's ready. Look through the sights then pull
the trigger, ok? Nothing to it. Safety's internal, so there's nothing
to release. Just pull the trigger. You haven't used one?"

"Not this type. Years ago, when I was a kid, I fired a .38."

"Well, pretty different gun. But the basics of shooting are the
same. Remember, once you slide it back, it's loaded and ready to
fire. Got the dough?"

"Can I leave the cartridges in the magazine?"

"It actually has three safety mechanisms, ok? But do you want
to take the chance? Anyway, I got things to do. The cash?"

Bradley reached into a front jeans pocket and handed over a
folded, stuffed white envelope. After counting the contents, the
manager wrapped the gun and cartridges in the green towel and
handed them to Bradley. "Nice doing business with you."

"Will this thing kill a bear?" Bradley asked as he put the gun in his briefcase.

"A bear?" the manager asked, again looking surprised. "Most people use a shotgun for that, man. Up close, sure."

"Good. That's what I need it for."

"Hey man, have a good day. I don't need to know, ok?" he said, nudging Bradley out of the office.

In his car, Bradley moved the green towel and its contents from his briefcase to the bottom of the glove compartment. That was another problem with the M3, he said to himself irritably; the glove compartment was too damn small, with much less space than in his old five series. He covered the towel as best he could with the car manual, a map and some Scotch minis he had for emergencies. After locking the compartment, he took his legal briefcase to the trunk of his car, put the laptop, cord and documents back in, and jammed it among the gear for the cottage.

Ten minutes later Bradley made a point of buying gas close to Highway 401, the first highway on the route to the cottage. But after filling up he turned south on Yonge, back in the direction of downtown. Less than a half hour later, as the sun was poised over the horizon, Bradley parked his car across the intersection from Amato's house.

At 7:00 p.m., punctual as always, Amato burst out of the front door of his house for his evening run. After a few quick stretches of arms and legs, he kicked into his run, crossing the lawn and jumping the hedge. Bradley imagined parking his car Sunday evening in front of the house, and under cover of the setting sun shooting Amato as he bolted off his porch. The thought of him found dead on his front lawn from a bloody bullet wound to the chest had dramatic appeal. But Airdrie was busy and a shot near the house would be far too loud. Bradley needed a better idea.

Once again he followed Amato along Airdrie and south on

Bayview. He kept his eyes open for locations for a drive-by shooting, but everywhere there were parked cars or traffic, and he doubted he could be accurate enough. The more Bradley thought about it, the more the trail down to the abandoned railway track interested him.

On the Bayview S-curve to Nesbitt, Bradley sped ahead and found a spot to pull his car over across from the playground. In the rear-view mirror, he watched Amato turn the corner onto Nesbitt then cross to True Davidson Drive and disappear into the forest. Five minutes later, with twilight beginning, Bradley walked across the playground and looked for the two blue spruces that marked the beginning of the path into the forest. This time he anticipated the street lamps along True Davidson buzzing to life. When they did, the two spruces were easy to see.

Bradley entered the path and went down the six steps after the spruces. At the bottom of the steps he stopped. Once again he noted the earthy smells and humidity around him. But he was more interested in the contours of the path and its surrounding ground, and he continued on. After a few steps another path joined in from the left. The combined paths led to the ridge of the first of the series of undulations to the abandoned railway track. Bradley stood at the precipice of the ridge, observing the severe dip that followed. At the bottom of the dip there were several large trees with thick trunks. And to the right of that there was slanted, even ground covered with low-level green plants.

With budding excitement, Bradley lurched down the dip and stopped at the bottom at the largest tree. He stepped behind its trunk and peered around, looking back up the path. His right forefinger became an ersatz gun, and he aimed and fired at an imaginary Amato hurtling down the steps and along the path. Then he followed with a second fictional shot, guessing that Amato would veer off the path and stumble past him with the force of the first bullet.

But Bradley judged that the tree trunk was too thin to hide him fully. Amato, another runner, or even someone above crossing the True Davidson bridge might see him. Bradley walked a few yards to the slanted ground to the side of the path. He squatted and looked back up toward the path. A clean shot was available. Better yet, he was much harder to see from the path or bridge.

Forty-five minutes later, Bradley took the Yonge on-ramp to Highway 401. As he flung the M3 hard around the corner, he ran through everything he had to do. There was the cottage to close and his plans for Charlie Chaplin to finalize. And all in less than twenty-four hours, so he could scope out the path one more time and get into the office Sunday morning to work on Platz's transaction.

Yes, he had a lot to do, but he had done more in less time before. He felt the same wave of energy that consumed him when a big corporate deal was on. After cranking up "Won't Get Fooled Again" he emitted a noise somewhere between a laugh and a growl and crushed the car's accelerator pedal.

CHAPTER 51

I had my meeting. All I have to do is deliver the money. I'll do that tomorrow night. I was shaking like a leaf through the whole thing. I can't believe I negotiated him down to fifty thousand. I told him that's all I have. I assumed he would tell me it was my problem to get more, but eventually he bought it.

I have never met a person so icy cold and desensitized to life. That may sound odd coming from me, the person "placing the order", so to speak. But I am driven by anger and vengeance. He was driven by nothing except money. I could have been buying a car, it was all the same to him. There was nothing inside him except emotionless calculation. I'm already dreading seeing him again tomorrow evening.

We talked about Sunday. If I get him the money by tomorrow evening, then he will do it Sunday. If it doesn't work out Sunday, then Monday. I had never imagined it so fast. I was planning for the middle of October. I don't mind. I really need to be free of this, and at peace.

I gave him PB's home address, work address and schedules. I told him the Collins, Shaw website, where he can see PB's picture. He's going to do some research now and tell me more tomorrow evening. He said that making it look like an accident — a botched robbery, say — is much harder and asked me if it was really necessary. I insisted on it. I told him I thought a carjacking was best. He didn't like being told what to do. I don't care how he does it; I just want things done properly.

I needed to check, though — I asked him if he'd done this before. He looked at me like I was going to be his victim. "Of course," he said in a clear voice. It could have been someone I went to high school with. "I am a professional. Don't worry — relax."

For a second or two I wanted to know how he does this for a living. What has happened to him that his actions don't bother him? I think he must have seen the questions in my eyes. "People have always killed other people — an eye for an eye, war, tribal terrorism — all that stuff," he said. "We've grown softer over the last century. You still have to do what you need to do to survive, right?" Of course I knew that his history was skewed. I also thought I caught an implication that I'm no different than him. But this is a one-off to right an awful wrong. I'm not a soulless mercenary.

Anyway, he tells me not to worry, but that's impossible. But I'm going to revel in this, too. I am imagining PB up at his cottage, surrounded by the bliss of nature, thinking all is well. Little does he realize what, completely unexpectedly, is going to strike him. He may think he's prepared for everything, so that, as usual, life goes his way. But he's not prepared for this.

CHAPTER 52

It was shortly after 11:00 p.m. when Bradley parked his car in the semi-circle gravel driveway at the front of his cottage near the end of Prior Lane on Otter Lake. Less than an hour earlier, a wall of thunderstorms had passed over, slowing him down. By the time he took the Rankin Lake Road exit just before Parry Sound the storms had cleared, taking with them late September's surprising humidity. Moisture on the branches of large pine trees around the driveway continued to form into large drops at the tips of needles. As they fell, a few made loud, metallic noises on the car, but most landed softly on the gravel or nearby earth. There was no breeze and everything was still.

Bradley unlocked the glove compartment; the green towel with the gun and cartridges lay safe at the bottom. He locked the compartment again, released the trunk from inside, and stepped out. Using the back door onto the lakeside deck that he always left unlocked, he made several trips transporting his briefcase and gear from the car into the cottage. It was a log-house design with a kitchen and small dining area at the back on one side, and the living room on the other. In the kitchen, Bradley dumped everything on a dining table pushed up against one of a series of large windows that overlooked the lake. When he was done he walked through the cottage, turning lights on and off and inspecting that everything was in order. The only light he left on was a lamp hung above the dining table.

Bradley still was not tired. Instead, his mind was alive with a plan that had laid deep roots on the drive to the cottage. He poured himself a large Scotch and stepped onto the deck. Except for a spray of light out the cottage window from the dining table lamp, it was dark, and a sea of stars was breaking through the cloud cover. Bradley sipped as he listened to the peaceful lapping of water against the shore down below.

After a few minutes he returned inside and topped off his drink. He moved most of the gear from the dining table to the kitchen floor and placed his legal briefcase on one of the chairs. After removing his laptop, he turned it on and inserted his USB key. In the Project Pizza folder he opened the document containing a map of Amato's running route and deleted the "to-do" list. Then he began the outline of his plan for his new colleague.

At 2:00 a.m., in the crystal-clear silence of his surroundings, Bradley reread his plan.

Saturday, September 29

- *In cottage bedroom, locate old green tracksuit, track shoes and gym bag; deface tread of track shoes; put everything in trunk of car*

- *In boathouse, locate old tarpaulin with draw strings to move body and remove all fingerprints; also put in trunk of car, in recycling bag*

- *Cover top and bottom of car seat with plastic garbage bags (for fibres)*

- *On drive home, invite Carver and wife over for casual dinner around 5:00 on Sunday*

- *Park near True Davidson Drive (where?); put on tracksuit/ track shoes and pretend I'm jogger; final check of forest path off of True Davidson*

- *Back at car, strip off tracksuit and change shoes; put in gym bag; put on boat shoes I wore to cottage*

- *After, locate spot to dump gym bag with tracksuit and shoes Sunday evening*

- *At some point Saturday evening, bring gym bag into house, and add T-shirt and jeans I wore to cottage.*

Sunday, September 30

- *Go to office*

- *Come home around 5:00; leave car on Gregory as usual*

- *John and Joan arrive for dinner (5:00); serve lots of wine; talk up Carver about Amato*

- *Claim that I have to work on Platz transaction and prepare for board meeting (mark up documents Sunday morning) (6:30)*

- *Run Law Society professional development webcast (6:32)*

- *Change into clothes I wore to cottage (6:37)*

- *Leave house with gym bag (6:40)*

- *Put gym bag in trunk of car (6:42)*

- *Call to Platz (6:43)*

- *Drive off (6:44)*

- *Park car (again, where? how long to drive from Gregory to Nesbitt?) (6:50)*

- *Put on tracksuit overtop clothing; put on track shoes and leave boat shoes in gym bag (6:52)*

- *Enter forest path east side of True Davidson Drive at two spruces and take position fifteen yards in, below ridge, to the right on ground (7:00)*

- *Two shots at Amato as he comes down path, when he's past steps and near ridge (7:05 but need to confirm)*

- *Make sure he is dead; remove personal belongings to suggest robbery; wrap body in tarpaulin (7:10)*

- *Cover area where he falls to hide any blood (7:12)*

- *Carry/drag body (to where? Also, how to avoid getting blood on me?) (7:22)*

- *Wipe gun clean of prints and dispose (where?) (7:25)*

- *At car, strip off tracksuit/shoes; put in gym bag; put on boat shoes (7:35)*

- *Driving home, dump gym bag (where?); arrive home, park on Gregory as usual (7:45 but need to confirm); dispose of plastic garbage bags on car seat*

- *Sneak back into study; shower; return to party (8:00)*

- *After dinner party, send email to Collins/Abrams/Amato with more revenue ideas*

- *Monday, dispose of clothes I had under tracksuit (where?); have monthly car detailing done.*

Bradley sat back. He was relatively satisfied with his work, but there were problems. The whole plan took too long and needed tightening up. He wondered if it was necessary to move Amato's body, and if so, what distance his strength would allow him to cover. And he had watched enough crime movies to know that he could not leave any trace of himself behind, whether fingerprints, fibres or gun residue. His plan went to great pains to avoid that, but he needed more careful review to be sure.

At the top of the document his eyes fell on the map of Amato's running route that he had downloaded Thursday night. A blip of panic coursed through him as he realized that the map, as well as Monday evening's research, had left an electronic trace of his interest in Amato. After some thought he reasoned that the map covered enough area for him to say that he had merely wanted to know where Amato lived relative to him and that the other research was natural curiosity about a new partner. Still, it had been a mistake. "You've *got* to be more careful," he muttered. "You've handled much more complicated things at the office. Stay on your game."

Finally feeling fatigue under his eyes, Bradley turned off the dining table lamp and in the dark worked his way down the small hall to the master bedroom. After setting the alarm on his watch for 7:00 a.m., he fell into bed. The last thing he thought of before falling deep asleep was the admonition of the pizza shop manager: "Remember, once you slide it back, it's loaded and ready to fire."

CHAPTER 53

The morning light was gaining strength when Bradley's alarm went off. As he awoke, he lay on his back with his eyes closed and thought how nice it was going to be to have his usual Saturday morning coffee and newspaper read at Café Sorrento. Then he allowed his eyes to open and remembered his drive to the cottage, and the enormity of the events he had planned.

Bradley jumped out of bed. After putting on the same clothes he'd arrived in, he added a sweater from an old cedar chest of drawers. He reviewed what he had to do that day: close the cottage; let himself be seen in the area; collect together the things he needed for his plan; and, before 6:00 p.m., complete the three-hour drive back to True Davidson Drive so he could survey the path one last time. And one other important thing: a little shooting practice.

Ignoring breakfast, Bradley started preparing the cottage for winter. Any food that could spoil was put in the garbage or into containers to take home. After unplugging all electrical devices, he protected everything mice might use for food or nesting. He grunted and groaned through draining the water system.

Around nine, when he thought it wasn't too early, he wandered over to see if any of his Otter Lake neighbours were up for the weekend. None had made the trip. To make his presence known, he decided to drive into Parry Sound. In the sunny and crisp day with the vaguely rotten smells of early fall fanned by a brisk breeze, Bradley made the trip in less than fifteen minutes. At an all-purpose service station he filled the voracious M3 with gas and bought coffee and brunch, paying with his debit card and making sure he had an engaging chat with the proprietor.

Returning to the cottage, Bradley pulled his car to a stop in the front driveway under the swaying pines. He unlocked the glove compartment and eased the bundle in the green towel into the plastic bag with the coffee and brunch. Inside the cottage he carefully withdrew the bundle and placed it on the dining table next to his laptop. After rushing through the coffee and brunch, he licked his lips and pulled both hands down his face. Then, slowly, he unfolded the towel.

The unloaded Glock 22 lay on its side. It looked more like a child's plaything than a real weapon. Grey-black, with a stamp that said "Austria", it was about two hundred millimetres long. The barrelling was smooth and rectangular, with a front and back sight. The grip had a stippled surface on all four sides and grooves for three fingers on the front strap.

Gingerly, Bradley picked up the gun, letting it lie in the palm of his hand, and, with a bobbing motion, assessed its weight. Next to the dining table, looking toward the lake, he assumed the shooting stance he'd learned as a boy at Camp Massassauga. He held the gun in his outstretched right hand and steadied it with his left. Spying a red-tail squirrel, upright and motionless on a rock halfway down to the lake, he lined up the white dot in the far sight of the gun with the U-shaped front sight. His right forefinger curled around the trigger and yielded three clicks with three firm tugs. Each time an imaginary bullet blew the squirrel off the rock.

Like the pizza shop manager had shown him, Bradley released the magazine, inserted the fifteen cartridges, and shoved the magazine back up the body of the Glock's grip. Then he popped the magazine back out, unloaded it, and repeated the entire exercise enough times that it began to feel like second nature. With the magazine loaded, he stroked the barrel. Like the evening before, the manager's words returned: "Remember, once you slide it back, it's loaded and ready to fire." Carefully, he set the gun down on the dining table.

Bradley went to the master bedroom. He changed into ancient underwear and jeans he found in the cedar chest of drawers. Then he slipped into an old pair of boat shoes and a windbreaker he located in the closet. Returning to the kitchen, he zipped the gun into the right pocket of the breaker.

He exited the lakeside deck door and walked down a series of landscaped rock steps to the boathouse. When he opened the boathouse door his eyes first went to a sleek, large white motorboat with an oversized engine in front of him, lightly rising and dipping in the lake waves. But instead he crossed over to the other side of the boathouse, and ignoring lifejackets hanging on a wall, lurched into a neighbouring aluminum outboard. After snapping the engine's cord he reversed the boat out of the boathouse through clouds of blue exhaust. Then he jammed the rudder hard left, blew open the throttle, and began bouncing the boat hard into the wind and over small whitecaps toward Snake Island.

It was a twenty-minute ride to the small, uninhabited island. On the way Bradley saw only two other boats, but he made sure their owners responded to his fervent waving. Once there, he circled the island, looking for signs of other visitors. When he didn't see any he veered the boat sharply toward sand in a crevice between two bulges of granite. Ten feet from the tiny beach Bradley cut the motor and let the boat drift until its bow scratched to a stop.

He heaved himself onto one of the bulges of granite and pulled the boat as far onto the beach as he could. Though he'd bought his cottage ten years before, it was only his second visit to Snake Island. In a sea of tall pines interspersed with birch in the centre of the island, he remembered a clearing. Sure enough, after following a faint path for less than a hundred steps, the trees parted to reveal a large mound of lichen-covered granite.

At the top of the mound Bradley made two 360-degree turns to ensure he was alone. At one end, no more than ten yards away, someone had built an inukshuk among loose rock. Wanting to ensure that he kept track of empty casings, Bradley allotted himself three practice shots. With his right hand he took the gun out of his breaker, and then with his left deliberately pulled back the slide of the barrel to load the first cartridge into the gun's chamber. Gingerly he lowered himself to the granite rock and propped himself in the prone position with his two elbows. He felt the stipples and finger grooves of the gun's grip in his right hand and used his left hand as a cradle. Licking his dry lips, his right forefinger began to tease the trigger. He lowered his head slightly, locating the inukshuk in the gun's sights with his right eye while pressing the left shut. As he summoned his maximum concentration, the tip of his tongue dangled out the left corner of his mouth.

Bradley increased the pressure on the trigger, but it did not yield. For several seconds he lost his nerve, and releasing his forefinger, he rearranged his body for greater comfort. Then he steadied himself and found the trigger again. His hands felt clammy, but he was intent on firing. Harder and harder, he pulled on the trigger until he felt some give. Through the sights, as beads of sweat pearled on his brow, his right eye stayed steady on the sculpture. He imagined having to pull harder, when, unexpectedly, the gun cracked, emitting a flash of orange flame, and recoiled. Bradley had no idea where the shot had gone, but a small cloud of dust hovered to the left of the inukshuk. "Got to be better than that Sunday," he muttered. "*Much* better."

His ears ringing, Bradley took careful aim again. With a better feel for the trigger action, his sole objective became hitting his target. After a few seconds the gun cracked again, and looking up, he saw the inukshuk's centre blown out, then the sculpture collapse in on itself. Several boulders to the right, something slithered away. Hastily, he lined up the gun's sights and shot. The bullet caromed somewhere into the distance. Bradley got up and ran over in search of a victim to hold up in triumph. He found nothing, and, disappointed, turned his attention to the inukshuk's remains. With a chuckle he kicked a few of the strewn rocks. Once again quite satisfied with himself, Bradley found the three cartridge casings and sauntered back to his boat. After throwing the casings far into the water, he made good time to the cottage with the wind at his back.

Bradley knew that the practice shots had left gun residue on his hands and clothes. On the deck to the side of the boathouse he stripped down to nothing and in a neighbouring storage shed found an old hunk of soap. Light shivers became shudders as he eased his flaccid body down a ladder into the cold lake water. After soaping himself in wild thrashing motions, he bolted back out of the water, removed the gun from the breaker, and ran naked up to the cottage.

Inside, he carefully placed the gun on the dining table. Then, in the master bedroom, he toweled off, and put on the T-shirt, jeans and boat shoes in which he'd arrived, and the sweater he'd found in the cedar chest of drawers that morning.

On the floor at the back of a closet, he found a dusty leather gym bag. Inside were a vintage dark green tracksuit and a pair of stiff track shoes imagined for cottage workouts. He'd added pounds since buying the tracksuit but he guessed it would still fit. He stuffed it back in the bag along with an old Green Bay Packers cap from the top of the closet.

Bradley walked with the track shoes back down to the shed next to the boathouse. He found a rusty shaving tool and carved

down the tread on the shoes until he was sure they were uniden-
tifiable. After brushing the filings into the water, he heaved the
tool as far out into Otter Lake as he could.

In the shed he also located an old pair of yard gloves, two
clear plastic bags for recycling garden debris and a tarpaulin with
draw strings. With the yard gloves on, he opened one recycling
bag and employed a small spade to deposit the breaker, the old
pair of boat shoes and other clothing he'd worn to Snake Island.
Bradley's mother had bought the tarpaulin years before for fall
leaf collection, and he'd taken it to the cottage for the same purpose. With lake water and an old broom, he scrubbed it hard to
remove fingerprints. Then, with the yard gloves still on, he folded the tarpaulin, put it in the second recycling bag and walked
the track shoes and two recycling bags to the cottage. With the
shoes back in the gym bag, he put everything in the M3's trunk.

Nearing the end of his tasks, Bradley winterized the engine
and fuel lines of both boats then covered and lifted them with
mechanical hoists out of the water. He added food containers
and bags of garbage from the cottage to the car trunk. In the cottage kitchen he found two large green garbage bags, and spread
one over the bottom of the driver's seat and one over its reclining
portion. Lastly, he balanced his briefcase with his laptop inside
on the passenger seat.

Only the Glock was left to take care of. He removed the unused cartridges from the magazine, laid out the green towel on
the dining table and placed the gun and cartridges on top. Carefully, he folded together the edges of the towel. After checking
each room of the cottage to make sure he hadn't left anything
behind, with the towel in his right hand he left the cottage by
the lakeside deck door.

The afternoon had become warm and the wind blew steadily.
Bradley stopped on the deck to suck in the early fall air. Then he
walked to his car and returned the green towel to the bottom of

the glove compartment. His watch showed it was only two thirty, plenty of time to get back to True Davidson Drive before six.

First, however, to register his location and to begin false détente, he wanted to call Amy. He considered what to say and how to find a pacifying tone. Clearing his throat among the pine trees, he said out loud, "Hi, it's me. How's everything going?" Too casual. "Hello dear, how are you? We need to talk." Obviously fake. "How are John and Dominic? And your friends at Maximus?" Tempting, but unhelpful.

He placed the call. Amy picked up but didn't greet him.

"Hi, Amy," Bradley said. Still nothing. He soldiered on. "So, I'll be leaving the cottage in an hour and a half. Nearly finished closing it. I guess I'll be home around seven thirty."

At least she didn't hang up. After tightening his jaw muscles Bradley managed a conciliatory sigh and said, "I'm sorry about what I said to you yesterday afternoon. I hope you'll be there when I get home."

He wondered if he needed to extend another olive branch, but Amy eventually spoke up. "Just so you know, I've pretty much stopped caring, Peter."

Bradley began to pace over pine needles and soft earth. "Well, I don't want that. There's been a lot of — of client pressure at work."

"If you didn't want me to stop caring, you should have paid some attention to me. Some *positive* attention."

Wincing at the beating, Bradley said, "Let's take some vacation. End of October? What do you think?"

"And maybe to my brother, as well."

Bradley nearly gagged. "What do you think about a vacation?"

"Like I said Peter, I've stopped caring."

"I'm serious about this. We'll rent a place in Tuscany for two weeks. Collins and his wife were just there and loved it."

"Whatever, Peter."

"And I had another idea. Let's have John Carver and his wife over for dinner tomorrow evening."

"Tomorrow?"

"Yes. I'll be home from the office around five. They can come over then."

"I have plans, actually."

"Plans?"

"But it might be a good idea. I like John."

Another beating. "Sure, did you want to call Joan? It'll be good to have some fun for a change. I may have to cut out a little while for a deal I'm working on, but after eight or so, I can rejoin and we can have a late dinner."

"You call him. He's your friend."

"So, it's ok then?"

"Sure. I don't care."

"All right, I'll call and let you know. See you at seven thirty."

Bradley tried Carver but had to leave a message. In his car, he accustomed himself to the slipperiness of the plastic bags on the driver's seat, then drove out the driveway and down Prior Lane. At Blue Lake Road, he turned left and went to the local bear-proof recycling and garbage bins. He deposited the recycling bag with the clothing he'd used for Snake Island and the bags of garbage from the cottage.

As he finished, he remembered Amy's comment about her brother. "Pay positive attention to Reggie? She's got to be fucking kidding." Bradley roared north on Blue Lake Road, bound for Rankin Lake Road and Highway 400, telling himself they'd find the three empty cartridge casings in Otter Lake before that happened.

CHAPTER 54

After the call with her husband, Amy looked around her brother's forlorn wreck of a condo and muttered to herself, "I'm surrounded by crazy people."

"What did you say?" Reggie asked anxiously.

Curling some hair between her fingertips, Amy ignored the question. Her brother looked sallow and unkempt. "We have to get some fresh air in here," she said.

She worked her way through discarded clothes on the floor to the balcony and heaved the sliding door open a few inches. The rush of traffic from the Gardiner Expressway filled the tiny condo.

"Peter doesn't give a shit about me," Reggie blurted. "I know that guy. That's why I had to do it."

Amy returned to her perch at the end of Reggie's sofa bed. Reggie sat on the swivel chair in front of his digital audio workstation. Nervously, he rotated back and forth on the chair, sometimes eying his sister, but most times finding something else, anything else, to focus on.

Amy looked at her brother pityingly. "You *had* to break into my house yesterday morning, and you *had* to transfer sixty thousand."

"You left the back door open."

"You're right, I'm responsible," Amy said. "That sixty thousand screwed everything up, Reggie. How do I explain it to Peter? Or the other transfers? There's a limit how much I can manipulate him, you know. And recently, it hasn't been very much." She paused. "Reggie, do we need to get you help? Do we?"

"What do you mean?"

"I keep pretending everything will be ok with you, but — but it doesn't get better. You still have no direction, you're still up and down like a kite, you still cut. I had to find you here — *again*. So what if things went badly Thursday? Shit happens." Amy looked at her brother for a response. "What am I supposed to do? Just tell me that. Is it time to take you back to the hospital?"

"You said we'd never do that again. We agreed."

"But what am I supposed to do? *What?*"

Reggie turned the swivel chair and looked disconsolately out the balcony window. "I'm gonna be fine. I'm gonna find my way."

"It took the asshole master and ruler all of two hours to figure out the transfers. You've seriously screwed things up for me, Reggie — very seriously."

"I'm not sick. I need time. I need some money."

"Is that why you transferred the money?" Reggie stayed silent. "Did Dominic call you? He said he has someone new for you to interview."

"I don't need to do that anymore. I've got everything figured out."

"Then just stay away for a while, Reggie. I need space right now. I've got things to do. And when you start doing these — these crazy things, it just — just fucks everything up."

"It's not crazy, Amy," Reggie said. For the first time he stopped moving his chair and looked hard at his sister. "I told you everything's about payoffs. Remember?"

"Vaguely. Seriously, what the hell are you talking about?"

"Give me the sixty thousand. Pay me off, Amy, and I'll leave you alone — forever."

Amy rolled her eyes and sighed heavily. "Oh for Christ's sake. I don't want to be left alone forever. Just for a little while."

"No, it should be forever. These guys, Peter, Dominic, everyone who stares at you. They're the ones you should be paying attention to."

"They're just men. Dime a dozen."

"Not Peter. It hasn't been the same since him. I'm a pain in the ass. Let me go. Give me the cash, and let me go."

"No, the cash is going back to Peter. You're not getting it. And I already have what I need."

"Give it to me, Amy — and let me go. It's all figured out. Don't worry."

"I always worry about you. Except right now I don't have time."

Reggie turned back toward the balcony, away from Amy's piercing eyes. "Then I just don't know what I'm going to do."

"Why don't you fucking go to work?" Amy asked shrilly.

Reggie stroked the skin under his left eye. The swelling was gone. "I missed the Friday afternoon shift. They fired me."

CHAPTER 55

An hour and a half into Bradley's drive home from the cottage, Carver called back. Bradley let the call go to voicemail then checked the message. Sounding fatigued, Carver accepted the invitation for dinner Sunday evening, provided no one talked politics. Bradley called Amy to let her know the plans were set; she did not pick up.

Close to six, Bradley had finished battling heavy traffic on Highway 401 and Yonge Street and was heading south on Mount Pleasant. At Whitehall Road, he turned left, and two short blocks later was at Gregory. His first order of business was timing the drive from his home on the west side of North Rosedale to Nesbitt on the east. He set the stopwatch feature on his Rolex, then drove to the end of Whitehall and found his way east along Summerhill Avenue.

At Astley Avenue he started across Governor's Bridge. He reached a roundabout for Nesbitt, Governor's Road and Douglas Crescent. After a half-turn through the roundabout, Bradley slowly drove straight along Governor's Road and pulled his car into a parking spot at the end. Diagonally to his left was the playground on Nesbitt and further east True Davidson Drive and the patch of forest. On both sides of his car there were houses with lush gardens that offered some cover. It was a perfect spot to park his car, Bradley thought. The Rolex told him the drive from Gregory had taken just under five minutes.

Bradley checked for pedestrians and saw none. He popped open the trunk of his car and got out. As he unzipped the gym bag, he stepped out of his boat shoes. Arduously, he pulled the tracksuit pants over his jeans; after some stretching, the jacket fit quite well over his sweater. He dropped the track shoes to the ground, stuffed his feet inside and laced them up. With a hard tug he put on the Packers cap, and after stuffing the boat shoes in the gym bag, he gently closed the trunk.

At the passenger side of his car, as discreetly as possible, Bradley leaned into the car and removed the unloaded gun from the towel in the glove compartment. Hurriedly, he stuffed it in the side pocket of his tracksuit. From here on in, he told himself, the key was to act like a jogger, a role no one would associate with him. After a few surprisingly painful stretches and twists, Bradley loped off like a shot animal across the playground to True Davidson Drive.

On the other side of True Davidson, he easily found the two spruces that marked the path into the forest. He pushed in like a seasoned runner trying to keep his pace. Behind the spruces, just before the steps down, he stopped and, slumped over at the waist, hands on knees, he tried to catch his breath. Half a minute later, with slightly wobbly legs, he went down the steps onto the dirt path. The ground was mostly dry despite the previous night's rain. When he reached the ridge of the large dip, he paused then spilled down. At the bottom he checked the path both ways to ensure he was alone and headed right toward the slanted ground that he'd scouted the evening before.

After studying the angles for two shots, Bradley concluded again that the location was ideal. He stood, and as he found more normal breathing, carefully assessed whether it was worth moving the body, and to where. Amato might be lean and mean, weighing maybe one hundred sixty pounds, but after the agonizing thirty-second run from Governor's Road, Bradley doubted he could move him far.

Two female voices emerged near the spruces. Bradley threw himself to the ground and held his head down. Amidst conversation about what he said and she said, running feet pattered by. After a few moments Bradley looked up; the joggers were heading down the undulating path toward the abandoned railway track. The low-level green plants around him had protected him, but Amato's body, closer to the path without similar cover, would be seen. Bradley resolved to roll the body into the tarpaulin, pull the drawstrings tight and carry or drag it farther from the path. After standing up and wiping debris off his tracksuit, he went in search of a place to toss the body.

Returning to the path, Bradley headed down to the railway track. Rather than walk east where police might look for Amato, he walked west under the True Davidson bridge. To his left, a sharp crevice marked the beginning of a deepening ravine. He knew it was one of several formed by creeks that ran into the Don River as it wound through Crothers Woods. Houses in the new subdivision were perched on the other side, but foliage obscured their view of the bottom of the ravine and track. Bradley's mind kicked into overdrive with the possibilities.

He continued a short distance in the slanted light of early evening. To his surprise an abandoned road appeared. From the track it declined steeply down the west side of the ravine. Bradley guessed it was an old service road for rusted signal equipment at the side of the track. Its remaining asphalt had deep cracks with weeds and was covered with fallen branches. Bradley walked down. A simple toss of Amato's body deep into the ravine to the left of the road might work well.

Then Bradley heard a trickle of water and continued down the road a few more steps. He stumbled upon four rusting horizontal metal plates in the centre of the road, and the outline of a subterranean metal box to which three plates were chained and locked. The sound of water came from underneath the plates and continued toward the ravine. He followed it to an old sewer installation above the ravine from which a tiny, steady stream of water fell.

Bradley returned to the metal plates. The fourth one, closest to the track, was partly covered by earth and debris, and was unlocked. Bradley kicked away dirt until the entire plate was exposed. He leaned over and with the sleeve of his tracksuit jacket pulled over his hand gave several hard heaves until the plate groaned open. His eyes took several seconds to adjust to the darkness inside the box. But then, more than a yard down, Bradley saw water trickling in the direction of the sewer. It was a perfect spot to stuff a body.

Flush with his find, Bradley let the metal plate fall shut and redistributed the debris he'd pushed aside. He returned to the railway track and then the path, stopping where he guessed Amato would fall after being shot. He'd counted out fewer than three hundred steps. It would be a heroic effort, but with the tarpaulin drawn tightly together, he was sure he could move the body to the metal plates. Then he would only need to lift the unlocked plate and let the body fall in. It would be worth it, he counselled himself. No one would know where on his running route Amato had disappeared, and moving his body would delay its discovery by many hours. Bradley would have all the time he needed to cover his tracks and resume his usual pattern of life.

He checked his watch. It was nearly seven and Amato was about to leave his house. Bradley walked over to the slanted ground to the side of the path and, after taking the Glock out of the pocket of his tracksuit, he dropped himself into a prone position. The sun was on the cusp of setting, and there was a lull in the forest.

Bradley kept a careful eye on his Rolex: 7:02, and Amato had already run along Airdrie; 7:03, and he was beginning the S-curve down Bayview; 7:04, and he would soon pass under the train bridge, then run right on Nesbitt, and left on True Davidson.

The Rolex flipped past 7:05. Bradley lowered his head a bit more and waited, steadying his grip on the Glock with his left hand. He braced himself, letting his tongue dangle out the side of his mouth. Without warning, Amato punched through the two spruces. Breathing heavily and closely watching his feet, he charged down the steps onto the dirt path. As best he could, surprised at how quickly Amato moved, Bradley lined him up in the two gun sights. When Amato reached the ridge of the large dip, Bradley pulled the trigger of the unloaded gun and, hearing it click, he guessed he would have connected. In a flash Amato was down the dip, pressing further along the path toward the railway track. Bradley curled on his side and took a second mock shot at Amato's receding back. Another hit, he told himself. Seconds later Amato became invisible. Bradley looked at his watch; it was 7:06.

A few minutes later, as twilight moved in, Bradley stood and stretched. After brushing off his torso, he returned the gun to the pocket of his tracksuit. At the two spruces he resumed a painful jog to his car. Once there, he opened the passenger door and snuck the gun into the green towel in the glove compartment. Then he opened the trunk and quickly pulled off the tracksuit and shoes, put them with the Packers cap in the gym bag and changed back into his boat shoes. Closing the trunk with the gym bag inside, he got into the driver's seat. He wiped sweat from his face with the bottom of his T-shirt then ran a comb through his damp hair. Slowly, his heart settled back to normal pace.

Bradley sat still in his car and asked himself if he was ready. He replayed Collins' actions and Amato's unwelcome presence in his mind, and the same feelings of unsolicited menace and need to assert his pre-eminence swelled up. Fortunately, like the last pieces of a puzzle, the details of his plan of ruin were fitting together nicely, as if the plan had been predetermined. He felt in command, relying on his great gift for finding solutions, however unorthodox, to difficult situations.

Yet, a few qualms flitted through his gut. He drilled down to understand them. Closest to the top was a concern that he was a natural suspect, but he was sure he wasn't. No one would conceive of his plan to exact revenge and protect his success because they hadn't been there for his emasculation at his father's hands. Instead the world would be diverted by his efforts, apparent through the weekend, to reconcile with his beautiful back-stabbing wife.

And a bit farther down there was a tension about being caught and handing over his freedom, however unlikely it was that the police would see through his crafty plan. Years before, hurrying along Clare's end by tampering with her medication, he'd felt a similar qualm. But he'd understood then, too, that his action was justifiable, aimed, as it had been, at saving her pain. Qualms were nature's way of ensuring that he had thought everything through. Softly, but distinctly, Bradley said, "It seems to me the die is cast." He started his car, eased out of the parking spot and found his way back to Governor's Bridge.

It was nearly dark as Bradley returned along Summerhill toward Gregory. He still had to figure out where, in twenty-four hours, he would dump the gun and the gym bag with the tracksuit, shoes and cap. He thought about waiting until Monday morning and finding somewhere downtown, but that created an unnecessary exposure. Bradley passed the fruit market where he'd found the pay phone to call Dominic Thursday evening. Just beyond there was a sewer grate in the road. Sunday evening, it would be straightforward to pull over and drop the gun between the grate's bars. As for the gym bag, only a few hundred yards farther west Bradley remembered a mind-boggling renovation of a house on Whitehall, the backyard of which faced Summerhill. He drove by slowly. Several dumpsters crowded the outer perimeter of the backyard, and one, overflowing with sheets of broken drywall, was sure to be emptied Monday. He would squeeze the bag down the side of the dumpster to the bottom.

Twenty minutes later, his hands full of food containers, other gear from the cottage and his briefcase, Bradley struggled to the front door of his house. Inside, he called out Amy's name. There was no response. On the side table in the hallway he found a note that said she'd gone to see her brother.

A short while later Bradley had put the clothing he'd worn to the cottage in a dry cleaner's bag and taken a shower. He went to his study, where he pulled the laptop out of his briefcase onto his desk and inserted the USB stick. In the Project Pizza folder, he opened the document with the outline of his plan. After deleting all the entries for that day, he updated Sunday's entries, with his own version of the underlining used by law offices to show changes in legal documents.

Sunday, September 30

- *Go to office _in morning (gym bag and tarpaulin left in car Saturday)_*

- *Come home around 5:00; leave car on Gregory as usual*

- *John and Joan arrive for dinner (5:00); serve lots of wine; talk up Carver about Amato*

- *Claim that I have to work on Platz transaction and prepare for board meeting (mark up documents Sunday morning) (6:30)*

- *Run Law Society professional development webcast (6:32)*

- *Change into clothes I wore to cottage (6:35)*

- *Leave house <u>and get into car</u> (6:<u>38</u>)*

- *Call to Platz (6:<u>39</u>)*

- *<u>Load gun</u> (6:<u>42</u>)*

- *Drive <u>to Governor's Road (start 6:<u>45</u>)</u>*

- *Park car <u>east end of Governor's Road</u> (6:50)*

- *Put on tracksuit overtop clothing; put on track shoes and leave boat shoes in gym bag; <u>add gun to tracksuit pocket; start jog-ging with recycling bag containing tarpaulin</u> (6:<u>53</u>)*

- *Enter forest path east side of True Davidson Drive at two spruces and take position fifteen yards in, below ridge, to the right on ground (<u>6:56</u>)*

- *Two shots at Amato as he comes down path, when he's past steps and near ridge (7:05:<u>30</u>)*

- *Make sure he is dead; <u>put gun back in tracksuit pocket;</u> remove personal belongings to suggest robbery; wrap body in tarpau-lin; <u>put my hands inside plastic recycling bag to avoid prints on tarpaulin</u> (7:10)*

- *Cover area where he falls to hide any blood (7:1<u>3</u>)*

- *Carry/drag body <u>to metal box on old road at side of abandoned railway track</u> (7:2<u>0</u>)*

- *<u>Jog back to</u> car; <u>put gun in towel in glove compartment;</u> strip off tracksuit/shoes; put in gym bag; <u>add recycling bag from tar-paulin;</u> put on boat shoes (7:<u>30</u>)*

- *Driv<u>e</u> home; <u>dump gun and Amato's personal belongings through sewer near fruit market; dump gym bag <u>in dumpster off of Summerhill;</u></u> arrive home, park on Gregory as usual (7:4<u>0</u>); dispose of plastic garbage bags on car seat*

- *Sneak back into study; shower; return to party (<u>7:55</u>)*

- *After dinner party, send email to Collins/Abrams/Amato with more revenue ideas <u>and throw away USB stick</u>*

- *Monday, dispose of clothes I had under tracksuit (where?); have monthly car detailing done.*

Bradley congratulated himself on his work. There was only one question: what to do with the T-shirt, jeans and boat shoes he'd worn to the cottage. He'd pulled the tracksuit over the T-shirt and jeans that evening, and would again Sunday evening. The tracksuit would end up in the dumpster inside the gym bag, but he didn't want any clothing with residual fibres lying about.

His ruminations were overtaken by the sound of the front door opening. A few seconds later stiletto heels walked down the hallway to the kitchen. Bradley saved his work and shut down the laptop. Glancing at the bust of Caesar on the coffee table, he whispered, "Yes indeed, the die is cast." Then he went to find Amy and begin the solicitudes necessary to regain her affections.

CHAPTER 56

I've done it. I handed over the money, and it will happen Sunday evening — Monday evening at the latest. That's all I know, and that it will look like some other type of crime.

Sunday evening. I asked him to make sure no one else gets hurt. "Do you think I'm an idiot?" he asked me, very irritated. He could use some customer service skills.

Of course, part of me wants to know the exact when, where and how. Whether he intended to or not, he answered that question. "Don't even ask for more details," he said. "I never give them. And you'll never see me again. Got it? You'll never see me again."

It shook me when he said that last sentence. At first I thought he meant he would make sure our paths would never cross again. Then I realized it was a warning to stay away. Actually, more like a threat.

At that point I just wanted to get out, but I hung around a bit longer to make sure everything was taken care of. He got even more irritated. "I never met anybody who stared at me so much. You're creeping me out." Then he kind of laughed at me and said, "If you're looking for my soul, I sold it a long time ago. It's not there." Great, I thought, now you're getting philosophical. *I felt like telling him not to bother. But I just stayed quiet.*

I started to leave but wanted to ask him, how could I be certain he wasn't just going to steal my money?

But he said, "This is it. Are you doing this?"

That comforted me. I said yes.

So now I'm going to delete this file, smash the hard drive it's on and bury the resentments of the past. In less than twenty-four hours, I will have freedom. At long last. I can't believe it.

CHAPTER 57

On Sunday morning, Bradley awoke with an instant stab of anticipation. Though it energized him, at the same time it distracted him. On the quiet drive to the office, despite the bright, clear September weather, he nearly missed a red light. When he stopped for coffee and a doughnut, he forgot to ask for regular and was handed a black. And at his office he found some of the documents Platz had given him were missing from his briefcase, and he had to print them fresh.

Behind his desk, Bradley told himself it was time to bear down and summon every ounce of focus. Platz wanted the competition law analysis of his transaction by the end of Monday, and because he was such a rainmaker, Bradley had decided to do most of the work himself. Despite his internal urgings, his mind flitted again and again to the day's key events: meet Anand and Murphy on Platz's file at two; leave the office at four; greet Carver and his wife at five. Then an hour and a half of careful partying, for which he already wore pressed pants, a shirt and a jacket, and finally into action. The minutes ticked by slowly.

At midday Bradley conceded that his best professional work was MIA. He conceived of a different way to ensure Platz got his work on time. He would ask Anand to prepare an initial analysis, which he would mark up the next day. Anand, who already was falling behind on other work, would likely resent the demand, but Bradley didn't care. If he needed to, Anand could ask Murphy for support. To distract himself, Bradley printed up materials for his upcoming board of directors' meeting. As he'd planned, he flipped through the pages and scratched a few comments here and there. At the top of the first page he wrote "Reviewed September 30, 2012 @ 7:15 p.m." then added the board materials to his briefcase.

Bradley left his office and walked down the hall. A few other lawyers were at their desks, and he chatted casually with each. Every time, it was the usual one-upmanship about who was carrying the toughest workload.

Soon he passed by Amato's office. The door was shut, but checking the hall both ways, Bradley pushed it open and went in. Instantly, he knew he was showing far too much interest in Amato; he told himself to leave but couldn't resist a quick scan. For a person whose first day had been Thursday, Amato had done a lot of personal decorating. Furniture had been repositioned, art and university degrees hung, and a few small running trophies crowded onto a side table. And then the ubiquitous family pictures, all framed, some on the walls, others in one kind of stand or another. Bradley glanced at each one. Everyone was clutching another family member. The children seemed happy but Amato's wife, Maria, looked dour, as if sentenced to a personal hell. "What a fucking fraud that guy is," Bradley snorted and stole out of the office.

Bradley was at a loss what to do. He wasn't used to watching time pass. He found a place to buy a sandwich and returned to his office to eat it in silence, waiting for Anand and Murphy. Twice he closed the door and lay prone on the floor, practicing his shooting position.

Anand and Murphy showed at the appointed 2:00 p.m. time. Anand, in slacks, a shirt and a zip-up cardigan, looked sharp as usual; Murphy had on a plain blouse, a colourful sweater and tight jeans. After a few muted greetings, the three took their usual places at the oval meeting table. The air in Bradley's office was heavy and expectant.

Documents were dropped in the middle of the table; Anand and Murphy's laptops were positioned and launched; smartphones lay at everyone's ready. Anand released a long yawn, remembering at the last second to cover his mouth. It initiated a similar urge in Murphy, but she was more successful in suppressing the yawn. Impatiently, Bradley looked back and forth between his colleagues, drumming his fingers on the table. "Are we ready?" he asked.

"Apologies," Anand said. He paused and stared quite hard at Bradley. "The baby is colicky again. The usual story."

"How much sleep is Anita getting?" Murphy asked.

"About Platz's transaction —" Bradley started.

"Not much. And neither am I," Anand said, not releasing his eyes from Bradley.

"About Platz's transaction, this is what I thought we should do. Unfortunately, this evening we're having a dinner party, and I have a board meeting to prepare for."

"You're still on a board?" Anand asked.

Bradley tried to hide his irritation. "It's just a private company. Been doing it for years; cleared with the Management Committee. Anyway, we need to understand Platz's transaction. It's one of these pain-in-the-ass deals to get at tax losses and I'm not even sure it's a merger. But if it is, then we have to see if the thresholds for notification to the Bureau are met. They may be, but I won't have time to do the analysis thoroughly." Bradley returned Anand's stare. "Platz wants the memo for the end of tomorrow."

With an involuntary tinge of sarcasm, Anand said, "I'd be happy to help out."

"I need a draft of the memo for late tomorrow morning,"

Bradley said without skipping a beat. "You know the precedents."

"Walter, do you want me to take a first crack?" Murphy asked. "You look like you should be taking a nap."

Anand laughed. "That bad, is it? I should say I feel fine and do the memo this afternoon. Right, Peter?"

Bradley looked a bit startled.

"I don't mind, Walter," Murphy said.

"Do whatever works for you, Walter," Bradley added curtly. "I just need it by noon tomorrow."

Anand paused, curling his lips. "Carolyn, if you send me something for first thing tomorrow, I'll come in early and look at it."

"Sure."

"Platz sent me these documents," Bradley said, pointing to the stack in the middle of the table. "We should take a little time and go through them, just to make sure we're on the right track."

"Conveniently, he sent me copies, too," Anand said. "They're in my office." Wearily, he got up and went to get them.

When Anand was out of earshot, Bradley looked at Murphy and asked, "What's his problem?"

She stared back, uncomprehendingly. "You don't know?"

"No."

"Partnership and a colicky child."

Bradley smirked and shook his head. "Sometimes you just have to get over stuff."

"I don't mind helping out. I need to be distracted. I dumped Kyle two days ago."

"Kyle?"

"My boyfriend — my ex-boyfriend."

"Oh yes, him. How is he?"

"You mean how am I?"

"Of course, that's what I meant."

"I'm fine. Thanks for asking."

Bradley stared at Murphy, unsure if she was mocking him. As Anand returned, she released a suppressed laugh and said, "Am I irritating you, Peter?"

"Not a bit, Carolyn."

"This is what I have," Anand said, heavily dropping another thick pile of documents on the table and taking his seat again.

"I'm sorry to hear that," Murphy said before wiping away a smile.

"You know what's not here?" Bradley mumbled, ignoring Murphy. "The binder of background materials that the client sent Platz on Friday." He got up to rummage through his briefcase next to his desk. "He left it with Margaret, but she's been away so much, I didn't get it until just before I left Friday."

"Where has Margaret been anyway?" Murphy asked. "She's looked very distracted and upset."

Bradley stood perplexed in front of his briefcase. "It's not here. Margaret — yes, well, she might have been taking me into confidence, but her daughter is being tested for MS. Just keep that to yourself. She's very stressed, as you can imagine."

"Oh my," Murphy said. "That's awful."

"It is," Bradley said, rummaging again, then scanning his desk. "It's not here. That's a problem — hate losing track of documents. I told Margaret to get the best specialist possible, even in the U.S. — whatever it costs."

"Can she afford that?" Murphy added.

"Probably not. Goddamn, it's not here. Maybe it's in the car." Bradley took his seat with a look of exasperation. "I said I would help her. That part should be the least of her worries. Yes, it must be in the car. I'm sure I saw it Saturday when I was leaving the cottage. Took the parking ramp fast this morning. The briefcase fell over on the passenger seat and things fell out. Coffee spilt, too."

"What was the rush?" Anand asked drily.

"It's an M3, Walter," Bradley said irritably.

"Smoke on the Water" belched from Bradley's smartphone. "Amy" showed on the screen. "Yes?" Bradley said curtly.

"I haven't heard from Reggie since yesterday afternoon. I have to find him."

A tremor ran through Bradley's body. "Just a minute." He turned to Murphy, pointing to the name on the screen. "Carolyn — would you mind?"

Murphy looked surprised. "Getting the binder?"

"Yes."

"Ah, sure," Murphy said.

"I just need to talk to Amy. Let me get my car keys." Bradley returned to his phone. "Just give me a second."

"Don't mind a little excursion before I start writing that exciting memo," Murphy said to Anand.

Bradley went to his jacket hung on the back of the office door. From an inside pocket he fished out a jangle of keys that included his car fob and tossed it to Murphy. "You press the top button to unlock and the middle button to lock. P1, just as you come out of the elevator. I have a red M3 now."

"I remember your spot. And it's the sixth time you told me about the new car."

"The binder's probably on the floor on the passenger side. If there's anything else, can you bring that up, too?" Bradley remembered the glove compartment. "You know what," he started, but Amy blared into the phone.

"Seriously, Peter, are you there?"

Murphy was already out the door, derisively rattling the jangle of keys. "Don't worry about it, I've got it."

Bradley swiped his face with his free hand. Locked in the glove compartment; the key hidden in the fob; everything wrapped in a green towel, he reasoned.

"*Peter!*"

There was nothing to worry about, Bradley assured himself.

"Yes, what?"

"Wait, he's on the other line. I'll call you back. Thank goodness."

Amy hung up, leaving Bradley to stare at his phone. A few seconds later he turned around, intending to take his seat again at the oval meeting table. To his surprise Anand was standing right behind him. Bradley stared into his murky face.

CHAPTER 58

On the elevator rides to P1 of the Bay Wellington Tower, Carolyn Murphy was annoyed. She had given up her Sunday afternoon to draft a memorandum, and all he cared about was Anand's state of mind. She had confided about exiting her relationship — an undemanding exercise, but only she knew that — and his first question was how Kyle was doing. And then he had ordered her down to his car to get some stupid binder, like she was still a law student or some other minion at his disposal. But for Margaret's daughter, he would move heaven and earth. Murphy caught herself on the last thought, sensing what anxiety Margaret must feel, and sent a quick wish that the diagnosis would be negative. Still, it all seemed so disproportionate. Entering P1, Murphy shook her head at Peter Bradley's sheer impenetrability.

Murphy approached the M3 and pushed the top button of the fob. The car's parking lights flashed and its doors unlocked. When she opened the passenger-side door, a light in the wheel well illuminated a black binder as well as a few documents haphazardly scattered on the floor. She grabbed what she saw, organized it into a pile and put the pile on the roof of the car.

Murphy slammed the door shut and aimed the fob at the car. But after a moment's hesitation she chose not to press the middle button to lock the car. Instead she casually looked around the parking area and confirmed she was alone. Surveillance cameras didn't concern her, because she could claim she was still looking for missing documents. Walking around to the other side of the car, she opened the driver's-side door and snuck in behind the steering wheel.

"So this is the master's view from his hot little new car," Murphy mused. "You really do have to sit back quite far to accommodate that gut of yours, don't you?"

From the back seat Murphy plucked a facial tissue from a box. As she glanced around the inside of the car, she dabbed her nose with the tissue in her left hand. With her right hand, she opened the ashtray but finding only loose change quickly closed it again. In the centre console she found CDs by Black Sabbath and AC/DC and laughed out loud at the retrograde musical taste. In a cubbyhole at the end of the long driver's-side door, old theatre brochures, a pair of outlandish sunglasses and a thumbed copy of *How to Find the Power within You* slummed together.

Murphy looked at the bottom button on the fob to open the trunk. The temptation to inspect was nearly irresistible, but she held off, knowing any surveillance image would be impossible to explain. Instead she leaned across the centre console toward the passenger-side wheel well, pretending to check one more time for lost items. "Oh, for Christ's sake," she blurted. Sticking out from under the passenger seat was the corner of a document she'd overlooked.

She caught the corner of the document in a pincer grip between her forefinger and thumb. As her right hand passed near the glove compartment, her middle and third fingers snuck under the compartment's latch and gave a pull. Murphy paused, puzzled why Bradley would lock the compartment.

It wasn't evident how to unlock the glove compartment. She fumbled with the fob, careful to avoid the emergency button, until at last a small key popped out the side. The key fit and the glove compartment fell open; inside a light came on. Leaning over further, she looked inside. At first she saw only the car manual and some maps. Then, to the left, she saw some miniature bottles of Scotch, mostly empty. Guessing they were his secret, and feeling a little embarrassed, she decided to close the compartment.

At the last second, she saw a strip of green towel underneath the car manual. Her hand snuck between for a quick probe of the towel. She guessed it was a dust rag, but to her surprise, her fingers encountered a variety of rigid edges. She clutched harder. One large item dominated, with a protrusion angling downward, and another that ran lengthwise. To its side, there was a collection of smaller items, pointed and tubular, that she easily rolled through the towel between her fingertips.

Murphy's tactile impressions rendered an image that made her gasp. After a moment's hesitation, she carefully withdrew the green towel and laid it on the passenger seat. Slowly she pulled the edges apart, then put her right hand to her open mouth. The overhead light was strong; there was no doubt what was in front of her. Swallowing hard, she rewrapped the towel, replaced it under the car manual and locked the glove compartment. She yanked herself out of the car and locked it, then rushed back to Bradley's office with the binder and documents she'd found.

CHAPTER 59

Initially, Anand's walk with his father Wednesday afternoon had calmed him; Anita even commented as much. But as hours and days passed, his resentments toward Bradley and the worries about his world spiralling out of control had regained strength. Only by assuring himself that he would honour his integrity, lay down boundaries — and keep his enemies closer — did he prevent himself from falling into impenetrable silence.

On the way to work Sunday he had decided to stop being Bradley's lackey and to breed a physical presence and scornful, ironic tone. It would be delicious to see Peter Bradley cower, if only for brief spurts. As Bradley handed the keys with the car fob to Murphy for the missing binder, Anand had walked behind his back, solely to invade his space and induce discomfort.

Startled, Bradley was lost for words. Finally he landed on the failsafe. "How is your kid, Walter — your baby?" he asked. Moving around Anand, he went to stand behind his desk.

Anand followed. With an air of casual contempt, he stood at the side of Bradley's desk, one hand in a pocket. "My child is fine. I've made a decision on resignation."

Bradley eyed Anand, asking himself why the man was so damn close. "Tomorrow would be a better day to talk about this."

"Tomorrow is too late. However, you have to swear on your honour."

"Swear on what?" Bradley said testily.

Anand did not flinch. "Your honour."

"My honour. Ok. Swear what?"

"That I will be made partner next year. In fact, I want it in writing — from Ted and you."

"Can I tell you, Walter? You seem a bit naïve on the process of being made partner. You don't get in by pressuring people."

"I think it's a fair request."

"You do, do you?" Bradley said with a sardonic smile. Still trying to escape Anand, he walked over to the oval meeting table and took his seat. Anand sat directly across from him. "It's highly unusual. You're worrying me again about your judgment." He didn't like the threatening look in Anand's eyes and stared back.

"It *is* a fair request, Peter. Not a lot to ask, really, in the circumstances."

Bradley didn't bite. "You're saying you won't resign if I guarantee you'll be partner next year."

"In writing, preferably."

Bradley purposely let a few moments pass. "I'll do that, provided you act professionally during the year and continue to do good work. And there has to be a business case. Swear."

"How do I know —?"

"I'll email you about this. You'll have to trust me that I'll evaluate you fairly. And if you don't trust me, well, I'll copy Ted on the email."

Anand kept his eyes locked; he had to swallow hard to get any moisture down his dry throat. This was his enemy, and he would keep him close — so close, in fact, he would smother him.

"And I assure you," Bradley continued, "this is the last time I'm talking about this. Well, what do you think, Walter, are you in or out?"

Anand was surprised how successful his aggression had been. *Push Peter Bradley and good things happen*, he told himself. *Push harder, Walter, push as hard as you can.*

"Could you send me a draft email? I'll respond to it tomorrow, probably with a few clarifications."

Bradley tried to hide the anger flushing into his epidermal cells. "Sure. I'll send you something tomorrow morning. Think very carefully what's best for you, Walter. One needs to be happy in life. Now maybe you want to go home and take your nap."

Fuck you, Anand said to himself, invoking unfamiliar words. *One day you're going to slip up, and I am going to be there to pick up the pieces.*

CHAPTER 60

A short time later Murphy returned to Bradley's office with the black binder and documents. Platz's transaction was far more complicated than Bradley had realized, and the group meeting dragged on. Anand, who chose to stay, was dark and humourless, and Murphy kept her eyes down. Bradley grew increasingly worried that Amy would cancel the dinner party because of her brother's obscure comings and goings. After a half hour, he excused himself and called her. She was aloof and distracted.

"Yes, I think he's fine. He said he's with a friend, though I didn't recognize the name."

"So, the dinner party — we're going ahead? I — I was hoping we would have some fun together this evening."

"Yes, yes. Everything will be ready," Amy said and hung up.

At three thirty the meeting finally broke. Bradley hoped it hadn't been too evident that he raised more questions than he answered. After Anand and Murphy left, Bradley closed his office door and sat behind his desk. He found the USB stick in a side pocket of his legal briefcase, inserted it into his laptop, and opened the Project Pizza folder. He went over the details one more time. Here and there a small refinement darted into his mind, but he made no changes. That time had passed; he was now in the realm of action.

After shutting down the laptop, knowing he could travel lightly that evening, Bradley threw only the board of directors materials and some documents for the Platz transaction in his briefcase. He was interrupted once more by Amy.

"I was going to get a few more bottles of wine. But I haven't had time with Reggie and everything. Pick something up on the way home, ok?"

Chafing under the last-minute change, Bradley looked at his watch. It was 3:45 p.m. Quickly, he calculated that he could walk to the St. Lawrence Market liquor store and back without any material impact on his plan. In the calmest tone he could muster, he agreed.

The liquor store was open until five on Sundays. With large steps, Bradley ate up sidewalk along Wellington, carrying his briefcase so he could return directly to his car. Once in the store, he asked a wannabe sommelier for some recommendations; always good to be seen, he said to himself. Clutching two Pinot noirs against his chest with one hand and his briefcase in the other, Bradley joined a long cashier line.

His eyes widened and he cursed so loudly that the person in front of him turned to look. In his office he'd forgotten the USB stick in the side of his laptop. It wasn't the minimal risk that bothered him; it was the sign that he wasn't one hundred percent focused. Anxiously waiting for the cashier, Bradley pounded the message into his head: *Get on your game, man; get on your* fucking *game. If there ever was a time, it's* now.

Bradley charged back to his office at double-speed, the expensive bottles of wine sloshing in his briefcase. At his office tower he hurriedly checked in with the security guard, then impatiently waited for the elevator. His watch showed it already was past four thirty. He was at risk of being late for the dinner party, but he comforted himself thinking that was his usual pattern. Any further delays, however, were not an option.

The elevator pinged at the twenty-ninth floor. Rounding the

corner into the hall toward his office, Bradley was surprised to see Anand and Murphy at the other end, huddled in conversation outside their offices. Anand had his jacket on and a thin brief-case at his side, ready to leave. Their heads were tilted together as if conspiring, and both looked with astonishment as Bradley strode down the hall. Bradley eyed them circumspectly. Murphy turned away, but Anand rejoined with a surly glare. They must be discussing Anand's partnership, Bradley thought. The last thing that interested him just then was prolonged conversation.

"Ah, Peter," Anand said in an overly silky voice. "We were just saying that we have a question for you."

Bradley slowed, but in an effort to signal haste, he glided by. Anand had adopted one of his faux smiles, while Murphy edged into her office. "I'm very late for this dinner party — can it wait till tomorrow?"

"It will only take a second," Anand said.

"All right. Just give me a minute."

Bradley walked to the closed door of his office, careful the others didn't follow. Grabbing the door's long vertical handle, he noticed with surprise that the door was only halfway jammed into its frame. He turned his head to look at Anand and Murphy for signs of complicity, but both had lost interest in him. Pushing the door open, he walked over to his desk and ripped the USB stick out of its laptop socket. Once he'd dropped the stick in a side pocket of his briefcase, he grabbed a random pink message slip from his desk and hurried out his office, closing the door hard behind him.

Anand stood alone, leaning against the doorway of Murphy's office, still in conversation. Bradley joined him, glancing at Murphy. She sat at her desk, the black binder splayed open on one side and an unopened notebook on the other. A document head-ed "Memorandum" addressed to Platz and Bradley waited on her laptop's screen.

"Got what I needed," Bradley said, waving the pink slip. "What's the question? I literally have a minute." For effect, he looked at his watch but was startled to see it was 4:45.

"I solved it," Murphy said. "Off you go to your dinner function."

"That's what I like to hear," Bradley said. "I thought you were going to take a nap," he added, looking at Anand.

"I'm going home in a few minutes."

"I'd wait, but I really have to go."

"Don't hold yourself up for me," Anand said, dismissively waving off Bradley.

As he drove home through light traffic, Bradley felt anxiety grip his gut. He calmed himself as much as possible, telling himself everything was well planned out. Nonetheless, in the car he fidgeted constantly and couldn't wait for the drive to be over. Stopped at a red light before Mount Pleasant, he glanced at the clock in his car. It read 4:58; he might still arrive home before Carver and his wife got there. The light turned green and Bradley ran the M3 hard through its first three gears.

Mount Pleasant curled left and down a gentle slope. In his rear-view mirror, Bradley became aware of a car following close behind his. It was a dirty small brown sedan, but he couldn't determine the make. At the bridge over Rosedale Valley Road, Bradley purposely slowed, worried that it might be driven by a cop. The car nudged even closer, to the point where Bradley couldn't see the front grill. He kept his speed steady as he approached the intersection with Elm Avenue, hoping that the brown sedan's driver simply was impatient to turn right. The car drove straight through along with Bradley's, keeping pace directly behind.

The brown sedan receded somewhat and its headlights flashed. Deciding the driver could not be a cop, Bradley tried to

stay patient and ignore him. They passed South Drive and the sedan came up close to Bradley's car again. Bradley abandoned caution. With parkland greenery on either side of Mount Pleasant,
he accelerated. The M3 closed in on cars ahead, but the brown
sedan stayed near. Again its headlights flash.

Bradley thought of the exit to Rosedale at Roxborough Drive,
before his usual right at Whitehall. He punched his car's accelerator, passing the car in front of him, then braked hard into the
sharp, lunging right turn. The driver of the brown sedan was not
fooled. The sedan squeezed in behind Bradley's car, and tipping
perilously, made the exit.

Bradley dropped a gear and gunned the M3 up Roxborough.
He attacked every speed bump with a hard brake, then, once
over, vicious acceleration. The brown sedan flailed over the
bumps and Bradley gained distance. Then, between parked cars
on the right, an old lady in a walker began to cross. Bradley punished his car's brakes. The old lady was nowhere in sight of a
crosswalk, but as she inched across the road she gave Bradley
the evil eye.

The brown sedan bore down on Bradley's car. For a second
Bradley was sure it was going to hit him. With inches to spare
between the old lady's struggling feet and his car's front bumper,
Bradley released the M3's clutch, smoking the back tires. Yet
again the brown sedan's headlights flashed, and this time the
driver waved at Bradley to pull over. Ignoring the invitation,
Bradley put the M3 through its paces.

The two cars approached a roundabout. Highland Avenue
veered right while Roxborough continued the other side, and
Schofield Avenue exited left. Bradley was not going to lead a crazy man to his house. Seeing a car approaching from the opposite
direction on Roxborough, he was seized with an idea. He approached the roundabout, purposely allowing the brown sedan
to catch up. The two cars went together into the circular path,

past the exit to Highland.

With the brown sedan on his tail, Bradley pointed his car toward the continuation of Roxborough. The car on the other side released its yield and began entering the roundabout. At the last moment Bradley swung the M3 violently to the left, then right onto Schofield. Cut off, the car entering the intersection came to a pitched stop. For a nanosecond the driver of the brown sedan tried to follow Bradley's maneuver but abandoned it to miss the other car. As the sedan pulled onto Roxborough, Bradley tore away, leaving behind a virulent exchange of honks.

Bradley bolted home. Repeatedly, he checked his rear-view mirror but saw no sign of his pursuer. Rattled, he tried to fathom what had happened. His best guess was that it had been a car-jacker, drawn in by the alluring red of his car.

Bradley approached his house, his mouth bone dry. Carver and his wife were getting out of their car. Amy had taken Bradley's usual parking spot on Gregory so Carver could park in the driveway. Bradley was happy to park on the other side of Gregory, facing north, with the protection of one neighbour's hedge to his right, and another's fence to his left.

As Bradley got out with his briefcase, Carver came over to greet him holding a bottle of wine. "Move my car?" he asked. A furrow crossed his brow. "Looking a little shaken there."

Bradley decided to minimize his harrowing drive home. It was time to get back to the plan. "Just encountered some crazy guy with road rage," he said dismissively. "Anyway, I can see I didn't have to go to the liquor store," he added, laughing engagingly and opening his briefcase for Carver to see his purchase. "No, leave your car there. Where's Joan?" He shut his car door and walked with Carver toward his house.

"Went in to see Amy. Nice of you to have us over. By the way, thanks again for the help last week."

"McLeavey's DUI pretty much blew over, didn't it?"

"Very funny, Peter. Like a charm. Premier's very happy."

Bradley stopped shortly before the front door. "I left something in the car. Do you mind taking my briefcase in?"

"Not at all. I'll go say hi to your beautiful wife."

I bet you will, Bradley thought.

When Carver stepped inside, Amy scampered down the hallway to greet him, leaving Joan in the kitchen.

"Hi, John," she said loudly, "nice to have Joan and you over." With a quick look back to make sure Carver's wife hadn't followed her, she added in a whisper, "Did you see Peter out there?"

"Just getting something out of the car," Carver responded in a hushed voice. "You look lovely."

"I don't feel lovely," she said. "Seriously, my brother's driving me crazy." She knew she didn't have time to disclose more. Instead she ran two long fingers down Carver's left cheek and said, "I need to see you again — soon."

Standing in front of the open trunk of his car, Bradley nodded. The gym bag and recycling bag with the tarpaulin were exactly where they should be. Licking his dry lips, he slipped the trunk shut, then walked toward his house. He did not see the dirty brown sedan come to a slow stop around the corner from Gregory with a view north toward the M3.

CHAPTER 61

I can't believe it. He's ruined everything — again.

And he's just as criminal as I thought. Worse.

I'm panicking. I've got people around me. I have a drink. I'm still panicking.

For Christ's sake, I really am no different than him.

Stop! Stop beating yourself up about this. It is *different. What I am doing is righting a wrong. I can't think of any explanation for what he is doing, other than trivial self-interest.*

I just want this to be over. I need him gone, but he won't go. All the plans have been turned upside down.

I'm being punished again. First, abandoned. Then, when I finally want to act, I'm thwarted. Where is the justice???

I think I'm screwed. Maybe, there's another way — and, maybe, it's as satisfying. But don't I have to find the guy I hired first? Think.

I'll never see the fifty thousand; I've lost that, too.

I didn't choose you, PB — you chose me. Why do I have to suffer at your hands? I want you in front of me so I can shake you till you die. I want to scream in your face, as loud as I can – You should have treated me better.

What an idiot you are. A gun in your car. I kept asking myself — what are you doing with a gun? The thought of murder only crept into my mind slowly. At first I thought of Amy. Wednesday evening, you told me she's out of control. And then I remembered, just before, you calling Amato and Collins "dicks". I heard you. And then the possibility rose in my mind.

And Project Pizza? What kind of ridiculous name is that? It was obvious to open the files on the USB stick — it's not like I've ever seen one inserted in your computer before. You think you're so damn smart. It's been easy to keep track of your password over the years. Did you think I hovered close to you at your desk out of reverence? Your birthday and sequential numbers — very sophisticated security. You're a fool.

No, I'm the fool. I thought PB had a routine. A routine all about him, but still a routine. And my hire was supposed to take advantage of that, jumping in on an average Sunday or Monday evening with a mock robbery or carjacking. As well as I know PB, not even I could guess a plan like the one for Tony Amato. It changes everything.

My mother dies and you desert me? So thoughtful of you, permitting a few of her belongings to come to me after she died. Toys, pictures, the diary of her last six months. Did you even read it yourself? She gets weaker and weaker, and all she thinks about is that you were tuning her out — he's a different man, she keeps writing — and what would happen to me. You promised her you would be there for me. Arranging an interview for a new family — that's how you were there for me.

Am I really screwed? Have I got this right??? If my hire kills PB after Amato is dead, for sure the police will be all over Collins, Shaw, and then they'll figure me out. And even if PB is wasted by the hire before he gets to Amato, the police will still find the USB stick and the plan for Amato. They'll be all over the law firm — and me — then, too. I saw the USB stick was gone. PB must have it on him.

Single father, career everything, so much to prove, because your daddy wasn't nice. You could have had your career, and me, too. Lots of daddies aren't nice.

It makes me laugh that you never suspected. Once I committed to it as my own sixteenth birthday present, it was easy to figure you out and get closer and closer. Spending the night later with John Carver and one or two of your erstwhile friends helped as well. I acknowledge it —

you've given me a good career. Law must be in the genes, though it never feels to me like we're related. Not a bit. I'm ashamed we share DNA.

I am so tired of thinking about this. You've made my life a waste. For Christ's sake, I've come full circle. After deleting my electronic diary last night, here I am, journaling in a school notebook again, just like when I was a teen.

I am screwed. Unless I find the hire — and take that extra step. You — you, Carolyn Ann — you are being told something by these crazy last-minute changes. Think about the other way. It can be enough. The more I think it over, it is enough.

But first I have to find the hire — because, like a bad dream, now I'm saying he can't kill PB. But how do I find him? The cell number he gave me is out of service. I have no choice — I have to go there. There's a dinner party, I know that much. Maybe I'll be in time. Can I do this? I need to move now. Seriously, can I do this? You've done much more recently. Leave this pub and get your car, right now.

Postscript: I flashed some cleavage and stole a drunken guy's phone. No password either. God, what is happening to me???

CHAPTER 62

Calmly, the hire waited in the elderly brown Focus. Stolen years earlier, and with fake license plates, it was used exclusively for special occasions. He liked his spot around the corner from Gregory. If Bradley emerged from his house, Bradley was unlikely to see him, but with his sharp eyes, the hire would easily spot Bradley. The sidewalks were quiet. So far, he had only seen two dog-walkers, both on the other side of the street.

Feeling comfortable and alert, he slumped further down the driver's-side seat to avoid neighbours' prying eyes. He had great patience in these situations; taking one's time was part of an effective hunt. He never took his eyes off Bradley's house, even when the smoke of the odd cigarette made him squint. The exception was an occasional check of his appearance in the mirror. A balaclava sat on his head, rolled up above his eyes, and the collar of his jacket was pushed up. He drank and ate nothing. Occasionally he checked that his thin gloves were on tight. A happy bladder and keeping one's DNA to oneself were key requirements of the job.

So, Bradley hadn't pulled over when he'd wanted him to. Quite a surprise trick in the roundabout, too. Perhaps his first idea of attacking Bradley on his drive home would have been all too easy. He was content to wait. Others — especially the new boys on the block, those part-time Russians — easily got nervous and wanted everything to happen just so. Despite the best planning, it often didn't turn out that way. That was part of the game, part of being a professional. Let the events unfold, seize the right opportunity, and know when to pull back and leave things for another day.

He'd been there since shortly after five. The car's dusty clock turned over to six. Time was on his side. He also had the benefit of falling light and the security of experience. Continuing to watch Bradley's house, he dropped his left hand to the door compartment and felt the outline of his gun. The beauty of guns was that they were always ready when you needed them, no matter what time of day or night. Unlike people, they were the best of friends.

CHAPTER 63

Carolyn Murphy tried to save every second she could. Outside the pub she bravely stepped into Yonge Street traffic and flagged down the first cab she saw. In the semi-circle driveway of her condo building at Adelaide and Jarvis Streets, she dropped a twenty on the passenger seat without asking the astonished driver for change. She didn't bother with her usual greetings to the concierge, and after a painfully slow elevator ride to the fifth floor, she ran down the hall to her unit, leaving the door open while searching for car keys. At 6:15 p.m. she charged back out without bothering to lock the door, car keys and purse in hand.

She drove her car hard up the straight incline out of underground parking. Turning northbound onto George Street, she jerked to a stop for a delivery truck making a laborious U-turn. Her fist pounded the horn; the driver looked at her disbelievingly and tapped his right temple with a forefinger. Slamming the gear selector into reverse, Murphy curled her car backwards, then re-engaged drive and headed south. She turned right at King and then Jarvis. She guessed it was only a ten-minute drive to Bradley's house — if she could remember how to get there.

As Murphy drove along Jarvis, images of violence swirled in her head: the hire pulling the trigger; Bradley's body lying somewhere unnoticed in a pool of blood; Amato's body sprawled across some forest path. She pressed the speed limit as much as she could, weaving between lanes and ignoring yellow lights. The leisurely Sunday evening traffic took her onto Mount Pleasant. *Get to the hire then make the call*, she instructed herself. That was the only way to satisfaction.

At South Drive, Murphy was forced to stop for a red light. Banging the steering wheel rim with a fist, she looked down at her purse on the passenger seat. Peeking out was a corner of the smartphone she'd stolen at the pub. For a second she worried that it had already been reported missing. She reached over and pressed the bottom button; four full bars of service and a large "6:28" shone brightly at the top. Desperately, she hoped that she was not too late.

CHAPTER 64

In the last hour, standing next to his wife, Carver had rounded into his best form: telling stories, laughing loudly, running the show. Bradley had tried his best to add to the dinner party's lively atmosphere, but he was more than thankful for Carver's bonhomie.

In his right hand Bradley studiously held a glass of Chardonnay, but for once no wine passed his lips. As he'd done twice before, he stepped unnoticed to the kitchen sink and emptied half the contents of the glass down the drain. Not a minute later Carver found a wine bottle and offered a refill.

"I have to work shortly," Bradley implored.

"You keep saying that," Carver replied. "Getting boring. Here, hand over the glass."

Amy and Joan laughed. Bradley relented with a rueful smile and shake of the head.

"Now, about the premier's wife," Carver began again with an insidious grin. "She has a thing for those funny little costumes they wear in the Legislature. You laugh, but I'm not kidding." Once more Carver had command of the floor.

Bradley looked at his watch. It was 6:20. Amidst the whirl of activity, Bradley caught Amy alone for a second. "You did a great job," he said, trying to meet her eyes. He'd made sure she knew to serve dinner late. To appease hunger, in the middle of the kitchen dining table Amy had spread a variety of enticing appetizers. At the back of the table, bottles of wine and glasses were arranged in semi-circles, with a single tall glass in the middle if Carver preferred one of the beers Amy had put cold for him. "You really look beautiful this evening," Bradley added.

"I try," she said blandly. Avoiding her husband's eyes, she continued to circulate.

For a moment Bradley watched his wife. Long fingers gracefully corrected the flow of her blond hair; a tight red dress accented by a string of white pearls and black stilettos teased out her lines. Bradley glanced at Joan, who had taken a seat near the dining table. Pretty in her own right, she was quiet, seeming intimidated by Amy.

Bradley was working his way to the kitchen sink when Carver surprised him. "So how's that Amato fellow working out?" he asked. "At least as far as you can tell after two whole days."

Bradley felt himself flush. When he tried to answer, he faltered. He was dismayed by the anxiety and weakness he was showing. Carver was playing into his hands, and he needed to take full advantage.

"Fine," he said in an overcompensating, booming voice. He toned it down. "Fine. It's going to be very interesting."

"Who are you talking about?" Joan asked, looking back and forth between Bradley and her husband.

"Another hotshot lawyer like Peter who's forsaken his old firm and joined Peter's group," her husband said.

"I see," Joan said without much interest.

"Have I met him?" Amy asked.

"I don't think so," Bradley said cautiously. "He was at Bergheim's. We never had anything to do with him socially."

As Joan and Amy diverted into their own chat, Carver lowered his voice and drew closer to Bradley.

"So you didn't really explain to me why Amato left."

Bradley paused. "He says he wasn't getting the support he expected at his old firm. More opportunity. More money, too, he says."

"Come to terms with him, then, have you?"

"Absolutely. Gretzky and Crosby, De Niro and Streep, all that stuff."

"Pardon?"

"It'll be a great team."

"I see." Carver's face grew more animated, presaging a new topic. "Interesting chat with the premier yesterday. Can't really tell you much about it."

But he did, in a manner Bradley knew would consume too many minutes. Repeatedly, Bradley stole a glance at his Rolex: 6:23; then 6:25; and soon, 6:27. What he really wanted to do was think over the details of his plan one last time, not desperately try to follow Carver's train of thought. His body felt heavy and slow, like a reptile in the cold, and Carver's voice was reduced to a low, incomprehensible drone.

"I have to go," Bradley blurted.

"Sorry?" Carver said.

Bradley realized he'd interrupted Carver in mid-sentence. It was so important to appear nonchalant. His lips were dry again and he licked them. "I have to start working on some files. May have a few calls to make."

"Right, you mentioned," Carver said, somewhat startled. "Obviously important. Off you go."

Bradley walked over to Amy and gave her a kiss on the cheek. She appeared surprised. "Need to start in on my work. Take till about eight or so."

"Ok, don't let us disturb you. We'll try to be quiet."

"Be as loud as you like," Bradley said. Hurriedly, he slunk out of the kitchen and headed up to the study.

The Rolex showed 6:31. Waiting for the desktop computer to grind to life, Bradley grabbed his briefcase and distributed the board materials and Platz's documents across his desk. On the computer he launched the media player and started a two-hour recording of a law conference. It played loudly enough to be heard outside the study.

Bradley had stuffed the dry cleaner's bag with the clothing he'd worn back and forth from the cottage in the bottom left drawer of his desk. As quickly as he could he maneuvered his large body out of his party clothing and into the T-shirt, jeans and boat shoes. He put the bag with the party clothing back in the drawer. When he returned he would restore the cottage clothing to the bag and dispose of everything the next morning on his way to work.

After a fateful glance at Caesar's bust on the coffee table and a slow swipe of his face, Bradley slipped the study door shut. He walked to the edge of the stairs. Carver had Amy and Joan laughing in near fits with imitations of well-known politicians. Swallowing hard, Bradley eased down the stairs. At the bottom, he peered around the corner of the hallway to the kitchen. He could see the back of Joan's head shaking with laughter; no one else was in sight. He moved to the front door and opened it a crack to peer onto the street. Everything was quiet on Gregory. He opened the door a bit more, enough to slither around its edge and step outside onto the front landing. Gently, he closed the door and released a large, controlled breath.

Bradley stepped down the landing and strode past Carver's car in the driveway. Late-day sunlight bouncing off the second-floor windows of a neighbour's house hit his eyes. He shifted his head to avoid the glare and saw his car across the street under the deep shade of an arching maple. He unlocked the car and fell into the driver's-side seat, the plastic bags covering the seat rustling.

The hire's patience had been rewarded. He rolled down his

balaclava then slowly dropped his gloved left hand to the compartment in the car door. Without looking, he found his gun and slid the barrel with his other hand to load the first cartridge. Easing the gun into the left pocket of his jacket, he whispered, "Ready, set, go," and reached to open his car door. But he hesitated, seeing Bradley raise his smartphone to an ear.

Bradley waited for Platz's voicemail recording to finish. "Robert, it's Peter Bradley," he said. "Leaving a message to say that we met on your transaction this afternoon. Carolyn is doing a draft memo on it this evening and I'm also going to spend some time on it this evening, in my study here, to review a couple of specific points. So we'll have the memo to you before the end of business tomorrow, as you asked. Hope you had an enjoyable Sunday."

The hire paused for Bradley to finish his call. He watched Bradley lean over to the passenger seat of his car and start fussing with something in the glove compartment. The hire let a minute pass then decided the moment was opportune. After a short inspection all around for pedestrians and cars, he slipped out of the Focus and walked quickly and silently toward the M3.

When he reached the car, the hire could see Bradley through the back window, still leaning over the centre console, just closing the glove compartment. He made a last check up and down Gregory. Removing the gun from his left jacket pocket, he walked alongside the car until he reached the driver's-side door. In one elegant movement, he whisked open the door twelve inches with his gloved right hand, caught the door with his left knee to hold it open, and pointed the gun in his left hand at Bradley's head. Then he steadied himself with his right hand on the car's door-frame.

Without moving from the console, Bradley snapped his head back to see who had opened the door.

"This is a robbery," the hire hissed. "This is a gun, loaded and ready to shoot. Don't fuck around. Give me your wallet." The look of panic on Bradley's face amused the hire. "I'll give you three more seconds. Give me your fucking wallet."

It started to fit for Bradley; this was the guy who had followed him. He doubted his assailant fully understood with whom he was dealing.

"Let me get it," Bradley said. "It's down here."

"Where?"

"Down here. In this compartment." Bradley turned slowly from the car console and reached with his left hand for the cubbyhole at the end of the driver's-side door. The hire followed Bradley's hand. "I keep it under this book."

Bradley shoved aside *How to Find the Power within You*. Empowered, he grabbed the edge of the cubbyhole and pulled as hard as he could. The door clipped the hire's gun, sending it to the ground, and slammed against three fingers of the hire's right hand on the car's doorframe. Bradley heard a crunch and a compressed scream. Holding the door as tightly as he could, he reached with his right hand for the loaded Glock on the passenger seat. He pointed the gun at his assailant through the glass and hissed, "Weren't expecting this, were you, asshole? You don't know who you're fucking with here."

CHAPTER 65

Murphy's memory of how to get to Bradley's house had failed her. From Mount Pleasant she had mistakenly entered Rosedale by way of Roxborough and continued on after the roundabout at Highland. In a maze of curving streets narrow with parked cars and mansions either side, she'd soon become disoriented. To her dismay she arrived back at South Drive. She pulled her car over and with the ceiling light on pounded the screen of the stolen smartphone until she got the maps function. "Oh my god, I needed to take Whitehall," she exclaimed.

She returned to Mount Pleasant, cursing herself for the valuable lost time. At Whitehall she brought her car to a crawl; if she was going to see whether the hire was staking out Bradley's dinner party, she needed to be inconspicuous. She decided to approach Gregory from the north end, off Summerhill. When she made the slow right onto Gregory, her breath caught in her throat. Clutching the steering wheel so hard every knuckle and vein in her hands jumped out, she stopped her car. In horror, she saw someone down the street standing next to Bradley's car wearing a balaclava. It could only be the hire.

Desperately, Murphy tried to make out what was happening. For a second she feared Bradley was already dead in his car, but to her relief, she saw his face, alive and growling at the hire. Then, leaning as far as possible over the steering wheel, her eyes opened wide, she realized everything was out of control. The hire seemed contorted in pain, somehow pinned to Bradley's car, and Bradley appeared to be pointing his gun at him. Murphy felt utterly helpless.

"Let my fingers out!" the hire cried. "Let them out! I'll leave you alone. Please!"

"So listen, you little piece of shit," Bradley hissed. "A car just pulled over up the road. I don't want trouble, you don't want trouble. You just want your fingers back, right?"

"Yes, fuck, yes!"

"Then I'm going to start this car and drive off, and let your fingers go when I please. Don't ever come back. I will shoot next time. I'm good at it."

"Ok, ok, fucking let go."

With the Glock still in his right hand, Bradley pushed the "Start" button of the M3. He slowly engaged the clutch, letting the car pull forward. Groaning, the hire stumbled along. When Bradley was sure his assailant was too far away from his gun to retrieve it, he jerked his car forward to elicit a final scream then released the car door a few inches. In his rear-view mirror he watched his assailant come to an agonizing stop. A smug smile curled onto Bradley's face.

Murphy saw Bradley drive toward her on Gregory and slumped onto the passenger seat of her car. But she did not hear his car pass. Instead, its throaty tone receded east. After a few seconds, she guessed that he had turned onto Whitehall. She let a few more seconds pass, then breathlessly straightened up.

At the other end of Gregory, in a loping run with his right hand dangling at his side, the hire rounded a small brown sedan and quickly got in. Given the pain he was in, he must have had enough, she told herself. And that would be perfect. She could make her call and everything would be set. For all she cared, the hire could keep her money.

With his functioning left hand, the hire slammed the brown sedan's gear selector into drive and yanked the steering wheel hard right. He tore up Gregory in Murphy's direction. She started to wave to get his attention and make sure he understood everything was called off. To her astonishment he made another hard right, onto Whitehall. Murphy's heart pounded anew. She realized the hire was nowhere near done.

CHAPTER 66

It had just passed 6:45 p.m., and Tony Amato put down his tablet. "Going for my run," he said.

Maria, seated across from him in the living room and immersed in a book, took no notice. Amato gave a slight shrug and walked over to one of the front windows. The sun was burning the horizon. He headed downstairs to locate one of his neatly folded sets of running gear in the laundry room.

At the same time, Peter Bradley eased onto Summerhill Avenue in the direction of Governor's Bridge and Nesbitt. With all his will he tried to block out the attack and concentrate on his plan. But the truth was it had deeply shaken him. He drove behind a slow-moving delivery truck, maintaining a large distance. White-knuckling the steering wheel with his left hand, he brought a trembling bottle of water to his parched lips with his right. Attempted armed robbery? In his neighbourhood? Unbelievable.

For a fleeting moment a thought poked into his head that the attack was a warning to him to stay home. But with a shake of his head and a glance at the Glock's outline under the green towel on the passenger seat, he dismissed the intrusive idea. He snorted with derision, imagining his assailant's astonishment when, with three stuck, crushed fingers, a Glock was pointed at him. "Things didn't go quite as he planned," Bradley blurted. "Asshole." A swell of confidence rolled through his body.

He checked the car clock. Because of the attack and the delivery truck in front of him, he was a minute behind schedule. Somehow he would have to make up the time, but not by driving faster. It was not the night to help a traffic cop make his quota. He was content driving behind the truck under the speed limit, making full stops at every intersection. Stop sign by stop sign, Bradley grew calmer.

He drove across Governor's Bridge and came to the roundabout for Nesbitt Drive, Governor's Road and Douglas Crescent. Like the evening before, he chose Governor's Road straight ahead. With parked cars either side, he drove carefully to the end, where the road met up again with a looping Douglas Crescent. There were several free parking spots to his right. He signalled and eased his car into the last one, finally focused on the fact that his quarry would soon head his way.

* * *

Carolyn Murphy felt only angst. She had turned onto Whitehall just in time to see the hire's car at the other end, making a left toward Summerhill. Her little car had groaned in displeasure when she pressed the gas pedal to the floor to catch up. Two turns later, she was a car behind the hire, trying to figure out a way to close the distance and stop him. Occasionally, much farther down Summerhill in the dimming light, she thought she caught the red of Bradley's car, but she wasn't sure.

The hire had nearly completed his assignment, and that would have been a disaster. But more horrible was that he hadn't given up. Had he forgotten that Bradley had a *gun?* Why didn't he just disappear with her money and get his damn hand fixed? This was customer service taken to an unnecessary extreme. The absurdity of it all, she told herself. Both she and the hire were following a man who intended to kill another. "I need to make the call," she hissed. "I need to stop him and then make the call. If there is a god, please, please, give me the chance."

Murphy had never been on Governor's Bridge before; she only identified it from a sign at the bridge's entrance. Halfway across, she strained to see the hire one car beyond. In her mind, she feverishly tried to recall details of Project Pizza. Parking at the east end of Governor's Road, a path off True Davidson Drive. She didn't know the area, but if this was Governor's Bridge, Governor's Road had to be ahead. And between 7:05 and 7:06, Bradley would shoot Amato. The hire stopped at the roundabout at the end of the bridge. The clock in her car changed to 6:51; she had run out of time and choices.

Murphy tromped the gas pedal and once again the engine groaned. Ignoring the solid middle line between the narrow lanes on the bridge, she swung left and began passing the car ahead. In the distance the high beams of an oncoming car flashed, and the driver of the car she was passing looked at her in astonishment. With a few feet to spare, Murphy cut in front and continued hard toward the intersection. The brake lights of the hire's car faded and the car entered the roundabout. Murphy made sure the hire couldn't ignore her. With a screeching stop, she played bumper cars.

* * *

Bradley stared at the Nesbitt playground diagonally to his left. Sunset was close at hand and the playground was quiet. He took another sip of water. The drive had gone smoothly and he was slightly ahead of schedule.

In his car's rear- and side-view mirrors, he looked back down Governor's Road. The roundabout at the other end was clogged, but no cars were coming in his direction. Pedestrians concerned him more. On the other side of the road, well down, a teenager picked up a piece of two-by-four at the edge of a renovation site. He tossed it into the foundation of a new house then proudly continued walking in the other direction. Approaching Bradley's car from behind on the passenger side, a woman was walking a large black Labrador. At every telephone pole the dog insisted on arching its back and releasing a stream. "Come on. Be done with it, already," Bradley muttered.

* * *

Murphy took a few seconds to recover from the surprising force of the fender-bender. She could see the hire, his balaclava rolled up above his eyes, looking in his rear-view mirror in anger. Other drivers stopped to size up the situation then worked their cars past, throwing eye daggers Murphy's way. She waved hectically at the hire to pull into Douglas Crescent. After a few seconds, he accommodated. He veered right and made a U-turn as she parked on the other side. Nervously, she got out and approached him.

Murphy was surprised that he didn't get out of his car. Instead, he rolled down his window and kept his face out of sight.

"Don't worry about it," he began. "I have to get going. Just don't worry —" Then there was a pause. "What the fuck?" he said. "What the hell are you doing here?"

Murphy didn't want to attract attention. She walked around the hire's car and stepped onto the neighbouring sidewalk near a metal telephone pole densely covered in vines. She motioned at the hire to join her, and reluctantly he stepped out of the car. When he got close, she saw he was unshaven and that sweat from under the balaclava was collecting in his eyebrows. Deep creases of pain etched from the corners of his eyes, and dilated pupils screamed anger. Murphy could hardly get coherent words out.

"Stop following him! It's over, ok? Keep the money. Just go, *please*."

The hire held up his right hand. His first three fingers were swollen in his glove and askew above the middle knuckle. "No one fucking does this to me. No one," he hissed viciously, spraying Murphy with foul saliva.

"You don't understand. I'm going to —" she began.

Murphy hardly heard the "Fuckoff." Her head snapped forward from the violent push to her chest and she flew backwards, lifted off her feet like a ragdoll. The back of her head slammed against the vine-covered pole. The world swam before her eyes and her ears rang like a house alarm. As her head began to pound, her stomach rose in protest. Vaguely, she heard the door of the hire's car slam shut and the car driving away.

* * *

Bradley's watch flicked past 6:53; he was falling behind schedule again. At long last, the woman and her black Lab disappeared at the end of Governor's Road. No one else was close by. He got out of the car and opened the trunk. As fast as he could, he pulled the green tracksuit over his clothes and changed from his boat shoes to the track shoes. With the Packers cap pulled over his head and the tarpaulin in the bag under his left arm, he closed the trunk and went to the passenger side of the car. In a second he had the loaded Glock in the right pocket of his tracksuit. He didn't notice how the early evening air cooled his moist skin. Instead, he bobbed through a few stretches and ran as fast as his spindly legs would go toward True Davidson Drive.

* * *

In the house across the street, a small poodle yapped at Murphy, its paws up against the sill of a bay window. Struggling to sit up, Murphy leaned against the metal pole, enveloped by vine either side, and felt the back of her head. A horrendous bump was swelling up fast and she felt a trickle down the nape of her neck. Pulling her fingers away, even in the poor light, she could see a reddish-brown smear of blood.

Bracing herself against the pole, Murphy stumbled to her feet. She slowly crossed the street, not knowing which discomfort to assuage first. Of all the people in the world, she thought of Tony Amato. She no longer cared about the hire; he and Bradley each had a gun and as far as she was concerned they could duke it out like it was high noon. At her car she opened the door and slumped into the driver's-side seat. The difference was Amato was innocent, like her. Letting Bradley cause even more pain was insufferable. She grabbed the stolen smartphone, and in the deepest voice her nausea permitted, said what she had to say. Leaning her head back against the seat's headrest, on the cusp of a dry heave, she felt powerless to do more.

* * *

On the other side of True Davidson, Bradley pushed between the two spruces. His chest heaved and his heart ran amok. He took fifteen seconds to catch his breath then nervously checked his watch again. In less than five minutes, Amato would leave his house and start his run to doom along Airdrie. Bradley ran the left sleeve of his tracksuit under his cap and across his brow to mop up perspiration. Clear-headed despite a wave of anticipation, he told himself that he had to get into position.

By the end of the steps, the only sounds were the light crunch of loose stones under his track shoes, and the distant, dull rush of traffic on Bayview. For the tenth time since he'd gotten out of his car he checked for the Glock's outline in his jacket pocket.

At first, the voice behind him did not register.

"Don't make me repeat it again," Bradley heard. "I said, stop the fuck there."

CHAPTER 67

Bradley halted in his tracks.

"Drop whatever's under your arm there and put your hands up, like it's the movies. Very slowly. No doubt you have that gun with you — you probably don't even know how to use it."

Every drop of saliva in Bradley's mouth dried up. For a second he wondered if he could extract the Glock, then whirl around, pump the first cartridge in the barrel and shoot. But he knew who stood overhead; he wouldn't have a chance. He let the recycling bag with the tarpaulin drop and raised both hands above his head.

"Now, you prick, turn around. Like I said, very fucking slowly. That's it."

Little by little, Bradley turned then looked up the steps he'd just descended. The hire, short and stocky, balaclava down, stood on the first step. He breathed heavily, like he'd run faster than Bradley. Once again his left hand pointed a gun straight and steady at Bradley. The balaclava hid all expression, but that didn't matter — rage dripped from every word.

"Nobody does what you did to me and gets away with it. Don't even fucking look at me. Lower your head."

Bradley did as he was told. It was surreal — he was going to be shot when he was supposed to do the shooting.

"Who are you anyway?" Bradley squeaked. "Some punk thief? What is your problem anyway?"

"Oh, mister fucking brave guy. Don't move, don't say anything until I ask you. Where's your wallet?"

Bradley felt an ounce of hope. "In the back pocket of my jeans. Underneath my track pants." He began to lower his right hand.

"I said, don't fucking move until I tell you."

"Ok, ok."

"Use your left hand. Now get the fucking thing out and throw it halfway toward me. Hurry up. We don't have all day."

"I can't reach it with my left hand —"

"Make it work, asshole. Fast."

Lowering his left hand, Bradley contorted himself to reach behind his back. Underneath the track pants, in the right back pocket of his jeans, he just caught the corner of his wallet. Gradually, he brought it around to his front, raising it high in the air for his assailant to see.

"Throw it up here," the hire said. Bradley complied. "Well done," the hire added.

Without moving for the wallet, the hire let a few pregnant seconds pass. "Ok, we're done," he finally said. Bradley's heart leapt. "Oh, wait. There's one more thing. You also have to die." The hire held up his right hand, grimacing as he glanced at his bent fingers. "At this point, really because of this."

Bradley's brief hope that the wallet would suffice disintegrated. An involuntary tremble reverberated throughout his body. What in god's name was happening, his mind pleaded. As whimpers emitted from his lips, he pressed his eyes together and tensed his entire body, waiting for the impact.

"So, as they say in the movies, prepare to meet your —"

A large crack, like the sound of a baseball bat making home run contact, resounded in the quiet air. For a horrible instant, Bradley thought it was the shot from his assailant's gun. But there was no impact, no searing pain — just a surprised grunt from above. Bradley opened his eyes; beads of sweat clogged his vision and burned. Wiping his eyes, he only caught a glimpse of a length of two-by-four receding from between the spruces.

In slow motion, the hire cowered and dropped his gun. A second later he began to stumble down the steps. Lurching toward him, Bradley tried to understand what had happened. All he could come up with was some kind of Good Samaritan near the forest. A Good Samaritan who'd instantly disappeared.

Bradley decided not to wait for clarification. Before the hire nearly fell into his arms, Bradley stepped aside, grabbed him by the shoulders, and with a vicious shove propelled him farther down the path. The hire stumbled even harder, trying desperately to catch his step. But before he could stabilize himself, he was at the precipice of the large dip in the path. He couldn't hold himself and catapulted down, falling at the bottom on his right hand and screaming in pain.

Bradley was hard on his heels. As the hire, moaning loudly, tried to lift himself, Bradley kicked as hard as he could, landing a toe of his track shoe deep in the hire's stomach. The hire rolled onto his back, clutching his gut. Bradley kicked him again, in the side. The hire writhed in pain, gasping for breath.

As Bradley drew in large gulps of air, Tony Amato did the same. Finishing the last stretches on the front step of his house, Amato let his watch tick down to 7:00 p.m. As he prepared to thrust himself across the lawn, over the hedge and onto Airdrie, he looked up at the sky. It was a wonderful evening for a run. The sun was just down, and the air was still and pleasantly cool.

Bradley was eaten alive with anger. He pawed at the gun in his right jacket pocket, feeling its outline with his fingertips. There was an easy way to put his assailant out of his agony, he thought. Bradley looked up and down the path. It was quiet both ways, but nervously he thought about the Good Samaritan. He pushed his legs up the path and steps then parted the two spruces. In the twilight and dim glow of the street lamps, it was hard to see across True Davidson. Eventually, his eyes grew accustomed. The gully on the other side was still. In the Nesbitt playground, diagonally to the right, a small figure scurried toward Douglas Crescent.

Bradley charged back down the path, but when he got to the bottom of the dip, the hire was gone. He spun around, looking for his wounded assailant. About to curse out loud for having lost him, Bradley saw the stooped figure stealing away right. He was close to the slanted ground Bradley had chosen to shoot from, heading toward the bridge on True Davidson that ran over the abandoned railway track.

Bradley bolted after him, thrashing through brush. Hearing Bradley, the hire tried to kick into a run, but for once Bradley was the faster one, and closed in quickly. He reached inside his tracksuit pocket and pulled the gun halfway out. With all his heart, he wanted to pump a bullet into his assailant's head. But he was here for Tony Amato. *If I'm going to shoot this gun, it's for Tony Amato*, he barked at himself. He let the gun slip back into his pocket.

The ground near the bridge rose steeply to True Davidson Drive and dropped precipitously to the railway track. The hire stumbled to a momentary stop, trying to figure out which way to go. Bradley was upon him. As hard as he could, Bradley unleashed a kick, catching the hire in the lower back. The hire went concave and his arms splayed in a desperate attempt to balance on terra firma. Bradley kicked one last time. The hire fell forward, unable to keep to his feet, rolling and somersaulting over hard ground, rocks and stumps, until he landed at the base of the bridge. For twenty seconds, Bradley watched. His assailant didn't move.

CHAPTER 68

"Take that, you fuck," Bradley uttered breathlessly. His body heaving and soaked in sweat, he bent over to catch his breath. Anxiously, he looked at his watch. All kinds of valuable time had been lost. It was coming up to 7:03, and Amato would be there in two and a half minutes. Bradley's mind raged. His indomitable self-confidence surged with his manhandling of his assailant, but another part of his brain flashed red to call off his plan. Instead of order there was chaos; instead of a plan, there was improvisation. And who the fuck was that Good Samaritan? Wiping the sweat from his brow, he stood up and made a momentary attempt to mask his footsteps in the brush. Then he ran back to the path.

He had to make a decision. Seconds were ticking by mercilessly. He ran up the path once more and collected the tarpaulin in the recycling bag and his wallet on one of the bottom steps. In the twilight Bradley saw a familiar outline on the step above. It was the hire's gun, and it looked just like his.

The thought blindsided him with full force. Kill Amato with his assailant's gun and leave Amato and the gun for discovery. Then his assailant, having accidentally fallen trying to get away, would be found. It was the perfect alibi. Bradley raced the idea through his mind. He could not leave fingerprints — that was his only concern. Bradley's right hand clutched his left wrist and he glared at his watch. Amato was sixty seconds away. *In or out*, he demanded of himself. *In or fucking out?* "In," he hissed.

With his tracksuit sleeve pulled down over his right hand, Bradley grabbed the gun. He threw himself down the path, the bag with the tarpaulin under his arm and his wallet back in his pocket, and plunged down the dip. Veering hard right, he found the slanted ground. *Lots of time*, he told himself, *lots of time*. He dropped the tarpaulin and then fell into a prone position. A last glance at his watch showed he had thirty seconds.

Set yourself and control your breathing, Bradley told himself. Filling his lungs, he propped himself on his elbows and held the gun as steady as he could in his sleeved right hand, cradled by his left. Slowly, he allowed the forefinger of his right hand to escape the sleeve and coil around the trigger. "Wipe the trigger when you're done," he muttered.

No more than ten seconds until a sweaty and gasping Amato would come running down the steps, keeping his knees high and carefully planting his feet. Bradley's heart leapt as never before, and perspiration drenched his brow and back. He shook his head to catapult a few beads of sweat off his forehead. Finally the sound of footsteps came toward the spruces. He counted down in his head — five, four, three — the footsteps, surprisingly loud and heavy, were very close. Two, one — and the footsteps stopped.

Bradley thought he heard other footsteps, softer and less discernible, but otherwise there was deep and eerie silence. Something was wrong, he knew it. He guessed that Amato was retying a shoelace or maybe catching his breath. But the seconds ticked on. Bradley's neck muscles ached in the prone position; rage took hold of his heart. Nothing was fucking working out. But somehow, some way, he would make sure it did.

"Put the gun down!"

Bradley's entire body jolted.

"I repeat! Put the gun down! Then get to your feet, show us

your hands and freeze!"

Bradley searched. At the top of the stairs, a figure, nearly un-detectable in head-to-toe black, lay on the ground between the spruces, aiming the biggest rifle he'd ever seen at him. He wasn't sure, but there might have been a second rifle poking through the branches of one of the spruces.

"I will, I will," Bradley said, gritting his teeth.

"Do it now! Do it slowly! Now, now, now!"

More steps came at him up the path.

"I'm putting the gun down now," Bradley said slowly. "I'm do-ing it now."

Ever so slightly, he moved his hands as if to drop the gun. They didn't realize who they were dealing with, Bradley thought. Rolling hard to his left, he pulled the trigger as fast and many times as he could. Loud cracking return fire thudded into the earth to his right, but he'd found a large rock for cover.

All he needed to do was to get to where his assailant had fall-en. That led down to the base of the bridge and along the railway track. From there, one way or another, he was sure he could find his way back up to his car.

Bradley crouched close to the rock. He prepared himself for a stooped run toward the bridge. Counting to three, he heaved to his feet and scurried as fast as he could. A few steps from the precipitous drop, a Remington 700 rifle boomed from atop the bridge. Bradley spun with the force of a bullet ripping through his right shoulder. He realized he hadn't thought about how *many* of them there were. The pain burned so intensely that he dropped the hire's gun. He kicked violently to grip the earthy ground with his treadless shoes, and used every ounce of energy to lunge over the precipice.

The second bullet screamed into his thigh, a direct hit to the bone. He yelled in agony, but now his tumble had started. His limbs flailed helplessly through somersaults, rolls and cartwheels, and his head and ribs bounced off rock outcroppings, roots and trees. The blur of random, violent motion coupled with excruciating pain seemed endless. Eventually, near the base of the bridge, Bradley came to rest.

Briefly, the curious thought entered his mind that he must have landed close to his assailant. With all his strength he lifted his head and looked around. From all sides there was wild activity racing toward him. But the hire, stumbling well down the railway track out of harm's way, had finally left him alone.

Bradley welcomed the clouds of unconsciousness that overtook him.

CHAPTER 69

I can live in peace now — even with this throbbing headache.

And I quote from the breaking local news. "At the last minute, police have thwarted an apparent murder attempt in Rosedale. They say a man armed with a handgun was waiting to shoot another man in a wooded area, just east of True Davidson Drive. There was an exchange of gunfire with the Emergency Task Force before the suspect was shot twice and apprehended. No police were injured. Fifty-two year old Peter Bradley, a prominent lawyer, has been arrested on multiple charges, including attempted murder. He is expected to survive..."

So like you, PB. Had to show your fangs and shoot back at the police. You played right into my hands. I was just counting on one conviction — for the attempted murder of Tony Amato. But now you're going to get multiple attempt convictions. And the police will have something to say about possessing an unregistered handgun, too.

What did you tell me at drinks Wednesday? A long incarceration can be worse than death, and everybody has their number for what is "long". I can't see how that's true but it sounds like it is for you. Twenty years, you said. Let's see. As I remember from law school, the maximum sentence for attempted murder is life imprisonment. Now, I know your lawyer will work hard to get it a lot lower. But with the help of that USB stick, could any attempted murder be more premeditated than Tony Amato's? Then add attempted murders of police officers? And you a lawyer to boot? With that kind of contempt for life and your profession, I think you'll get close to twenty.

I have to admit, when you explained about helping Margaret's daughter in the office today, I thought that I might have misread you for my entire life. But then I saw your plan for Tony. You are a slippery one.

I was so worried that they would think it was just a crank call, with a stolen phone and all. I gave them a few excerpts from PB's document. I said I saw a guy in a green tracksuit with a gun entering a forest path on the east side of True Davidson Drive, just north of a bridge. And that it looked like he was going to shoot someone, from ground about fifteen yards in, below a ridge. Obviously they couldn't trace me, but I thought I gave them enough information to take it seriously. And they did — but, my god, they sure left everything to the last possible moment.

But my bigger worry was what happened to that damn hire. I got him good with that two-by-four. If he had been caught — I don't even want to think about that. But I saw his car when I returned down Governor's Road and waited in my own long enough to see him return.

Now I'm going to reread this piece of paper ten times and savour every word — and then burn it.

And to you, Peter Bradley, I say rest in peace. Curled up in a deep, dark hole — for a very long time.

Acknowledgements

Many thanks to the folowing friends and family who toiled through drafts of this book: Peter Armstrong, Janet Bolton, Simone Davis, Renate Fritze, Hellen Hajikostantinou and Lelia McDonald. Special thanks also to Lisa Charters and Jennie Painter.

About the Author

Peter Fritze was a partner in a downtown Toronto law firm and general counsel of a Canadian multinational. Visit his website/blog at **www.peterfritze.com**. He's met many lawyers but none like Peter Bradley.

Made in the USA
Charleston, SC
16 June 2014